INTERNATIONAL

THE
SHELTERING
SKY

THE SHELTERING SKY

PAUL BOWLES

VINTAGE INTERNATIONAL

VINTAGE BOOKS

A DIVISION OF RANDOM HOUSE, INC.

NEW YORK

FIRST VINTAGE INTERNATIONAL EDITION, MARCH 1990

Library of Congress Cataloging-in-Publication Data
Bowles, Paul, 1910–
The sheltering sky / Paul Bowles.
p.   cm.
ISBN 0-679-72979-8
I. Title.
PS3552.0874S5   1990
813'.54—dc20   89-28905
CIP

Book design by Maura Fadden Rosenthal

Manufactured in the United States of America

10 9 8 7 6 5

FOR JANE

BOOK ONE

TEA IN THE SAHARA

"Each man's destiny is personal only insofar as it may happen to resemble what is already in his memory."

—EDUARDO MALLEA

He awoke, opened his eyes. The room meant very little to him; he was too deeply immersed in the non-being from which he had just come. If he had not the energy to ascertain his position in time and space, he also lacked the desire. He was somewhere, he had come back through vast regions from nowhere; there was the certitude of an infinite sadness at the core of his consciousness, but the sadness was reassuring, because it alone was familiar. He needed no further consolation. In utter comfort, utter relaxation he lay absolutely still for a while, and then sank back into one of the light momentary sleeps that occur after a long, profound one. Suddenly he opened his eyes again and looked at the watch on his wrist. It was purely a reflex action, for when he saw the time he was only confused. He sat up, gazed around the tawdry room, put his hand to his forehead, and sighing deeply, fell back onto the bed. But now he was awake; in another few seconds he knew where he was, he knew that the time was late afternoon, and that he had been sleeping since lunch. In the next room he could hear his wife stepping about in her mules on the smooth tile floor, and this sound now comforted him, since he had reached another level of consciousness where the mere certitude of being alive was not sufficient. But how difficult it was to accept the high, narrow room with its beamed ceiling, the huge apathetic designs stenciled in indifferent colors around the walls, the closed window of red and orange glass. He yawned: there was no air in the room. Later he would climb down from the high bed and fling the window open, and at that moment he would remember his dream. For although he could not recall a detail of it, he knew he had dreamed. On the other side of the window there would be air, the roofs, the town, the sea. The evening wind would cool his face as he stood looking, and at that moment the dream would be there. Now he only could lie as he was, breathing slowly, almost ready to fall asleep again, paralyzed in the airless room, not waiting for twilight but staying as he was until it should come.

2

On the terrace of the Café d'Eckmühl-Noiseux a few Arabs sat drinking mineral water; only their fezzes of varying shades of red distinguished them from the rest of the population of the port. Their European clothes were worn and gray; it would have been hard to tell what the cut of any garment had been originally. The nearly naked shoeshine boys squatted on their boxes looking down at the pavement, without the energy to wave away the flies that crawled over their faces. Inside the café the air was cooler but without movement, and it smelled of stale wine and urine.

At the table in the darkest corner sat three Americans: two young men and a girl. They conversed quietly, and in the manner of people who have all the time in the world for everything. One of the men, the thin one with a slightly wry, distraught face, was folding up some large multicolored maps he had spread out on the table a moment ago. His wife watched the meticulous movements he made with amusement and exasperation; maps bored her, and he was always consulting them. Even during the short periods when their lives were stationary, which had been few enough since their marriage twelve years ago, he had only to see a map to begin studying it passionately, and then, often as not, he would begin to plan some new, impossible trip which sometimes eventually became a reality. He did not think of himself as a tourist; he was a traveler. The difference is partly one of time, he would explain. Whereas the tourist generally hurries back home at the end of a few weeks or months, the traveler, belonging no more to one place than to the next, moves slowly, over periods of years, from one part of the earth to another. Indeed, he would have found it difficult to tell, among the many places he had lived, precisely where it was he had felt most at home. Before the war it had been Europe and the Near East, during the war the West Indies and South America. And she had accompanied him without reiterating her complaints too often or too bitterly.

At this point they had crossed the Atlantic for the first time since 1939, with a great deal of luggage and the intention of keeping as far as possible from the places which had been touched by the war. For, as he claimed, another important difference between tourist and traveler is that the former accepts his own civilization without question; not so the traveler, who compares it with the others, and rejects those elements he finds not to his liking. And the war was one facet of the mechanized age he wanted to forget.

In New York they had found that North Africa was one of the few places they could get boat passage to. From his earlier visits, made during his student days in Paris and Madrid, it seemed a likely place to spend a year or so; in any case it was near Spain and Italy, and they could always cross over if it failed to work out. Their little freighter had spewed them out from its comfortable maw the day before onto the hot docks, sweating and scowling with anxiety, where for a long time no one had paid them the slightest attention. As he stood there in the burning sun, he had been tempted to go back aboard and see about taking passage for the continuing voyage to Istanbul, but it would have been difficult to do without losing face, since it was he who had cajoled them into coming to North Africa. So he had cast a matter-of-fact glance up and down the dock, made a few reasonably unflattering remarks about the place, and let it go at that, silently resolving to start inland as quickly as possible.

The other man at the table, when he was not talking, kept whistling aimless little tunes under his breath. He was a few years younger, of sturdier build, and astonishingly handsome, as the girl often told him, in his late Paramount way. Usually there was very little expression of any sort to be found on his smooth face, but the features were formed in such a manner that in repose they suggested a general bland contentment.

They stared out into the street's dusty afternoon glare.

"The war has certainly left its mark here." Small, with blonde hair and an olive complexion, she was saved from prettiness by the intensity of her gaze. Once one had seen her eyes, the rest of the face grew vague, and when one tried to recall her image afterwards, only the piercing, questioning violence of the wide eyes remained.

"Well, naturally. There were troops passing through for a year or more."

"It seems as though there might be some place in the world they could have left alone," said the girl. This was to please her husband, because she regretted having felt annoyed with him about the maps a moment ago. Recognizing the gesture, but not understanding why she was making it, he paid no attention to it.

The other man laughed patronizingly, and he joined in.

"For your special benefit, I suppose?" said her husband.

"For us. You know you hate the whole thing as much as I do."

"What whole thing?" he demanded defensively. "If you mean this colorless mess here that calls itself a town, yes. But I'd still a damned sight rather be here than back in the United States."

She hastened to agree. "Oh, of course. But I didn't mean this place or any other particular place. I meant the whole horrible thing that happens after every war, everywhere."

"Come, Kit," said the other man. "You don't remember any other war."

She paid him no attention. "The people of each country get more like the people of every other country. They have no character, no beauty, no ideals, no culture—nothing, nothing."

Her husband reached over and patted her hand. "You're right. You're right," he said smiling. "Everything's getting gray, and it'll be grayer. But some places'll withstand the malady longer than you think. You'll see, in the Sahara here . . ."

Across the street a radio was sending forth the hysterical screams of a coloratura soprano. Kit shivered. "Let's hurry up and get there," she said. "Maybe we could escape that."

They listened fascinated as the aria, drawing to a close, made the orthodox preparations for the inevitable high final note.

Presently Kit said: "Now that that's over, I've got to have another bottle of Oulmès."

"My God, more of that gas? You'll take off."

"I know, Tunner," she said, "but I can't get my mind off water. It doesn't matter what I look at, it makes me

8

thirsty. For once I feel as if I could get on the wagon and stay there. I can't drink in the heat."

"Another Pernod?" said Tunner to Port.

Kit frowned. "If it were real Pernod—"

"It's not bad," said Tunner, as the waiter set a bottle of mineral water on the table.

"*Ce n'est pas du vrai Pernod?*"

"*Si, si, c'est du Pernod,*" said the waiter.

"Let's have another set-up," Port said. He stared at his glass dully. No one spoke as the waiter moved away. The soprano began another aria.

"She's off!" cried Tunner. The din of a street car and its bell passing across the terrace outside, drowned the music for a moment. Beneath the awning they had a glimpse of the open vehicle in the sunshine as it rocked past. It was crowded with people in tattered clothes.

Port said: "I had a strange dream yesterday. I've been trying to remember it, and just this minute I did."

"No!" cried Kit with force. "Dreams are so dull! Please!"

"You don't want to hear it!" he laughed. "But I'm going to tell it to you *anyway.*" The last was said with a certain ferocity which on the surface appeared feigned, but as Kit looked at him she felt that on the contrary he actually was dissimulating the violence he felt. She did not say the withering things that were on the tip of her tongue.

"I'll be quick about it," he smiled. "I know you're doing me a favor by listening, but I can't remember it just thinking about it. It was daytime and I was on a train that kept putting on speed. I thought to myself: 'We're going to plough into a big bed with the sheets all in mountains.'"

Tunner said archly: "Consult Madame La Hiff's *Gypsy Dream Dictionary.*"

"Shut up. And I was thinking that if I wanted to, I

9

could live over again—start at the beginning and come right on up to the present, having exactly the same life, down to the smallest detail."

Kit closed her eyes unhappily.

"What's the matter?" he demanded.

"I think it's extremely thoughtless and egotistical of you to insist this way when you know how boring it is for us."

"But I'm enjoying it so much." He beamed. "And I'll bet Tunner wants to hear it, anyway. Don't you?"

Tunner smiled. "Dreams are my cup of tea. I know my La Hiff by heart."

Kit opened one eye and looked at him. The drinks arrived.

"So I said to myself: 'No! No!' I couldn't face the idea of all those God-awful fears and pains again, *in detail.* And then for no reason I looked out the window at the trees and heard myself say: 'Yes!' Because I knew I'd be willing to go through the whole thing again just to smell the spring the way it used to smell when I was a kid. But then I realized it was too late, because while I'd been thinking 'No!' I'd reached up and snapped off my incisors as if they'd been made of plaster. The train had stopped and I held my teeth in my hand, and I started to sob. You know those terrible dream sobs that shake you like an earthquake?"

Clumsily Kit rose from the table and walked to a door marked *Dames.* She was crying.

"Let her go," said Port to Tunner, whose face showed concern. "She's worn out. The heat gets her down."

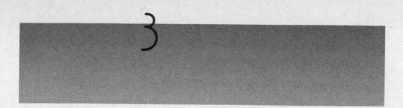

3

He sat up in bed reading, wearing only a pair of shorts. The door between their two rooms was open, and so were the windows. Over the town and harbor a lighthouse played its beam in a wide, slow circle, and above the desultory traffic an insistent electric bell shrilled without respite.

"Is that the movie next door?" called Kit.

"Must be," he said absently, still reading.

"I wonder what they're showing."

"What?" He laid down his book. "Don't tell me you're interested in going!"

"No." She sounded doubtful. "I just wondered."

"I'll tell you what it is. It's a film in Arabic called *Fiancée for Rent*. That's what it says under the title."

"It's unbelievable."

"I know."

She wandered into the room, thoughtfully smoking a

cigarette, and walked about in a circle for a minute or so. He looked up.

"What is it?" he asked.

"Nothing." She paused. "I'm just a little upset. I don't think you should have told that dream in front of Tunner."

He did not dare say: "Is that why you cried?" But he said: "In *front* of him! I told it *to* him, as much as to you. What's a dream? Good God, don't take everything so seriously! And why shouldn't he hear it? What's wrong with Tunner? We've known him for five years."

"He's such a gossip. You know that. I don't trust him. He always makes a good story."

"But who's he going to gossip with here?" said Port, exasperated.

Kit in turn was annoyed.

"Oh, not here!" she snapped. "You seem to forget we'll be back in New York some day."

"I know, I know. It's hard to believe, but I suppose we will. All right. What's so awful if he remembers every detail and tells it to everybody we know?"

"It's such a humiliating dream. Can't you see?"

"Oh, crap!"

There was a silence.

"Humiliating to whom? You or me?"

She did not answer. He pursued: "What do you mean, you don't trust Tunner? In what way?"

"Oh, I trust him, I suppose. But I've never felt completely at ease with him. I've never felt he was a close friend."

"That's nice, now that we're here with him!"

"Oh, it's all right. I like him very much. Don't misunderstand."

"But you must mean something."

"Of course I mean something. But it's not important."

She went back into her own room. He remained a moment, looking at the ceiling, a puzzled expression on his face.

He started to read again, and stopped.

"Sure you don't want to see *Fiancée for Rent?*"

"I certainly don't."

He closed his book. "I think I'll take a walk for about a half an hour."

He rose, put on a sports shirt and a pair of seersucker trousers, and combed his hair. In her room, she was sitting by the open window, filing her nails. He bent over her and kissed the nape of her neck, where the silky blonde hair climbed upward in wavy furrows.

"That's wonderful stuff you have on. Did you get it here?" He sniffed noisily, with appreciation. Then his voice changed when he said: "But what did you mean about Tunner?"

"Oh, Port! For God's sake, stop *talking* about it!"

"All right, baby," he said submissively, kissing her shoulder. And with an inflection of mock innocence: "Can't I even *think* about it?"

She said nothing until he got to the door. Then she raised her head, and there was pique in her voice: "After all, it's much more your business than it is mine."

"See you soon," he said.

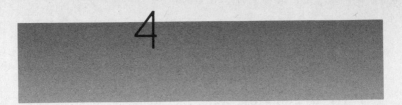

He walked through the streets, unthink-ingly seeking the darker ones, glad to be alone and to feel the night air against his face. The streets were crowded. People pushed against him as they passed, stared from door-ways and windows, made comments openly to each other about him—whether with sympathy or not he was unable to tell from their faces—and they sometimes ceased to walk merely in order to watch him.

"How friendly are they? Their faces are masks. They all look a thousand years old. What little energy they have is only the blind, mass desire to live, since no one of them eats enough to give him his own personal force. But what do they think of me? Probably nothing. Would one of them help me if I were to have an accident? Or would I lie here in the street until the police found me? What motive could any one of them *have* for helping me? They have no religion left. Are they Moslems or Christians? They don't know. They know money, and when they get it, all they want is to eat. But what's wrong with that? Why do I feel this way about them? Guilt at being well fed and healthy among them? But suffering is equally divided among all men; each has the same amount to undergo. . . ." Emotionally he felt that this last idea was untrue, but at the moment it was a necessary belief: it is not always easy to support the stares of hungry people. Thinking that way he could walk on through the streets. It was as if either he or they did not exist. Both suppositions were possible. The Spanish maid at the hotel had said to him that noon: *"La vida es pena."* "Of course," he had replied, feeling false even as he spoke, asking himself if any American can truthfully accept a definition of life which makes it synonymous with suffering. But at the moment he had approved her sentiment because she was old, withered, so clearly of the people. For years it had been one of his superstitions that reality and true perception were to be found in the conversation of the laboring classes. Even though now he saw clearly that their formulas of thought and speech are as strict and as patterned, and thus as far removed from any profound expression of truth as those of any other class, often he found himself still in the act of waiting, with the unreasoning belief that gems of wisdom might yet issue from their mouths. As he walked along, his nervousness was made manifest to him by the sudden consciousness that he was repeatedly tracing rapid figure-eights with his right index finger. He sighed and made himself stop doing it.

His spirits rose a bit as he came out onto a square that was relatively brightly lighted. The cafés on all four sides of the little plaza had put tables and chairs not only across the sidewalks, but in the street as well, so that it would have been impossible for a vehicle to pass through without upsetting them. In the center of the square was a tiny park adorned by four plane trees that had been trimmed to look like open parasols. Underneath the trees there were at least a dozen dogs of various sizes, milling about in a close huddle, and all barking frantically. He made his way slowly across the square, trying to avoid the dogs. As he moved along cautiously under the trees he became aware that at each step he was crushing something beneath his feet. The ground was covered with large insects; their hard shells broke with little explosions that were quite audible to him even amidst the noise the dogs were making. He was aware that ordinarily he would have experienced a thrill of disgust on contact with such a phenomenon, but unreasonably tonight he felt instead a childish triumph. "I'm in a bad way and so what?" The few scattered people sitting at the tables were for the most part silent, but when they spoke, he heard all three of the town's tongues: Arabic, Spanish and French.

Slowly the street began to descend; this surprised him because he imagined that the entire town was built on the slope facing the harbor, and he had consciously chosen to walk inland rather than toward the waterfront. The odors in the air grew ever stronger. They were varied, but they all represented filth of one sort or another. This proximity with, as it were, a forbidden element, served to elate him. He abandoned himself to the perverse pleasure he found in continuing mechanically to put one foot in front of the other, even though he was quite clearly aware of his fatigue. "Suddenly I'll find myself turning around and going back," he thought. But not until then, because he would not make the decision to do it. The impulse to retrace his steps delayed itself from moment to moment. Finally he ceased being surprised: a faint vision began to haunt his mind. It was Kit, seated by the open window, filing her nails and looking out over the town. And as he found his fancy returning more often, as the minutes went by, to that scene, unconsciously he felt himself the protagonist, Kit the spectator. The validity of his existence at that moment was predicated on the assumption that she had not moved, but was still sitting there. It was as if she could still see him from the window, tiny and far away as he was, walking rhythmically uphill and down, through light and shadow; it was as if only she knew when he would turn around and walk the other way.

The street lights were very far apart now, and the streets had left off being paved. Still there were children in the gutters, playing with the garbage and screeching. A small stone suddenly hit him in the back. He wheeled about, but it was too dark to see where it had come from. A few seconds later another stone, coming from in front of him, landed against his knee. In the dim light, he saw a group of small children scattering before him. More stones came from the other direction, this time without hitting him. When he got beyond, to a point where there was a light, he stopped and tried to watch the two groups in battle, but they all ran off into the dark, and so he started up again, his gait as mechanical and rhythmical as before. A wind that was dry and warm, coming up the street out of the blackness before him, met him head on. He sniffed at the fragments of mystery in it, and again he felt an unaccustomed exaltation.

Even though the street became constantly less urban, it seemed reluctant to give up; huts continued to line it on both sides. Beyond a certain point there were no more lights, and the dwellings themselves lay in darkness. The wind, straight from the south, blew across the barren mountains that were invisible ahead of him, over the vast flat sebkha to the edges of the town, raising curtains of dust that climbed to the crest of the hill and lost themselves in the air above the harbor. He stood still. The last possible suburb had been strung on the street's thread. Beyond the final hut the garbage and rubble floor of the road sloped abruptly downward in three directions. In the dimness below were shallow, crooked canyon-like formations. Port raised his eyes to the sky: the powdery course of the Milky Way was like a giant rift across the heavens that let the faint white light through. In the distance he heard a motorcycle. When its sound was finally gone, there was nothing to hear but an occasional cockcrow, like the highest part of a repeated melody whose other notes were inaudible.

He started down the bank to the right, sliding among the fish skeletons and dust. Once below, he felt out a rock that seemed clean and sat down on it. The stench was overpowering. He lit a match, saw the ground thick with chicken feathers and decayed melon rinds. As he rose to his feet he heard steps above him at the end of the street. A figure stood at the top of the embankment. It did not speak, yet Port was certain that it had seen him, had followed him, and knew he was sitting down there. It lit a cigarette, and for a moment he saw an Arab wearing a chechia on his head. The match, thrown into the air, made a fading parabola, the face disappeared, and only the red point of the cigarette remained. The cock crowed several times. Finally the man cried out.

"Qu'est-ce ti cherches là?"

"Here's where the trouble begins," thought Port. He did not move.

The Arab waited a bit. He walked to the very edge of the slope. A dislodged tin can rolled noisily down toward the rock where Port sat.

"Hé! M'sieu! Qu'est-ce ti vo?"

He decided to answer. His French was good.

"Who? Me? Nothing."

The Arab bounded down the bank and stood in front of him. With the characteristic impatient, almost indignant gestures he pursued his inquisition. What are you doing here all alone? Where do you come from? What do you want here? Are you looking for something? To which Port answered wearily: Nothing. That way. Nothing. No.

For a moment the Arab was silent, trying to decide what direction to give the dialogue. He drew violently on his cigarette several times until it glowed very bright, then he flicked it away and exhaled the smoke.

"Do you want to take a walk?" he said.

"What? A walk? Where?"

"Out there." His arm waved toward the mountains.

"What's out there?"

"Nothing."

There was another silence between them.

"I'll pay you a drink," said the Arab. And immediately on that: "What's your name?"

"Jean," said Port.

The Arab repeated the name twice, as if considering its merits. "Me," tapping his chest, "Smaïl. So, do we go and drink?"

"No."

"Why not?"

"I don't feel like it."

"You don't feel like it. What do you feel like doing?"

"Nothing."

All at once the conversation began again from the beginning. Only the now truly outraged inflection of the Arab's voice marked any difference: *"Qu'est-ce ti fi là? Qu'est-ce ti cherches?"* Port rose and started to climb up the slope, but it was difficult going. He kept sliding back down. At once the Arab was beside him, tugging at his arm. "Where are you going, Jean?" Without answering Port made a great effort and gained the top. *"Au revoir,"* he called, walking quickly up the middle of the street. He heard a desperate scrambling behind him; a moment later the man was at his side.

"You didn't wait for me," he said in an aggrieved tone.

"No. I said good-bye."

"I'll go with you."

Port did not answer. They walked a good distance in silence. When they came to the first street light, the Arab reached into his pocket and pulled out a worn wallet. Port glanced at it and continued to walk.

"Look!" cried the Arab, waving it in his face. Port did not look.

"What is it?" he said flatly.

"I was in the Fifth Battalion of Sharpshooters. Look at the paper! Look! You'll see!"

Port walked faster. Soon there began to be people in the street. No one stared at them. One would have said that the presence of the Arab beside him made him invisible. But now he was no longer sure of the way. It would never do to let this be seen. He continued to walk straight ahead as if there were no doubt in his mind. "Over the crest of the hill and down," he said to himself, "and I can't miss it."

Everything looked unfamiliar: the houses, the streets, the cafés, even the formation of the town with regard to the hill. Instead of finding a summit from which to begin the downward walk, he discovered that here the streets all led perceptibly upward, no matter which way he turned; to descend he would have had to go back. The Arab walked solemnly along with him, now beside him, now slipping behind when there was not enough room to walk two abreast. He no longer made attempts at conversation; Port noticed with relish that he was a little out of breath.

"I can keep this up all night if I have to," he thought, "but how the hell will I get to the hotel?"

All at once they were in a street which was no more than a passageway. Above their heads the opposite walls jutted out to within a few inches of each other. For an instant Port hesitated: this was not the kind of street he wanted to walk in, and besides, it so obviously did not lead to the hotel. In that short moment the Arab took charge. He said: "You don't know this street? It's called Rue de la Mer Rouge. You know it? Come on. There are *cafés arabes* up this way. Just a little way. Come on."

Port considered. He wanted at all costs to keep up the pretense of being familiar with the town.

"Je ne sais pas si je veux y aller ce soir," he reflected, aloud.

The Arab began to pull Port's sleeve in his excitement. *"Si, si!"* he cried. *"Viens!* I'll pay you a drink."

"I don't drink. It's very late."

Two cats nearby screamed at each other. The Arab made a hissing noise and stamped his feet; they ran off in opposite directions.

"We'll have tea, then," he pursued.

Port sighed. *"Bien,"* he said.

The café had a complicated entrance. They went through a low arched door, down a dim hall into a small garden. The air reeked of lilies, and it was also tinged with the sour smell of drains. In the dark they crossed the garden and climbed a long flight of stone steps. The staccato sound of a hand drum came from above, tapping indolent patterns above a sea of voices.

"Do we sit outside or in?" the Arab asked.

"Outside," said Port. He sniffed the invigorating smell of hashish smoke, and unconsciously smoothed his hair as they arrived at the top of the stairs. The Arab noticed even that small gesture. "No ladies here, you know."

"Oh, I know."

Through a doorway he caught a glimpse of the long succession of tiny, brightly-lit rooms, and the men seated everywhere on the reed matting that covered the floors. They all wore either white turbans or red chechias on their heads, a detail which lent the scene such a strong aspect of homogeneity that Port exclaimed: "Ah!" as they passed by the door. When they were on the terrace in the starlight, with an oud being plucked idly in the dark nearby, he said to his companion: "But I didn't know there was anything like this left in this city." The Arab did not understand. "Like this?" he echoed. "How?"

"With nothing but Arabs. Like the inside here. I thought all the cafés were like the ones in the street, all mixed up; Jews, French, Spanish, Arabs together. I thought the war had changed everything."

The Arab laughed. "The war was bad. A lot of people died. There was nothing to eat. That's all. How would that change the cafés? Oh no, my friend. It's the same as always." A moment later he said: "So you haven't been here since the war! But you were here before the war?"

"Yes," said Port. This was true; he had once spent an afternoon in the town when his boat had made a brief call there.

The tea arrived; they chatted and drank it. Slowly the image of Kit sitting in the window began to take shape again in Port's mind. At first, when he became conscious of it, he felt a pang of guilt. Then his fantasy took a hand, and he saw her face, tight-lipped with fury as she undressed and flung her flimsy pieces of clothing across the furniture. By now she had surely given up waiting and gone to bed. He shrugged his shoulders and grew pensive, rinsing what was left of his tea around and around in the bottom of the glass, and following with his eyes the circular motion he was making.

"You're sad," said Smaïl.

"No, no." He looked up and smiled wistfully, then resumed watching the glass.

"You live only a short time. *Il faut rigoler.*"

Port was impatient; he was not in the mood for café philosophizing.

"Yes, I know," he said shortly, and he sighed. Smaïl pinched his arm. His eyes were shining.

"When we leave here, I'll take you to see a friend of mine."

"I don't want to meet him," said Port, adding: "Thank you anyway."

"Ah, you're really sad," laughed Smaïl. "It's a girl. Beautiful as the moon."

Port's heart missed a beat. "A girl," he repeated automatically, without taking his eyes from the glass. He was perturbed to witness his own interior excitement. He looked at Smaïl.

"A girl?" he said. "You mean a whore."

Smaïl was mildly indignant. "A whore? Ah, my friend, you don't know me. I wouldn't introduce you to that. *C'est de la saloperie, ça!* This is a friend of mine, very elegant, very nice. When you meet her, you'll see."

The musician stopped playing the oud. Inside the café they were calling out numbers for the lotto game: *"Ouahad aou tletine! Arbaine!"*

Port said: "How old is she?"

Smaïl hesitated. "About sixteen. Sixteen or seventeen."

"Or twenty or twenty-five," suggested Port, with a leer.

Again Smaïl was indignant. "What do you mean, twenty-five? I tell you she's sixteen or seventeen. You don't believe me? Listen. You meet her. If you don't like her, you just pay for the tea and we'll go out again. Is that all right?"

"And if I do like her?"

"Well, you'll do whatever you want."

"But I'll pay her?"

"But of course you'll pay her."

Port laughed. "And you say she's not a whore."

Smaïl leaned over the table towards him and said with a great show of patience: "Listen, Jean. She's a dancer. She only arrived from her bled in the desert a few weeks ago. How can she be a whore if she's not registered and doesn't live in the quartier? Eh? Tell me! You pay her because you take up her time. She dances in the quartier, but she has no room, no bed there. She's not a whore. So now, shall we go?"

Port thought a long time, looked up at the sky, down into the garden, and all around the terrace before answering: "Yes. Let's go. Now."

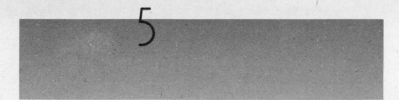

5

When they left the café it seemed to him that they were going more or less in the same direction from which they had just come. There were fewer people in the streets and the air was cooler. They walked for a good distance through the Casbah, making a sudden exit through a tall gateway onto a high, open space outside the walls. Here it was silent, and the stars were very much in evidence. The pleasure he felt at the unexpected freshness of the air and the relief at being in the open once more, out from under the overhanging houses, served to delay Port in asking the question that was in his mind: "Where are we going?" But as they continued along what seemed a parapet at the edge of a deep, dry moat, he finally gave voice to it. Smaïl replied vaguely that the girl lived with some friends at the edge of town.

"But we're already in the country," objected Port.

"Yes, it's the country," said Smaïl.

It was perfectly clear that he was being evasive now;

his character seemed to have changed again. The beginning of intimacy was gone. To Port he was once more the anonymous dark figure that had stood above him in the garbage at the end of the street, smoking a bright cigarette. *You can still break it up. Stop walking. Now.* But the combined even rhythm of their feet on the stones was too powerful. The parapet made a wide curve and the ground below dropped steeply away into a deeper darkness. The moat had ended some hundred feet back. They were now high above the upper end of an open valley.

"The Turkish fortress," remarked Smaïl, pounding on the stones with his heel.

"Listen to me," began Port angrily; "where are we going?" He looked at the rim of uneven black mountains ahead of them on the horizon.

"Down there." Smaïl pointed to the valley. A moment later he stopped walking. "Here are the stairs." They leaned over the ledge. A narrow iron staircase was fastened to the side of the wall. It had no railing and led straight downward at a steep angle.

"It's a long way," said Port.

"Ah, yes, it's the Turkish fortress. You see that light down there?" He indicated a faint red glimmer that came and went almost directly beneath them. "That's the tent where she lives."

"The tent!"

"There are no houses down here. Only tents. There are a lot of them. *On descend?*"

Smaïl went first, keeping close to the wall. "Touch the stones," he said.

As they approached the bottom, he saw that the feeble glow of light was a dying bonfire built in an open space between two large nomad tents. Smaïl suddenly stopped to listen. There was an indistinguishable murmur of male voices. *"Allons-y,"* he muttered; his voice sounded satisfied.

They reached the end of the staircase. There was hard ground beneath their feet. To his left Port saw the black silhouette of a huge agave plant in flower.

"Wait here," whispered Smaïl. Port was about to light a cigarette; Smaïl hit his arm angrily. "No!" he whispered. "But what is it?" began Port, highly annoyed at the show of secrecy. Smaïl disappeared.

Leaning against the cold rock wall, Port waited to hear a break in the monotonous, low-pitched conversation, an exchange of greetings, but nothing happened. The voices went on exactly as before, an uninterrupted flow of expressionless sounds. "He must have gone into the other tent," he thought. One side of the farther tent flickered pink in the light of the bonfire; beyond was darkness. He edged a few steps along the wall, trying to see the entrance of the tent, but it faced in the other direction. Then he listened for the sound of voices there, but none came. For no reason at all he suddenly heard Kit's parting remark as he had left her room: "After all, it's much more your business than it is mine." Even now the words meant nothing in particular to him, but he remembered the tone in which she had said it: she had sounded hurt and rebellious. And it was all about Tunner. He stood up straight. "He's been after her," he whispered aloud. Abruptly he turned and went to the staircase, started up it. After six steps he stopped and looked around. "What can I do tonight?" he thought. "I'm using this as an excuse to get out of here, because I'm afraid. What the hell, he'll never get her."

A figure darted out from between the two tents and ran lightly to the foot of the stairs. "Jean!" it whispered. Port stood still.

"Ah! ti es là! What are you doing up there? Come on!"

Port walked slowly back down. Smaïl stepped out of his way, took his arm.

"Why can't we talk?" whispered Port. Smaïl squeezed his arm. "Shh!" he said into his ear. They skirted the nearer tent, brushing past a clump of high thistles, and made their way over the stones to the entrance of the other.

"Take off your shoes," commanded Smaïl, slipping off his sandals.

"Not a good idea," thought Port. "No," he said aloud.

"Shh!" Smaïl pushed him inside, shoes still on.

The central part of the tent was high enough to stand up in. A short candle stuck on top of a chest near the entrance provided the light, so that the nether parts of the tent were in almost complete darkness. Lengths of straw matting had been spread on the ground at senseless angles; objects were scattered everywhere in utter disorder. There was no one in the tent waiting for them.

"Sit down," said Smaïl, acting the host. He cleared the largest piece of matting of an alarm clock, a sardine can, and an ancient, incredibly greasy pair of overalls. Port sat down and put his elbows on his knees. On the mat next to him lay a chipped enamel bedpan, half filled with a darkish liquid. There were bits of stale bread everywhere. He lit a cigarette without offering one to Smaïl, who returned to stand near the entrance, looking out.

And suddenly she stepped inside—a slim, wild-looking girl with great dark eyes. She was dressed in spotless white, with a white turbanlike headdress that pulled her hair tightly backward, accentuating the indigo designs tattooed on her forehead. Once inside the tent, she stood quite still, looking at Port with something of the expression, he thought, the young bull often wears as he takes the first few steps into the glare of the arena. There was bewilderment, fear, and a passive expectancy in her face as she stared quietly at him.

"Ah, here she is!" said Smaïl, still in a hushed voice. "Her name is Marhnia." He waited a bit. Port rose and stepped forward to take her hand. "She doesn't speak French," Smaïl explained. Without smiling, she touched Port's hand lightly with her own and raised her fingers to her lips. Bowing, she said, in what amounted almost to a whisper: *"Ya sidi, la bess âlik? Eglès, baraka 'laou'fik."* With gracious dignity and a peculiar modesty of movement, she unstuck the lighted candle from the chest, and walked across to the back of the tent, where a blanket stretched from the ceiling formed a partial alcove. Before disappearing behind the blanket, she turned her head to them, and said, gesturing: *"Agi! Agi menah!"* The two men followed her into the alcove, where an old mattress had been laid on some low boxes in an attempt to make a salon. There was a tiny tea table beside the improvised divan, and a pile of small, lumpy cushions lay on the mat by the table. The girl set the candle down on the bare earth and began to arrange the cushions along the mattress.

"Essmah!" she said to Port, and to Smaïl: *"Tsekellem bellatsi."* Then she went out. He laughed and called after her in a low voice: *"Fhemtek!"* Port was intrigued by the girl, but the language barrier annoyed him, and he was even more irritated by the fact that Smaïl and she could converse together in his presence. "She's gone to get fire," said Smaïl. "Yes, yes," said Port, "but why do we have to whisper?" Smaïl rolled his eyes toward the tent's entrance. "The men in the other tent," he said.

Presently she returned, carrying an earthen pot of bright coals. While she was boiling the water and preparing the tea, Smaïl chatted with her. Her replies were always grave, her voice hushed but pleasantly modulated. It seemed to Port that she was much more like a young nun than a café dancer. At the same time he did not in the least trust her, being content to sit and marvel at the delicate movements of her nimble, henna-stained fingers as she tore the stalks of mint apart and stuffed them into the little teapot.

When she had sampled the tea several times and eventually had found it to her liking, she handed them each a glass, and with a solemn air sat back on her haunches and began to drink hers. "Sit here," said Port, patting the couch beside him. She indicated that she was quite happy where she was, and thanked him politely. Turning her attention to Smaïl, she proceeded to engage him in a lengthy conversation during which Port sipped his tea and tried to relax. He had an oppressive sensation that daybreak was near at hand—surely not more than an hour or so away, and he felt that all this time was being wasted. He looked anxiously at his watch; it had stopped at five minutes of two. But it was still going. Surely it must be later than that. Marhnia addressed a question to Smaïl which seemed to include Port. "She wants to know if you have heard the story about Outka, Mimouna and Aïcha," said Smaïl. "No," said Port. *"Goul lou, goul lou,"* said Marhnia to Smaïl, urging him.

"There are three girls from the mountains, from a place near Marhnia's bled, and they are called Outka, Mimouna and Aïcha." Marhnia was nodding her head slowly in affirmation, her large soft eyes fixed on Port. "They go to seek their fortune in the M'Zab. Most girls from the mountains go to Alger, Tunis, here, to earn money, but these girls want one thing more than everything else. They want to drink tea in the Sahara." Marhnia continued to nod her head; she was keeping up with the story solely by means of the place-names as Smaïl pronounced them.

"I see," said Port, who had no idea whether the story was a humorous one or a tragic one; he was determined to be careful, so that he could pretend to savor it as much as she clearly hoped he would. He only wished it might be short.

"In the M'Zab the men are all ugly. The girls dance in the cafés of Ghardaia, but they are always sad; they still want to have tea in the Sahara." Port glanced again at Marhnia. Her expression was completely serious. He nodded his head again. "So, many months pass, and they are still in the M'Zab, and they are very, very sad, because the men are all so ugly. They are very ugly there, like pigs. And they don't pay enough money to the poor girls so they can go and have tea in the Sahara." Each time he said "Sahara," which he pronounced in the Arabic fashion, with a vehement accent on the first syllable, he stopped for a moment. "One day a Targui comes, he is tall and handsome, on a beautiful mehari; he talks to Outka, Mimouna and Aïcha, he tells them about the desert, down there where he lives, his bled, and they listen, and their eyes are big. Then he says: 'Dance for me,' and they dance. Then he makes love with all three, he gives a silver piece to Outka, a silver piece to Mimouna, and a silver piece to Aïcha. At daybreak he gets on his mehari and goes away to the south. After that they are very sad, and the M'Zabi look uglier than ever to them, and they only are thinking of the tall Targui who lives in the Sahara." Port lit a cigarette; then he noticed Marhnia looking expectantly at him, and he passed her the pack. She took one, and with a crude pair of tongs elegantly lifted a live coal to the end of it. It ignited immediately, whereupon she passed it to Port, taking his in exchange. He smiled at her. She bowed almost imperceptibly.

"Many months go by, and still they can't earn enough

money to go to the Sahara. They have kept the silver pieces, because all three are in love with the Targui. And they are always sad. One day they say: 'We are going to finish like this—always sad, without ever having tea in the Sahara—so now we must go anyway, even without money.' And they put all their money together, even the three silver pieces, and they buy a teapot and a tray and three glasses, and they buy bus tickets to El Goléa. And there they have only a little money left, and they give it all to a bachhamar who is taking his caravan south to the Sahara. So he lets them ride with his caravan. And one night, when the sun is going to go down, they come to the great dunes of sand, and they think: 'Ah, now we are in the Sahara; we are going to make tea.' The moon comes up, all the men are asleep except the guard. He is sitting with the camels playing his flute." Smaïl wriggled his fingers in front of his mouth. "Outka, Mimouna and Aïcha go away from the caravan quietly with their tray and their teapot and their glasses. They are going to look for the highest dune so they can see all the Sahara. Then they are going to make tea. They walk a long time. Outka says: 'I see a high dune,' and they go to it and climb up to the top. Then Mimouna says: 'I see a dune over there. It's much higher and we can see all the way to In Salah from it.' So they go to it, and it is much higher. But when they get to the top, Aïcha says: 'Look! There's the highest dune of all. We can see to Tamanrasset. That's where the Targui lives.' The sun came up and they kept walking. At noon they were very hot. But they came to the dune and they climbed and climbed. When they got to the top they were very tired and they said: 'We'll rest a little and then make tea.' But first they set out the tray and the teapot and the glasses. Then they lay down and slept. And then"—Smaïl paused and looked at Port—"Many days later another caravan was passing and a man saw something on top of the highest dune there. And when they went up to see, they found Outka, Mimouna and Aïcha; they were still there, lying the same way as when they had gone to sleep. And all three of the glasses," he held up his own little tea glass, "were full of sand. That was how they had their tea in the Sahara."

There was a long silence. It was obviously the end of the story. Port looked at Marhnia; she was still nodding her head, her eyes fixed on him. He decided to hazard a remark. "It's very sad," he said. She immediately inquired of Smaïl what he had said. *"Gallik merhmoum bzef,"* translated Smaïl. She shut her eyes slowly and continued to nod her head. *"Ei oua!"* she said, opening them again. Port turned quickly to Smaïl. "Listen, it's very late. I want to arrange a price with her. How much should I give her?"

Smaïl looked scandalized. "You can't do that as if you were dealing with a whore! *Ci pas une putain, je t'ai dit!*"

"But I'll pay her if I stay with her?"

"Of course."

"Then I want to arrange it now."

"I can't do that for you, my friend."

Port shrugged his shoulders and stood up. "I've got to go. It's late."

Marhnia looked quickly from one man to the other. Then she said a word or two in a very soft voice to Smaïl, who frowned but stalked out of the tent yawning.

They lay on the couch together. She was very beautiful, very docile, very understanding, and still he did not trust her. She declined to disrobe completely, but in her delicate gestures of refusal he discerned an ultimate yielding, to bring about which it would require only time. With time he could have had her confidence; tonight he could only have that which had been taken for granted from the beginning. He reflected on this as he lay, looking into her untroubled face, remembered that he was leaving for the south in a day or two, inwardly swore at his luck, and said to himself: "Better half a loaf." Marhnia leaned over and snuffed the candle between her fingers. For a second there was utter silence, utter blackness. Then he felt her soft arms slowly encircle his neck, and her lips on his forehead.

Almost immediately a dog began to howl in the distance. For a while he did not hear it; when he did, it troubled him. It was the wrong music for the moment. Soon he found himself imagining that Kit was a silent onlooker. The fantasy stimulated him—the lugubrious howling no longer bothered him.

Not more than a quarter of an hour later, he got up and peered around the blanket, to the flap of the tent: it was still dark. He was seized with an abrupt desire to be out of the place. He sat down on the couch and began to arrange his clothing. The two arms stole up again, locked themselves about his neck. Firmly he pulled them away, gave them a few playful pats. Only one came up this time; the other slipped inside his jacket and he felt his chest being caressed. Some indefinable false movement there made him reach inside to put his hand on hers. His wallet was already between her fingers. He yanked it away from her and pushed her back down on the mattress. "Ah!" she cried, very loud. He rose and stumbled noisily through the welter of objects that lay between him and the exit. This time she screamed, briefly. The voices in the other tent became audible. With his wallet still in his hand he rushed out, turned sharply to the left and began to run toward the wall. He fell twice, once against a rock and once because the ground sloped unexpectedly down. As he rose the second time, he saw a man coming from one side to cut him off from the staircase. He was limping, but he was nearly there. He did get there. All the way up the stairs it seemed to him that someone immediately behind him would have hold of one of his legs during the next second. His lungs were an enormous pod of pain, would burst instantly. His mouth was open, drawn down at the sides, his teeth clenched, and the air whistled between them as he drew breath. At the top he turned, and seizing a boulder he could not lift, he did lift it, and hurled it down the staircase. Then he breathed deeply and began to run along the parapet. The sky was palpably lighter, an immaculate gray clarity spreading upward from behind the low hills in the east. He could not run very far. His heart was beating in his head and neck. He knew he never could reach the town. On the side of the road away from the valley there was a wall, too high to be climbed. But a few hundred feet farther on, it had been broken down for a short distance, and a talus of stones and dirt made a perfect stile. He cut back inside the wall in the direction from which he had just come, and hurried panting up a gradual side hill studded with the flat stone beds which are Moslem tombstones. Finally he sat down for a minute, his head in his hands, and was conscious of several things at once: the pain of his head and chest, the fact that he no longer held his wallet, and the loud sound of his own heart, which, however, did not keep him from thinking he heard the excited voices of his pursuers below in the road a moment later. He rose and staggered on upward over the graves. Eventually the hill sloped downward in the other direction. He felt a little safer. But each minute the light of day was nearer; it would be easy to spot his solitary figure from a distance, wandering over the hill. He began to run again, downhill, always in the same direction, staggering now and then, never looking up for fear he should fall; this went on for a long time; the graveyard was left behind. Finally he reached a high spot covered with bushes and cactus, but from which he could dominate the entire immediate countryside. He sat down among the bushes. It was perfectly quiet. The sky was white. Occasionally he stood up carefully and peered out. And so it was that when the sun came up he looked between two oleanders and saw it reflected red across the miles of glittering salt sebkha that lay between him and the mountains.

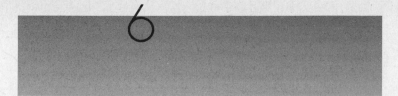

6

Kit awoke in a sweat with the hot morning sun pouring over her. She stumbled up, closed the curtains, and fell back into bed. The sheets were wet where she had lain. The thought of breakfast turned her stomach. There were days when from the moment she came out of sleep, she could feel doom hanging over her head like a low rain cloud. Those were difficult days to live through, not so much because of the sensation of suspended disaster of which she was acutely conscious then, but because the customary smooth functioning of her system of omens was wholly upset. If on ordinary days on her way out to go shopping she turned her ankle or scraped her shin on the furniture, it was easy to conclude that the shopping expedition would be a failure for one reason or another, or that it might be actually dangerous for her to persist in making it. At least on those days she knew a good omen from a bad one. But the other days were treacherous, for the feeling of doom was so strong that it became a hostile consciousness just behind or beside her, foreseeing her attempts to avoid flying in the face of the evil omens, and thus all too able to set traps for her. In this way what at first sight might seem a propitious sign could easily be nothing more than a kind of bait to lure her into danger. Then, too, the turned ankle could be a thing to disregard in such cases, since it had been brought upon her so that she might abandon her intention of going out, and thus might be at home when the furnace boiler exploded, the house caught on fire, or someone she particularly wanted to avoid stopped by to see her. And in her personal life, in her relationships with her friends, these considerations reached monstrous proportions. She was capable of sitting all morning long, attempting to recall the details of a brief scene or conversation, in order to be able to try out in her mind every possible interpretation of each gesture or sentence, each facial expression or vocal inflection, together with their juxtapositions. A great part of her life was dedicated to the categorizing of omens. And so it is not surprising that when she found it impossible to exercise that function, because of her doubt, her ability to go through the motions of everyday existence was reduced to a minimum. It was as if she had been stricken by a strange paralysis. She had no reactions at all; her entire personality withdrew from sight; she had a haunted look. On these days of doom friends who knew her well would say: "Oh, this is one of Kit's *days.*" If on these days she was subdued and seemed most reasonable, it was only because she was imitating mechanically what she considered rational behavior. One reason she had such a strong dislike of hearing dreams recounted was that the telling of them brought straightway to her attention the struggle that raged in her—the war between reason and atavism. In intellectual discussions she was always the proponent of scientific method; at the same time it was inevitable that she should regard the dream as an omen.

A further complexity was brought to the situation by the fact that also she lived through still other days when vengeance from above seemed the remotest of possibilities. Every sign was good; an unearthly aura of beneficence glowed from behind each person, object and circumstance. On those days, if she permitted herself to act as she felt, Kit could be quite happy. But of late she had begun to believe that such days, which were rare enough, to be sure, were given her only to throw her off her guard, so that she would not be able to deal with her omens. A natural euphoria was then transformed into a nervous and slightly hysterical peevishness. In conversation repeatedly she would catch herself up, trying to pretend that her remarks had been made in wilful jest, when actually they had been uttered with all the venom of which a foul humor is capable.

She was no more disturbed by other people as such, than the marble statue is by the flies that crawl on it; however, as possible harbingers of undesirable events and wielders of unfavorable influence in her own life, she accorded other people supreme importance. She would say: "Other people rule my life," and it was true. But she allowed them to do it only because her superstitious fancy had invested them with magical importance regarding her own destiny, and never because their personalities awoke any profound sympathy or understanding in her.

A good part of the night she had lain awake, thinking. Her intuition generally let her know when Port was up to something. She told herself always that it did not matter what he did, but she had repeated the statement so often in her mind that long ago she had become suspicious of its truth. It had not been an easy thing to accept the fact that she did care. Against her will she forced herself to admit that she still belonged to Port, even though he did not come to claim her—and that she still lived in a world illumined by the distant light of a possible miracle: he might yet return to her. It made her feel abject, and therefore, of course, furious with herself to realize that everything depended on him, that she was merely waiting for some unlikely caprice on his part, something which might in some unforeseen manner bring him back. She was far too intelligent to make the slightest effort in that direction herself; even the subtlest means would have failed, and to fail would be far worse than never to have tried. It was merely a question of sitting tight, of being there. Perhaps some day he would see her. But in the meantime so many precious months were going past, unused!

Tunner annoyed her because although his presence and his interest in her provided a classical situation which, if exploited, actually might give results where nothing else could, she was for some reason incapable of playing up to him. He bored her; she involuntarily compared him with Port, and always to Port's advantage. As she had been thinking in the night she had tried again and again to direct her fantasies in such a way as to make Tunner an object of excitement. Naturally this had been a failure. Nevertheless she had resolved to attempt the building of a more intimate relationship with him, despite the fact that even as she had made the decision she was quite aware that not only would it be a thoroughly unsavory chore for her, but also that she would be doing it, as she always did everything that required a conscious effort, for Port.

There was a knock at the door into the hall.

"Oh, God, who is it?" Kit said aloud.

"Me." It was Tunner's voice. As usual, he sounded offensively chipper. "Are you awake?"

She scrambled about in the bed, making a loud noise that mingled sighs, flapping sheet, and creaking bedspring. "Not very," she groaned, at last.

"This is the best time of day. You shouldn't miss it!" he shouted.

There was a pointed silence, during which she remembered her resolution. In a martyred voice she called: "Just a minute, Tunner."

"Right!" A minute, an hour—he would wait, and show the same good-natured (and false, she thought) smile when he finally was let in. She dashed cold water into her face, rubbed it with a flimsy turkish towel, put on some lipstick and ran a comb through her hair. Suddenly frantic, she began to look about the room for the right bathrobe. Through the partially open door into Port's room she caught sight of his big white terry-cloth robe hanging on the wall. She knocked rapidly on the door as she went in, saw that he was not there, and snatched up the robe. As she pulled the belt about her waist in front of her mirror she reflected with satisfaction that no one ever could accuse her of coquetry in having chosen this particular garment. It came to the floor on her, and she had to roll the sleeves back twice to uncover her hands.

She opened the door.

"Hi!"

There was the smile.

"Hello, Tunner," she said apathetically. "Come in."

He rumpled her hair with his left hand as he walked past her on his way to the window, where he pulled the curtains aside. "You holding a séance in here? Ah, now I can see you." The sharp morning light filled the room, the polished floor-tiles reflecting the sun on the ceiling as if they had been water.

"How are you?" she said vacantly as she stood beside the mirror again, combing her hair where he had tousled it.

"Wonderful." He beamed at her image in the mirror, making his eyes sparkle, and even, she noted with great distaste, moving a certain facial muscle that emphasized the dimples in his cheeks. "He's such a fake," she thought. "What in God's name's he doing here with us? Of course, it's Port's fault. He's the one who encouraged him to drag along."

"What happened to Port last night?" Tunner was saying. "I sort of waited up for him, but he didn't show up."

Kit looked at him. "Waited for up him?" she repeated, incredulous.

"Well, we more or less had a date at our café, you know the one. For a nightcap. But no hide, no hair. I got in bed and read until pretty late. He hadn't come in by three." This was completely false. Actually Tunner had said: "If you go out, look into the Eckmühl; I'll probably be in there." He had gone out shortly after Port, had picked up a French girl and stayed with her at her hotel until five. When he had come back at dawn he had managed to look through the low glass transoms into their rooms, and had seen the empty bed in one and Kit asleep in the other.

"Really?" she said, turning back to the mirror. "He can't have had much sleep, then, because he's already gone out."

"You mean he hasn't come in yet," said Tunner, staring at her intently.

She did not answer. "Will you push that button there, please?" she said presently. "I think I'll have a cup of their chicory and one of those plaster croissants."

When she thought enough time had passed, she wandered into Port's room and glanced at the bed. It had been turned down for the night and not touched since. Without knowing precisely why, she pulled the sheet all the way down and sat on the bed for a moment, pushing dents in the pillows with her hands. Then she unfolded the laid-out pajamas and dropped them in a heap at the foot. The servant knocked at her door; she went back into her room and ordered breakfast. When the servant had left she shut the door and sat in the armchair by the window, not looking out.

"You know," Tunner said musingly, "I've thought a lot about it lately. You're a very curious person. It's hard to understand you."

Kit clicked her tongue with exasperation. "Oh, Tunner! Stop trying to be interesting." Immediately she blamed herself for showing her impatience, and added, smiling: "On you it looks terrible."

His hurt expression quickly changed into a grin. "No, I mean it. You're a fascinating case."

She pursed her lips angrily; she was furious, not so much because of what he was saying, although she considered it all idiotic, but because the idea of having to converse with him at all right now seemed almost more than she could bear. "Probably," she said.

Breakfast arrived. He sat with her while she drank her coffee and ate her croissant. Her eyes had assumed a dreamy expression, and he had the feeling that she had completely forgotten his presence. When she had nearly finished her breakfast, she turned to him and said politely: "Will you excuse me if I eat?"

He began to laugh. She looked startled.

"Hurry up!" he said. "I want to take you out for a walk before it gets too hot. You had a lot of stuff on your list anyway."

"Oh!" she moaned. "I don't feel—" But he cut her short. "Come on, come on. You dress. I'll wait in Port's room. I'll even shut the door."

She could think of nothing to say. Port never gave her orders; he hung back, hoping thereby to discover what she really wanted. He made it more difficult for her, since she seldom acted on her own desires, behaving instead according to her complex system of balancing those omens to be observed against those to be disregarded.

Tunner had already gone into the adjacent room and closed the door. It gratified Kit to think that he would see the disheveled bedclothes. As she dressed she heard him whistling. "A bore, a bore, a bore!" she said under her breath. At that moment the other door opened; Port stood there in the hall, running his left hand through his hair.

"May I come in?" he asked.

She was staring at him.

"Well, obviously. What's the matter with you?"

He still stood there.

"What in God's name's wrong with you?" she said impatiently.

"Nothing." His voice rasped. He strode to the center of the room and pointed to the closed connecting door. "Who's in there?"

"Tunner," she said with unfeigned innocence, as if it were a most natural occurrence. "He's waiting for me while I get dressed."

"What the hell goes on here?"

Kit flushed and turned away vehemently. "Nothing. Nothing," she said quickly. "Don't be crazy. What do you *think* goes on, anyway?"

He did not lower his voice. "I don't know. *I'm* asking *you.*"

She pushed him in the chest with her outspread hands and walked toward the door to open it, but he caught her arm and pulled her around.

"Please stop it!" she whispered furiously.

"All right, all right. I'll open the door myself," he said, as if by allowing her to do it he might be running too great a risk.

He went into his room. Tunner was leaning out the window looking down. He swung around, smiling broadly. "Well, well!" he began.

Port was staring at the bed. "What *is* this? What's the matter with your room that you have to be in here?" he demanded.

But Tunner appeared not to take in the situation at all, or else he refused to admit that there was any. "So! Back from the wars!" he cried. "And do you look it! Kit and I are going for a walk. You probably want some sleep." He dragged Port over in front of the mirror. "Look at yourself!" he commanded. At the sight of his smeared face and red-rimmed eyes, Port wilted.

"I want some black coffee," he grumbled. "And I want to go down and get a shave." Now he raised his voice. "And I wish to hell you'd both get out of here and take your walk." He pushed the wall button savagely.

Tunner gave him a fraternal pat on the back. "See you later, old man. Get some sleep."

Port glared at him as he went out, and sat down on the bed when he had gone. A large ship had just steamed into the harbor; its deep whistle sounded below the street noises. He lay back on the bed, gasping a little. When the knocking came at the door, he never heard it. The servant stuck his head in, said: *"Monsieur,"* waited a few seconds, quietly shut the door and went away.

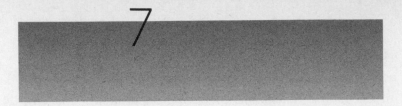

7

He slept all day. Kit came back at lunch time; she went in softly, and having coughed once to see if he would wake, went to eat without him. Before twilight he awoke, feeling greatly cleansed. He rose and undressed slowly. In the bathroom he drew a hot tub, bathed at length, shaved, and searched for his white bathrobe. He found it in Kit's room, but she was not there. On her table was a variety of groceries she had bought to take on the trip. Most of the items were black-market goods from England, and according to the labels they had been manufactured by appointment to H.M. King George VI. He opened a package of biscuits and began to eat one after another, voraciously. Framed by the window, the town below was growing dim. It was that moment of twilight when light objects seem unnaturally bright, and the others are restfully dark. The town's electricity had not yet been turned on, so that the only lights were those on the few ships anchored in the harbor, itself neither light nor dark—merely an empty area between the buildings and the sky. And to the right were the mountains. The first one coming up out of the sea looked to him like two knees drawn up under a huge sheet. For a fraction of a second, but with such force that he felt the change's impact as a physical sensation, he was somewhere else, it was long ago. Then he saw the mountains again. He wandered downstairs.

They had made a point of not patronizing the hotel bar because it was always empty. Now, going into the gloomy little room, Port was mildly surprised to see sitting alone at the bar a heavy-looking youth with a formless face which was saved from complete non-existence by an undefined brown beard. As he installed himself at the other end, the young man said with a heavy English accent: *"Otro Tio Pepe,"* and pushed his glass toward the barman.

Port thought of the cool subterranean bodegas at Jerez where Tio Pepe of 1842 had been tendered him, and ordered the same. The young man looked at him with a certain curiosity in his eyes, but said nothing. Presently a large, sallow-skinned woman, her hair fiery with henna, appeared in the doorway and squealed. She had the glassy black eyes of a doll; their lack of expression was accentuated by the gleaming make-up around them. The young man turned in her direction.

"Hello, Mother. Come in and sit down."

The woman moved to the youth's side but did not sit. In her excitement and indignation she seemed not to have noticed Port. Her voice was very high. "Eric, you filthy toad!" she cried. "Do you realize I've been looking for you everywhere? I've never seen such behavior! And what are you drinking? What do you *mean* by drinking, after what Doctor Levy told you? You *wretched* boy!"

The young man did not look at her. "Don't scream so, Mother."

She glanced in Port's direction, saw him. "What *is* that you're drinking, Eric?" she demanded again, her voice slightly more subdued, but no less intense.

"It's just sherry, and it's quite delightful. I wish you wouldn't get so upset."

"And who do you think's going to pay for your caprices?" She seated herself on the stool beside him and began to fumble in her bag. "Oh, blast! I've come off without my key," she said. "Thanks to your thoughtlessness. You'll have to let me in through your room. I've discovered the sweetest mosque, but it's covered with brats all shrieking like demons. Filthy little beasts, they are! I'll show it to you tomorrow. Order a glass of sherry for me, if it's dry. I think it might help me. I've felt wretched all day. I'm positive it's the malaria coming back. It's about time for it, you know."

"Otro Tio Pepe," said the youth imperturbably.

Port watched, fascinated as always by the sight of a human being brought down to the importance of an automaton or a caricature. By whatever circumstances and in whatever manner reduced, whether ludicrous or horrible, such persons delighted him.

The dining room was unfriendly and formal to a degree which is acceptable only when the service is impeccable; this was not the case here. The waiters were impassive and moved slowly. They seemed to have difficulty in understanding the wants even of the French; certainly they showed no sign of interest in pleasing anyone. The two English people were given a table near the corner where Port and Kit were eating; Tunner was out with his French girl.

"Here they are," whispered Port. "Keep an ear open. But try and keep a straight face."

"He looks like a young Vacher," said Kit, leaning far over the table, "the one who wandered across France slicing children into pieces, you remember?"

They were silent a few minutes, hoping to be diverted by the other table, but mother and son appeared to have nothing to say to each other. Finally Port turned to Kit and said: "Oh, while I think of it, what was all that this morning?"

"Do we have to go into it now?"

"No, but I was just asking. I thought maybe you could answer."

"You saw all there was to see."

"I wouldn't ask you if I thought so."

"Oh, can't you see—" Kit began in a tone of exasperation; then she stopped. She was about to say: "Can't you see that I didn't want Tunner to know you hadn't come back last night? Can't you see he'd be interested to know that? Can't you see it would give him just the wedge he's looking for?" Instead she said: "Do we have to discuss it? I told you the whole story when you came in. He came while I was having breakfast and I sent him into your room to wait while I got dressed. Isn't that perfectly proper?"

"It depends on your conception of propriety, baby."

"It certainly does," she said acidly. "You notice I haven't mentioned what *you* did last night."

Port smiled and said smoothly: "You couldn't very well, since you don't know."

"And I don't want to." She was letting her anger show in spite of herself. "You can think whatever you want to think. I don't give a damn." She glanced over at the other table and noticed that the large bright-eyed woman was following what she could of their conversation with acute interest. When that lady saw that Kit was aware of her attention, she turned back to the youth and began a loud monologue of her own.

"This hotel has the most extraordinary plumbing system; the water taps do nothing but sigh and gurgle constantly, no matter how tightly one shuts them off. The stupidity of the French! It's unbelievable! They're all mental defectives. Madame Gautier herself told me they have the lowest national intelligence quotient in the world. Of course, their blood is thin; they've gone to seed. They're all part Jewish or Negro. Look at them!" She made a wide gesture which included the whole room.

"Oh, here, perhaps," said the young man, holding his glass of water up to the light and studying it carefully.

"In France!" the woman cried excitedly. "Madame Gautier told me herself, and I've read it in ever so many books and papers."

"What revolting water," he murmured. He set the glass on the table. "I don't think I shall drink it."

"What a fearful sissy you are! Stop complaining! I don't want to hear about it! I can't bear to hear any more of your talk about dirt and worms. *Don't* drink it. No one cares whether you do or not. It's frightful for you, anyway, washing everything down with liquids the way you do. Try to grow up. Have you got the paraffin for the Primus, or did you forget that as well as the Vittel?"

The young man smiled with poisonous mock benevolence, and spoke slowly, as if to a backward child: "No, I did not forget the paraffin as well as the Vittel. The tin is in the back of the car. Now, if I may, I think I shall take a little walk." He rose, still smiling most unpleasantly, and moved away from the table.

"Why, you rude puppy! I'll box your ears!" the woman called after him. He did not turn around.

"Aren't they something?" whispered Port.

"Very amusing," said Kit. She was still angry. "Why don't you ask them to join us on our great trek? It's all we'd need."

They ate their fruit in silence.

After dinner, when Kit had gone up to her room, Port wandered around the barren street floor of the hotel, to the writing room with its impossible, dim lights far overhead; to the palm-stuffed foyer where two ancient French women in black sat on the edges of their chairs, whispering to one another; to the front entrance, in which he stood a few minutes staring at a large Mercedes touring car parked opposite; and back to the writing room. He sat down. The sickly light from above scarcely illumined the travel posters on the walls: *Fès la Mystérieuse, Air-France, Visitez l'Espagne.* From a grilled window over his head came hard female voices and the metallic sound of kitchen activities, amplified by the stone walls and tile floors. This room, even more than the others, reminded him of a dungeon. The electric bell of the cinema was audible above all the other noises, a constant, nerveracking background. He went to the writing tables, lifted the blotters, opened the drawers, searching for stationery; there was none. Then he shook the inkwells; they were dry. A violent argument had broken out in the kitchen. Scratching the fleshy parts of his hands, where the mosquitoes had just bitten him, he walked slowly out of the room through the foyer, along the corridor into the bar. Even here the light was weak and distant, but the array of bottles behind the bar formed a focal point of interest for the eyes. He had a slight indigestion—not a sourness, but the promise of a pain which at the moment was only a tiny physical unhappiness in some unlocatable center. The swarthy barman was staring at him expectantly. There was no one else in the room. He ordered a whiskey and sat savoring it, drinking slowly. Somewhere in the hotel a toilet was flushed, making its sounds of choking and regurgitation.

The unpleasant tension inside him was lessening; he felt very much awake. The bar was stuffy and melancholy. It was full of the sadness inherent in all deracinated things. "Since the day the first drink was served at this bar," he thought, "how many moments of happiness have been lived through, here?" The happiness, if there still was any, existed elsewhere: In sequestered rooms that looked onto bright alleys where the cats gnawed fish-heads; in shaded cafés hung with reed matting, where the hashish smoke mingled with the fumes of mint from the hot tea; down on the docks, out at the edge of the sebkha in the tents (he passed over the white image of Marhnia, the placid face); beyond the mountains in the great Sahara, in the endless regions that were all of Africa. But not here in this sad colonial room where each invocation of Europe was merely one more squalid touch, one more visible proof of isolation; the mother country seemed farthest in such a room.

As he sat regularly swallowing small mouthfuls of warm whiskey, he heard footsteps approaching in the corridor. The young Englishman came into the room, and without looking in Port's direction sat down at one of the small tables. Port watched him order a liqueur, and when the barman was back behind the bar, he walked over to the table. *"Pardon, monsieur,"* he said. *"Vous parlez français?"* *"Oui, oui,"* the young man answered, looking startled. "But you also speak English?" pursued Port quickly. "I do," he replied, setting his glass down and staring at his interlocutor in a manner which Port suspected was completely theatrical. His intuition told him that flattery was the surest approach in this case. "Then maybe you can give me some advice," he went on with great seriousness.

The young man smiled weakly. "If it's about Africa, I daresay I can. I've been mucking about here for the past five years. Fascinating place, of course."

"Wonderful, yes."

"You know it?" He looked a bit worried; he wanted so much to be the only traveler.

"Only certain parts," Port reassured him. "I've traveled a good deal in the north and west. Roughly Tripoli to Dakar."

"Dakar's a filthy hole."

"But so are ports all over the world. What I wanted advice about is the exchange. What bank do you think it's best to use? I have dollars."

The Englishman smiled. "I think I'm rather a good person to give you such information. I'm actually Australian myself, but my mother and I live mostly on American dollars." He proceeded to offer Port a complete exposition of the French banking system in North Africa. His voice took on the inflections of an old-fashioned professor; his manner of expressing himself was objectionably pedantic, Port thought. At the same time there was a light in his eyes which not only belied the voice and manner but also managed to annul whatever weight his words might carry. It seemed to Port that the young man was speaking to him rather as if he thought he were dealing with a maniac, as if the subject of conversation had been chosen as one proper to the occasion, one which could be extended for as long a time as necessary, until the patient was calmed.

Port allowed him to continue his discourse, which presently left banking behind and went into personal experiences. This terrain was more fertile; it obviously was where the young man had been heading from the start. Port offered no comments, save for an occasional polite exclamation which helped to give the monologue the semblance of a conversation. He learned that prior to their arrival in Mombasa the young man and his mother, who wrote travel books and illustrated them with her own photographs, had lived for three years in India, where an elder son had died; that the five African years, spent in every part of the continent, had managed to give them both an astonishing list of diseases, and they still suffered intermittently from most of them. It was difficult, however, to know what to believe and what to discount, since the report was decorated with such remarks as: "At that time I was manager of a large import-export firm in Durban," "The government put me in charge of three thousand Zulus," "In Lagos I bought a command car and drove it through to Casamance," "We were the only whites ever to have penetrated into the region," "They wanted me to be cameraman for the expedition, but there was no one in Cape Town I could trust to keep the studios running properly, and we were making four films at the time." Port began to resent his not knowing better how far to go with his listener, but he let it all pass, and was delighted with the ghoulish pleasure the young man took in describing the dead bodies in the river at Douala, the murders in Takoradi, the self-immolating madman in the market at Gao. Finally the talker leaned back, signaled to the barman to bring him another liqueur, and said: "Ah, yes, Africa's a great place. I wouldn't live anywhere else these days."

"And your mother? Does she feel the same way?"

"Oh, she's in love with it. She wouldn't know what to do if you put her down in a civilized country."

"She writes all the time?"

"All the time. Every day. Mostly about out-of-the-way places. We're about to go down to Fort Charlet. Do you know it?"

He seemed reasonably sure that Port would not know Fort Charlet. "No, I don't," said Port. "But I know where it is. How're you going to get there? There's no service of any kind, is there?"

"Oh, we'll get there. The Touareg will be just Mother's meat. I have a great collection of maps, military and otherwise, which I study carefully each morning before we set out. Then I simply follow them. We have a car," he added, seeing Port's look of bewilderment. "An ancient Mercedes. Powerful old thing."

"Ah, yes, I saw it outside," murmured Port.

"Yes," said the young man smugly. "We always get there."

"Your mother must be a very interesting woman," said Port.

The young man was enthusiastic. "Absolutely amazing. You must meet her tomorrow."

"I should like very much to."

"I've packed her off to bed, but she won't sleep until I get in. We always have communicating rooms, of course, so that unfortunately she knows just when I go to bed. Isn't married life wonderful?"

Port glanced at him quickly, a little shocked at the crudity of his remark, but he was laughing in an open and unaware fashion.

"Yes, you'll enjoy talking with her. Unluckily we have an itinerary which we try to follow exactly. We're leaving tomorrow noon. When are you pulling out of this hell-hole?"

"Oh, we've been planning to get the train tomorrow for Bousif, but we're not in any hurry. So we may wait until Thursday. The only way to travel, at least for us, is to go when you feel like going and stay where you feel like staying."

"I quite agree. But surely you don't feel like staying here?"

"Oh God, no!" laughed Port. "We hate it. But there are three of us, and we just haven't all managed to get up the necessary energy at one time."

"Three of you? I see." The young man appeared to be considering this unexpected news. "I see." He rose and reached in his pocket, pulling out a card which he handed to Port. "I might give you this. My name is Lyle. Well, cheer-o, and I hope you work up the initiative. May see you in the morning." He spun around as if in embarrassment, and walked stiffly out of the room.

Port slipped the card into his pocket. The barman was asleep, his head on the bar. Deciding to have a last drink, he went over and tapped him lightly on the shoulder. The man raised his head with a groan.

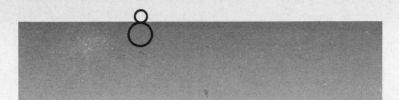

8

"Where have you been?" said Kit. She was sitting up in bed reading, having dragged the little lamp to the very edge of the night-table. Port moved the table against the bed and pushed the lamp back to a safe distance from the edge. "Guzzling down in the bar. I have a feeling we're going to be invited to drive to Boussif."

Kit looked up, delighted. She hated trains. "Oh, no! Really? How marvelous!"

"But wait'll you hear by whom!"

"Oh God! Not those monsters!"

"They haven't said anything. I just have a feeling they will."

"Oh well, that's absolutely out, of course."

Port went into his room. "I wouldn't worry about it either way. Nobody's said anything. I got a long story from the son. He's a mental case."

"You know I'll worry about it. You *know* how I hate train rides. And you come in calmly and say we may have an invitation to go in a car! You might at least have waited till morning and let me have a decent night's sleep before having to make up my mind which of the two tortures I want."

"Why don't you begin your worrying once we've been asked?"

"Oh, don't be ridiculous!" she cried, jumping out of bed. She stood in the doorway, watching him undress. "Good night," she said suddenly, and shut the door.

Things came about somewhat as Port had imagined they would. In the morning, as he was standing in the window wondering at the first clouds he had seen since mid-Atlantic, a knock came at the door; it was Eric Lyle, his face suffused and puffy from having just awakened.

"Good morning. I say, do forgive me if I've awakened you, but I've something rather important to talk about. May I come in?" He glanced about the room in a strangely surreptitious manner, his pale eyes darting swiftly from object to object. Port had the uncomfortable feeling that he should have put things away and closed all his luggage before letting him in.

"Have you had tea?" said Lyle.

"Yes, only it was coffee."

"Aha!" He edged nearer to a valise, toyed with the straps. "You have some nice labels on your bags." He lifted the leather tag with Port's name and address on it. "Now I see your name. Mr. Porter Moresby." He crossed the room. "You must forgive me if I snoop. Luggage always fascinates me. May I sit down? Now, look, Mr. Moresby. That *is* you, isn't it? I've been talking at some length with Mother and she agrees with me that it would be much pleasanter for you and Mrs. Moresby—I suppose that's the lady you were with last night—" he paused.

"Yes," said Port.

"—if you both came along with us to Boussif. It's only

five hours by car, and the train ride takes ages; something like eleven hours, if I remember. And eleven hours of utter hell. Since the war the trains are completely impossible, you know. We think—"

Port interrupted him. "No, no. We couldn't put you out to that extent. No, no."

"Yes, *yes*," said Lyle archly.

"Besides, we're three, you know."

"Ah, yes, of course, said Lyle in a vague voice. "Your friend couldn't come along on the train, I suppose?"

"I don't think he'd be very happy with the arrangement. Anyway, we couldn't very well go off and leave him."

"I see. That's a shame. We can scarcely take him along, with all the luggage there'd be, you know." He rose, looked at Port with his head on one side like a bird listening for a worm, and said: "Come along with us; do. You can manage it, I know." He went to the door, opened it, and leaned through toward Port, standing on tiptoe. "I'll tell you what. You come by and let me know in an hour. Fifty-three. And I do hope your decision is favorable." Smiling, and letting his gaze wander once more around the room, he shut the door.

Kit literally had not slept at all during the night; at daybreak she had dozed off, but her sleep was troubled. She was not in a receptive mood when Port rapped loudly on the communicating door and opened it immediately afterward. Straightway she sat up, holding the sheet high around her neck with her hand, and staring wildly. She relaxed and fell back.

"What *is* it?"

"I've got to talk to you."

"I'm so sleepy."

"We have the invitation to drive to Boussif."

Again she bobbed up, this time rubbing her eyes. He sat on the bed and kissed her shoulder absently. She drew back and looked at him. "From the monsters? Have you accepted?"

He wanted to say "Yes," because that would have avoided a long discussion; the matter would have been settled for her as well as for him.

"Not yet."

"Oh, you'll have to refuse."

"Why? It'll be much more comfortable. And quicker. And certainly safer."

"Are you trying to terrify me so I won't budge out of the hotel?" She looked toward the window. "Why is it so dark out still? What time is it?"

"It's cloudy today for some strange reason."

She was silent; the haunted look came into her eyes.

"They won't take Tunner," said Port.

"Are you stark, raving mad?" she cried. "I wouldn't dream of going without him. Not for a second!"

"Why not?" said Port, nettled. "He could get there all right on the train. I don't know why we should lose a good ride just because he happens to be along. We don't have to stick with him every damned minute, do we?"

"You don't have to; no."

"You mean you do?"

"I mean I wouldn't consider leaving Tunner here and going off in a car with those two. She's an hysterical old hag, and the boy—! He's a real criminal degenerate if I ever saw one. He gives me the creeps."

"Oh, come on!" scoffed Port. "*You* dare use the word hysterical. My God! I wish you could see yourself this minute."

"You do exactly what you like," said Kit, lying back. "I'll go on the train with Tunner."

Port's eyes narrowed. "Well, by God, you can *go* on

the train with him, then. And I hope there's a wreck!" He went into his room and dressed.

Kit rapped on the door. *"Entrez,"* said Tunner with his American accent. "Well, well, this is a surprise! What's up? To what do I owe this unexpected visit?"

"Oh, nothing in particular," she said, surveying him with a vague distaste which she hoped she managed to conceal. "You and I've got to go alone to Boussif on the train. Port has an invitation to drive there with some friends." She tried to keep her voice wholly inexpressive.

He looked mystified. "What's all this? Say it again slowly. Friends?"

"That's right. Some English woman and her son. They've asked him."

Little by little his face began to beam. This was not false now, she noted. He was just incredibly slow in reacting.

"Well, well!" he said again, grinning.

"What a dolt he is," she thought, observing the utter lack of inhibition in his behavior. (The blatantly normal always infuriated her.) "His emotional maneuvers all take place out in the open. Not a tree or a rock to hide behind."

Aloud she said: "The train leaves at six and gets there at some God-forsaken hour of the morning. But they say it's always late, and that's good, for once."

"So we'll just go together, the two of us."

"Port'll be there long before, so he can get rooms for us. I've got to go now and find a beauty parlor, God forbid."

"What do you need of that?" protested Tunner. "Let well enough alone. You can't improve on nature."

She had no patience with gallantry; nevertheless she smiled at him as she went out. "Because I'm a coward," she thought. She was quite conscious of a desire to pit Tunner's magic against Port's, since Port had put a curse on the trip. And as she smiled she said, as if to nobody: "I think we can avoid the wreck."

"Huh?"

"Oh, nothing. I'll see you for lunch in the dining room at two."

Tunner was the sort of person to whom it would occur only with difficulty that he might be being used. Because he was accustomed to imposing his will without meeting opposition, he had a highly developed and very male vanity which endeared him, strangely enough, to almost everyone. Doubtless the principal reason why he had been so eager to accompany Port and Kit on this trip was that with them as with no one else he felt a definite resistance to his unceasing attempts at moral domination, at which he was forced, when with them, to work much harder; thus unconsciously he was giving his personality the exercise it required. Kit and Port, on the other hand, both resented even the reduced degree to which they responded to his somewhat obvious charm, which was why neither one would admit to having encouraged him to come along with them. There was no small amount of shame involved where they were concerned, since both of them were conscious of all the acting and formula-following in his behavior, and yet to a certain degree both were willingly ensnared by it. Tunner himself was an essentially simple individual irresistibly attracted by whatever remained just beyond his intellectual grasp. Contenting himself with not quite being able to seize an idea was a habit he had acquired in adolescence, and it operated in him now with still greater force. If he could get on all sides of a thought, he concluded that it was an inferior one; there had to be an inaccessible part of it for his interest to be aroused. His attention, however, did not spur him to additional thought. On the contrary, it merely provided him with an emotional satisfaction *vis-à-vis* the idea, making it possible for him to relax and admire it at a distance. At the beginning of his friendship with Port and Kit he had been inclined to treat them with the careful deference he felt was due them, not as individuals, but as beings who dealt almost exclusively with ideas, sacred things. Their discouraging of this tactic had been so categorical that he had been obliged to adopt a new one, in using which he felt even less sure of himself. This consisted of gentle prods, ridicule so faint and unfocused that it always could be given a flattering turn if necessary, and the adoption of an attitude of amused, if slightly pained resignation, that made him feel like the father of a pair of impossibly spoiled prodigies.

Light-hearted now, he moved about the room whistling at the prospect of being alone with Kit; he had decided she needed him. He was not at all sure of being able to convince her that the need lay precisely in the field where he liked to think it did. Indeed, of all the women with whom he hoped some day to have intimate relations he considered Kit the most unlikely, the most difficult. He caught a glimpse of himself as he stood bent over a suitcase, and smiled inscrutably at his image; it was the same smile that Kit thought so false.

At one o'clock he went to Port's room to find the door open and the luggage gone. Two maids were making the bed up with fresh linen. *"Se ha marchao,"* said one. At two he met Kit in the dining room; she was looking exceptionally well groomed and pretty.

He ordered champagne.

"At a thousand francs a bottle!" she remonstrated. "Port would have a fit!"

"Port isn't here," said Tunner.

9

A few minutes before twelve Port stood outside the entrance of the hotel with all his luggage. Three Arab porters, acting under the direction of young Lyle, were piling bags into the back of the car. The slow-moving clouds above were interspersed now with great holes of deep blue sky; when the sun came through its heat was unexpectedly powerful. In the direction of the mountains the sky was still black and frowning. Port was impatient; he hoped they would get off before Kit or Tunner happened by.

Precisely at twelve Mrs. Lyle was in the lobby complaining about her bill. The pitch of her voice rose and fell in sharp scallops of sound. Coming to the doorway she cried: "Eric, will you come in here and tell this man I did *not* have biscuits yesterday at tea? Immediately!"

"Tell him yourself," said Eric absently. *"Celle-là on va mettre ici en bas,"* he went on to one of the Arabs, indicating a heavy pigskin case.

"You idiot!" She went back in; a moment later Port heard her squealing: *"Non! Non! Thé seulement! Pas gateau!"*

Eventually she appeared again, red in the face, her handbag swinging on her arm. Seeing Port she stood still and called: "Eric!" He looked up from the car, came over and presented Port to his mother.

"I'm very glad you can come with us. It's an added protection. They say in the mountains here it's better to carry a gun. Although I must say I've never seen an Arab I couldn't handle. It's the beastly French one really needs protection from. Filthy lot! Fancy their telling me what I had yesterday for tea. But the insolence! Eric, you coward! You let me do all the fighting at the desk. *You* probably ate the biscuits they were charging me for!"

"It's all one, isn't it?" Eric smiled.

"I should think you'd be ashamed to admit it. Mr. Moresby, look at that hulking boy. He's never done a day's work in his life. I have to pay all his bills."

"Come *on,* Mother! Get in." This was said despairingly.

"What do you mean, *get in?*" Her voice went very high. "Fancy talking to me like that! You need a good slap in the face. That might help you." She climbed into the front of the car. "I've never had such talk from anyone."

"We shall all three sit in front," said Eric. "Do you mind, Mr. Moresby?"

"I'm delighted. I prefer the front," said Port. He was determined to remain wholly on the periphery of this family pattern; the best way of assuring that, he thought, would be to have no visible personality whatever, merely to be civil, to listen. It was likely that this ludicrous wrangling was the only form of conversation these two had ever managed to devise for themselves.

They started up, Eric at the wheel, racing the motor first. The porters shouted: *"Bon voyage!"*

"I noticed several people staring at me when I left,"

said Mrs. Lyle, settling back. "Those filthy Arabs have done their work here, the same as everywhere else."

"Work? What do you mean?" said Port.

"Why, their spying. They spy on you all the time here, you know. That's the way they make their living. You think you can do anything without their knowing it?" She laughed unpleasantly. "Within an hour all the miserable little touts and undersecretaries at the consulates know everything."

"You mean the British Consulate?"

"*All* the consulates, the police, the banks, everyone," she said firmly.

Port looked at Eric expectantly. "But—"

"Oh, yes," said Eric, apparently happy to reinforce his mother's statement. "It's a frightful mess. We never have a moment's peace. Wherever we go, they hold back our letters, they try to keep us out of hotels by saying they have no rooms, and when we do get rooms they search them while we're out and steal our things, they get the porters and chambermaids to eavesdrop—"

"But *who?* Who does all this? And why?"

"The Arabs!" cried Mrs. Lyle. "They're a stinking, low race of people with nothing to do in life but spy on others. How else do you think they live?"

"It seems incredible," Port ventured timidly, hoping in this way to call forth more of the same, for it amused him.

"Hah!" she said in a tone of triumph. "It may seem incredible to you because you don't know them, but look out for them. They hate us all. And so do the French. Oh, *they* loathe us!"

"I've always found the Arabs very sympathetic," said Port.

"Of course. That's because they're servile, they flatter

you and fawn on you. And the moment your back is turned, off they rush to the consulate."

Said Eric: "Once in Mogador—" His mother cut him short.

"Oh, shut up! Let someone else talk. Do you think anyone wants to hear about your blundering stupidities? If you'd had a little sense you'd not have got into that business. What right did you have to go to Mogador, when I was dying in Fez? Mr. Moresby, I was dying! In the hospital, on my back, with a terrible Arab nurse who couldn't even give a proper injection—"

"She could!" said Eric stoutly. "She gave me at least twenty. You just happened to get infected because your resistance was low."

"*Resistance!*" shrieked Mrs. Lyle. "I refuse to talk any more. Look, Mr. Moresby, at the colors of the hills. Have you ever tried infra-red on landscapes? I took some exceptionally fine ones in Rhodesia, but they were stolen from me by an editor in Johannesburg."

"Mr. Moresby's not a photographer, Mother."

"Oh, be quiet. Would that keep him from knowing about infra-red photography?"

"I've seen samples of it," said Port.

"Well, of course you have. You see, Eric, you simply don't know what you're saying, ever. It all comes from lack of discipline. I only wish you had to earn your living for one day. It would teach you to think before you speak. At this point you're no better than an imbecile."

A particularly arid argument ensued, in which Eric, apparently for Port's benefit, enumerated a list of unlikely sounding jobs he claimed to have held during the past four years, while the mother systematically challenged each item with what seemed convincing proof of its falsity. At each new claim she cried: "What lies! What a liar! You don't even know what the truth is!" Finally Eric replied in an aggrieved tone, as if capitulating: "You'd never let me stick at any work, anyway. You're terrified that I might become independent."

Mrs. Lyle cried: "Look, look! Mr. Moresby! That sweet burro! It reminds me of Spain. We just spent two months there. It's a horrible country," (she pronounced it *hawibble*) "all soldiers and priests and Jews."

"Jews?" echoed Port incredulously.

"Of course. Didn't you know? The hotels are full of them. They run the country. From behind the scenes, of course. The same as everywhere else. Only in Spain they're very clever about it. They will *not* admit to being Jewish. In Córdoba—this will show you how wily and deceitful they are. In Córdoba I went through a street called Judería. It's where the synagogue is. Naturally it's positively teeming with Jews—a typical ghetto. But do you think one of them would admit it? Certainly not! They all shook their fingers back and forth in front of my face, and shouted: '*Católico! Católico!*' at me. But fancy that, Mr. Moresby, their claiming to be Roman Catholics. And when I went through the synagogue the guide kept insisting that no services had been held in it since the fifteenth century! I'm afraid I was dreadfully rude to him. I burst out laughing in his face."

"What did he say?" Port inquired.

"Oh, he merely went on with his lecture. He'd learned it by rote, of course. He did stare. They all do. But I think he respected me for not being afraid. The ruder you are to them the more they admire you. I showed him I knew he was telling me the most fearful lot of lies. Catholics! I daresay they think that makes them superior. It was too funny, when they were all most Jewy; one had only to look at them. Oh, I know Jews. I've had too many vile experiences with them not to know them."

The novelty of the caricature was wearing off. Port was beginning to feel smothered sitting there between them; their obsessions depressed him. Mrs. Lyle was even more objectionable than her son. Unlike him, she had no exploits, imaginary or real, to recount; her entire conversation consisted of descriptions in detail of the persecutions to which she believed she had been subjected, and of word-by-word accounts of the bitter quarrels in which she had been engaged with those who harassed her. As she spoke, her character took shape before him, although already he was far less inclined to be interested in it. Her life had been devoid of personal contacts, and she needed them. Thus she manufactured them as best she could; each fight was an abortive attempt at establishing some kind of human relationship. Even with Eric, she had come to accept the dispute as the natural mode of talking. He decided that she was the loneliest woman he had ever seen, but he could not care very much.

He ceased listening. They had left the town, traversed the valley, and were climbing a large, bare hill on the other side. As they swung around one of the many S-curves, he realized with a start that he was looking straight at the Turkish fortress, small and perfect as a toy at this distance, on the opposite side of the valley. Under the wall, scattered about on the yellow earth, were several tiny black tents; which one he had been in, which one was Marhnia's, he could not say, for the staircase was not visible from here. And there she was, doubtless, somewhere below in the valley, having her noonday sleep in the airless heat of a tent, alone or with a lucky Arab friend—not Smaïl, he thought. They turned again, mounting ever higher; there were cliffs above them. By the road sometimes were high clumps of dead thistle plants, coated with white dust, and from the plants the locusts called, a high, unceasing scream like the sound of heat itself. Again and again the valley came into view, always a little smaller, a little farther away, a little less real. The Mercedes roared like a plane; there was no muffler on the exhaust pipe. The mountains were there ahead, the sebkha was spread out below. He turned to get a last look at the valley; the shape of each tent was still discernible, and he realized that the tents looked like the mountain peaks behind them on the horizon.

As he watched the heat-covered landscape unfold, his thoughts took an inward turn, dwelt briefly on the dream that still preoccupied him. At the end of a moment, he smiled; now he had it. The train that went always faster was merely an epitome of life itself. The unsureness about the *no* and the *yes* was the inevitable attitude one had if one tried to consider the value of that life, and the hesitation was automatically resolved by one's involuntary decision to refuse participation in it. He wondered why it had upset him; it was a simple, classic dream. The connections were all clear in his head. Their particular meaning with regard to his own life scarcely mattered. For in order to avoid having to deal with relative values, he had long since come to deny all purpose to the phenomenon of existence—it was more expedient and comforting.

He was pleased to have solved his little problem. He looked around the countryside; they were still climbing, but they had gone over the first crest. About them now were barren, rounded hills, without details to give them scale. And on every side was the same uneven, hard line of the horizon, with the blinding white sky behind. Mrs. Lyle was saying: "Oh, they're a foul tribe. A rotten lot, I can tell you." "I'll kill this woman yet," he thought savagely. As the gradient lessened and the car added speed, the fleeting illusion of a breeze was created, but when the road curved upward again and they resumed the slow ascent, he realized that the air was motionless.

"There's a sort of belvedere up ahead, according to the map," said Eric. "We ought to have a superb view."

"Do you think we should stop?" Mrs. Lyle inquired anxiously. "We must be at Boussif for tea."

The vantage point proved to be a slightly perceptible widening of the road at a spot where the latter made a hairpin curve. Some boulders which had rolled down from the cliff on the inner side made the passage even more hazardous. The drop from the edge was sheer, and the view inland was spectacular and hostile.

Eric stopped the car for a moment, but no one got out. The rest of the drive was through stony territory, too parched to shelter even the locusts, yet now and then Port caught a glimpse in the distance of a mud-walled hamlet, the color of the hills, fenced round about with cactus and thorny shrubs. A silence fell upon the three, and there was nothing to hear but the steady roaring of the motor.

When they came in sight of Boussif with its modern white concrete minaret, Mrs. Lyle said: "Eric, I want you to attend to the rooms. I shall go directly to the kitchen and set about showing them how to make tea." To Port she said, holding up her handbag: "I always carry the tea here in my bag with me when we're on a voyage. Otherwise I should have to wait forever while that wretched boy attended to the automobile and the luggage. I believe there's nothing at all to see in Boussif, so we shall be spared going into the streets."

"Derb Ech Chergui," said Port. And as she turned to

look at him in astonishment, "I was just reading a sign," he said reassuringly. The long main street was empty, cooking in the afternoon sun, whose strength seemed doubled by the fact that over the mountains ahead to the south still hung the massive dark clouds that had been there since the early morning.

10

It was a very old train. From the low ceiling in the corridor of their carriage hung a row of kerosene lamps that swung violently back and forth in unison as the ancient vehicle rocked along. When they had been about to pull out of the station, Kit, in the usual desperation she felt at the beginning of a train ride, had jumped down, run over to the newsstand, and bought several French magazines, getting back aboard just as they were starting up. Now, in the indistinct mixture of fading daylight and the yellow glow cast by the dim lamps, she held them on her lap and opened one after the other, trying to see what was in them. The only one she could see at all was full of photographs: *Ciné Pour Tous.*

They had the compartment to themselves. Tunner sat opposite her.

"You can't read in this light," he said.

"I'm just looking at pictures."

"Oh."

"You'll excuse me, won't you? In a minute I won't even be able to do this much. I'm a little nervous on trains."

"Go right ahead," he said.

They had brought a cold supper with them, put up by the hotel. From time to time Tunner eyed the basket speculatively. Finally she looked up and caught him at it. "Tunner! Don't tell me you're hungry!" she cried.

"Only my tapeworm."

"You're revolting." She lifted the basket, glad to be able to engage in any manual activity. One by one she pulled out the thick sandwiches, separately wrapped in flimsy paper napkins.

"I told them not to give us any of that lousy Spanish ham. It's raw, and you can *really* get worms from it. I'm sure some of these are made of it, though. I think I can smell it. They always think you're talking just to hear the sound of your voice."

"I'll eat the ham if there is any," said Tunner. "It's good stuff, if I remember."

"Oh, it tastes all right." She brought out a package of hard-boiled eggs, wrapped with some very oily black olives. The train shrieked and plunged into a tunnel. Kit hastily put the eggs into the basket and looked apprehensively at the window. She could see the outline of her face reflected in the glass, pitilessly illumined by the feeble glare from overhead. The stench of coal smoke increased each second; she could feel it constricting her lungs.

"Phew!" Tunner choked.

She sat still, waiting. If the accident were going to come, it would probably be either in a tunnel or on a trestle. "If I could only be sure it would happen tonight," she thought. "I could relax. But the uncertainty. You never know, so you always wait."

Presently they emerged, breathed again. Outside, over the miles of indistinct rocky land, the mountains loomed, jet-black. Above their sharp crests what little light was left in the sky came from between heavy threatening clouds.

"How about those eggs?"

"Oh!" She handed him the whole package.

"I don't want 'em all!"

"You must eat them," she said, making a great effort to be present, to take part in the little life going on inside the creaking wooden walls of the car. "I only want some fruit. And a sandwich."

But she found the bread hard and dry; she had difficulty chewing it. Tunner was busy leaning over, dragging out one of his valises from under the seat. She slipped the uneaten sandwich into the space between her seat and the window.

He sat up, his face triumphant, holding a large dark bottle; he fished in his pocket a moment, and brought out a corkscrew.

"What is it?"

"You guess," he said grinning.

"Not—champagne!"

"The first time."

In her nervousness she reached out and clasped his head in her two hands, kissing him noisily on the forehead.

"You *darling!*" she cried. "You're marvelous!"

He tugged at the cork; there was a pop. A haggard woman in black passed along the corridor and stared in at them. Holding the bottle in his hand, Tunner rose and drew the shades. Kit watched him, thinking: "He's very different from Port. Port would never have done this."

And as he poured it out into the plastic traveling cups, she continued to debate with herself. "But it means nothing except that he spent the money. It's something bought, that's all. Still, being willing to spend the money. . . . And having thought of it, more than anything."

They touched cups in a toast. There was no familiar clink—only a dead paper-like sound. "Here's to Africa," said Tunner, suddenly bashful. He had meant to say: "Here's to tonight."

"Yes."

She looked at the bottle where he had set it on the floor. Characteristically, she decided at once that it was the magic object which was going to save her, that through its power she might escape the disaster. She drained her cup. He refilled it.

"We must make it last," she cautioned, suddenly fearful lest the magic give out.

"You think so? Why?" He pulled out the valise and opened it again. "Look." There were five more bottles. "That's why I made such a fuss about carrying this bag myself," he said, smiling to make his dimples deep. "You probably thought I was nuts."

"I didn't notice," she said faintly, not even noticing the dimples she disliked so strongly. The sight of so much magic had somewhat overcome her.

"So, drink up. Fast and furious."

"Don't you worry about me," she laughed. "I don't need any exhortations." She felt absurdly happy—much too happy for the occasion, she reminded herself. But it was always a pendulum; in another hour she would be back where she had been a minute ago.

The train came slowly to a stop. Beyond the window it was black night; there was not a light to be seen. Somewhere outside, a voice was singing a strange, repetitious melody. Always beginning high and wandering downward until the breath gave out, only to recommence again at the top of the scale, the song had the pattern of a child's weeping.

"Is that a man?" said Kit incredulously.

"Where?" said Tunner, looking around.

"Singing."

He listened a moment. "Hard to tell. Drink up."

She drank, and smiled. Soon she was staring out the window at the black night. "I think I was never meant to live," she said ruefully.

He looked worried. "Now see here, Kit. I know you're nervous. That's why I brought the fizz-water along. But you've just got to calm down. Take it easy. Relax. Nothing's that important, you know. Who was it said—"

"No. That's something I don't want," she interrupted. "Champagne, yes. Philosophy, no. And I think you were incredibly sweet to have thought of it, especially now that I see why you brought it along."

He stopped chewing. His face changed expression; his eyes grew a little bit hard. "What do you mean?"

"Because you realized I was a nervous fool on trains. And you couldn't possibly have done anything I'd have appreciated more."

He chewed again, and grinned. "Oh, forget it. I'm doing all right by it, too, you may have noticed. So here's to good old Mumm!" He uncorked the second bottle. Painfully the train started up again.

The fact that they were moving once more exhilarated her. *"Díme ingrato, porqué me abandonaste, y sola me dejaste . . ."* she sang.

"More?" He held the bottle.

"Claro que si," she said, downing it at one gulp, and stretching forth her cup again, immediately.

The train jolted along, stopping every little while, each time in what looked like empty countryside. But always there were voices out beyond in the darkness, shouting in the guttural mountain tongue. They completed their supper; as Kit was eating her last fig, Tunner bent over to pull out another bottle from the valise. Without quite knowing what she was doing, she reached into the space where she had hidden her sandwich, drew it out and stuffed it into her handbag on top of her compact. He poured her some champagne.

"The champagne's not as cool as it was," she said, sipping it.

"Can't have everything."

"Oh, but I love it! I don't mind it warm. You know, I think I'm getting quite high."

"Bah! Not on the little bit you've had." He laughed.

"Oh, you don't know me! When I'm nervous or upset, right off I'm high."

He looked at his watch. "Well, we've got another eight hours at least. We might as well dig in. Is it all right with you if I change seats and sit with you?"

"Of course. I asked you to when we first got on, so you wouldn't have to ride backwards."

"Fine." He rose, stretched, yawned, and sat down beside her very hard, bumping against her. "I'm sorry," he said. "I miscalculated the beast's gyrations. God, what a train." His right arm went around her, and he pulled her toward him a little. "Lean against me. You'll be more comfortable. Relax! You're all tense and tight."

"Tight, yes! I'm afraid so." She laughed; to her it sounded like a titter. She reclined partially against him, her head on his shoulder. "This should make me feel comfortable," she was thinking, "but it only makes everything worse. I'm going to jump out of my skin."

For a few minutes she made herself sit there without moving. It was difficult not to be tense, because it seemed to her that the motion of the train kept pushing her toward him. Slowly she felt the muscles of his arm tightening around her waist. The train came to a halt. She bounded up, crying: "I want to go to the door and see what it looks like outside."

He rose, put his arm around her again, held it there with insistence, and said: "You know what it looks like. Just dark mountains."

She looked up into his face. "I know. Please, Tunner." She wriggled slightly, and felt him let go. At that moment the door into the corridor opened, and the ravaged-looking woman in black made as if to enter the compartment.

"Ah, pardon. Je me suis trompée," she said, scowling balefully, and going on without shutting the door behind her.

"What does that old harpy want?" said Tunner.

Kit walked to the doorway, stood in it, and said loudly: "She's just a *voyeuse.*" The woman, already halfway down the corridor, turned furiously and glared at her. Kit was delighted. The satisfaction she derived from knowing that the woman had heard the word struck her as absurd. Yet there it was, a strong, exultant force inside her. "A little more and I'll be hysterical. And then Tunner *will* be helpless!"

In normal situations she felt that Port was inclined to lack understanding, but in extremities no one else could take his place; in really bad moments she relied on him utterly, not because he was an infallible guide under such circumstances, but because a section of her consciousness annexed him as a buttress, so that in part she identified herself with him. "And Port's not here. So no hysteria, please." Aloud she said: "I'll be right back. Don't let the witch in."

"I'll come with you," he said.

"Really, Tunner," she laughed. "I'm afraid where I'm going you'd be just a little in the way."

He strove not to show his embarrassment. "Oh! Okay. Sorry."

The corridor was empty. She tried to see out the windows, but they were coated with dust and fingermarks. Up ahead she could hear the noise of voices. The doors onto the quai were closed. She went into the next coach; it was marked "II," and it was more brightly lighted, more populous, much shabbier. At the other end she met people coming into the car from outside. She crowded past them, got off and walked along the ground toward the front of the train. The fourth-class passengers, all native Berbers and Arabs, were milling about in the midst of a confusion of bundles and boxes, piled on the dirt platform under the faint light of a bare electric bulb. A sharp wind swept down from the nearby mountains. Quickly she slipped in among the people and climbed aboard.

As she entered the car, her first impression was that she was not on the train at all. It was merely an oblong area, crowded to bursting with men in dun-colored burnouses, squatting, sleeping, reclining, standing, and moving about through a welter of amorphous bundles. She stood still an instant taking in the sight; for the first time she felt she was in a strange land. Someone was pushing her from behind, obliging her to go on into the car. She resisted, seeing no place to move to, and fell against a man with a white beard, who stared at her sternly. Under his gaze she felt like a badly behaved child. *"Pardon, monsieur,"* she said, trying to bend out of the way in order to avoid the growing pressure from behind. It was useless; she was impelled forward in spite of all her efforts, and staggering over the prostrate forms and the piles of objects, she moved into the middle of the car. The train lurched into motion. She glanced around a little fearfully. The idea occurred to her that these were Moslems, and that the odor of alcohol on her breath would scandalize them almost as much as if she were suddenly to remove all her clothing. Stumbling over the crouched figures, she worked her way to one side of the windowless wall and leaned against it while she took out a small bottle of perfume from her bag and rubbed it over her face and neck, hoping it would counteract, or at least blend with, whatever alcoholic odor there might be about her. As she rubbed, her fingers struck a small, soft object on the nape of her neck. She looked: it was a yellow louse. She had partly crushed it. With disgust she wiped her finger against the wall. Men were looking at her, but with neither sympathy nor antipathy. Nor even with curiosity, she thought. They had the absorbed and vacant expression of the man who looks into the handkerchief after blowing his nose. She shut her eyes for a moment. To her surprise she felt hungry. She took the sandwich out and ate it, breaking off the bread in small pieces and chewing them violently. The man leaning against the wall beside her was also eating—small dark objects which he kept taking out of the hood of his garment and crunching noisily. With a faint shudder she saw that they were red locusts with the legs and heads removed. The babble of voices which had been constant suddenly ceased; people appeared to be listening. Above the rumbling of the train and the rhythmical clacking of the wheels over the rails she could hear the sharp, steady sound of rain on the tin roof of the car. The men were nodding their heads; conversation started up again. She determined to fight her way back to the door in order to be able to get down at the next stop. Holding her head slightly lowered in front of her, she began to burrow wildly through the crowd. There were groans from below as she stepped on sleepers, there were exclamations of indignation as her elbows came in contact with faces. At each step she cried: *"Pardon! Pardon!"* She had got herself wedged into a corner at the end of the car. Now all she needed was to get to the door. Barring her way was a wild-faced man holding a severed sheep's head, its eyes like agate marbles staring from their sockets. "Oh!" she moaned. The man looked at her stolidly, making no movement to let her by. Using all her strength, she fought her way around him, rubbing her skirt against the bloody neck as she squeezed past. With relief she saw that the door onto the platform was open; she would have only to get by those who filled the entrance. She began her cries of *"Pardon!"* once more, and charged through. The platform itself was less crowded because the cold rain was sweeping across it. Those sitting there had their heads covered with the hoods of their burnouses. Turning her back to the rain she gripped the iron railing and looked directly into the most hideous human face she had ever seen. The tall man wore cast-off European clothes, and a burlap bag over his head like a haïk. But where his nose should have been was a dark triangular abyss, and the strange flat lips were white. For no reason at all she thought of a lion's muzzle; she could not take her eyes away from it. The man seemed neither to see her nor to feel the rain; he merely stood there. As she stared she found herself wondering why it was that a diseased face, which basically means nothing, should be so much more horrible to look at than a face whose tissues are healthy but whose expression reveals an interior corruption. Port would say that in a nonmaterialistic age it would not be thus. And probably he would be right.

She was drenched through and shivering, but she still held on to the cold metal railing and looked straight ahead of her—sometimes into the face, and sometimes to one side into the gray, rain-filled air of the night behind it. It was a *tête-à-tête* which would last until they came to a station. The train was laboring slowly, noisily, up a steep grade. From time to time, in the middle of the shaking and racket, there was a hollow sound for a few seconds as it crossed a short bridge or a trestle. At such moments it seemed to her that she was moving high in the air and that far below there was water rushing between the rocky walls of the chasms. The driving rain continued. She had the impression of living a dream of terror which refused to come to a finish. She was not conscious of time passing; on the contrary, she felt that it had stopped, that she had become a static thing suspended in a vacuum. Yet underneath was the certainty that at a given moment it would no longer be this way—but she did not want to think of that, for fear that she should become alive once more, that time should begin to move again and that she should be aware of the endless seconds as they passed.

And so she stood unmoving, always shivering, holding herself very erect. When the train slowed down and came to a stop, the lion-faced man was gone. She got off and hurried through the rain, back toward the end of the train. As she climbed into the second-class carriage, she remembered that he had stepped aside like any normal man, to let her pass. She began to laugh to herself, quietly. Then she stood still. There were people in the corridor, talking. She turned and went back to the toilet, locked herself in, and began to make up by the flickering lantern overhead, looking into the small oval mirror above the washstand. She was still trembling with cold, and water ran down her legs onto the floor. When she felt she could face Tunner again, she went out, down the corridor, and crossed over into the first-class coach. The door of their compartment was open. Tunner was staring moodily out the window. He turned as she went in, and jumped up.

"My God, Kit! Where have you been?"

"In the fourth-class carriage?" She was shaking violently, so that it was impossible for her to sound nonchalant, as she had intended.

"But look at you! Come in here." His voice was suddenly very serious. He pulled her firmly into the compartment, shut the door, helped her to sit down, and immediately began to go through his luggage, taking things out and laying them on the seat. She watched him in a stupor. Presently he was holding two aspirin tablets and a plastic cup in front of her face. "Take these," he commanded. The cup contained champagne. She did as she was told. Then he indicated the flannel bathrobe on the seat across from her. "I'm going out into the passageway here, and I want you to take off every stitch you have on, and put on that. Then you rap on the door and I'll come in and massage your feet. No excuses, now. Just do it." He went out and rolled the door shut after him.

She pulled down the shades at the outside windows and did as he had told her. The robe was soft and warm; she sat huddled in it on the seat for a while, her legs drawn up under her. And she poured herself three more cups of champagne, drinking them quickly one after the other. Then she tapped softly on the glass. The door opened a little. "All clear?" said Tunner.

"Yes, yes. Come in."

He sat down opposite her. "Now, stick your foot out here. I'm going to give them an alcohol rub. What's the matter with you, anyway? Are you crazy? Want to get pneumonia? What happened? Why were you so long? You had me nuts here, running up and down the place, in and out of cars asking everybody if they'd seen you. I didn't know *where* the hell you'd gone to."

"I told you I was in the fourth-class with the natives. I couldn't get back because there's no bridge between the cars. That feels wonderful. You'll wear yourself out."

He laughed, and rubbed more vigorously. "Never have yet."

When she was completely warm and comfortable he reached up and turned the lantern's wick very low. Then he moved across and sat beside her. The arm went around her, the pressure began again. She could think of nothing to say to stop him.

"You all right?" he asked softly, his voice husky.

"Yes," she said.

A minute later she whispered nervously: "No, no, no! Someone may open the door."

"No one's going to open the door." He kissed her. Over and over in her head she heard the slow wheels on the rails saying: "Not *now* not now, not *now* not now . . ." And underneath she imagined the deep chasms in the rain, swollen with water. She reached up and caressed the back of his head, but she said nothing.

"Darling," he murmured. "Just be still. Rest."

She could no longer think, nor were there any more images in her head. She was aware only of the softness of the woolen bathrobe next to her skin, and then of the nearness and warmth of a being that did not frighten her. The rain beat against the window panes.

11

The roof of the hotel in the early morning, before the sun had come from behind the nearby mountainside, was a pleasant place for breakfast. The tables were set out along the edge of the terrace, overlooking the valley. In the gardens below, the fig trees and high stalks of papyrus moved slightly in the fresh morning wind. Farther down were the larger trees where the storks had made their huge nests, and at the bottom of the slope was the river, running with thick red water. Port sat drinking his coffee, enjoying the rain-washed smell of the mountain air. Just below, the storks were teaching their young to fly; the ratchet-like croaking of the older birds was mingled with shrill cries from the fluttering young ones.

As he watched, Mrs. Lyle came through the doorway from downstairs. It seemed to him that she looked unusually distraught. He invited her to sit with him, and she ordered her tea from an old Arab waiter in a shoddy rose-colored uniform.

"Gracious! Aren't we ever picturesque!" she said.

Port called her attention to the birds; they watched them until her tea was brought.

"Tell me, has your wife arrived safely?"

"Yes, but I haven't seen her. She's still asleep."

"I should think so, after that damnable trip."

"And your son. Still in bed?"

"Good heavens, no! He's gone off somewhere, to see some caïd or other. That boy has letters of introduction to Arabs in every town of North Africa, I expect." She became pensive. After a moment she said, looking at him sharply: "I do hope you don't go near them."

"Arabs, you mean? I don't know any personally. But it's rather hard not to go near them, since they're all over the place."

"Oh, I'm talking about social contact with them. Eric's an absolute fool. He wouldn't be ill today if it hadn't been for those filthy people."

"Ill? He looks well enough to me. What's wrong with him?"

"He's very ill." Her voice sounded distant; she looked down toward the river. Then she poured herself some more tea, and offered Port a biscuit from a tin she had brought upstairs with her. Her voice more definite, she continued. "They're all contaminated, you know, of course. Well, that's it. And I've been having the most *beastly* time trying to make him get proper treatment. He's a young idiot."

"I don't think I quite understand," said Port.

"An infection, an infection," she said impatiently. "Some filthy swine of an Arab woman," she added, with astonishing violence.

"Ah," said Port, noncommittal.

Now she sounded less sure of herself. "I've been told

that such infections can even be transmitted among men directly. Do you believe that, Mr. Moresby?"

"I really don't know," he answered, looking at her in some surprise. "There's so much uninformed talk about such things. I should think a doctor would know best."

She passed him another biscuit. "I don't blame you for not wanting to discuss it. You must forgive me."

"Oh, I have no objection at all," he protested. "But I'm not a doctor. You understand."

She seemed not to have heard him. "It's disgusting. You're quite right."

Half of the sun was peering from behind the rim of the mountain; in another minute it would be hot. "Here's the sun," said Port. Mrs. Lyle gathered her things together.

"Shall you be staying long in Boussif?" she asked.

"We have no plans at all. And you?"

"Oh, Eric has some mad itinerary worked out. I believe we go on to Aïn Krorfa tomorrow morning, unless he decides to leave this noon and spend the night in Sfissifa. There's supposed to be a fairly decent little hotel there. Nothing so grand as this, of course."

Port looked around at the battered tables and chairs, and smiled. "I don't think I'd want anything much less grand than this."

"Oh, but my dear Mr. Moresby! This is positively luxurious. This is the best hotel you'll find between here and the Congo. There's nothing after this with running water, you know. Well, we shall see you before we go, in any case. I'm being baked by this horrible sun. Please say good morning to your wife for me." She rose and went downstairs.

Port hung his coat on the back of the chair and sat a while, pondering the unusual behavior of this eccentric woman. He could not bring himself to attribute it to mere irresponsibility or craziness; it seemed much more likely that her deportment was a roundabout means of communicating an idea she dared not express directly. In her own confused mind the procedure was apparently logical. All he could be certain of was that her basic motivation was fear. And Eric's was greed; of that also he was sure. But the compound made by the two together continued to mystify him. He had the impression that the merest indication of a design was beginning to take shape; what the design was, what it might end by meaning, all that was still wholly problematical. He guessed however that at the moment mother and son were working at cross-purposes. Each had a reason for being interested in his presence, but the reasons were not identical, nor even complementary, he thought.

He consulted his watch: it was ten-thirty. Kit would probably not be awake yet. When he saw her he intended to discuss the matter with her, if she were not still angry with him. Her ability to decipher motivations was considerable. He decided to take a walk around the town. Stopping off in his room, he left his jacket there and picked up his sun glasses. He had reserved the room across the hall for Kit. As he went out he put his ear against the door of her room and listened; there was no sound within.

Boussif was a completely modern town, laid out in large square blocks, with the market in the middle. The unpaved streets, lined for the most part with box-shaped one-story buildings, were filled with a rich red mud. A steady procession of men and sheep moved through the principal thoroughfare toward the market, the men walking with the hoods of their burnouses drawn up over their heads against the sun's fierce attack. There was not a tree to be seen anywhere. At the ends of the transversal streets the bare wasteland sloped slowly upward to the base of the mountains, which were raw, savage rock without vegetation. Except for the faces he found little of interest in the enormous market. At one end there was a tiny café with one table set outside under a cane trellis. He sat down and clapped his hands twice. *"Ouahad atai,"* he called; that much Arabic he remembered. While he sipped the tea, which he noticed was made with dried mint leaves instead of fresh, he observed that the same ancient bus kept passing the café, sounding its horn insistently. He watched it as it went by. Filled with native passengers, it made the tour of the market again and again, the boy on the back platform pounding its resonant tin body rhythmically, and shouting: *"Arfâ! Arfâ! Arfâ! Arfâ!"* without stopping.

He sat there until lunchtime.

12

The first thing Kit knew when she awoke was that she had a bad hangover. Then she noticed the bright sun shining into the room. What room? It was too much effort for her to think back. Something moved at her side on the pillow. She rolled her eyes to the left, and saw a shapeless dark mass beside her head. She cried out and sprang up, but even as she did so she knew it was only Tunner's black hair. In his sleep he stirred, and stretched out his arm to embrace her. Her head pounding painfully, she jumped out of bed and stood staring at him. "My God!" she said aloud. With difficulty she aroused him, made him get up and dress, forced him out into the hall with all his luggage, and quickly locked the door after him. Then, before he had thought of finding a boy to help him with the bags, while he was still standing there stupidly, she opened the door and made a whispered demand for a bottle of champagne. He got one out, passed it in to her, and she shut the door again. She sat down on the bed and drank the whole bottle. Her need for the drink was partly physical, but particularly she felt she could not face Port until she had engaged in an inner dialogue from which she might emerge in some measure absolved for last night. She also hoped the champagne would make her ill, so that she could have a legitimate reason for staying in bed all day. It had quite the opposite effect: no sooner had she finished it than her hangover was gone, and she felt slightly tipsy, but very well. She went to the window and looked out onto the glaring courtyard where two Arab women were washing clothes in a large stone basin, spreading them out over the bushes to dry in the sun. She turned quickly and unpacked her overnight case, scattering the objects about the room. Then she began a careful search for any trace of Tunner that might be left in the room. A black hair on the pillow caused her heart to skip a beat; she dropped it out the window. Meticulously she made the bed, spread the woolen cover over it. Next she called the maid and asked her to have the fathma come and wash the floor. That way, if Port should arrive soon, it would look as though the maid had already finished the room. She dressed and went downstairs. The fathma's heavy bracelets jangled as she scrubbed the tiles.

When he got back to the hotel Port knocked on the door of the room opposite his. A male voice said: *"Entrez,"* and he walked in. Tunner had partially undressed and was unpacking his valises. He had not thought to unmake the bed, but Port did not notice this.

"What the hell!" said Port. "Don't tell me they've given Kit the lousy back room I reserved for you."

"I guess they must have. But thanks anyway." Tunner laughed.

"You don't mind changing, do you?"

"Why? Is the other room so bad? No, I don't mind. It just seems like a lot of damned nonsense for just a day. No?"

"Maybe it'll be more than a day. Anyway, I'd like Kit to be here across from me."

"Of course. Of course. Better let her know too, though. She's probably in the other room there in all innocence, thinking it's the best in the hotel."

"It's not a bad room. It's just on the back, that's all. It was all they had yesterday when I reserved them."

"Righto. We'll get one of these monkeys to make the shift for us."

At lunch the three were reunited. Kit was nervous; she talked steadily, mainly about post-war European politics. The food was bad, so that none of them was in a very pleasant humor.

"Europe has destroyed the whole world," said Port. "Should I be thankful to it and sorry for it? I hope the whole place gets wiped off the map." He wanted to cut short the discussion, to get Kit aside and talk with her privately. Their long, rambling, supremely personal conversations always made him feel better. But she hoped particularly to avoid just such a *tête-à-tête*.

"Why don't you extend your good wishes to all humanity, while you're at it?" she demanded.

"Humanity?" cried Port. "What's that? Who is humanity? I'll tell you. Humanity is everyone but one's self. So of what interest can it possibly be to anybody?"

Tunner said slowly: "Wait a minute. Wait a minute. I'd like to take issue with you on that. I'd say humanity *is* you, and that's just what makes it interesting."

"Good, Tunner!" cried Kit.

Port was annoyed. "What rot!" he snapped. "You're

never humanity; you're only your own poor hopelessly isolated self." Kit tried to interrupt. He raised his voice and went on. "I don't have to justify my existence by any such primitive means. The fact that I breathe is my justification. If humanity doesn't consider that a justification, it can do what it likes to me. I'm not going to carry a passport to existence around with me, to prove I have the right to be here! I'm here! I'm in the world! But my world's not humanity's world. It's the world as *I* see it."

"Don't yell," said Kit evenly. "If that's the way you feel, it's all right with me. But you ought to be bright enough to understand that not everybody feels the same way."

They got up. The Lyles smiled from their corner as the trio left the room.

Tunner announced: "I'm off for a siesta. No coffee for me. See you later."

When Port and Kit stood alone in the hall, he said to her: "Let's have coffee out in the little café by the market."

"Oh, please!" she protested. "After that leaden meal? I couldn't ever walk anywhere. I'm still exhausted from the trip."

"All right; up in my room?"

She hesitated. "For a few minutes. Yes, I'd love it." Her voice did not sound enthusiastic. "Then I'm going to have a nap, too."

Upstairs they both stretched out on the wide bed and waited for the boy to arrive with the coffee. The curtains were drawn, but the insistent light filtered through them, giving objects in the room a uniform, pleasant rose color. It was very quiet outside in the street; everything but the sun was having a siesta.

"What's new?" said Port.

"Nothing, except as I told you, I'm worn out from the train trip."

"You could have come with us in the car. It was a fine ride."

"No, I couldn't. Don't start that again. Oh, I saw Mr. Lyle this morning downstairs. I still think he's a monster. He insisted on showing me not only his own passport, but his mother's, too. Of course they were both crammed with stamps and visas. I told him you'd want to see them, that you liked that sort of thing more than I did. She was born in Melbourne in 1899 and he was born in 1925, I don't remember where. Both British passports. So there's all your information."

Port glanced sideways at her admiringly. "God, how did you get all that without letting him see you staring?"

"Just shuffling the pages quickly. And she's down as a journalist and he as a student. Isn't that ridiculous? I'm sure he never opened a book in his life."

"Oh, he's a halfwit," said Port absently, taking her hand and stroking it. "Are you sleepy, baby?"

"Yes, terribly, and I'm only going to take a tiny sip of coffee because I don't want to get waked up. I want to sleep."

"So do I, now that I'm lying down. If he doesn't come in a minute I'll go down and cancel the order."

But a knock came at the door. Before they had time to reply, it was flung open, and the boy advanced bearing a huge copper tray. *"Deux cafés,"* he said grinning.

"Look at that mug," said Port. "He thinks he's come in on a hot romance."

"Of course. Let the poor boy think it. He has to have some fun in life."

The Arab set the tray down discreetly by the window

and tiptoed out of the room, looking back once over his shoulder at the bed, almost wistfully, it seemed to Kit. Port got up and brought the tray to the bed. As they had their coffee he turned to her suddenly.

"Listen!" he cried, his voice full of enthusiasm.

Looking at him, she thought: "How like an adolescent he is."

"Yes?" she said, feeling like a middle-aged mother.

"There's a place that rents bicycles near the market. When you wake up, let's hire a couple and go for a ride. It's fairly flat all around Boussif."

The idea appealed to her vaguely, although she could not imagine why.

"Perfect!" she said. "I'm sleepy. You can wake me at five, if you think of it."

13

They rode slowly out the long street toward the cleft in the low mountain ridge south of the town. Where the houses ended the plain began, on either side of them, a sea of stones. The air was cool, the dry sunset wind blew against them. Port's bicycle squeaked slightly as he pedaled. They said nothing, Kit riding a little ahead. In the distance, behind them, a bugle was being blown; a firm, bright blade of sound in the air. Even now, when it would be setting in a half-hour or so, the sun burned. They came to a village, went through it. The dogs barked wildly and the women turned away, covering their mouths. Only the children remained as they were, looking, in a paralysis of surprise. Beyond the village, the road began to rise. They were aware of the grade only from their pedaling; to the eye it looked flat. Soon Kit was tired. They stopped, looked back across the seemingly level plain to Boussif, a pattern of brown blocks at the base of the mountains. The breeze blew harder.

"It's the freshest air you'll ever smell," said Port.

"It's wonderful," said Kit. She was in a dreamy, amiable state of mind, and she did not feel talkative.

"Shall we try and make the pass there?"

"In a minute. I just want to catch my breath."

Presently they started out again, pedaling determinedly, their eyes on the gap in the ridge ahead. As they approached it, already they could see the endless flat desert beyond, broken here and there by sharp crests of rock that rose above the surface like the dorsal fins of so many monstrous fish, all moving in the same direction. The road had been blasted through the top of the ridge, and the jagged boulders had slid down on both sides of the cut. They left the bicycles by the road and started to climb upward among the huge rocks, toward the top of the ridge. The sun was at the flat horizon; the air was suffused with redness. As they stepped around the side of a boulder they came all at once on a man, seated with his burnous pulled up about his neck—so that he was stark naked from the shoulders down—deeply immersed in the business of shaving his pubic hair with a long pointed knife. He glanced up at them with indifference as they passed before him, immediately lowering his head again to continue the careful operation.

Kit took Port's hand. They climbed in silence, happy to be together.

"Sunset is such a sad hour," she said, presently.

"If I watch the end of a day—any day—I always feel it's the end of a whole epoch. And the autumn! It might as well be the end of everything," he said. "That's why I hate cold countries, and love the warm ones, where there's no winter, and when night comes you feel an opening up of the life there, instead of a closing down. Don't you feel that?"

"Yes," said Kit, "but I'm not sure I prefer the warm countries. I don't know. I'm not sure I don't feel that it's wrong to try to escape the night and winter, and that if you do you'll have to pay for it somehow."

"Oh, Kit! You're really crazy." He helped her up the side of a low cliff. The desert was directly below them, much farther down than the plain from which they had just climbed.

She did not answer. It made her sad to realize that in spite of their so often having the same reactions, the same feelings, they never would reach the same conclusions, because their respective aims in life were almost diametrically opposed.

They sat down on the rocks side by side, facing the vastness below. She linked her arm through his and rested her head against his shoulder. He only stared straight before him, sighed, and finally shook his head slowly.

It was such places as this, such moments that he loved above all else in life; she knew that, and she also knew that he loved them more if she could be there to experience them with him. And although he was aware that the very silences and emptinesses that touched his soul terrified her, he could not bear to be reminded of that. It was as if always he held the fresh hope that she, too, would be touched in the same way as he by solitude and the proximity to infinite things. He had often told her: "It is your only hope," and she was never sure what he meant. Sometimes she thought he meant that it was *his* only hope, that only if she were able to become as he was, could he find his way back to love, since love for Port meant loving her—there was no question of anyone else. And now for so long there had been no love, no possibility of it. But in spite of her willingness to become whatever he wanted her to become, she could not change that much: the terror was always there inside her ready to take command. It was useless to pretend otherwise. And just as she was unable to shake off the dread that was always with her, he was unable to break out of the cage into which he had shut himself, the cage he had built long ago to save himself from love.

She pinched his arm. "Look there!" she whispered. Only a few paces from them, atop a rock, sitting so still that they had not noticed him, was a venerable Arab, his legs tucked under him, his eyes shut. At first it seemed as though he might be asleep, in spite of his erect posture, since he made no sign of being conscious of their presence. But then they saw his lips moving ever so little, and they knew he was praying.

"Do you think we should watch like this?" she said, her voice hushed.

"It's all right. We'll just sit here quietly." He put his head in her lap and lay looking up at the clear sky. Over and over, very lightly, she stroked his hair. The wind from the regions below gathered force. Slowly the sky lost its intensity of light. She glanced up at the Arab; he had not moved. Suddenly she wanted to go back, but she sat perfectly still for a while looking tenderly down at the inert head beneath her hand.

"You know," said Port, and his voice sounded unreal, as voices are likely to do after a long pause in an utterly silent spot, "the sky here's very strange. I often have the sensation when I look at it that it's a solid thing up there, protecting us from what's behind."

Kit shuddered slightly as she said: "From what's behind?"

"Yes."

"But what *is* behind?" Her voice was very small.

"Nothing, I suppose. Just darkness. Absolute night."

"Please don't talk about it now." There was agony in her entreaty. "Everything you say frightens me, up here. It's getting dark, and the wind is blowing, and I can't stand it."

He sat up, put his arms about her neck, kissed her, drew back and looked at her, kissed her again, drew back again, and so on, several times. There were tears on her cheeks. She smiled forlornly as he rubbed them away with his forefingers.

"You know what?" he said with great earnestness. "I think we're both afraid of the same thing. And for the same reason. We've never managed, either one of us, to get all the way into life. We're hanging on to the outside for all we're worth, convinced we're going to fall off at the next bump. Isn't that true?"

She shut her eyes for a moment. His lips on her cheek had awakened the sense of guilt, and it swept over her now in a great wave that made her dizzy and ill. She had spent her siesta trying to wipe her conscience clean of the things that had happened the night before, but now she was clearly aware that she had not been able to do it, and that she never would be able to do it. She put her hand to her forehead, holding it there. At length she said: "But if we're not in, then we *are* more likely to—fall off."

She had hoped he would offer some argument to this, that he would find his own analogy faulty, perhaps—that some consolation would be forthcoming. All he said was: "I don't know."

The light was growing palpably dimmer. Still the old Arab sat buried in his prayers, severe and statue-like in the advancing dusk. It seemed to Port that behind them, back on the plain, he could hear one long-drawn-out bugle note, but it went on and on. No man could hold his breath that long: it was his imagination. He took her hand and pressed it. "We must go back," he whispered. Quickly they rose and went leaping over the rocks down to the road. The bicycles were there where they had left them. They coasted silently back toward the town. The dogs in the village set up a clamor as they sped past. At the market place they left the bicycles, and walked slowly through the street that led to the hotel, head on into the parade of men and sheep that continued its steady advance into the town, even at night.

All the way back to town Kit had been turning an idea over and over in her head: "Somehow Port knows about Tunner and me." At the same time she did not believe he was conscious of knowing it. But with a deeper part of his intelligence she was certain he felt the truth, felt what had happened. As they walked along the dark street she was almost tempted to ask him how he knew. She was curious about the functioning of a purely animal sense like that, in a man as complex as Port. But it would have done no good; as soon as he had been made aware of his knowledge he would have decided to be furiously jealous, immediately there would have been a scene, and all the implicit tenderness between them would have vanished, perhaps never to be recovered. To have not even that tenuous communion with him would be unbearable.

Port did a curious thing when dinner was over. Alone he went out to the market, sat in the café for a few minutes watching the animals and men by the flickering carbide lamps, and on passing the open door of the shop where he had rented the bicycles, went in. There he asked for a bicycle equipped with a headlight, told the man to wait for him until he returned, and quickly rode off in the direction of the gap. Up there among the rocks it was cold, the night wind blew. There was no moon; he could not see the desert in front of him, down below—only the hard stars above that flared in the sky. He sat on the rock and let the wind chill him. Riding down to Boussif he realized he never could tell Kit that he had been back there. She would not understand his having wanted to return without her. Or perhaps, he reflected, she would understand it too well.

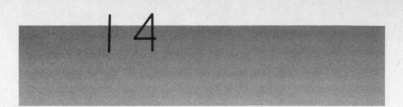

14

Two nights later they got on the bus for Aïn Krorfa, having chosen the night car to avoid the heat, which is oppressive along that route. Somehow, too, the dust seems less heavy when one cannot see it. Daytime, as the bus makes its way across this part of the desert, winding down and up through the small canyons, one watches the trail of dust that rises in the car's wake, sometimes breathing it in when the road doubles back on itself sharply. The fine powder piles up on every surface which is anywhere near to being horizontal, and this includes the wrinkles in the skin, the eyelids, the insides of the ears, and even, on occasions, hidden spots like the navel. And by day, unless the traveler is accustomed to such quantities of dust, he is supremely conscious of its presence, and is likely to magnify the discomfort it causes him. But at night, because the stars are bright in the clear sky, he has the impression, so long as he does not move, that there is no dust. The steady hum of the motor lulls him into a trance-like state in which his entire attention goes to watching the road move endlessly toward him as the headlights uncover it. That is, until he falls asleep, to be awakened later by the stopping of the bus at some dark, forsaken bordj, where he gets out chilled and stiff, to drink a glass of sweet coffee inside the gates.

Having received their places in advance, they had been able to get the most desirable seats in the bus, which were those in front with the driver. There was less dust here, and the heat from the motor, although excessive and a bit uncomfortable for the feet, was welcome by eleven o'clock, when the warmth of the day had totally disappeared and they became conscious of the dry, intense cold that always comes at night in this high region. And so all three of them were squeezed together with the driver, on the front seat. Tunner, who sat by the door, seemed to be asleep. Kit, with her head resting heavily against Port's arm, stirred a little now and then, but her eyes were closed. Straddling the emergency brake, and with his ribs continually being prodded by the driver's elbow as he steered, Port had by far the least comfortable spot, and consequently he was wide awake. He sat staring ahead through the windshield at the flat road that kept coming on, always toward him, and always being devoured by the headlights. Whenever he was en route from one place to another, he was able to look at his life with a little more objectivity than usual. It was often on trips that he thought most clearly, and made the decisions that he could not reach when he was stationary.

Since the day he and Kit had gone bicycling together he had felt a definite desire to strengthen the sentimental bonds between them. Slowly it was assuming an enormous importance to him. At times he said to himself that subconsciously he had had that in mind when he had conceived this expedition with Kit from New York into the unknown; it was only at the last minute that Tunner had been asked to come along, and perhaps that, too, had been subconsciously motivated, but out of fear; for much as he desired the rapprochement, he knew that also he dreaded the emotional responsibilities it would entail. But now, here in this distant and unconnected part of the world, the longing for closer ties with her was proving stronger than the fear. To forge such a bond required that they be alone together. The last two days at Boussif had been agonizing ones. It was almost as if Tunner had been aware of Port's desire and were determined to frustrate it. He had been present with them all day and half the night, ceaselessly talking, and apparently without a wish in the world save that of sitting with them, eating with them, taking walks with them, and even going with them to Kit's room at night, when of all times Port wanted to be alone with her, and standing for an hour or so in the doorway making pointless conversation. (It occurred to him, naturally, that Tunner might still have hopes of getting his way with her. The exaggerated attention he paid her, the banal flattery which was supposed to pass for gallantry, made him think this likely; but because Port ingenuously believed that his own feeling for Kit was identical in every respect with hers for him, he remained convinced that never under any circumstances would she yield to a person like Tunner.)

The only time he had succeeded in getting Kit out of the hotel alone had been while Tunner was still having his siesta, and then they had gone a scant hundred yards down the street and run into Eric Lyle, who straightway had announced that he would be delighted to accompany them on their walk. This he had done, to Port's silent fury, and Kit's visible disgust; indeed, Kit had been so annoyed by his presence that she had scarcely sat down at the café in the market when she had complained of a headache and rushed back to the hotel, leaving Port to cope with Eric. The objectionable youth was looking particularly pale and pimply in a flamboyant shirt decorated with giant tulips. He had bought the material, he said, in the Congo.

Once alone with Port, he had had the effrontery to ask him to lend him ten thousand francs, explaining that his mother was eccentric about money, and often flatly refused for weeks at a time to give him any.

"Not a chance. Sorry," Port had said, determining to be adamant. The sum had gradually been reduced, until at last he had remarked wistfully: "Even five hundred francs would keep me in smokes for a fortnight."

"I never lend anyone money," Port had explained with annoyance.

"But you will me." His voice was of honey.

"I will not."

"I'm not one of those stupid English who think all Americans have pots of money. It isn't that at all. But my mother's mad. She simply refuses to give me money. What am I to do?"

"Since he has no shame," thought Port, "I'll have no mercy." So he said: "The reason I won't lend you money is that I know I'll never get it back, and I haven't enough to give away. You see? But I'll give you three hundred francs. Gladly. I notice you smoke the *tabac du pays*. Fortunately it's very cheap."

In Oriental fashion Eric had bowed his head in agreement. Then he held forth his hand for the money. It made Port uncomfortable even now to recall the scene. When he had got back to the hotel he had found Kit and Tunner drinking beer together in the bar, and since then he had not had her to himself a minute, save the night before, when she had bidden him good night in the doorway. It did not make it easier for him, the fact that he suspected she was trying to keep from being alone with him.

"But there's plenty of time," he said to himself. "The only thing is, I must get rid of Tunner." He was pleased to have reached at last a definite decision. Perhaps Tunner would take a hint and leave of his own accord; if not, they would have to leave him. Either way, it must be done, and immediately, before they found a place they wanted to stay in long enough for Tunner to begin using it as a mail address.

He could hear the heavy valises sliding about on the top of the bus above his head; with conveyances no better than this he wondered if they had been wise to bring so much. However, it was too late now to do anything about it. There would be no place along the way where they could leave anything, because it was more than likely they would be coming back by some other route, if, indeed, they returned to the Mediterranean coast at all. For he had hopes of being able to continue southward; only, since no data on transportation and lodging facilities ahead of them were available, they would have to take their chances on what each place had to offer, hoping at best to gather some information each time about the next town, as they moved along. It was merely that the institution of tourist travel in this part of the world, never well developed in any case, had been, not interrupted, but utterly destroyed by the war. And so far there had been no tourists to start it up again. In a sense this state of affairs pleased him, it made him feel that he was pioneering—he felt more closely identified with his great-grandparents, when he was rolling along out here in the desert than he did sitting at home looking out over

the reservoir in Central Park—but at the same time he wondered how seriously one ought to take the travel bulletins
in their attempts to discourage such pioneering: "At present
travelers are strongly advised not to undertake land trips
into the interiors of French North Africa, French West Africa, or French Equatorial Africa. As more is learned on the
subject of touristic conditions in this part of the world, such
information will be made available to the public." He had
not shown any such paragraphs to Kit while he was making
his campaign speeches for Africa as against Europe. What
he had shown her was a carefully chosen collection of photographs he had brought back from previous trips: views of
oases and markets, as well as attractive vistas of the lobbies
and gardens of hotels which no longer operated. So far she
was being quite sensible—she had not objected once to the
accommodations—but Mrs. Lyle's vivid warning worried him
a little. It would not be amusing for very long to sleep in
dirty beds, eat inedible meals, and wait an hour or so every
time one wanted to wash one's hands.

The night went by slowly; yet to Port, watching the
road was hypnotic rather than monotonous. If he had not
been journeying into regions he did not know, he would
have found it insufferable. The idea that at each successive
moment he was deeper into the Sahara than he had been
the moment before, that he was leaving behind all familiar
things, this constant consideration kept him in a state of
pleasurable agitation.

Kit moved from time to time, lifted her head, and
murmuring something unintelligible, let it fall back against
him. Once she shifted and allowed it to fall in the other
direction, against Tunner who gave no sign of being awake.
Firmly Port grasped her arm and pulled her around so that
she leaned once more upon his shoulder. About once every

hour he and the chauffeur had a cigarette together, but otherwise they engaged in no words. At one point, waving his hands toward the dark, the chauffeur said: "Last year they say they saw a lion around here. The first time in years. They say it ate a lot of sheep. It was probably a panther, though."

"Did they catch it?"

"No. They're all afraid of lions."

"I wonder what became of it."

The driver shrugged his shoulders and lapsed into the silence he obviously preferred. Port was pleased to hear the beast had not been killed.

Just before dawn, at the coldest time of the night, they came to a bordj, bleak and austere in the windswept plain. Its single gate was opened, and more asleep than awake, the three staggered in, following the crowd of natives from the back of the bus. The vast courtyard was packed with horses, sheep and men. Several fires blazed; the red sparks flew wildly in the wind.

On a bench near the entrance of the room where the coffee was served there were five falcons, each with a black leather mask over its head, and each fastened to a peg in the bench by a delicate chain attached to its leg. They all perched in a row, quite unmoving, as if they had been mounted and ranged there by a taxidermist. Tunner became quite excited about them and rushed around inquiring if the birds were for sale. His questions were answered by polite stares. Finally he returned to the table looking somewhat confused, and sat down saying: "No one seems to know who they belong to."

Port snorted. "You mean nobody understood anything you said. What the hell would you want with them anyway?"

Tunner reflected a second. Then he laughed and said: "I don't know. I liked them, that's all."

When they went out again, the first signs of light were pushing up from behind the plain. And now it was Port's turn to sit by the door. By the time the bordj had become only a tiny white box far behind them, he was asleep. In this way he missed the night's grand finale: the shifting colors that played on the sky from behind the earth before the rising of the sun.

15

Even before Aïn Krorfa was in sight, the flies had made their presence known. As the first straggling oases appeared and the road darted between the high mud walls of the outlying settlements, all at once the bus was mysteriously full of them—small, grayish and tenacious. Some of the Arabs remarked about them, and covered their heads; the rest seemed not to be conscious of them. The driver said: *"Ah, les salauds! On voit bien que nous sommes à Aïn Krorfa!"*

Kit and Tunner went into a frenzy of activity, waving their arms about, fanning their faces, and blowing sideways frantically to drive the insects off their cheeks and noses, all of which was next to useless. They clung with surprising determination, and had practically to be lifted off; at the last instant they would rise swiftly, and then descend almost simultaneously to the same spot.

"We're being attacked!" cried Kit.

Tunner set about fanning her with a piece of newspaper. Port was still asleep by the door; the corners of his mouth bristled with flies.

"They stick when it's cool," said the driver. "Early in the morning you can't get rid of them."

"But where do they come from?" demanded Kit.

The outraged tone of her voice made him laugh.

"This is nothing," he said, with a deprecatory wave of the hand. "You must see them in the town. Like black snow, over everything."

"When will there be a bus leaving?" she said.

"You mean back to Boussif? I go back tomorrow."

"No, no! I mean toward the south."

"Ah, that! You must ask in Aïn Krorfa. I know only about the Boussif service. I think they have a line that makes Bou Noura once a week, and you can always get a ride on a produce truck to Messad."

"Oh, I don't want to go there," said Kit. She had heard Port say Messad was of no interest.

"Well, I do," interrupted Tunner in English with some force. "Wait a week in a place like this? My God, I'd be dead!"

"Don't get excited. You haven't seen it yet. Maybe the driver's just having us on, as Mr. Lyle would say. Besides, it probably wouldn't be a week, the bus to Bou Noura. It might be leaving tomorrow. It could even be today, as far as that goes."

"No," Tunner said obstinately. "One thing I can't stand is filth."

"Yes, you're a real American, I know." She turned her head to look at him, and he felt she was making fun of him. His face grew red.

"You're damned right."

Port awoke. His first gesture was to drive away the

flies from his face. He opened his eyes and stared out the window at the increasing vegetation. High palms shot up behind the walls; beneath them in a tangled mass were the oranges, figs and pomegranates. He opened the window and leaned out to sniff the air. It smelled of mint and wood-smoke. A wide river-bed lay ahead; there was even a meandering stream of water in the middle of it. And on each side of the road, and of all the roads that branched from it, were the deep seguias running with water that is the pride of Aïn Krorfa. He withdrew his head and said good morning to his companions. Mechanically he kept brushing away the insistent flies. It was not until several minutes later that he noticed Kit and Tunner doing the same thing. "What are all these flies?" he demanded.

Kit looked at Tunner and laughed. Port felt that they had a secret between them. "I was wondering how long it would be before you discovered them," she said.

Again they discussed the flies, Tunner calling upon the driver to attest to their number in Aïn Krorfa—this for Port's benefit, because he hoped to gain a recruit for his projected exodus to Messad—and Kit repeating that it would be only logical to examine the town before making any decisions. So far she found it the only visually attractive place she had seen since arriving in Africa.

This pleasant impression, however, was based wholly upon her appreciation of the verdure she could not help noticing behind the walls as the bus sped onward toward the town; the town itself, once they had arrived, seemed scarcely to exist. She was disappointed to see that it rather resembled Boussif, save that it appeared to be much smaller. What she could see of it was completely modern and geometrically laid out, and had it not been for the fact that the buildings were white instead of brown, and for the sidewalks bordering the principal street, which lay in the shadows of projecting arcades, she easily could have thought herself still in the other town. Her first view of the Grand Hotel's interior quite unnerved her, but Tunner was present and she felt impelled to sustain her position as one who had the right to twit him about his fastidiousness.

"Good heavens, what a mess!" she exclaimed; actually her epithet fell far short of describing what she really felt about the patio they had just entered. The simple Tunner was horrified. He merely looked, taking in each detail as it reached his gaze. As for Port, he was too sleepy to see much of anything, and he stood in the entrance, waving his arms around like a windmill in an attempt to keep the flies away from his face.

Originally having been built to shelter an administrative office of the colonial government, the building since had fallen on evil days. The fountain which at one time had risen from the basin in the center of the patio was gone, but the basin remained. In it reposed a small mountain of reeking garbage, and reclining on the sides of the mountain were three screaming, naked infants, their soft formless bodies troubled with bursting sores. They looked human there in their helpless misery, but somehow not quite so human as the two pink dogs lying on the tiles nearby—pink because long ago they had lost all their hair, and their raw, aged skin lay indecently exposed to the kisses of the flies and sun. One of them feebly raised its head an inch or so off the floor and looked at the newcomers vacantly through its pale yellow eyes; the other did not move. Behind the columns which formed an arcade at one side were a few amorphous and useless pieces of furniture piled on top of each other. A huge blue and white agateware pitcher stood near the central basin. In spite of the quantity of garbage in the patio, the predominating odor was of the latrine. Above the crying of the babies there was the shrill sound of women's voices in dispute, and the thick noise of a radio boomed in the background. For a brief instant a woman appeared in a doorway. Then she shrieked and immediately disappeared again. In the interior there were screams and giggles; one woman began to cry out: "Yah, Mohammed!" Tunner swung about and went into the street, where he joined the porters who had been told to wait outside with the luggage. Port and Kit stood quietly until the man called Mohammed appeared: he was wrapping a long scarlet sash around and around his waist; the end still trailed along the floor. In the course of the conversation about rooms, he kept insisting that they take one room with three beds—it would be cheaper for them and less work for the maids.

"If I could only get out of here," Kit thought, "before Port arranges something with him!" But her sense of guilt expressed itself in allegiance; she could not go out into the street because Tunner was there and she would appear to be choosing sides. Suddenly she, too, wished Tunner were not with them. She would feel much freer in expressing her own preferences. As she had feared, Port went upstairs with the man, returning presently to announce that the rooms were not really bad at all.

They engaged three smelly rooms, all giving onto a small court whose walls were bright blue. In the center of the court was a dead fig tree with masses of barbed wire looped from its branches. As Kit peered from the window a hungry-looking cat with a tiny head and huge ears walked carefully across the court. She sat down on the great brass bed, which, besides the jackal skin on the floor by it, was the only furnishing in the room. She could scarcely blame

Tunner for having refused at first even to look at the rooms. But as Port said, one always ends by getting used to anything, and although at the moment Tunner was inclined to be a little unpleasant about it, by night he would probably have grown accustomed to the whole gamut of incredible odors.

At lunch they sat in a bare, well-like room without windows, where the temptation was to whisper, since the spoken word was attended by distorting echoes. The only light came from the door into the main patio. Port clicked the switch of the overhead electric bulb: nothing happened. The barefoot waitress giggled. "No light," she said, setting their soup on the table.

"All right," said Tunner, "we'll eat in the patio."

The waitress rushed out of the room and returned with Mohammed, who frowned but set about helping them move the table and chairs out under the arcade.

"Thank heavens they're Arabs, and not French," said Kit. "Otherwise it would have been against the rules to eat out here."

"If they were French we could eat inside," said Tunner.

They lighted cigarettes in the hope of counteracting some of the stench that occasionally was wafted toward them from the basin. The babies were gone; their screams came from an inner room now.

Tunner stopped eating his soup and stared at it. Then he pushed his chair back and threw his napkin onto the table. "Well, by God in heaven, this may be the only hotel in town, but I can find better food than this in the market. Look at the soup! It's full of corpses."

Port examined his bowl. "They've weevils. They must have been in the noodles."

"Well, they're in the soup now. It's thick with 'em. You all can eat here at Carrion Towers if you like. I'm going to dig up a native restaurant."

"So long," said Port. Tunner went out.

He returned an hour later, less belligerent and slightly crest-fallen. Port and Kit were still in the patio, sitting over coffee and waving away flies.

"How was it? Did you find anything?" they asked.

"The food? Damned good." He sat down. "But I can't get any information on how to get out of this place."

Port, whose opinion of his friend's mastery of the French language had never been high, said: "Oh." A few minutes later he got up and went out into the town to collect by himself whatever bits of knowledge he could relating to the transportation facilities of the region. The heat was oppressive, and he had not eaten well. In spite of these things he whistled as he walked along under the deserted arcades, because the idea of getting rid of Tunner made him unaccountably lively. Already he was noticing the flies less.

Late in the afternoon a large automobile drew up in front of the hotel entrance. It was the Lyles' Mercedes.

"Of all the utterly idiotic things to have done! To try to find some lost village no one ever heard of!" Mrs. Lyle was saying. "You nearly made me miss tea. I suppose you'd have thought that amusing. Now drive away these wretched brats and come in here. Mosh! Mosh!" she cried, suddenly charging at a group of native youngsters who had approached the car. "Mosh! *Imshi!*" She raised her handbag in a menacing gesture; the bewildered children slowly backed away from her.

"I must find the right term to get rid of them with here," said Eric, jumping out and slamming the door. "It's no use saying you'll get the police. They don't know what that is."

"What nonsense! Police, indeed! Never threaten natives with the local authorities. Remember, we don't recognize French sovereignty here."

"Oh, that's in the Rif, Mother, and it's Spanish sovereignty."

"Eric! Will you be quiet? Don't you think I know what Madame Gautier told me? What do you *mean?*" She stopped as she saw the table under the arcade, still laden with the dirty dishes and glasses left by Port and Kit. "Hello! Someone else has arrived," she said in a tone that denoted the greatest interest. She turned accusingly to Eric. "And they've eaten outside! I told you we could have eaten outside, if you'd only insisted a bit. The tea's in your room. Will you bring it down? I must see about that putrid fire in the kitchen. And get out the sugar and open a new tin of biscuits."

As Eric returned through the patio with the box of tea, Port came in the door from the street.

"Mr. Moresby!" he cried. "What a pleasant surprise!"

Port tried to keep his face from falling. "Hello," he said. "What are you doing here? I thought I'd recognized your car outside."

"Just one second. I've got to deliver this tea to Mother. She's in the kitchen waiting for it." He rushed through the side door, stepping on one of the obscene dogs that lay exhausted just inside in the dark. It yelped lengthily. Port hurried upstairs to Kit and imparted the latest bad news to her. A minute later Eric pounded on the door. "I say, do have tea with us in ten minutes in room eleven. How nice to see you, Mrs. Moresby."

Room eleven was Mrs. Lyle's, longer but no less bare

than the others, and directly over the entrance. While she drank her tea, she kept rising from the bed where everyone was sitting for lack of chairs, going to the window and crying "Mosh! Mosh!" into the street.

Presently Port could no longer contain his curiosity. "What is that strange word you're calling out the window, Mrs. Lyle?"

"I'm driving those thiving little niggers away from my car."

"But what are you saying to them? Is it Arabic?"

"It's French," she said, "and it means get out."

"I see. Do they understand it?"

"They'd jolly well better. More tea, Mrs. Moresby!"

Tunner had begged off, having heard enough about the Lyles from Kit's description of Eric. According to Mrs. Lyle, Aïn Krorfa was a charming town, especially the camel market, where there was a baby camel they must photograph. She had taken several shots of it that morning. "It's too sweet," she said. Eric sat devouring Port with his eyes. "He wants more money," Port thought. Kit noticed his extraordinary expression, too, but she put a different interpretation on it.

When tea was over, and they were taking their leave, since they seemed to have exhausted all the possible subjects for conversation, Eric turned to Port. "If I don't see you at dinner, I'll drop in on you tonight afterward. What time do you go to bed?"

Port was vague. "Oh, any time, more or less. We'll probably be out fairly late looking around the town."

"Righto," said Eric, patting his shoulder affectionately as he shut the door.

When they got back to Kit's room she stood gazing out the window at the skeletal fig tree. "I wish we'd gone to Italy," she said. Port looked up quickly. "Why do you say that? Is it because of them, because of the hotel?"

"Because of everything." She turned toward him, smiling. "But I don't really mean it. This is just the right hour to go out. Let's."

Aïn Krorfa was beginning to awaken from its daily sun-drugged stupor. Behind the fort, which stood near the mosque on a high rocky hill that rose in the very middle of the town, the streets became informal, there were vestiges of the original haphazard design of the native quarter. In the stalls, whose angry lamps had already begun to gutter and flare, in the open cafés where the hashish smoke hung in the air, even in the dust of the hidden palm-bordered lanes, men squatted, fanning little fires, bringing their tin vessels of water to a boil, making their tea, drinking it.

"Teatime! They're really Englishmen dressed for a masquerade," said Kit. She and Port walked very slowly, hand in hand, perfectly in tune with the soft twilight. It was an evening that suggested languor rather than mystery.

They came to the river, here merely a flat expanse of white sand stretching away in the half light, and followed it a while until the sounds of the town became faint and high in the distance. Out here the dogs barked behind the walls, but the walls themselves were far from the river. Ahead of them a fire burned; seated by it was a solitary man playing a flute, and beyond him in the shifting shadows cast by the flames, a dozen or so camels rested, chewing solemnly on their cuds. The man looked toward them as they passed, but continued his music.

"Do you think you can be happy here?" asked Port in a hushed voice.

Kit was startled. "Happy? Happy? How do you mean?"

"Do you think you'll like it?"

"Oh, I don't know!" she said, with an edge of annoyance in her voice. "How can I tell? It's impossible to get into their lives, and know what they're really thinking."

"I didn't ask you that," Port remarked, nettled.

"You should have. That's what's important here."

"Not at all," he said. "Not for me. I feel that this town, this river, this sky, all belong to me as much as to them."

She felt like saying: "Well, you're crazy," but she confined herself to: "How strange."

They circled back toward the town, taking a road that led between garden walls.

"I wish you wouldn't ask me such questions," she said suddenly. "I can't answer them. How could I say: yes, I'm going to be happy in Africa? I like Aïn Krorfa very much, but I can't tell whether I want to stay a month or leave tomorrow."

"You couldn't leave tomorrow, for that matter, even if you did want to, unless you went back to Boussif. I found out about the buses. It's four days before the one for Bou Noura leaves. And it's forbidden to get rides on trucks to Messad now. They have soldiers who check along the way. There's a heavy fine for the drivers."

"So we're stuck in the Grand Hotel."

With Tunner," thought Port. Aloud: "*With* the Lyles."

"God forbid," Kit murmured.

"I wonder how long we've got to keep on running into them. I wish to hell they'd either get ahead of us once and for all, or let us get ahead of them and stay there."

"Things like that have to be arranged," said Kit. She, too, was thinking of Tunner. It seemed to her that if presently she were not going to have to sit opposite him over a meal, she could relax completely now, and live in the moment, which was Port's moment. But it seemed useless even to try, if in an hour she was going to be faced with the living proof of her guilt.

It was completely dark when they got back to the hotel. They ate fairly late, and after dinner, since no one felt like going out, they went to bed. This process took longer than usual because there was only one wash basin and water pitcher—on the roof at the end of the corridor. The town was very quiet. Some café radio was playing a transcription of a record by Abd-el-Wahab: a dirge-like popular song called: *I Am Weeping Upon Your Grave.* Port listened to the melancholy notes as he washed; they were broken into by nearby outbursts of dogs barking.

He was already in bed when Eric tapped on his door. Unfortunately he had not turned off his light, and for fear that it showed under the door he did not dare pretend to be asleep. The fact that Eric tiptoed into the room, a conspiratorial look on his face, displeased him. He pulled his bathrobe on.

"What's the matter?" he demanded. "Nobody's asleep."

"I hope I'm not disturbing you, old man." As always, he appeared to be talking to the corners of the room.

"No, no. But it's lucky you came when you did. Another minute and my light would have been out."

"Is your wife asleep?"

"I believe she's reading. She usually does before she goes to sleep. Why?"

"I wondered if I might have that novel she promised me this afternoon."

"When, now?" He passed Eric a cigarette and lit one himself.

"Oh, not if it will disturb her."

"Tomorrow would be better, don't you think?" said Port, looking at him.

"Right you are. What I actually came about was that money—" He hesitated.

"Which?"

"The three hundred francs you lent me. I want to give them back to you."

"Oh, that's quite all right." Port laughed, still looking at him. Neither one spoke for a moment.

"Well, of course, if you like," Port said finally, wondering if by any unlikely chance he had misjudged the youth, and somehow feeling more convinced than ever that he had not.

"Ah, excellent," murmured Eric, fumbling about in his coat pocket. "I don't like to have these things on my conscience."

"You didn't need to have it on your conscience, because if you'll remember, I gave it to you. But if you'd rather return it, as I say, naturally, that's fine with me."

Eric had finally extracted a worn thousand-franc note, and held it forth with a faint, propitiatory smile. "I hope you have change for this," he said, finally looking into Port's face, but as though it were costing him a great effort. Port sensed that this was the important moment, but he had no idea why. "I don't know," he said, not taking the proffered bill. "Do you want me to look?"

"If you could." His voice was very low. As Port clumsily got out of bed and went to the valise where he kept his money and documents, Eric seemed to take courage. "I do feel like a rotter, coming here in the middle of the night and bothering you this way, but first of all I want to get this off my mind, and besides, I need the change badly, and they don't seem to have any here in the hotel, and Mother and I are leaving first thing in the morning for Messad and I was afraid I might not see you again—"

"You are? Messad?" Port turned, his wallet in his hand. "Really? Good Lord! And our friend Mr. Tunner wants so much to go!"

"Oh?" Eric stood up slowly. 'Oh?" he said again. "I daresay we could take him along." He looked at Port's face and saw it brighten. "But we're leaving at daybreak. You'd better go immediately and tell him to be ready downstairs at six-thirty. We've ordered tea for six o'clock. You'd better have him do likewise."

"I'll do that," said Port, slipping his wallet into his pocket. "I'll also ask him for the change, which I don't seem to have."

"Good. Good," Eric said with a smile, sitting down again on the bed.

Port found Tunner naked, wandering distractedly around his room with a DDT bomb in his hand. "Come in," he said. "This stuff is no good."

"What have you got?"

"Bedbugs, for one thing."

"Listen. Do you want to go to Messad tomorrow morning at six-thirty?"

"I want to go tonight at *eleven*-thirty. Why?"

"The Lyles will drive you."

"And then what?"

Port improvised. "They'll be coming back here in a few days and going straight on to Bou Noura. They'll take you down and we'll be there expecting you. Lyle's in my room now. Do you want to talk with him?"

"No."

There was a silence. The electric light suddenly went off, then came on, a feeble orange worm inside the bulb, so that the room looked as if it were being viewed through heavy black glasses. Tunner glanced at his disordered bed and shrugged. "What time did you say?"

"Six-thirty they're going."

"Tell him I'll be down at the door." He frowned at Port, a faint suspicion in his face. "And you. Why aren't you going?"

"They'll only take one," he lied, "and besides, I like it here."

"You won't once you've gotten into your bed," said Tunner bitterly.

"You'll probably have them in Messad too," Port suggested. He felt safe now.

"I'll take my chances on any hotel after this one."

"We'll look for you in a few days in Bou Noura. Don't crash any harems."

He shut the door behind him and went back to his room. Eric was still sitting in the same position on the bed, but he had lighted another cigarette.

"Mr. Tunner is delighted, and'll meet you at six-thirty down at the door. Oh, damn! I forgot to ask him about the change for your thousand francs." He hesitated, about to go back out.

"Don't bother, please. He can change it for me tomorrow on the way, in case I need it changed."

Port opened his mouth to say: 'But I thought you wanted to pay me back the three hundred." He thought better of it. Now that the thing was settled, it would be tragic to risk a slip-up, just for a few francs. So he smiled and said: "Surely. Well, I hope we'll see you when you come back."

"Yes, indeed," smiled Eric, looking at the floor. He got up suddenly and went to the door. "Good night."

"Good night."

Port locked the door after him and stood by it, musing. Eric's behavior had impressed him as being unusually eccentric, yet he still suspected that it was explainable. Being sleepy, he turned off what remained of the light and got into bed. The dogs barked in chorus, far and nearby, but he was not molested by vermin.

That night he awoke sobbing. His being was a well a thousand miles deep; he rose from the lower regions with a sense of infinite sadness and repose, but with no memory of any dream save the faceless voice that had whispered: "The soul is the weariest part of the body." The night was silent, save for a small wind that blew through the fig tree and moved the loops of wire hanging there. Back and forth they rubbed, creaking ever so slightly. After he had listened a while, he fell asleep.

16

Kit sat up in bed, her breakfast tray on her knees. The room was lighted by the reflection of the sun on the blue wall outside. Port had brought her her breakfast, having decided after observing their behavior that the servants were incapable of carrying out any orders whatever. She had eaten, and now was thinking of what he had told her (with ill-concealed relish) about having got rid of Tunner. Because she, too, had secretly wished him gone, it seemed to her a doubly ignoble thing to have done. But why? He had gone of his own free will. Then she realized that intuitively she already was aware of Port's next move: he would contrive to miss connections with Tunner at Bou Noura. She could tell by his behavior, in spite of whatever he said, that he had no intention of meeting him there. That was why it seemed unkind. The deceit of the maneuver, if she were correct, was too bald; she determined not to be a party to it. "Even if Port runs out on him, I'll stay and meet him." She reached over and set the tray on the jackal skin;

badly cured, the pelt gave off a sour odor. "Or am I only trying to go on punishing myself by seeing Tunner in front of me every day?" she wondered. "Would it be better really to get rid of him?" If only it were possible to dig behind the coming weeks and know! The clouds above the mountains had been a bad sign, but not in the way she had imagined. Instead of the wreck there had been another experience which perhaps would prove more disastrous in its results. As usual she was being saved up for something worse than she expected. But she did not believe it was to be Tunner, so that it really was not important how she behaved now with regard to him. The other omens indicated a horror more vast, and surely ineluctable. Each escape merely made it possible for her to advance into a region of heightened danger. "In that case," she thought, "why not give in? And if I should give in, how would I behave? Exactly the same as now." So that giving in or not giving in had nothing to do with her problem. She was pushing against her own existence. All she could hope to do was eat, sleep and cringe before her omens.

She spent most of the day in bed reading, getting dressed only to have lunch with Port down in the stinking patio under the arcade. Immediately on returning to her room she pulled her clothes off. The room had not been made up. She straightened the bedsheet and lay down again. The air was dry, hot, breathless. During the morning Port had been out in the town. She wondered how he could support the sun, even with his helmet; it made her ill to be in it even for five minutes. His was not a rugged body, yet he had wandered for hours in the oven-like streets and returned to eat heartily of the execrable food. And he had unearthed some Arab who expected them both to tea at six. He had impressed it upon her that on no account must they be late. It was typical of him to insist upon punctuality in the case of an anonymous shopkeeper in Aïn Krorfa, when with his friends and with her he behaved in a most cavalier fashion, arriving at his appointments indifferently anywhere from a half-hour to two hours after the specified time.

The Arab's name was Abdeslam ben Hadj Chaoui; they called for him at his leather shop and waited for him to close and lock the front of it. He led them slowly through the twisting streets as the muezzin called, talking all the while in flowery French, and addressing himself principally to Kit.

"How happy I am! This is the first time I have the honor to invite a lady, and a gentleman, from New York. How I should like to go and see New York! What riches! Gold and silver everywhere! *Le grand luxe pour tout le monde,* ah! Not like Aïn Krorfa—sand in the streets, a few palms, hot sun, sadness always. It is a great pleasure for me to be able to invite a lady from New York. And a gentleman. New York! What a beautiful word!" They let him talk on.

The garden, like all the gardens in Aïn Krorfa, was really an orchard. Under the orange trees were small channels running with water fed from the well, which was built up on an artificial plateau at one end. The highest palms stood at the opposite end, near the wall that bordered the river-bed, and underneath one of these a great red and white wool rug was spread out. There they sat while a servant brought fire and the apparatus for making tea. The air was heavy with the odor of the spearmint that grew beside the water channels.

"We shall talk a little, while the water boils," said their host, smiling beneficently from one to the other. "We plant the male palm here because it is more beautiful. In Bou

Noura they think only of money. They plant the female. You know how *they* look? They are short and fat, they give many dates, but the dates are not even good, not in Bou Noura!" He laughed with quiet satisfaction. "Now you see how stupid the people are in Bou Noura!"

The wind blew and the palm trunks slowly moved with it, their lofty tops swaying slightly in a circular motion. A young man in a yellow turban approached, greeted them gravely, and seated himself a little in the background, at the edge of the rug. From under his burnous he brought forth an oud, whose strings he began to pluck casually, looking off under the trees all the while. Kit drank her tea in silence, smiling from time to time at M. Chaoui's remarks. At one point she asked Port in English for a cigarette, but he frowned, and she understood that it would shock the others to see a lady smoke. And so she sat drinking the tea, feeling that what she saw and heard around her was not really happening, or if it were, she was not really there herself. The light was fading; little by little the pots of coals became the eyes' natural focusing point. Still the lute music went on, a patterned background for the aimless talk; listening to its notes was like watching the smoke of a cigarette curl and fold in untroubled air. She had no desire to move, speak, or even think. But suddenly she was cold. She interrupted the conversation to say so. M. Chaoui was not pleased to hear it; he considered it a piece of incredible rudeness. He smiled, and said: "Ah, yes. Madame is blonde. The blondes are like the seguia when it has no water in it. The Arabs are like the seguias of Aïn Krorfa. The seguias of Aïn Krorfa are always full. We have flowers, fruit, trees."

"Yet you say Aïn Krorfa is sad," said Port.

"Sad?" repeated M. Chaoui with astonishment. "Aïn Krorfa is never sad. It is peaceful and full of joy. If one offered me twenty million francs and a palace, I would not leave my native land."

"Of course," Port agreed, and seeing that his host no longer desired to sustain the conversation, he said: "Since Madame is cold, we must go, but we thank you a thousand times. It has been a great privilege for us to be allowed to come to this exquisite garden."

M. Chaoui did not rise. He nodded his head, extended his hand, said: "Yes, yes. Go, since it is cold."

Both guests offered florid apologies for their departure: it could not be said that they were accepted with very good grace. "Yes, yes, yes," said M. Chaoui. "Another time perhaps it will be warmer."

Port restrained his mounting anger, which, even as he was feeling it, made him annoyed with himself.

"Au 'voir, cher monsieur," Kit suddenly said in a childish treble. Port pinched her arm. M. Chaoui had noticed nothing extraordinary; indeed, he unbent sufficiently to smile once more. The musician, still strumming on his lute, accompanied them to the gate, and solemnly said: *"B'slemah"* as he closed it after them.

The road was almost dark. They began to walk quickly.

"I hope you're not going to blame me for that," began Kit defensively.

Port slipped his arm around her waist. "Blame you! Why? How could I? And what difference does it make, anyway?"

"Of course it makes a difference," she said. "If it doesn't, what was the point of seeing the man in the first place?"

"Oh, *point!* I don't suppose there was any particular point. I thought it would be fun. And I still think it was; I'm glad we went."

"So am I, in a way. It gave me a first-hand opportunity of seeing what the conversations are going to be like here—just how unbelievably superficial they can be."

He let go of her waist. "I disagree. You don't say a frieze is superficial just because it has only two dimensions."

"You do if you're accustomed to having conversation that's something more than decoration. I don't think of conversation as a frieze, myself."

"Oh, nonsense! It's just another way of living they have, a completely different philosophy."

"I know that," she said, stopping to shake sand from her shoe. "I'm just saying I could never live with it."

He sighed: the tea-party had accomplished exactly the contrary to what he had hoped it might. She sensed what was in his mind, and presently she said: "Don't think about me. Whatever happens, I'll be all right if I'm with you. I enjoyed it tonight. Really." She pressed his hand. But this was not quite what he wanted; resignation was not enough. He returned her pressure halfheartedly.

"And what was that little performance of yours at the end?" he asked a moment later.

"I couldn't help it. He was being so ridiculous."

"It's not a good idea generally to make fun of your host," he said coldly.

"Oh, bah! If you noticed, he loved it. He thought I was being deferential."

They ate quietly in the nearly-dark patio. Most of the garbage had been cleared away, but the stench of the latrines was as strong as ever. After dinner they went to their rooms and read.

The next morning, when he took breakfast to her, he

said: "I nearly paid you a visit last night. I couldn't seem to sleep. But I was afraid of waking you."

"You should have rapped on the wall," she said. "I'd have heard you. I was probably awake."

All that day he was unaccountably nervous; he attributed it to the seven glasses of strong tea he had drunk in the garden. Kit, however, had drunk as much as he, and she seemed not in the least nervous. In the afternoon he walked by the river, watched the Spahis training on their perfect white horses, their blue capes flying behind in the wind. Since his agitation appeared to be growing rather than diminishing with the passage of time, he set himself the task of tracing it to its source. He walked along with his head bent over, seeing nothing but the sand and glistening pebbles. Tunner was gone, Kit and he were alone. Everything now depended on him. He could make the right gesture, or the wrong one, but he could not know beforehand which was which. Experience had taught him that reason could not be counted on in such situations. There was always an extra element, mysterious and not quite within reach, that one had not reckoned with. One had to know, not deduce. And he did not have the knowledge. He glanced up; the river-bed had become enormously wide, the walls and gardens had receded into the distance. Out here there was no sound but the wind blowing around his head on its way from one part of the earth to another. Whenever the thread of his consciousness had unwound too far and got tangled, a little solitude could wind it quickly back. His state of nervousness was remediable in that it had to do only with himself: he was afraid of his own ignorance. If he desired to cease being nervous he must conceive a situation for himself in which that ignorance had no importance. He must behave as if there was no question of his having Kit,

ever again. Then, perhaps, out of sheer inattention, automatically, it could happen. But should his principal concern
at the moment be the purely egocentric one of ridding himself of his agitation, or the accomplishment of his original
purpose in spite of it? "I wonder if after all I'm a coward?"
he thought. Fear spoke; he listened and let it persuade—the
classical procedure. The idea saddened him.

Not far away, on a slight elevation at a point where
the river's course turned sharply, was a small ruined building, without a roof, so old that a twisted tree had grown
up inside it, covering the area within the walls with its
shade. As he passed nearer to it and could see inside, he
realized that the lower branches were hung with hundreds
of rags, regularly torn strips of cloth that had once been
white, all moving in the same direction with the wind.
Faintly curious, he climbed the bank and went to investi-
gate, but on approaching he saw that the ruin was occupied:
an old, old man sat beneath the tree, his thin brown arms
and legs bound with ancient bandages. Around the base of
the trunk he had built a shelter; it was clear to see that he
lived there. Port stood looking at him a long time, but he
did not lift his head.

Going more slowly, he continued. He had brought
with him some figs, which he now pulled out and devoured.
When he had followed the river's complete turning, he
found himself facing the sun in the west, looking up a small
valley that lay between two gently graded, bare hills. At the
end was a steeper hill, reddish in color, and in the side of
the hill was a dark aperture. He liked caves, and was
tempted to set out for it. But distances here were deceptive,
and there might not be time before dark; besides, he did
not feel the necessary energy inside him. "Tomorrow I'll
come earlier and go up," he said to himself. He stood look-

ing up the valley a little wistfully, his tongue seeking the fig seeds between his teeth, with the small tenacious flies forever returning to crawl along his face. And it occurred to him that a walk through the countryside was a sort of epitome of the passage through life itself. One never took the time to savor the details; one said: another day, but always with the hidden knowledge that each day was unique and final, that there never would be a return, another time.

Under his sun helmet his head was perspiring. He removed the helmet with its wet leather band, and let the sun dry his hair for a moment. Soon the day would be finished, it would be dark, he would be back at the foul-smelling hotel with Kit, but first he must decide what course to take. He turned and walked back toward the town. When he came opposite the ruin, he peered inside. The old man had moved; he was seated just inside what had once been the doorway. The sudden thought struck him that the man must have a disease. He hastened his step and, absurdly enough, held his breath until he was well past the spot. As he allowed the fresh wind to enter his lungs again, he knew what he would do: he would temporarily abandon the idea of getting back together with Kit. In his present state of disquiet he would be certain to take all the wrong turnings, and would perhaps lose her for good. Later, when he least expected it, the thing might come to pass of its own accord. The rest of his walking was done at a brisk pace, and by the time he was back in the streets of Aïn Krorfa he was whistling.

They were having dinner. A traveling salesman eating inside in the dining room had brought a portable radio with him and was tuned in to Radio Oran. In the kitchen a louder radio was playing Egyptian music.

"You can put up with this sort of thing for just so

long. Then you go crazy," said Kit. She had found patches of fur in her rabbit stew, and unfortunately the light in that part of the patio was so dim that she had not made the discovery until after she had put the food into her mouth.

"I know," said Port absently. "I hate it as much as you."

"No, you don't. But I think you would if you didn't have me along to do your suffering for you."

"How can you say that? You know it's not so." He toyed with her hand: having made his decision he felt at ease with her. She, however, seemed unexpectedly irritable.

"Another town like this will fix me up fine," she said. "I shall simply go back and take the first boat out for Genoa or Marseille. This hotel's a nightmare, a *nightmare!*" After Tunner's departure she had vaguely expected a change in their relationship. The only difference his absence made was that now she could express herself clearly, without fear of seeming to be choosing sides. But rather than make any effort to ease whatever small tension might arise between them, she determined on the contrary to be intransigent about everything. It could come about now or later, that much-awaited reunion, but it must be all his doing. Because neither she nor Port had ever lived a life of any kind of regularity, they both had made the fatal error of coming hazily to regard time as non-existent. One year was like another year. Eventually everything would happen.

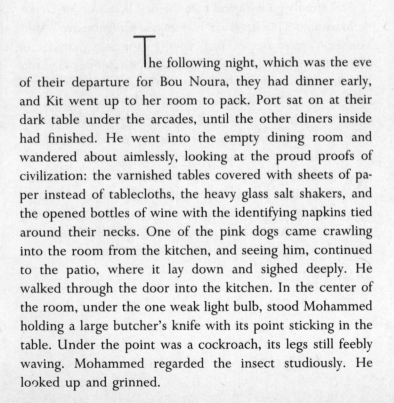

17

The following night, which was the eve of their departure for Bou Noura, they had dinner early, and Kit went up to her room to pack. Port sat on at their dark table under the arcades, until the other diners inside had finished. He went into the empty dining room and wandered about aimlessly, looking at the proud proofs of civilization: the varnished tables covered with sheets of paper instead of tablecloths, the heavy glass salt shakers, and the opened bottles of wine with the identifying napkins tied around their necks. One of the pink dogs came crawling into the room from the kitchen, and seeing him, continued to the patio, where it lay down and sighed deeply. He walked through the door into the kitchen. In the center of the room, under the one weak light bulb, stood Mohammed holding a large butcher's knife with its point sticking in the table. Under the point was a cockroach, its legs still feebly waving. Mohammed regarded the insect studiously. He looked up and grinned.

"Finished?" he asked.

"What?" said Port.

"Finished with dinner?"

"Oh, yes."

"Then I'll lock the dining room." He went and moved Port's table back into the room, turned off the lights and locked both doors. Then he put out the light in the kitchen. Port moved into the patio. "Going home to sleep?" he inquired.

Mohammed laughed. "Why do you think I work all day? Just to go home to sleep? Come with me. I'll show you the best place in Aïn Krorfa."

Port walked with him out into the street, where they conversed for a few minutes. Then they moved off down the street together.

The house was several houses, all with a common entrance through a large tiled courtyard. And each house had several rooms, all very small, and, with the exception of those on the ground floor, all at varying levels. As he stood in the courtyard in the faint light that was a blend of carbide-lamp glare and starlight, all the bright little boxlike interiors looked like so many ovens around him. Most of them had their door or windows open, and were filled to bursting with men and girls, both sexes uniformly dressed in flowing white garments. It looked festive, and it exhilarated him to see it; certainly he had no feeling that it was a vicious place, even though at first he tried hard to see it as such.

They went to the door of a room opposite the entrance, and Mohammed peered in, saluting certain of the men sitting inside on the couches along the walls. He entered, motioning to Port to follow him. Room was made for them, and they sat down with the others. A boy took their order for tea and quickly ran out of the room across the court. Mohammed was soon engaged in conversation with a man sitting nearby. Port leaned back and watched the girls as they drank tea and chatted with the men, sitting opposite them on the floor; he was waiting for a licentious gesture, at least a hint of a leer. None was forthcoming.

For some reason which he was unable to fathom, there were a good many small children running about the establishment. They were well behaved and quiet as they played in the gloomy courtyard, exactly as if it had belonged to a school instead of a brothel. Some of them wandered inside the rooms, where the men took them on their laps and treated them with the greatest affection, patting their cheeks and allowing them occasional puffs on their cigarettes. Their collective disposition toward contentment might easily be due, he thought, to the casual benevolence of their elders. If one of the younger ones began to shed tears, the men laughed and waved it away; it soon stopped.

A fat black police dog waddled in and out of the rooms, sniffing shoes; it was the object of everyone's admiration. "The most beautiful dog in Aïn Krorfa," said Mohammed as it appeared panting in the doorway near them. "It belongs to Colonel Lefilleul; he must be here tonight."

When the boy returned with the tea he was accompanied by another, not more than ten years old, but with an ancient, soft face. Port pointed him out to Mohammed and whispered that he looked ill.

"Oh, no! He's a singer." He signaled to the child, who began to clap his hands in a syncopated rhythm and utter a long repetitious lament built on three notes. To Port it seemed utterly incongruous and a little scandalous, hearing this recent addition to humanity produce a music so unchildlike and weary. While he was still singing, two girls came over and greeted Mohammed. Without any formalities he made them sit down and pour the tea. One was thin with a salient nose, and the other, somewhat younger, had the apple-like cheeks of a peasant; both bore blue tattoo marks on the foreheads and chins. Like all the women, their heavy robes were weighted down with an assortment of even heavier silver jewelry. For no particular reason neither one appealed to Port's fancy. There was something vaguely workaday about both of them; they were very much present. He could appreciate now what a find Marhnia had been, her treachery notwithstanding. He had not seen anyone here with half her beauty or style. When the child stopped singing Mohammed gave him some coins; he looked at Port expectantly as well, but Mohammed shouted at him, and he ran out. There was music in the next room: the sharp reedy rhaïta and the dry drums beneath. Since the two girls bored him, Port excused himself and went into the courtyard to listen.

In front of the musicians in the middle of the floor a girl was dancing, if indeed the motions she made could properly be called a dance. She held a cane in her two hands, behind her head, and her movements were confined to her agile neck and shoulders. The motions, graceful and of an impudence verging on the comic, were a perfect translation into visual terms of the strident and wily sounds of the music. What moved him, however, was not the dance itself so much as the strangely detached, somnambulistic expression of the girl. Her smile was fixed, and, one might have added, her mind as well, as if upon some object so remote that only she knew of its existence. There was a supremely impersonal disdain in the unseeing eyes and the curve of the placid lips. The longer he watched, the more fascinating the face became; it was a mask of perfect proportions, whose beauty accrued less from the configuration of features than from the meaning that was implicit in their expression—meaning, or the withholding of it. For what emotion lay behind the face it was impossible to tell. It was as if she were saying: "A dance is being done. I do not dance because I am not here. But it is my dance." When the piece drew to its conclusion and the music had stopped, she stood still for a moment, then slowly lowered the cane from behind her head, and tapping vaguely on the floor a few times, turned and spoke to one of the musicians. Her remarkable expression had not changed in any respect. The musician rose and made room for her on the floor beside him. The way he helped her to sit down struck Port as peculiar, and all at once the realization came to him that the girl was blind. The knowledge hit him like an electric shock; he felt his heart leap ahead and his head grow suddenly hot.

Quickly he went back into the other room and told Mohammed he must speak with him alone. He hoped to get him into the courtyard so as not to be obliged to go through his explanation in front of the girls, even though they spoke no French. But Mohammed was disinclined to move. "Sit down, my dear friend," he said, pulling at Port's sleeve. Port, however, was far too concerned lest his prey escape him to bother being civil. *"Non, non, non!"* he cried. *"Viens vite!"* Mohammed shrugged his shoulders in deference to the two girls, rose and accompanied him into the courtyard, where they stood by the wall under the light. Port asked him first if the dancing girls were available, and felt his spirits fall when Mohammed told him that many of them had lovers, and that in such cases they merely lived in the house as registered prostitutes, using it only as a home, and without engaging in the profession at all. Naturally those with lovers were given a wide berth by everyone else. *"Bsif! Forcément!* Throats are sliced for that," he laughed, his brilliant red gums gleaming like a dentist's model in wax. This was an angle Port had not considered. Still, the case merited a determined effort. He drew Mohammed over near the door of the adjacent cubicle, in which she sat, and pointed her out to him.

"Find out for me about that one there," he said. "Do you know her?"

Mohammed looked. "No," he said at length. "I will find out. If it can be arranged, I myself will arrange it and you pay me a thousand francs. That will be for her, and enough for me to buy coffee and breakfast."

The price was too high for Aïn Krorfa, and Port knew it. But this seemed to him a poor time to begin bargaining, and he accepted the arrangement, going back, as Mohammed bade him do, into the first room and sitting down again with the two dull girls. They were now engaged in a very serious conversation with each other, and scarcely noticed his arrival. The room buzzed with talk and laughter; he sat back and listened to the sound of it; even though he could not understand a word of what was being said he enjoyed studying the inflections of the language.

Mohammed was out of the room for quite a while. It began to be late, the number of people sitting about gradually diminished as the customers either retired to inner chambers or went home. The two girls sat on, talking, interspersing their words now with occasional fits of laughter in which they held onto one another for mutual support. He wondered if he ought to go in search of Mohammed. He tried to sit quietly and be part of the timelessness of the place, but the occasion scarcely lent itself to that kind of imaginative play. When he finally did go into the courtyard to look for him, he immediately caught sight of him in an opposite room, reclining on a couch smoking a hashish pipe with some friends. He went across and called to him, remaining outside because he did not know the etiquette of the hashish chamber. It appeared, however, that there was none.

"Come in," said Mohammed from the cloud of pungent smoke. "Have a pipe."

He went in, greeted the others, and said in a low voice to Mohammed: "And the girl?"

Mohammed looked momentarily blank. Then he laughed: "Ah, that one? You have bad luck, my friend. You know what she has? She is blind, the poor thing."

"I know, I know," he said impatiently, and with mounting apprehension.

"Well, you don't want her, do you? She is blind!"

Port forgot himself. *"Mais bien sûr que je la veux!"* he shouted. "Of course I do! Where is she?"

Mohammed raised himself a little on one elbow. "Ah!" he grunted. "By now, I wonder! Sit down here and have a pipe. It's among friends."

Port turned on his heel in a rage and strode out into the court, where he made a systematic search of the cubicles from one side of the entrance to the other. But the girl was gone. Furious with disappointment, he walked through the gate into the dark street. An Arab soldier and a girl stood just outside the portal, talking in low tones. As he went past them he stared intently into her face. The soldier glared at him, but that was all. It was not she. Looking up and down the ill-lit street, he could discern two or three white-robed figures in the distance to the left and to the right. He started walking, viciously kicking stones out of his path. Now that she was gone, he was persuaded, not that a bit of enjoyment had been denied him, but that he had lost love itself. He climbed the hill and sat down beside the fort, leaning against the old walls. Below him were the few lights of the town, and beyond was the inevitable horizon of the desert. She would have put her hands up to his coat lapels, touched his face tentatively, run her sensitive fingers slowly along his lips. She would have sniffed the brilliantine in his hair and examined his garments with care. And in bed, without eyes to see beyond the bed, she would have been completely there, a prisoner. He thought of the little games he would have played with her, pretending to have disappeared when he was really still there; he thought of the countless ways he could have made her grateful to him. And always in conjunction with his fantasies he saw the imperturbable, faintly questioning face in its masklike symmetry. He felt a sudden shudder of self pity that was almost pleasurable, it was such a complete expression of his mood. It was a physical shudder; he was alone, abandoned, lost, hopeless, cold. Cold especially—a deep interior cold nothing could change. Although it was the basis of his unhappiness, this glacial deadness, he would cling to it always, because it was also the core of his being, he had built the being around it.

But at the moment he felt bodily cold, too, and this was strange because he had just climbed the hill fast and was still panting a little. Seized by a sudden fear, akin to the terror of the child when it brushes against an unidentifiable object in the dark, he jumped up and ran along the crest of the hill until he came to the path that led below to the market place. Running assuaged his fear, but when he stopped and looked down at the ring of lights around the market he still felt the cold, like a piece of metal inside him. He ran on down the hill, deciding to go to the hotel and get the whiskey in his room, and since the kitchen was locked, take it back to the brothel where he could make himself a hot grog with some tea. As he went into the patio he had to step over the watchman lying across the threshold. The man raised himself slightly and called out: *"Echkoun? Qui?"*

"Numéro vingt!" he cried, hurrying through the foul smells.

No light came from under Kit's door. In his room he took up the bottle of whiskey and looked at his watch, which out of caution he had left behind on the night table. It was three-thirty. He decided that if he walked quickly he could get there and be back in his room by half-past four, unless they had let the fires go out.

The watchman was snoring when he went out into the street. There he forced himself to take strides so long that the muscles of his legs rebelled, but the exercise failed to mitigate the chill he felt everywhere within him. The town seemed completely asleep. No music was audible as he approached the entrance of the house. The courtyard was totally dark and so were most of the rooms. A few of them, however, were still open and had lights. Mohammed was there, stretched out, talking with his friends.

"Well, did you find her?" he said as Port entered the room. "What are you carrying there?" Port held up the bottle, smiling faintly.

Mohammed frowned. "You don't want that, my friend. That's very bad. It turns your head." He made spiral gestures with one hand and tried to wrest the bottle away from Port with the other. "Have a pipe with me," he urged. "It's better. Sit down."

"I'd like more tea," said Port.

"It's too late," said Mohammed with great assurance.

"Why?" Port asked stupidly. "I must."

"Too late. No fire," Mohammed announced, with a certain satisfaction. "After one pipe you forget you wanted tea. In any case you have already drunk tea."

Port ran out into the courtyard and clapped his hands loudly. Nothing happened. Thrusting his head into one of the cubicles where he saw a woman seated, he asked in French for tea. She stared at him. He asked in his halting Arabic. She answered that it was too late. He said, "A hundred francs." The men murmured among themselves; a hundred francs seemed an interesting and reasonable offer, but the woman, a plump, middle-aged matron, said: "No." Port doubled his offer. The woman rose and motioned him to accompany her. He walked behind her, beneath a curtain hung across the back wall of the room, and through a series of tiny, dark cells, until finally they were out under the stars. She stopped and indicated that he was to sit on the ground and wait for her. A few paces from him she disappeared into a separate hut, where he heard her moving about. Nearer still to him in the dark an animal of some sort was sleeping; it breathed heavily and stirred from time to time. The ground was cold and he began to shiver. Through the breaks in the wall he saw a flicker of light. The woman had lighted a candle and was breaking bundles of twigs. Presently he heard them crackling in flames as she fanned the fire.

The first cock was crowing when she finally came out of the shack with the pot of coals. She led the way, sparks trailing behind her, into one of the dark rooms through which they had passed, and there she set it down and put the water to boil. There was no light but the red glow of the burning charcoal. He squatted before the fire holding his hands fanwise for the warmth. When the tea was ready to drink, she pushed him gently back until he found himself against a mattress. He sat on it; it was warmer than the floor. She handed him a glass. *"Meziane, skhoun b'zef,"* she croaked, peering at him in the fading light. He drank half a glassful and filled it to the top with whiskey. After repeating the process, he felt better. He relaxed a bit and had another. Then for fear he should begin to sweat, he said: *"Baraka,"* and they went back to the room where the men lay smoking.

Mohammed laughed when he saw them. "What have you been doing?" he said accusingly. He rolled his eyes toward the woman. Port felt a little sleepy now and thought only of getting back to the hotel and into bed. He shook his head. "Yes, yes," insisted Mohammed, determined to have his joke. "I know! The young Englishman who went to Messad the other day, he was like you. Pretending always to be innocent. He pretended the woman was his mother, that he never would go near her, but I caught them together."

Port did not answer immediately. Then he jumped, and cried: "What!"

"Of course! I opened the door of room eleven, and there they are in the bed. Naturally. You believed him when he said she was his mother?" he added, noticing Port's incredulous expression. "You should have seen what I saw when I opened the door. Then you would know what a liar he was! Just because the lady is old, that does not stop her. No, no, no! Nor the man. So I say, what have you been doing with *her.* No?" He went on laughing.

Port smiled and paid the woman, saying to Mohammed: "Look. You see, I'm paying only two hundred francs I promised for the tea. You see?"

Mohammed laughed louder. "Two hundred francs for tea! Too much for such old tea! I hope you had two glasses, my friend."

"Good night," said Port to the room in general, and he went out into the street.

BOOK TWO

THE EARTH'S SHARP EDGE

" 'Good-bye,' says the dying man to
the mirror they hold in front of him.
'We won't be seeing each other any
more.' "

—VALÉRY

As commander of the military post of Bou Noura, Lieutenant d'Armagnac found the life there full if somewhat unvaried. At first there had been the novelty of his house; his books and furniture had been sent down from Bordeaux by his family, and he had experienced the pleasure of seeing them in new and unlikely surroundings. Then there had been the natives. The lieutenant was intelligent enough to insist on allowing himself the luxury of not being snobbish about the indigenous population. His overt attitude toward the people of Bou Noura was that they were an accessible part of a great, mysterious tribe from whom the French could learn a great deal if they only would take the trouble. And since he was an educated man, the other soldiers at the post, who would have enjoyed seeing all the natives put behind barbed wire and left there to rot in the sun ("... *comme on a fait en Tripolitaine*"), did not hold his insanely benevolent attitude against him, contenting themselves by saying to one another that some day he would come to his senses and realize what worthless scum they really were. The lieutenant's true enthusiasm for the natives had lasted three years. About the time he had grown tired of his half-dozen or so Ouled Naïl mistresses, the period of his great devotion to the Arabs came to an end. It was not that he became any less objective in meting out justice to them; it was rather that he suddenly ceased thinking about them and began taking them for granted.

That same year he had gone back to Bordeaux for a six weeks' stay. There he had renewed his acquaintance with a young lady whom he had known since adolescence; but she had acquired a sudden and special interest for him by declaring, as he was about to leave for North Africa to resume his duties, that she could imagine nothing more wonderful and desirable than the idea of spending the rest of her life in the Sahara, and that she considered him the luckiest of men to be on his way back there. A correspondence had ensued, and letters had gone back and forth between Bordeaux and Bou Noura. Less than a year later he had gone to Algiers and met her as she got off the boat. The honeymoon had been spent in a little bougainvillaea-covered villa up at Mustapha-Supérieur (it had rained every day), after which they had returned together to the sunlit rigors of Bou Noura.

It was impossible for the lieutenant to know how nearly her preconceived notion of the place had coincided with what she had discovered to be its reality; he did not know whether she was going to like it or not. At the moment she was already back in France waiting for their first child to be born. Soon she would return and they would be better able to tell.

At present he was bored. After Mme. d'Armagnac had left, the lieutenant had attempted to pick up his old life where he had broken it off, but he found the girls of the Bou Noura quartier exasperatingly uncomplicated after the more evolved relationship to which he latterly had become accustomed. Thus he had occupied himself with building an extra room onto his house to surprise his wife on her return. It was to be an Arab salon. Already he was having the coffee table and couches built, and he had bought a beautiful, large cream-colored wool rug for the wall, and two sheepskins for the floor. It was during the fortnight when he was arranging this room that the trouble began.

The trouble, while it was nothing really serious, had managed to interfere with his work, a fact which could not be overlooked. Moreover, being an active man, he was always bored when he was confined to his bed, and he had been there for several days. Actually it had been a question of bad luck; if only someone else had happened on it—a native, for instance, or even one of his inferiors—he would not have been obliged to give the thing so much attention. But he had had the misfortune to discover it himself one morning while making his semi-weekly tour of inspection of the villages. Thereby it became official and important. It had been just outside the walls of Igherm, which he always visited directly after Tolfa, passing on foot through the cemetery and then climbing the hill; from the big gate of Igherm he could see the valley below where a soldier from the Poste waited in a truck to pick him up and carry him on to Beni Isguen, which was too far to walk. As he had been about to go through the gate into the village, his attention had been drawn by something which ought to have looked perfectly normal. A dog was running along with something in its mouth, something large and suspiciously pink, part of which dragged along the ground. But he had stared at the object.

Then he had made a short walk along the outside of

the wall and had met two other dogs coming toward him with similar prizes. Finally he had come upon what he was looking for: it was only an infant, and in all likelihood it had been killed that morning. Wrapped in the pages of some old numbers of *L'Echo d'Alger*, it had been tossed into a shallow ditch. After questioning several people who had been outside the gate that morning he was able to ascertain that a certain Yamina ben Rhaïssa had been seen shortly after sunrise entering the gate, and that this was not a regular occurrence. He had no difficulty in locating Yamina; she lived nearby with her mother. At first she had denied hysterically all knowledge of the crime, but when he had taken her alone out of the house to the edge of the village and had talked with her in what he considered a "reasonable" fashion for five minutes she had calmly told him the entire story. Not the least surprising part of her tale was the fact that she had been able to conceal her pregnancy from her mother, or so she said. The lieutenant had been inclined to disbelieve this until he reflected upon the number of undergarments worn by the women of the region; then he decided that she was telling the truth. She had got the older woman out of the house by means of a stratagem, had given birth to the infant, strangled it and deposited it outside the gate wrapped in newspaper. By the time her mother had returned, she was already washing the floor.

Yamina's principal interest at this point seemed to be in finding out from the lieutenant the names of the persons who had made it possible for him to find her. She was intrigued by his swift detection of her act, and she told him so. This primitive insouciance rather amused him, and for a quarter of an hour or so he actually allowed himself to consider how he could best arrange to spend the night with her. But by the time he had made her walk with him down the hill to the road where the truck was waiting, already he viewed his fantasies of a few minutes back with astonishment. He canceled the visit to Beni Isguen and took the girl straight to his headquarters. Then he remembered the infant. Seeing that Yamina was safely locked up, he hurried with a soldier to the spot and collected for evidence what small parts of the body were still left. It was on the basis of these few bits of flesh that Yamina was installed in the local prison, pending removal to Algiers for trial. But the trial never took place. During the third night of her imprisonment a gray scorpion, on its way along the earthen floor of her cell, discovered an unexpected and welcome warmth in one corner, and took refuge there. When Yamina stirred in her sleep, the inevitable occurred. The sting entered the nape of the neck; she never recovered consciousness. The news of her death quickly spread around the town, with the detail of the scorpion missing from the telling of it, so that the final and, as it were, official native version was that the girl had been assaulted by the entire garrison, including the lieutenant, and thereafter conveniently murdered. Naturally, it was not everyone who lent complete credence to the tale, but there was the indisputable fact that she had died while in French custody. Whatever the natives believed, the prestige of the lieutenant went into a definite decline.

The lieutenant's sudden unpopularity had immediate results: the workmen failed to appear at his house in order to continue the construction of the new salon. To be sure, the mason did arrive, only to sit in the garden all morning with Ahmed the houseboy, trying to persuade him (and in the end successfully) not to remain another day in the employ of such a monster. And the lieutenant had the quite correct impression that they were going out of their way to avoid meeting him in the street. The women especially seemed to fear his presence. When the news got around that he was in the neighborhood the streets cleared of themselves; all he heard as he walked along was the bolting of doors. If men passed it was with their eyes averted. These things constituted a blow to his prestige as an administrator, but they affected him rather less than the discovery, made the very day he took to his bed with a singular combination of cramps, dizziness and nausea, that his cook, who for some reason had stayed on with him, was a first cousin of the late Yamina.

The arrival of a letter from his commanding officer in Algiers made him no happier. There was no question, it said, of the justice of his procedure: the bits of evidence were in a jar of formaldehyde at the Tribunal of Bou Noura, and the girl had confessed. But it did criticize the lieutenant's negligence, and, which was more painful to him, it raised the question of his fitness to deal with the "native psychology."

He lay in his bed and looked at the ceiling; he felt weak and unhappy. It was nearly time for Jacqueline to come and prepare him his noonday consommé. (At the first cramp he had immediately got rid of his cook; he knew that much about dealing with the native psychology.) Jacqueline had been born in Bou Noura of an Arab father—at least, so it was said, and from her features and complexion it was easy to believe—and a French mother who had died shortly after her birth. What the Frenchwoman had been doing in Bou Noura all alone no one ever knew. But it was all in the distant past; Jacqueline had been taken in by the Pères Blancs and raised in the Mission. She knew all the songs the Fathers labored so diligently to teach the children—indeed, she was the only one who did know them. Besides learning to sing and pray she had also learned how to cook, which last talent proved to be a true blessing for the Mission since the unfortunate Fathers had been living on the local cuisine for many years and all suffered with their livers. When Father Lebrun had learned of the lieutenant's dilemma he straightway had volunteered to send Jacqueline to replace his cook and prepare him two simple meals a day. The Father had come himself the first day, and after looking at the lieutenant had decided that there would be no danger in letting her visit him, at least for a few days. He relied upon Jacqueline to warn him of her patient's progress, because once he was on the road to recovery, the lieutenant's behavior could no longer be counted on. He had said, looking down at him as he lay in his tousled bed: "I leave her in your hands, and you in God's." The lieutenant had understood what he meant, and he had tried to smile, but he felt too sick. Still, now as he thought of it he smiled, since he considered Jacqueline a wretched, skinny thing at whom no one would look twice.

She was late that noon, and when she arrived she was in a breathless state because Corporal Dupeyrier had stopped her near the Zaouia and given her a very important message for him. It was a matter of a foreigner, an American, who had lost his passport.

"An American?" echoed the lieutenant. "In Bou Noura?" Yes, said Jacqueline. He was here with his wife, they were at Abdelkader's pension (which was the only place they could have been, since it was the only hostelry of any sort in the region), and they had already been in Bou Noura several days. She had even seen the gentleman: a young man.

"Well," said the lieutenant, "I'm hungry. How about a little rice today? Have you time to prepare it?"

"Ah, yes, monsieur. But he told me to tell you that it is important you see the American today."

"What are you talking about? Why should I see him? I can't find his passport for him. When you go back to the Mission, pass by the Poste and tell Corporal Dupeyrier to tell the American he must go to Algiers, to his consul. If he doesn't already know it," he added.

"*Ah, ce n'est pas pour ça!* It's because he accused Monsieur Abdelkader of stealing the passport."

"What?" roared the lieutenant, sitting up.

"Yes. He went yesterday to file a complaint. And Monsieur Abdelkader says that you will oblige him to retract it. That's why you must see him today." Jacqueline, obviously delighted with the degree of his reaction, went into the kitchen and began to rattle the utensils loudly. She was carried away by the idea of her importance.

The lieutenant slumped back into this bed and fell to worrying. It was imperative that the American be induced to withdraw his accusation, not only because Abdelkader was an old friend of his, and was quite incapable of stealing anything whatever, but particularly because he was one of the best known and highly esteemed men of Bou Noura. As proprietor of the inn he maintained close friendships with the chauffeurs of all the buses and trucks that passed through the territory; in the Sahara these are important people. Assuredly there was not one of them who at one time or another had not asked for, and received, credit from Abdelkader on his meals and lodgings; most of them had even borrowed money from him. For an Arab he was amazingly trusting and easy-going about money, both with Europeans and with his compatriots, and everyone liked him for it. Not only was it unthinkable that he should have stolen the passport—it was just as unthinkable that he should be formally accused of such a thing. For that reason the corporal was right. The complaint must be retracted immediately. "Another stroke of bad luck," he thought. "Why must it be an American?" With a Frenchman he would have known how to go about persuading him to do it without any unpleasantness. But with an American! Already he could see him: a gorilla-like brute with a fierce frown on his face, a cigar in the corner of his mouth, and probably an automatic in his hip pocket. Doubtless no complete sentences would pass between them because neither one would be able to understand enough of the other's language. He began trying to recall his English: "Sir, I must to you, to pray that you will—" "My dear sir, please I would make to you remark—" Then he remembered having heard that Americans did not speak English in any case, that they had a patois which only they could understand among themselves. The most unpleasant part of the situation to him was the fact that he would be in bed, while the American would be free to roam about the room, would enjoy all the advantages, physical and moral.

He groaned a little as he sat up to eat the soup Jacqueline had brought him. Outside the wind was blowing and the dogs of the nomad encampment up the road were barking; if the sun had not been shining so brightly that the moving palm branches by the window gleamed like glass, for a moment he would have said it was the middle of the night—the sounds of the wind and the dogs would have been exactly the same. He ate his lunch; when Jacqueline was ready to leave he said to her: "You will go to the Poste and tell Corporal Dupeyrier to bring the American here at three o'clock. He himself is to bring him, remember."

"*Oui, oui,*" she said, still in a state of acute pleasure. If she had missed out on the infanticide, at least she was in on the new scandal at the start.

19

Precisely at three o'clock Corporal Du-
peyrier ushered the American into the lieutenant's salon.
The house was absolutely silent. *"Un moment,"* said the
corporal, going to the bedroom door. He knocked, opened
it, the lieutenant made a sign with his hand, and the corporal relayed the command to the American, who walked
into the bedroom. The lieutenant saw what he considered
to be a somewhat haggard adolescent, and he immediately
decided that the young man was slightly peculiar, since in
spite of the heat he was wearing a heavy turtle-neck sweater
and a woolen jacket.

The American advanced to the bedside and, offering
his hand, spoke in perfect French. The lieutenant's initial
surprise at his appearance turned to delight. He had the
corporal draw up a chair for his guest and asked him to be
seated. Then he suggested that the corporal go on back to
the Poste; he had decided he could handle the American by
himself. When they were alone he offered him a cigarette
and said: "It seems you have lost your passport."

"That's exact," replied Port.

"And you believe it was stolen—not lost?"

"I *know* it was stolen. It was in a valise I always keep locked."

"Then how could it have been stolen from the valise?" said the lieutenant, laughing with an air of triumph. "Always is not quite the word."

"It could have been," pursued Port patiently, "because I left the valise open yesterday for a minute when I went out of my room to the bathroom. It was a foolish thing to do, but I did it. And when I returned to my door the proprietor was standing outside it. He claimed he had been knocking because lunch was ready. Yet he had never come himself before; it was always one of the boys. The reason I am sure it was the proprietor is that yesterday is the only time I have ever left the valise open when I have been out of the room, even for an instant. It seems clear to me."

"Pardon. Not to me. Not at all. Shall we make a detective story out of it? When is the last time you saw your passport?"

Port thought for a moment. "When I arrived in Aïn Krorfa," he said finally.

"Aha!" cried the lieutenant. "In Aïn Krorfa! And yet you accuse Monsieur Abdelkader, without hesitating. How do you explain that?"

"Yes, I accuse him," Port said stubbornly, nettled by the lieutenant's voice. "I accuse him because logic indicates him as the only possible thief. He's absolutely the only native who had access to the passport, the only one for whom it would have been physically possible."

Lieutenant d'Armagnac raised himself a little higher in bed. "And why precisely do you demand it be a native?"

Port smiled faintly. "Isn't it reasonable to suppose it was a native? Apart from the fact that no one else had the

161

opportunity to take it, isn't it the sort of thing that would naturally turn out to have been done by a native—charming as they may be?"

"No, monsieur. To me it seems just the kind of thing that would *not* have been done by a native."

Port was taken aback. "Ah, really?" he said. "Why? Why do you say that?"

The lieutenant said: "I have been with the Arabs a good many years. Of course they steal. And Frenchmen steal. And in America you have gangsters, I believe?" He smiled archly. Port was impassive: "That was a long time ago, the era of gangsters," he said. But the lieutenant was not discouraged. "Yes, everywhere people steal. And here as well. However, the native here," he spoke more slowly, emphasizing his words, "takes only money or an object he wants for himself. He would never take anything so complicated as a passport."

Port said: "I'm not looking for motives. God knows *why* he took it." His host cut him short. "But I *am* looking for motives!" he cried. "And I see no reason for believing that any native has gone to the trouble of stealing your passport. Certainly not in Bou Noura. And I doubt very much in Aïn Krorfa. One thing I can assure you, Monsieur Abdelkader did not take it. You can believe that."

"Oh?" said Port, unconvinced.

"Never. I have known him for several years—"

"But you have no more proof that he didn't than I have that he did!" Port exclaimed, annoyed. He turned up his coat collar and huddled in his chair.

"You aren't cold, I hope?" said the lieutenant in surprise.

"I've been cold for days," answered Port, rubbing his hands together.

The lieutenant looked at him closely for an instant. Then he went on: "Will you do me a favor if I do you one in return?"

"I suppose so. What?"

"I should be greatly obliged if you would withdraw your complaint against Monsieur Abdelkader at once—today. And I will try one thing to get you your passport back. *On ne sait jamais.* It may be successful. If your passport has been stolen, as you say, the only place for it logically to be now is Messad. I shall telegraph Messad to have a thorough search made of the Foreign Legion barracks."

Port was sitting quite still, looking straight ahead of him. "Messad," he said.

"You were not there, too, were you?"

"No, no!" There was a silence.

"And so, are you going to do me this favor? I shall have an answer for you as soon as the search has been carried out."

"Yes," said Port. "I'll go this afternoon. Tell me: there is a market for such things at Messad, then?"

"But of course. Passports bring high prices in Legion posts. Especially an American passport! *Oh, là, là!*" The lieutenant's spirits were soaring: he had attained his object; this could offset, at least partially, the damaging effects of the Yamina case to his prestige. "*Tenez,*" he said, pointing to a cupboard in the corner, "you are cold. Will you hand me that bottle of cognac over there? We shall each have a swallow." It was not at all what Port wanted, but he felt he scarcely could refuse the hospitable gesture.

Besides, what did he want? He was not sure, but he thought it was merely to sit quietly in a warm, interior place for a long time. The sun made him feel colder, made his head burn, seem enormous and top-heavy. If he had not had his normal appetite he would have suspected that perhaps he was not well. He sipped the cognac, wondering if it would make him warmer, or if he would regret having drunk it, for the heartburn it sometimes produced in him. The lieutenant appeared to have divined his thoughts, for he said presently: "It's fine old cognac. It won't hurt you."

"It's excellent," he replied, choosing to ignore the latter part of the remark.

The lieutenant's impression that here was a young man unhealthily preoccupied with himself was confirmed by Port's next words. "It's strange," he said with a deprecatory smile, "how, ever since I discovered that my passport was gone, I've felt only half alive. But it's a very depressing thing in a place like this to have no proof of who you are, you know."

The lieutenant stretched forth the bottle, which Port declined. "Perhaps after my little investigation in Messad you will recover your identity," he laughed. If the American wished to extend him such confidences, he was quite willing to be his confessor for the moment.

"You are here with your wife?" asked the lieutenant. Port assented absently. "That's it," said the lieutenant to himself. "He's having trouble with his wife. Poor devil!" It occurred to him that they might go together to the quartier. He enjoyed showing it off to strangers. But as he was about to say: "Fortunately my wife is in France—" he remembered that Port was not French; it would not be advisable.

While he was considering this, Port rose and politely took his leave—a little abruptly, it is true, but he could hardly be expected to remain by the bedside the whole afternoon. Besides, he had promised to stop by and withdraw the complaint against Abdelkader.

As he walked along the hot road toward the walls of Bou Noura he kept his head down, seeing nothing but the dust and the thousands of small sharp stones. He did not look up because he knew how senseless the landscape would appear. It takes energy to invest life with meaning, and at present this energy was lacking. He knew how things could stand bare, their essence having retreated on all sides to beyond the horizon, as if impelled by a sinister centrifugal force. He did not want to face the intense sky, too blue to be real, above his head, the ribbed pink canyon walls that lay on all sides in the distance, the pyramidal town itself on its rocks, or the dark spots of oasis below. They were there, and they should have pleased his eye, but he did not have the strength to relate them, either to each other or to himself; he could not bring them into any focus beyond the visual. So he would not look at them.

On arriving back at the pension, he stopped by the little room that served as office, and found Abdelkader seated in a dark corner on the divan, playing dominoes with a heavily turbaned individual. "Good day, monsieur," said Port. "I have been to the authorities and withdrawn the accusation."

"Ah, my lieutenant has arranged it," murmured Abdelkader.

"Yes," said Port, although he was vexed to see that no credit was to be given him for acceding to Lieutenant d'Armagnac's wishes.

"Bon, merci." Abdelkader did not look up again, and Port went on upstairs to Kit's room.

There he found that she had ordered all her luggage brought up and was unpacking it. The room looked like a bazaar: there were rows of shoes on the bed, evening gowns had been spread out over the footboard as if for a window display, and bottles of cosmetics and perfumes lined the night table.

"What in God's name are you doing?" he cried.

"Looking at my things," she said innocently. "I haven't seen them in a long time. Ever since the boat I've been living in one bag. I'm so sick of it. And when I looked out that window after lunch," she became more animated as she pointed to the window that gave onto the empty desert, "I felt I'd simply die if I didn't see something civilized soon. Not only that. I'm having a Scotch sent up and I'm opening my last pack of Players."

"You *must* be in a bad way," he said.

"Not at all," she retorted, but a bit too energetically. "It'd be abnormal if I were able to adapt myself too quickly to all this. After all, I'm still an American, you know. And I'm not even trying to be anything else."

"Scotch!" Port said, thinking aloud. "There's no ice this side of Boussif. And no soda either, I'll bet."

"I want it neat." She slipped into a backless gown of pale blue satin and went to make up in the mirror that hung on the back of the door. He decided that she should be humored; in any case it amused him to watch her building her pathetic little fortress of Western culture in the middle of the wilderness. He sat down on the floor in the center of the room and watched her with pleasure as she flitted about, choosing her slippers and trying on bracelets. When the servant knocked, Port himself went to the door and in the hall took the tray from his hands, bottle and all.

"Why didn't you let him in?" demanded Kit, when he had closed the door behind him.

"Because I didn't want him running downstairs with the news," he said, setting the tray on the floor and sitting down again beside it.

"What news?"

He was vague. "Oh, that you have fancy clothes and jewelry in your bags. It's the sort of thing that would go on ahead of us wherever we went, down here. Besides," he smiled at her, "I'd rather they didn't get a look at how pretty you can be."

"Well, really, Port! Make up your mind. Is it me you're trying to protect? Or do you think they'll add ten francs on to the bill downstairs?"

"Come here and have your lousy French whiskey. I want to tell you something."

"I will not. You'll bring it to me like a gentleman." She made room among the objects on the bed and sat down.

"Fine." He poured her a good-sized drink and took it to her.

"You're not having any?" she said.

"No. I had some cognac at the lieutenant's house, and it didn't do any good. I'm as chilly as ever. But I have news, and that's what I wanted to tell you. There's not much doubt that Eric Lyle stole my passport." He told her about the passport market for legionnaires at Messad. In the bus coming from Aïn Krorfa he had already informed her of Mohammed's discovery. She, showing no surprise, had repeated her story of having seen their passports, so that there was no doubt of their being mother and son. Nor was she surprised now. "I suppose he felt that since I'd seen theirs, he had a right to see yours," she said. "But how'd he get it? When'd he get it?"

"I know just when. The night he came to my room in Aïn Krorfa and wanted to give me back the francs I'd let him have. I left my bag open and him in the room while I went in to see Tunner, because I had my wallet with me and it certainly never occurred to me the louse was after my passport. But beyond a doubt that's what happened to it. The more I think about it the surer I am. Whether they find out anything at Messad or not, I'm convinced it was

Lyle. I think he intended to steal it the first time he ever saw me. After all, why not? Easy money, and his mother never gives him any."

"I think she does," said Kit, "on certain conditions. And I think he hates all that, and is only looking for a chance to escape, and will hook up with anybody, do anything, rather than that. And I think she's quite aware of it and is terrified he'll go, and will do everything she can to prevent his getting intimate with anybody. Remember what she told you about his being 'infected.' "

Port was silent. "My God! What a mess I got Tunner into!" he said after a moment.

Kit laughed. "What do you mean? He'll weather it. It'll be good for him. Besides, I can't see him being very friendly with either one of them."

"No." He poured himself a drink. "I shouldn't do this," he said. "It'll mess me up inside, with the cognac. But I can't let you sit there and go away by yourself, float off on a few drinks."

"You know I'm delighted to have company, but won't it make you sick?"

"I already feel sick," he exclaimed. "I can't go on forever taking precautions just because I'm cold all the time. Anyway, I think as soon as we get to El Ga'a I'll be better. It's a lot warmer there, you know."

"Again? We only just got *here.*"

"But you can't deny it's chilly here at night."

"I certainly do deny it. But that's all right. If we've got to go to El Ga'a, then let's go, by all means, but let's go soon, and stay awhile."

"It's one of the great Saharan cities," he said, as if he were holding it up for her to see.

"You don't have to sell it to me," she said. "And even

if you did, that wouldn't be the way. You know that means very little to me. El Ga'a, Timbuctoo, it's all the same to me, more or less; all equally interesting, but not anything I'm going to go mad about. But if you'll be happier there— I mean healthier—we should go, by all means." She made a nervous gesture with her hand, in the hope of driving away an insistent fly.

"Oh. You think my complaint is mental. You said happier."

"I don't think anything because I don't know. But it seems awfully peculiar to me that anybody should be constantly cold in September in the Sahara desert."

"Well, it'll have to seem peculiar," he said with annoyance. Then he suddenly exclaimed: "These flies have claws! They're enough to drive you completely off your balance. What do they want, to crawl down your throat?" He groaned and rose to his feet; she looked at him expectantly. "I'll fix it so we'll be safe from them. Get up." He burrowed into a valise and presently pulled out a folded bundle of netting. At his suggestion Kit cleared the bed of her clothing. Over the headboard and footboard he spread the net, remarking that there was no good reason why a mosquito net could not become a fly net. When it was well fastened they slid underneath with the bottle and lay there quietly as the afternoon wore on. By twilight they were pleasantly drunk, disinclined to move out from under their tent. Perhaps it was the sudden appearance of the stars in the square of the sky framed by the window, which helped to determine the course of their conversation. Each moment, as the color deepened, more stars came to fill the spaces which up until then had been empty. Kit smoothed her gown at the hips and said: "When I was young—"

"How young?"

"Before I was twenty, I mean, I used to think that life was a thing that kept gaining impetus. It would get richer and deeper each year. You kept learning more, getting wiser, having more insight, going further into the truth—" She hesitated.

Port laughed abruptly. "And now you know it's not like that. Right? It's more like smoking a cigarette. The first few puffs it tastes wonderful, and you don't even think of its ever being used up. Then you begin taking it for granted. Suddenly you realize it's nearly burned down to the end. And then's when you're conscious of the bitter taste."

"But I'm always conscious of the unpleasant taste *and* of the end approaching," she said.

"Then you should give up smoking."

"How mean you are!" she cried.

"I'm not mean!" he objected, almost upsetting his glass as he raised himself on his elbow to drink. "It seems logical, doesn't it? Or I suppose living's a habit like smoking. You keep saying you're going to give it up, but you go right on."

"*You* don't even threaten to stop, as far as I can see," she said accusingly.

"Why should I? I want to go on."

"But you complain so all the time."

"Oh, not about life; only about human beings."

"The two can't be considered separately."

"They certainly can. All it takes is a little effort. Effort, effort! Why won't anybody make any? I can imagine an absolutely different world. Just a few misplaced accents."

"I've heard it all for years," said Kit. She sat up in the near-dark, cocked her head and said: "Listen!"

Somewhere outside, not far away, perhaps in the market place, an orchestra of drums was playing, little by little gathering up the loose strands of rhythmic force into one mighty compact design which already was revolving, a still imperfect wheel of heavy sounds, lumbering ahead toward the night. Port was silent awhile, and said in a whisper: "That, for instance."

"I don't know," said Kit. She was impatient. "I know I don't feel any part of those drums out there, however much I may admire the sounds they make. And I don't see any reason why I should *want* to feel a part of them." She thought that such a straightforward declaration would put a quick end to the discussion, but Port was stubborn that evening.

"I know, you never like to talk seriously," he said, "but it won't hurt you for once."

She smiled scornfully, since she considered his vague generalities the most frivolous kind of chatter—a mere vehicle for his emotions. According to her, at such times there was no question of his meaning or not meaning what he said, because he did not know really what he was saying. So she was banteringly: "What's the unit of exchange in this different world of yours?"

He did not hesitate. "The tear."

"It isn't fair," she objected. "Some people have to work very hard for a tear. Others can have them just for the thinking."

"What system of exchange *is* fair?" he cried, and his voice sounded as if he were really drunk. "And whoever invented the concept of fairness, anyway? Isn't everything easier if you simply get rid of the idea of justice altogether? *You* think the quantity of pleasure, the degree of suffering is constant among all men? It somehow all comes out in the end? You think that? If it comes out even it's only because the final sum is zero."

"I suppose that's a comfort to you," she said, feeling that if the conversation went on she would get really angry.

"None at all. Are you crazy? I have no interest in

knowing the final figure. But I am interested in all the complicated processes that make it possible to get that result inevitably, no matter what the original quantity was."

"The end of the bottle," she murmured. "Perhaps a perfect zero is something to reach."

"Is it all gone? Hell. But we don't reach it. It reaches us. It's not the same thing."

"He's really drunker than I am," she thought. "No, it isn't," she agreed.

And as he was saying: "You're damned right," and flopping violently over to lie on his stomach, she went on thinking of what a waste of energy all this talk was, and wondering how she could stop him from working himself up into an emotional state.

"Ah, I'm disgusted and miserable!" he cried in a sudden burst of fury. "I should never take a drop because it always knocks me out. But it's not weakness the way it is with you. Not at all. It takes more will power for me to make myself take a drink than it does for you not to. I hate the results and I always remember what they'll be."

"Then why do you do it? Nobody asks you to."

"I told you," he said. "I wanted to be with you. And besides, I always imagine that somehow I'll be able to penetrate to the interior of somewhere. Usually I get just about to the suburbs and get lost. I don't think there *is* any interior to get to any more. I think all you drinkers are victims of a huge mass hallucination."

"I refuse to discuss it," said Kit haughtily, climbing down from the bed and struggling her way through the folds of netting that hung to the floor.

He rolled over and sat up.

"I know why I'm disgusted," he called after her. "It's something I ate. Ten years ago."

"I don't know what you're talking about. Lie down again and sleep," she said, and went out of the room.

"I do," he muttered. He crawled out of the bed and went to stand in the window. The dry desert air was taking on its evening chill, and the drums still sounded. The canyon walls were black now, the scattered clumps of palms had become invisible. There were no lights; the room faced away from the town. And this was what he meant. He gripped the windowsill and leaned out, thinking: "She doesn't know what I'm talking about. It's something I ate ten years ago. Twenty years ago." The landscape was there, and more than ever he felt he could not reach it. The rocks and the sky were everywhere, ready to absolve him, but as always he carried the obstacle within him. He would have said that as he looked at them, the rocks and the sky ceased being themselves, that in the act of passing into his consciousness, they became impure. It was slight consolation to be able to say to himself: "I am stronger than they." As he turned back into the room, something bright drew his eye to the mirror on the open door of the wardrobe. It was the new moon shining in through the other window. He sat down on the bed and began to laugh.

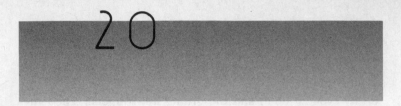

20

Port spent the next two days trying as-
siduously to gather information about El Ga'a. It was astonishing how little the people of Bou Noura knew about the
place. Everyone seemed in agreement that it was a large
city—always it was spoken of with a certain respect—that it
was far away, that the climate was warmer, and the prices
high. Beyond this, no one appeared able to give any description of it, not even the men who had been there, such as
the bus driver he spoke with, and the cook in the kitchen.
One person who could have given him a somewhat fuller
report on the town was Abdelkader, but intercourse between him and Port had been reduced to mere grunts of
recognition. When he considered it, he realized now that it
rather suited his fancy to be going off with no proof of his
identity to a hidden desert town about which no one could
tell him anything. So that he was not so much moved as he
might have been when on meeting Corporal Dupeyrier in
the street and mentioning El Ga'a to him, the corporal said:

"But Lieutenant d'Armagnac has spent many months there. He can tell you everything you want to know." Only then did he understand that he really wanted to know nothing about El Ga'a beyond the fact that it was isolated and unfrequented, that it was precisely those things he had been trying to ascertain about it. He determined not to mention the town to the lieutenant, for fear of losing his preconceived idea of it.

The same afternoon Ahmed, who had reinstated himself in the lieutenant's service, appeared at the pension and asked for Port. Kit, in bed reading, told the servant to send the boy to the hammam, where Port had gone to bask in the steam room in the hope of thawing out his chill once and for all. He was lying almost asleep in the dark, on a hot, slippery slab of rock, when an attendant came and roused him. With a wet towel around him he went to the entrance door. Ahmed stood there scowling; he was a light Arab boy from the ereg, and his face had the telltale, fiery gashes halfway down each cheek which debauchery sometimes makes in the soft skin of those too young to have pouches and wrinkles.

"The lieutenant wants you right away," said Ahmed.

"Tell him in an hour," Port said, blinking at the light of day.

"Right away," repeated Ahmed stolidly. "I wait here."

"Oh, he gives orders!" He went back inside and had a pail of cold water thrown over him—he would have liked more of it, but water was expensive here, and each pailful was a supplementary charge—and a quick massage before he dressed. It seemed to him that he felt a little better as he stepped out into the street. Ahmed was leaning against the wall talking with a friend, but he sprang to attention at

Port's appearance, and kept a few paces behind him all the way to the lieutenant's house.

Dressed in an ugly bathrobe of wine-colored artificial silk, the lieutenant sat in his salon smoking.

"You will pardon me if I remain seated," he said. "I am much better, but I feel best when I move least. Sit down. Will you have sherry, cognac or coffee?"

Port murmured that coffee would please him most. Ahmed was sent to prepare it.

"I don't mean to detain you, monsieur. But I have news for you. Your passport has been found. Thanks to one of your compatriots, who had also discovered his passport missing, a search had already been instigated before I got in contact with Messad. Both documents had been sold to legionnaires. But fortunately both have been recovered." He fumbled in his pocket and brought out a slip of paper. "This American, whose name is Tunner, says he knows you and is coming here to Bou Noura. He offers to bring your passport with him, but I must have your consent before notifying the authorities there to give it to him. Do you give your consent? Do you know this Monsieur Tunner?"

"Yes, yes," said Port absently. The idea horrified him; faced with Tunner's imminent arrival, he was appalled to realize that he had never expected really to see him again. "When is he coming?"

"I believe immediately. You are not in a hurry to leave Bou Noura?"

"No," said Port, his mind darting back and forth like a cornered animal, trying to remember what day the bus left for the south, what day it was then, how long it would take for Tunner to get from Messad. "No, no. I am not pressed for time." The words sounded ridiculous as he said them. Ahmed came in silently with a tray bearing two small tin canisters with steam rising from them. The lieutenant poured a glass of coffee from each and handed one to Port, who took a sip and sat back in his chair.

"But I do hope to get eventually to El Ga'a," he went on, in spite of himself.

"Ah, El Ga'a. You will find it very impressive, very picturesque, and very hot. It was my first Saharan post. I know every alley. It's a vast city, perfectly flat, not too dirty, but rather dark because the streets are built through the houses, like tunnels. Quite safe. You and your wife can wander wherever you please. It's the last town of any size this side of the Soudan. And that's a great distance away, the Soudan. *Oh, là, là!*"

"I suppose there's a hotel in El Ga'a?"

"Hotel? A kind of hotel," laughed the lieutenant. "You will find rooms with beds in them, and it may be clean. It is not so dirty in the Sahara as people say. The sun is a great purifier. With even a minimum of hygiene the people could be healthy here. But of course there is not that minimum. Unfortunately for us, *d'ailleurs.*"

"No. Yes, unfortunately," said Port. He could not bring himself back to the room and the conversation. He had just realized that the bus left that very night, and there would not be another for a week. Tunner would be there by then. With that realization, his decision seemed to have come automatically. Certainly he was not conscious of having made it, but a moment later he relaxed and began to question the lieutenant on the details of his daily life and work in Bou Noura. The lieutenant looked pleased; one by one the inevitable anecdotes of the colonist came out, all having to do with the juxtaposition, sometimes tragic, but usually ludicrous, of the two incongruous and incompatible cultures. Finally Port rose. "It's too bad," he said with a note of sincerity in his voice, "that I shan't be staying here longer."

"But you will be here several days more. I count absolutely on seeing you and Madame before your departure. In another two or three days I shall be completely well. Ahmed will let you know when and call for you. So, I shall notify Messad to give your passport to Monsieur Tunner." He rose, extended his hand; Port went out.

He walked through the little garden planted with stunted palms, and out the gate into the dusty road. The sun had set, and the sky was rapidly cooling. He stood still a moment looking upward, almost expecting to hear the sky crack as the nocturnal chill pressed against it from outside. Behind him in the nomad encampment the dogs barked in chorus. He began to walk quickly, to be out of their hearing as soon as he could. The coffee had accelerated his pulse to an unusual degree, or else it was his nervousness at the thought of missing the bus to El Ga'a. Entering the town gate, he turned immediately to the left and went down the empty street to the offices of the Transports Généraux.

The office was stuffy, without light. In the dimness behind the counter on a pile of burlap sacks sat an Arab, half asleep. Immediately Port said: "What time does the bus leave for El Ga'a?"

"Eight o'clock, monsieur."

"Are there seats still?"

"Oh, no. Three days ago they were all sold."

"*Ah, mon dieu!*" cried Port; his entrails seemed to grow heavier. He gripped the counter.

"Are you sick?" said the Arab, looking at him, and his face showed a little interest.

"Sick," thought Port. And he said: "No, but my wife is very sick. She must get to El Ga'a by tomorrow." He watched the Arab's face closely, to see if he were capable of believing such an obvious lie. Apparently here it was as logical for an ailing person to go away from civilization and medical care as to go in the direction of it, for the Arab's expression slowly changed to one of understanding and sympathy. Still, he raised his hands in a gesture that denoted his inability to help.

But already Port had pulled out a thousand-franc note and spread it on the counter with determination.

"You will have to give us two seats tonight," he said firmly. "This is for you. You persuade someone to go next week." Out of courtesy he did not suggest that the persuasion be used on two natives, although he knew that would be the case. "How much is the passage to El Ga'a?" He drew out more money.

The Arab rose to his feet and stood scratching his turban deliberately. "Four hundred and fifty francs each," he answered, "but I don't know—"

Port laid another twelve hundred francs before him and said: "That's nine hundred. And twelve hundred and fifty for you, after you take out for the tickets." He saw that the man's decision had been made. "I shall bring the lady at eight o'clock."

"Half-past seven," said the Arab, "for the luggage."

Back at the pension, in his excitement, he rushed into Kit's room without knocking. She was dressing, and cried with indignation: "Really, have you lost your mind?"

"Not at all," he said. "Only I hope you can travel in that dress."

"What do you mean?"

"We have seats on the bus tonight at eight."

"Oh, no! Oh, my God! For where? El Ga'a?" He nodded and there was a silence. "Oh, well," she said finally.

"It's all the same to me. You know what you want. But it's six now. All these grips—"

"I'll help you." There was a febrile eagerness in his manner now that she could not help observing. She watched him pulling her clothes out of the wardrobe and sliding them off the hangers with staccato gestures; his behavior struck her as curious, but she said nothing. When he had done all he could in her room he went into his own, where he packed his valises in ten minutes and dragged them out into the corridor himself. Then he ran downstairs and she heard him talking excitedly to the boys. At quarter of seven they sat down to their dinner. In no time he had finished his soup.

"Don't eat so fast. You'll have indigestion," Kit warned him.

"We've got to be at the bus office at seven-thirty," he said, clapping his hands for the next course.

"We'll make it, or they'll wait for us."

"No, no. There'll be trouble about the seats."

While they were still eating their cornes de gazelle he demanded the hotel bill and paid it.

"Did you see Lieutenant d'Armagnac?" she asked, as he was waiting for his change.

"Oh, yes."

"But no passport?"

"Not yet," he said, adding: "Oh, I don't think they'll ever find it. How could you expect them to? It's probably been sent off up to Algiers or Tunis by now."

"I still think you should have wired the consul from here."

"I can send a letter from El Ga'a by the same bus we go down in, when it makes the return trip. It'll only be two or three days later."

"I don't understand you," said Kit.

"Why?" he asked innocently.

"I don't understand anything. Your sudden indifference. Even this morning you were in the most awful state about not having any passport. Anyone would have thought you couldn't live another day without it. And now another few days make no difference. You *will* admit there's no connection?"

"You *will* admit they don't make much difference?"

"I will not. They might easily. And that's not my point. Not at all," she said, "and you know it."

"The main point right now is that we catch the bus." He jumped up and ran out to where Abdelkader was still trying to make change for him. Kit followed a moment later. By the flare of the tiny carbide lamps that swung on long wires from the ceiling the boys were bringing down the bags. It was a procession down the staircase; there were six boys, all laden with luggage. A small army of village gamins had gathered outside the door in the dark, with the tacit hope of being allowed to carry something along to the bus terminal.

Abdelkader was saying: "I hope you will like El Ga'a."

"Yes, yes," Port answered, putting his change into various pockets. "I hope I did not upset you too much with my troubles."

Abdelkader looked away. "Ah, that," he said. "It is better not to speak of it." The apology was too offhand; he could not accept it.

The night wind had risen. Windows and shutters were banging upstairs. The lamps rocked back and forth, sputtering.

"Perhaps we shall see you on our return trip," insisted Port.

Abdelkader should have answered: *"Incha'allah."* He merely looked at Port, sadly but with understanding. For a moment it seemed that he was about to say something; then he turned his head away. "Perhaps," he said finally, and when he turned back his lips were fixed in a smile—a smile that Port felt was not directed at him, did not even show consciousness of him. They shook hands and he hurried over to Kit, standing in the doorway carefully making up under the moving light of the lamp, while the curious young faces outside were upturned, following each movement of her fingers as she applied the lipstick.

"Come on!" he cried. "There's no time for that."

"I'm all done," she said, swinging around so he should not jostle her as she completed her handiwork. She dropped her lipstick into her bag and snapped it shut.

They went out. The road to the bus station was dark; the new moon gave no light. Behind them a few of the village urchins still straggled hopefully, most of them having given up when they saw the entire staff of the pension's boys accompanying the travelers.

"Too bad it's windy," said Port. "That means dust."

Kit was indifferent to the dust. She did not answer. But she noticed the unusual inflection in his speaking: he was unaccountably exhilarated.

"I only hope there are no mountains to cross," she said to herself, wishing again, but more fervently now, that they had gone to Italy, or any small country with boundaries, where the villages had churches and one went to the station in a taxi or a carriage, and could travel by daylight. And where one was not inevitably on display every time one stirred out of the hotel.

"Oh, my God, I forgot!" Port cried. "You're a very sick woman." And he explained how he had got the seats.

"We're almost there. Let me put my arm around your waist. You walk as though you had a pain. Shuffle a little."

"This is ridiculous," she said crossly. "What'll our boys think?"

"They're too busy. You've turned your ankle. Come on. Drag a bit. Nothing simpler." He pulled her against him as they walked along.

"And what about the people whose seats we're usurping?"

"What's a week to them? Time doesn't exist for them."

The bus was there, surrounded by shouting men and boys. The two went into the office, Kit walking with a certain real difficulty caused by the force with which Port was pressing her toward him. "You're hurting me. Let up a little," she whispered. But he continued to constrict her waist tightly, and they arrived at the counter. The Arab who had sold him the tickets said: "You have numbers twenty-two and twenty-three. Get in and take your seats quickly. The others don't want to give them up."

The seats were near the back of the bus. They looked at each other in dismay; it was the first time they had not sat in front with the driver.

"Do you think you can stand it?" he asked her.

"If you can," she said.

And as he saw an elderly man with a gray beard and a high yellow turban looking in through the window with what seemed to him a reproachful expression, he said: "Please lie back and be fatigued, will you? You've got to carry this off to the end."

"I hate deceit," she said with great feeling. Then suddenly she shut her eyes and looked quite ill. She was thinking of Tunner. In spite of the firm resolution she had made in Aïn Krorfa to stay behind and meet him according to their agreement, she was letting Port spirit her off to El Ga'a without even leaving a note of explanation. Now that it was too late to change the pattern of her behavior, suddenly it seemed incredible to her that she had allowed herself to do such a thing. But a second later she said to herself that if this was an unpardonable act of deceit toward Tunner, how much graver was the deception she still practiced with Port in not telling him of her infidelity. Immediately she felt fully justified in leaving; nothing Port asked of her could be refused at this point. She let her head fall forward contritely.

"That's right," said Port encouragingly, pinching her arm. He scrambled over the bundles that had just been piled into the aisle and got out to see that all the luggage was on top. When he got back in, Kit was still in the same attitude.

There were no difficulties. As the motor started up, Port glanced out and saw the old man standing beside a younger one. They were both close to the windows, looking wistfully in. "Like two children," he thought, "who aren't being allowed to go on a picnic with the family."

When they started to move, Kit sat up straight and began to whistle. Port nudged her uneasily.

"It's all over," she said. "You don't think I'm going to go on playing sick all the way, I hope? Besides, you're mad. No one's paying the slightest attention to us." This was true. The bus was full of lively conversation; their presence seemed quite unnoticed.

The road was bad almost immediately. At each bump Port slid down lower in his seat. Noticing that he made no effort to avoid slipping more, Kit said at length: "Where are you going? On to the floor?" When he answered, he said only: "What?" and his voice sounded so strange that she turned sharply and tried to see his face. The light was too dim. She could not tell what expression was there.

"Are you asleep?" she asked him.

"No."

"Is anything wrong? Are you cold? Why don't you spread your coat over you?"

This time he did not answer.

"Freeze, then," she said, looking out at the thin moon, low in the sky.

Some time later the bus began a slow, laborious ascent. The fumes from the exhaust grew heavy and acrid; this, combined with the intense noise of the grinding motor and the constantly increasing cold, served to jar Kit from the stupor into which she had sunk. Wide awake, she looked around the indistinct interior of the bus. The occupants all appeared to be asleep; they were resting at unlikely angles, completely rolled in their burnouses, so that not even a finger or a nose was visible. A slight movement beside her made her look down at Port, who had slid so low in his seat that he now was resting on the middle of his spine. She decided to make him sit up, and tapped him vigorously on the shoulder. His only reply was a slight moan.

"Sit up," she said, tapping again. "You'll ruin your back."

This time he groaned: "Oh-h-h!"

"Port, for heaven's sake, sit up," she said nervously. She began to tug at his head, hoping to rouse him enough to start him into making some effort himself.

"Oh, God!" he said, and he slowly wormed his way backward up onto the seat. "Oh, God!" he repeated when he was sitting up finally. Now that his head was near her, she realized that his teeth were chattering.

"You've got a chill!" she said furiously, although she was furious with herself rather than with him. "I told you to cover up, and you just sat there like an idiot!"

He made no reply, merely sat quite still, his head bent

forward and bouncing up and down against his chest with the pitching of the bus. She reached over and pulled at his coat, managing little by little to extricate it from under him where he had thrown it on the seat. Then she spread it over him, tucking it down at the sides with a few petulant gestures. On the surface of her mind, in words, she was thinking: "Typical of him, to be dead to the world, when I'm wide awake and bored." But the formation of the words was a screen to hide the fear beneath—the fear that he might be really ill. She looked out at the windswept emptiness. The new moon had slipped behind the earth's sharp edge. Here in the desert, even more than at sea, she had the impression that she was on the top of a great table, that the horizon was the brink of space. She imagined a cube-shaped planet somewhere above the earth, between it and the moon, to which somehow they had been transported. The light would be hard and unreal as it was here, the air would be of the same taut dryness, the contours of the landscape would lack the comforting terrestrial curves, just as they did all through this vast region. And the silence would be of the ultimate degree, leaving room only for the sound of the air as it moved past. She touched the window-pane; it was ice cold. The bus bumped and swayed as it continued upward across the plateau.

21

It was a long night. They came to a bordj built into the side of a cliff. The overhead light was turned on. The young Arab just in front of Kit, turning around and smiling at her as he lowered the hood of his burnous, pointed at the earth several times and said: *"Hassi Inifel!"*

"Merci," she said, and smiled back. She felt like getting out, and turned to Port. He was doubled up under his coat; his face looked flushed.

"Port," she began, and was surprised to hear him answer immediately. "Yes?" His voice sounded wide awake.

"Let's get out and have something hot. You've slept for hours."

Slowly he sat up. "I haven't slept at all, if you want to know."

She did not believe him. "I see," she said. "Well, do you want to go inside? I'm going."

"If I can. I feel terrible. I think I have grippe or something."

"Oh, nonsense! How could you? You probably have indigestion from eating dinner so fast."

"You go on in. I'll feel better not moving."

She climbed out and stood a moment on the rocks in the wind, taking deep breaths. Dawn was nowhere in sight.

In one of the rooms near the entrance of the bordj there were men singing together and clapping their hands quickly in complex rhythm. She found coffee in a smaller room nearby, and sat down on the floor, warming her hands over the clay vessel of coals. "He *can't* get sick here," she thought. "Neither of us can." There was nothing to do but refuse to be sick, once one was this far away from the world. She went back out and looked through the windows of the bus. Most of the passengers had remained asleep, wrapped in their burnouses. She found Port, and tapped on the glass. "Port!" she called. "Hot coffee!" He did not stir.

"Damn him!" she thought. "He's trying to get attention. He *wants* to be sick!" She climbed aboard and worked her way back to his seat, where he lay inert.

"Port! Please come and have some coffee. As a favor to me." She cocked her head and looked at his face. Smoothing his hair she asked: "Do you feel sick?"

He spoke into his coat. "I don't want anything. Please. I don't want to move."

She disliked to humor him; perhaps by waiting on him she would be playing right into his hands. But in the event he had been chilled he should drink something hot. She determined to get the coffee into him somehow. So she said: "Will you drink it if I bring it to you?"

His reply was a long time in coming, but he finally said: "Yes."

The driver, an Arab who wore a visored cap instead of a turban, was already on his way out of the bordj as she rushed in. "Wait!" she said to him. He stood still and turned around, looking her up and down speculatively. He had no one to whom he could make any remarks about her, since there were no Europeans present, and the other Arabs were not from the city, and would have failed completely to understand his obscene comments.

Port sat up and drank the coffee, sighing between swallows.

"Finished? I've got to give the glass back."

"Yes." The glass was relayed through the bus to the front, where a child waited for it, peering anxiously back lest the bus start up before he had it in his hands.

They moved off slowly across the plateau. Now that the doors had been open, it was colder inside.

"I think that helped," Port said. "Thanks an awful lot. Only I *have* got something wrong with me. God knows I never felt quite like this before. If I could only be in bed and lie out flat, I'd be all right, I think."

"But what do you think it *is?*" she said, suddenly feeling them all there in full force, the fears she had been holding at bay for so many days.

"You tell *me*. We don't get in till noon, do we? What a mess, what a mess!"

"Try and sleep, darling." She had not called him that in at least a year. "Lean over, way over, this way, put your head here. Are you warm enough?" For a few minutes she tried to break the jolts of the bus for him by posting with her body against the back of the seat, but her muscles soon tired; she leaned back and relaxed, letting his head bounce up and down on her breast. His hand in her lap sought hers, found it, held it tightly at first, then loosely. She decided he was asleep, and shut her eyes, thinking: "Of course, there's no escape now. I'm here."

At dawn they reached another bordj standing on a perfectly flat expanse of land. The bus drove through the entrance into a court, where several tents stood. A camel peered haughtily through the window beside Kit's face. This time everyone got out. She woke Port. "Want some breakfast?" she said.

"Believe it or not, I'm a little hungry."

"Why shouldn't you be?" she said brightly. "It's nearly six o'clock."

They had more of the sweet black coffee, some hard-boiled eggs, and dates. The young Arab who had told her the name of the other bordj walked by as they sat on the floor eating. Kit could not help noticing how unusually tall he was, what an admirable figure he cut when he stood erect in his flowing white garment. To efface her feeling of guilt at having thought anything at all about him, she felt impelled to bring him to Port's attention.

"Isn't that one striking!" she heard herself saying, as the Arab moved from the room. The phrase was not at all hers, and it sounded completely ridiculous coming out of her mouth; she waited uneasily for Port's reaction. But Port was holding his hand over his abdomen; his face was white.

"What is it?" she cried.

"Don't let the bus go," he said. He rose unsteadily to his feet and left the room precipitately. Accompanied by a boy he stumbled across the wide court, past the tents where fires burned and babies cried. He walked doubled over, holding his head with one hand and his belly with the other.

In the far corner was a little stone enclosure like a gun-turret, and the boy pointed to it. *"Daoua,"* he said. Port went up the steps and in, slamming the wooden door after him. It stank inside, and it was dark. He leaned back against the cold stone wall and heard the spiderwebs snap as his head touched them. The pain was ambiguous: it was a violent cramp and a mounting nausea, both at once. He stood still for some time, swallowing hard and breathing heavily. What faint light there was in the chamber came up through the square hole in the floor. Something ran swiftly across the back of his neck. He moved away from the wall and leaned over the hole, pushing with his hands against the other wall in front of him. Below were the fouled earth and spattered stones, moving with flies. He shut his eyes and remained in that expectant position for some minutes, groaning from time to time. The bus driver began to blow his horn; for some reason the sound increased his anguish. "Oh, God, shut up!" he cried aloud, groaning immediately afterward. But the horn continued, mixing short blasts with long ones. Finally came the moment when the pain suddenly seemed to have lessened. He opened his eyes, and made an involuntary movement upward with his head, because for an instant he thought he saw flames. It was the red rising sun shining on the rocks and filth beneath. When he opened the door Kit and the young Arab stood outside; between them they helped him out to the waiting bus.

As the morning passed, the landscape took on a gaiety and softness that were not quite like anything Kit had ever seen. Suddenly she realized that it was because in good part sand had replaced rock. And lacy trees grew here and there, especially in the spots where there were agglomerations of huts, and these spots became more frequent. Several times they came upon groups of dark men mounted on mehara. These held the reins proudly, their kohl-farded eyes were fierce above the draped indigo veils that hid their faces.

For the first time she felt a faint thrill of excitement. "It *is* rather wonderful," she thought, "to be riding past such people in the Atomic Age."

Port reclined in his seat, his eyes shut. "Just forget I'm here," he had said when they left the bordj, "and I'll be better able to do the same thing. It's only a few hours more—then bed, thank God."

The young Arab spoke just enough French to be undaunted by the patent impossibility of his engaging in an actual conversation with Kit. It appeared that in his eyes a noun alone or a verb uttered with feeling was sufficient, and she seemed to be of the same mind. He told her, with the usual Arab talent for making a legend out of a mere recounting of facts, about El Ga'a and its high walls with their gates that shut at sunset, its quiet dark streets and its great market where men sold many things that came from the Soudan and from even farther away: salt bars, ostrich plumes, gold dust, leopard skins—he enumerated them in a long list, unconcernedly using the Arabic term for a thing when he did not know the French. She listened with complete attention, hypnotized by the extraordinary charm of his face and his voice, and fascinated as well by the strangeness of what he was talking about, the odd way he was saying it.

The terrain now was a sandy wasteland, strewn with occasional tortured bushlike trees that crouched low in the virulent sunlight. Ahead, the blue of the firmament was turning white with a more fierce glare than she had thought possible: it was the air over the city. Before she knew it, they were riding along beside the gray mud walls. The children cried out as the bus went past, their voices like bright needles. Port's eyes were still shut; she decided not to disturb him until they had arrived. They turned sharply to the left, making a cloud of dust, and went through a big gate into an enormous open square—a sort of antechamber to the city, at the end of which was another gate, even larger.

Beyond that the people and animals disappeared into darkness. The bus stopped with a jolt and the driver got out abruptly and walked away with the air of wishing to have nothing further to do with it. Passengers still slept, or yawned and began looking about for their belongings, most of which were no longer in the places where they had put them the night before.

Kit indicated by word and gesture that she and Port would stay where they were until everyone else had left the vehicle. The young Arab said that in that event he would, too, because she would need him to help take Port to the hotel. As they sat there waiting for the leisurely travelers to get down, he explained that the hotel was across the town on the side by the fort, since it was operated exclusively for the few officers who did not have homes, it being very rare that anyone arriving by bus had need of a hotel.

"You are very kind," she said, sitting back in her seat.

"Yes, madame." His face expressed nothing but friendly solicitousness, and she trusted him implicitly.

When at last the bus was empty save for the debris of pomegranate peel and date pits on the floor and seats, he got out and called a group of men to carry the bags.

"We're here," said Kit in a loud voice. Port stirred, opened his eyes, and said: "I finally slept. What a hellish trip. Where's the hotel?"

"It's somewhere around," she said vaguely; she did not like to tell him that it was on the other side of the city.

He sat up slowly. "God, I hope it's near. I don't think I can make it if it isn't. I feel like hell. I really feel like hell."

"There's an Arab here who's helping us. He's taking us there. It seems it isn't right here by the terminal." She felt better letting him discover the truth about the hotel from the Arab; that way she would remain uninvolved in the matter, and whatever resentment Port might feel would not be directed against her.

Outside in the dust was the disorder of Africa, but for the first time without any visible sign of European influence, so that the scene had a purity which had been lacking in the other towns, an unexpected quality of being complete which dissipated the feeling of chaos. Even Port, as they helped him out, noticed the unified aspect of the place. "It's wonderful here," he said, "what I can see of it, anyway."

"What you can see of it!" echoed Kit. "Is something wrong with your eyes?"

"I'm dizzy. It's a fever, I know that much."

She felt his forehead, and said nothing but: "Well, let's get out of this sun."

The young Arab walked on his left and Kit on his right; each had a supporting arm about him. The porters had gone on ahead.

"The first decent place," said Port bitterly, "and I have to feel like this."

"You're going to stay in bed until you're absolutely well. We'll have plenty of time to explore later."

He did not answer. They went through the inner gate and straightway plunged into a long, crooked tunnel. Passersby brushed against them in the dark. People were sitting along the walls at the sides, from where muffled voices rose, chanting long repetitious phrases. Soon they were in the sunlight once more, then there was another stretch of darkness where the street burrowed through the thick-walled houses.

"Didn't he tell you where it was? I can't take much more of this," Port said. He had not once addressed the Arab directly.

"Ten, fifteen minutes," said the young Arab.

He still disregarded him. "It's out of the question," he told Kit, gasping a little.

"My dear boy, you've *got* to go. You can't just sit down in the street here."

"What is it?" said the Arab, who was watching their faces. And on being told, he hailed a passing stranger and spoke with him briefly. "There is a fondouk that way." He pointed. "He can—" He made a gesture of sleeping, his hand against his cheek. "Then we go hotel and get men and *rfed, très bien!*" He made as if to sweep Port off his feet and carry him in his arms.

"No, no!" cried Kit, thinking he really was about to pick him up.

He laughed and said to Port: "You want to go there?"

"Yes."

They turned around and made their way back through a part of the interior labyrinth. Again the young Arab spoke with someone in the street. He turned back to them smiling. "The end. The next dark place."

The fondouk was a small, crowded and dirty version of any one of the bordjes they had passed through during the recent weeks, save that the center was covered with a latticework of reeds as a protection from the sun. It was filled with country folk and camels, all of them reclining together on the ground. They went in and the Arab spoke with one of the guardians, who cleared the occupants from a stall at one side and piled fresh straw in its corner for Port to lie down on. The porters sat on the luggage in the courtyard.

"I can't leave here," said Kit, looking about the filthy cubicle. "Move your hand!" It lay on some camel dung, but he left it there. "Go on, please. *Now,*" he said. "I'll be all right until you get back. But hurry. Hurry!"

She cast a last anguished glance at him and went out

into the court, followed by the Arab. It was a relief to her to be able to walk quickly in the street.

"*Vite! Vite!*" she kept repeating to him, like a machine. They panted as they went along, threading their way through the slow-moving crowd, down into the heart of the city and out on the other side, until they saw the hill ahead with the fort on it. This side of the town was more open than the other, consisting in part of gardens separated from the streets by high walls, above which rose an occasional tall black cypress. At the end of a long alley there was an almost unnoticeable wooden plaque painted with the words: *Hôtel du Ksar,* and an arrow pointing left. "Ah!" cried Kit. Even here at the edge of town it was still a maze; the streets were constructed in such a way that each stretch seemed to be an impasse with walls at the end. Three times they had to turn back and retrace their steps. There were no doorways, no stalls, not even any passersby—only the impassive pink walls baking in the breathless sunlight.

At last they came upon a tiny, but well-bolted door in the middle of a great expanse of the wall. *Entrée de l'Hôtel,* said the sign above it. The Arab knocked loudly.

A long time passed and there was no answer. Kit's throat was painfully dry; her heart was still beating very fast. She shut her eyes and listened. She heard nothing.

"Knock again," she said, reaching up to do it herself. But his hand was still on the knocker, and he pounded with greater energy than before. This time a dog began to bark somewhere back in the garden, and as the sound gradually came closer it was mingled with cries of reproof. "*Askout!*" cried the woman indignantly, but the animal continued to bark. Then there was a period during which an occasional stone bumped on the ground, and the dog was quiet. In her impatience Kit pushed the Arab's hand away from the knocker and started an incessant hammering, which she did not stop until the woman's voice was on the other side of the door, screaming: *"Echkoun? Echkoun?"*

The young Arab and the woman engaged in a long argument, he making extravagant gestures while he demanded she open the door, and she refusing to touch it. Finally she went away. They heard her slippered feet shuffling along the path, then they heard the dog bark again, the woman's reprimands, followed by yelps as she struck it, after which they heard nothing.

"What is it?" cried Kit desperately. *"Pourquoi on ne nous laisse pas entrer?"*

He smiled and shrugged his shoulders. "Madame is coming," he said.

"Oh, good God!" she said in English. She seized the knocker and hammered violently with it, at the same time kicking the base of the door with all her strength. It did not budge. Still smiling, the Arab shook his head slowly from side to side. *"Peut pas,"* he told her. But she continued to pound. Even though she knew she had no reason to be, she was furious with him for not having been able to make the woman open the door. After a moment she stopped, with the sensation that she was about to faint. She was shaking with fatigue, and her mouth and throat felt as though they were made of tin. The sun poured down on the bare earth; there was not a square inch of shadow, save at their feet. Her mind went back to the many times when, as a child, she had held a reading glass over some hapless insect, following it along the ground in its frenzied attempts to escape the increasingly accurate focusing of the lens, until finally she touched it with the blinding pinpoint of light, when as if by magic it ceased running, and she watched it slowly wither and begin to smoke. She felt that if she looked up she would find the sun grown to monstrous proportions. She leaned against the wall and waited.

Eventually there were steps in the garden. She listened to their sound grow in clarity and volume, until they came right up to the door. Without even turning her head she waited for it to be opened; but that did not happen.

"Qui est là?" said a woman's voice.

Out of fear that the young Arab would speak and perhaps be refused entrance for being a native, Kit summoned all her strength and cried: *"Vous êtes la propriétaire?"*

There was a short silence. Then the woman, speaking with a Corsican or Italian accent, began a voluble entreaty: *"Ah, madame, allez vous en, je vous en supplie! . . . Vous ne pouvez pas entrer ici!* I regret! It is useless to insist. I cannot let you in! No one has been in or out of the hotel for more than a week! It is unfortunate, but you cannot enter!"

"But, madame," Kit cried, almost sobbing, "my husband is very ill!"

"Aie!" The woman's voice rose in pitch and Kit had the impression that she had retreated several steps into the garden; her voice, a little farther away, now confirmed it. *"Ah, mon dieu!* Go away! There is nothing I can do!"

"But where?" screamed Kit. "Where can I go?"

The woman already had started back through the garden. She stopped to cry: "Away from El Ga'a! Leave the city! You cannot expect me to let you in. So far we are free of the epidemic, here in the hotel."

The young Arab was trying to pull Kit away. He had understood nothing except that they were not to be let in. "Come. We find fondouk," he was saying. She shook him off, cupped her hands, and called: "Madame, what epidemic?"

The voice came from still farther away. "But, menin-

gitis. You did not know? *Mais oui, madame! Partez! Partez!"*
The sound of her hurried footsteps became fainter, was lost.
Around the corner of the passageway a blind man had appeared, and was advancing toward them slowly, touching
the wall as he moved. Kit looked at the young Arab; her
eyes had opened very wide. She was saying to herself: "This
is a crisis. There are only a certain number of them in life.
I must be calm, and think." He, seeing her staring eyes,
and still understanding nothing, put his hand comfortingly
on her shoulder and said: "Come." She did not hear him,
but she let him pull her away from the wall just before the
blind man reached them. And he led her along the street
back into the town, as she kept thinking: "This is a crisis."
The sudden darkness of a tunnel broke into her self-imposed
hypnosis. "Where are we going?" she said to him. The question pleased him greatly; into it he read a recognition of
her reliance upon him. "Fondouk," he replied, but some
trace of his triumph must have been implicit in the utter-
ance of his word, for she stopped walking and stepped away
from him. *"Balak!"* cried a voice beside her, and she was
jolted by a man carrying a bundle. The young Arab reached
out and gently pulled her toward him. "The fondouk," she
repeated vaguely. "Ah, yes." They resumed walking.

In his noisy stable Port seemed to be asleep. His hand
still rested on the patch of camel dung—he had not moved
at all. Nevertheless he heard them enter and stirred a little
to show them he was conscious of their presence. Kit
crouched in the straw beside him and smoothed his hair.
She had no idea what she was going to say to him, nor, of
course, what they were going to do, but it comforted her
to be this near to him. For a long time she squatted there,
until the position became too painful. Then she stood up.
The young Arab was sitting on the ground outside the door.

"Port has not said a word," she thought, "but he is expecting the men from the hotel to come and carry him there."
At this moment the most difficult part of her task was having to tell him that there was nowhere for him to stay in
El Ga'a; she determined not to tell him. At the same time
her course of action was decided for her. She knew just
what she would do.

And it was all done quickly. She sent the young Arab
to the market. Any car, any truck, any bus would do, she
had said to him, and price meant nothing. This last enjoin-
der was wasted on him, of course—he spent nearly an hour
haggling over the price three people would pay to be taken
in the back of a produce truck that was going to a place
called Sbâ that afternoon. But when he came back it was
arranged. Once the truck was loaded, the driver would call
with it at the New Gate, which was the gate nearest to the
fondouk, and would send his mechanic-*copain* to let them
know he was waiting for them, and to recruit the men
necessary for carrying Port through the town to the vehicle.
"It is good luck," said the young Arab. "Two times one
month they go to Sbâ." Kit thanked him. During all the
time of his absence Port had not stirred, and she had not
dared attempt to rouse him. Now she knelt down with her
mouth close to his ear and began to repeat his name softly
from time to time. "Yes, Kit," he finally said, his voice very
faint. "How are you?" she whispered.

He waited a good while before answering. "Sleepy,"
he said.

She patted his head. "Sleep a while longer. The men
will be here in a little while."

But they did not come until nearly sunset. Meanwhile
the young Arab had gone to fetch a bowl of food for Kit.
Even with her ravenous appetite, she could hardly manage

to swallow what he brought her: the meat consisted of various unidentifiable inner organs fried in deep fat, and there were some rather hard quinces cut in halves, cooked in olive oil. There was also bread, and it was of this that she ate most copiously. When the light already was fading, and the people outside in the courtyard were beginning to prepare their evening meal, the mechanic arrived with three fierce-looking Negroes. None of them spoke any French. The young Arab pointed Port out to them, and they unceremoniously lifted him up from his bed of straw and carried him out into the street, Kit following as near to his head as possible, to see that they did not let it fall too low. They walked quickly along the darkening passageways, through the camel and goat market, where there was no sound now but the soft bells worn by some of the animals. And soon they were outside the walls of the city, and the desert was dark beyond the headlights of the waiting truck.

"Back. He goes in back," said the young Arab to her by way of explanation, as the three let their burden fall limply on the sacks of potatoes. She handed him some money and asked him to settle with the Soudanese and the porters. It was not enough; she had to give him more. Then they went away. The chauffeur was racing the motor, the mechanic hopped into the front seat beside him and shut the door. The young Arab helped her up into the back, and she stood there leaning over a stack of wine cases looking down at him. He made as if to jump in with her, but at that instant the truck started to move. The young Arab ran after it, surely expecting Kit to call out to the driver to stop, since he had every intention of accompanying her. Once she had caught her balance, however, she deliberately crouched low and lay down on the floor among the sacks and bundles, near Port. She did not look out until they were miles into the desert. Then she looked with fear, lifting her head and peering quickly as if she expected to see him out there in the cold wasteland, running along the trail behind the truck after her.

The truck rode more easily than she had expected, perhaps because the trail was smooth and there were few curves; the way seemed to lie through a straight, endless valley on each side of which in the distance were high dunes. She looked up at the moon, still tiny, but visibly thicker than last night. And she shivered a little, laying her handbag on her bosom. It gave her momentary pleasure to think of that dark little world, the handbag smelling of leather and cosmetics, that lay between the hostile air and her body. Nothing was changed in there; the same objects fell against each other in the same limited chaos, and the names were still there, still represented the same things. Mark Cross, Caron, Helena Rubinstein. "Helena Rubinstein," she said aloud, and it made her laugh. "I'm going to be hysterical in one minute," she said to herself. She clutched one of Port's inert hands and squeezed the fingers as hard as she could. Then she sat up and devoted all her attention to kneading and massaging the hand, in the hope of feeling it grow warmer under her pressure. A sudden terror swept over her. She put her hand on his chest. Of course, his heart was beating. But he seemed cold. Using all her energy, she pushed his body over onto its side, and stretched herself out behind him, touching him at as many points as possible, hoping in this way to keep him warm. As she relaxed, it struck her that she herself had been cold and that she felt more comfortable now. She wondered if subconsciously part of her desire in lying beside Port had been to warm herself. "Probably, or I never should have thought of it." She slept a little.

And awoke with a start. It was natural, now her mind was clear, that there should be a horror. She tried to keep from thinking what it was. Not Port. That had been going on for a long time now. A new horror, connected with sunlight, dust. . . . She looked away with all her power as she felt her mind being swept into contact with the idea. In a split second it would no longer be possible not to know what it was. . . . There! Meningitis!

The epidemic was in El Ga'a and she had been exposed to it. In the hot tunnels of the streets she had breathed in the poisoned air, she had nestled in the contaminated straw at the fondouk. Surely by now the virus had lodged within her and was multiplying. At the thought of it she felt her back grow stiff. But Port could not be suffering from meningitis: he had been cold since Aïn Krorfa, and he had probably had a fever since the first days in Bou Noura, if they only had had the intelligence between them to find out. She tried to recall what she knew about symptoms, not only of meningitis, but of the other principal contagious diseases. Diphtheria began with a sore throat, cholera with diarrhea, but typhus, typhoid, the plague, malaria, yellow fever, kala azar—as far as she knew they all began with fever and malaise of one sort or another. It was a toss-up. "Perhaps it's amoebic dysentery combined with a return of malaria," she reasoned. "But whatever it is, it's already there in him, and nothing I do or don't do can change the outcome of it." She did not want to feel in any way responsible; that would have been too much to bear at this point. As it was, she felt that she was holding up rather well. She remembered stories of horror from the war, stories whose moral always turned out to be: "One never knows what a person is made of until the moment of stress; then often the most timorous person turns out to be the bravest." She wondered if she were being brave, or just resigned. Or cowardly, she added to herself. That, too, was possible, and there was no way of knowing. Port could never tell her because he knew even less about it. If she nursed him and got him through whatever he had, he doubtless would tell her she had been brave, a martyr, and many other things, but that would be out of gratitude. And then she wondered why she wanted to know—it seemed rather a frivolous consideration at the moment.

The truck roared on and on. Fortunately the back was completely open, or the exhaust fumes would have been troublesome. As it was, she caught a sharp odor now and then, but in the following instant it was dissipated in the cold night air. The moon set, the stars were there, she had no idea how late it was. The noise of the motor drowned out the sound of whatever conversation there may have been in front between the driver and the mechanic, and made it impossible for her to communicate with them. She put her arms about Port's waist, and hugged him closer for warmth. "Whatever he has, he's breathing it away from me," she thought. In her moments of sleep she burrowed with her legs beneath the sacks to keep warm; their weight sometimes woke her, but she preferred the pressure to the cold. She had put some empty sacks over Port's legs. It was a long night.

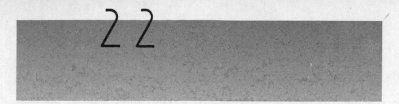

22

As he lay in the back of the truck, protected somewhat from the cold by Kit, now and then he was aware of the straight road beneath him. The twisting roads of the past weeks became alien, faded from his memory; it had been one strict, undeviating course inland to the desert, and now he was very nearly at the center.

How many times his friends, envying him his life, had said to him: "Your life is so simple." "Your life seems always to go in a straight line." Whenever they had said the words he heard in them an implicit reproach: it is not difficult to build a straight road on a treeless plain. He felt that what they really meant to say was: "You have chosen the easiest terrain." But if they elected to place obstacles in their own way—and they so clearly did, encumbering themselves with every sort of unnecessary allegiance—that was no reason why they should object to his having simplified his life. So it was with a certain annoyance that he would say: "Everyone makes the life he wants. Right?" as though there were nothing further to be said.

The immigration authorities at his disembarkation had not been satisfied to leave a blank after the word *Profession* on their papers as he had done in his passport. (That passport, official proof of his existence, racing after him, somewhere behind in the desert!) They had said: "Surely monsieur must do something." And Kit, seeing that he was about to contest the point, had interposed quickly: "Ah, yes. Monsieur is a writer, but he is modest!" They had laughed, filled in the space with the word *écrivain,* and made the remark that they hoped he would find inspiration in the Sahara. For a while he had been infuriated by their stubbornness in insisting upon his having a label, an *état-civil*. Then for a few hours the idea of his actually writing a book had amused him. A journal, filled in each evening with the day's thoughts, carefully seasoned with local color, in which the absolute truth of the theorem he would set forth in the beginning—namely, that the difference between something and nothing is nothing—should be clearly and calmly demonstrated. He had not even mentioned the idea to Kit; she surely would have killed it with her enthusiasm. Since the death of his father he no longer worked at anything, because it was not necessary, but Kit constantly held the hope that he would begin again to write—to write no matter what, so long as he worked at it. "He's a *little* less insupportable when he's working," she explained to others, and by no means totally in jest. And when he saw his mother, which was seldom, she too would say: "Been working?" and look at him with her large sad eyes. He would reply: "Nope," and look back at her insolently. Even as they were driving to the hotel in the taxi, with Tunner saying: "What a hellhole" as he saw the miserable streets, he had been thinking that Kit would be too delighted at the prospect; it would have to be done in secret—it was the only way he would be able to carry it off. But then when he had got settled in the hotel, and they had started their little pattern of café life at the Eckmühl-Noiseux, there had been nothing to write about—he could not establish a connection in his mind between the absurd trivialities which filled the day and the serious business of putting words on paper. He thought it was probably Tunner who prevented him from being completely at ease. Tunner's presence created a situation, however slight, which kept him from entering into the reflective state he considered essential. As long as he was living his life, he could not write about it. Where one left off, the other began, and the existence of circumstances which demanded even the vaguest participation on his part was sufficient to place writing outside the realm of possibility. But that was all right. He would not have written well, and so he would have got no pleasure from it. And even if what he might have written had been good, how many people would have known it? It was all right to speed ahead into the desert leaving no trace.

Suddenly he remembered that they were on their way to the hotel in El Ga'a. It was another night and they had not yet arrived; there was a contradiction somewhere, he knew, but he did not have the energy to look for it. Occasionally he felt the fever rage within him, a separate entity; it gave him the image of a baseball player winding up, getting ready to pitch. And he was the ball. Around and around he went, then he was flung into space for a while, dissolving in flight.

They stood over him. There had been a long struggle, and he was very tired. Kit was one; the other was a soldier. They were talking, but what they said meant nothing. He left them there standing over him, and went back where he had come from.

"He will be as well off here as anywhere else this side of Sidibel-Abbès," said the soldier. "With typhoid all you can do, even in a hospital, is to keep the fever as low as possible, and wait. We have little here in Sbâ in the way of medicine, but these"—he pointed to a tube of pills that lay on an overturned box by the cot—"will bring the fever down, and that is already a great deal."

Kit did not look at him. "And peritonitis?" she said in a low voice.

Captain Broussard frowned. "Do not look for complications, madame," he said severely. "It is always bad enough without that. Yes, of course, peritonitis, pneumonia, heart stoppage, who knows? And you, too, maybe you have the famous El Ga'a meningitis that Madame Luccioni was kind enough to warn you about. *Bien sûr!* And maybe there are fifty cases of cholera here in Sbâ at this moment. I would not tell you even if there were."

"Why not?" she said, finally looking up.

"It would be absolutely useless; and besides, it would lower your morale. No, no. I would isolate the sick, and take measures to prevent the spread of the disease, nothing more. What we have in our hands is always enough. We have a man here with typhoid. We must bring down the fever. That is all. And these stories of peritonitis for him, meningitis for you, do not interest me in the least. You must be realistic, madame. If you stray outside that, you do harm to everyone. You have only to give him his pills every two hours, and try to make him take as much soup as possible. The cook's name is Zina. It would be prudent to be in the kitchen with her now and then to be sure there is always a fire and a big pot of soup constantly hot and ready. Zina is magnificent; she has cooked for us twelve years. But all natives need to be watched, always. They forget. And now, madame, if you will pardon me, I shall get back to my work. One of the men will bring you the mattress I promised you from my house, this afternoon. It will not be very comfortable, doubtless, but what can you expect—you are in Sbâ, not in Paris." He turned in the doorway. *"Enfin, madame, soyez courageuse!"* he said, frowning again, and went out.

Kit stood unmoving, and slowly looked about the bare little room with the door on one side, and a window on the other. Port lay on the rickety cot, facing the wall, breathing regularly with the sheet pulled up around his head. This room was the hospital of Sbâ; it had the one available bed in the town, with real sheets and blankets, and Port was in it only because no member of the military force happened to be ill at the moment. A mud wall came halfway up the window outside, but above that the sky's agonizing light poured in. She took the extra sheet the captain had given her for herself, folded it into a small square the size of the window, got a box of thumbtacks out of Port's luggage, and covered the open space. Even as she stood in the window she was struck with the silence of the place. She could have thought there was not a living being within a thousand miles. The famous silence of the Sahara. She wondered if as the days went by each breath she took would sound as loud to her as it did now, if she would get used to the ridiculous noise her saliva made as she swallowed, and if she would have to swallow as often as she seemed to be doing at the moment, now that she was so conscious of it.

"Port," she said, very softly. He did not stir. She walked out of the room into the blinding light of the courtyard with its floor of sand. There was no one in sight. There was nothing but the blazing white walls, the unmoving sand at her feet and the blue depths of the sky above. She took a few steps, and feeling a little ill, turned and went back into the room. There was not a chair to sit on—only the cot and the little box beside it. She sat down on one of the valises. A tag hung from the handle by her hand. *Wanted on Voyage*, it said. The room had the utterly noncommittal look of a storeroom. With the luggage in the middle of the floor there was not even space for the mattress they were going to bring; the bags would have to be piled in one huge heap in a corner. She looked at her hands, she looked at her feet in their lizard-skin pumps. There was no mirror in the room; she reached across to another valise and seized her handbag, pulling out her compact and lipstick. When she opened the compact she discovered there was not enough light to see her face in its little mirror. Standing in the doorway, she made up slowly and carefully.

"Port," she said again, as softly as before. He went on breathing. She locked her handbag into a valise, looked at her wristwatch, and stepped forth once more into the bright courtyard, this time wearing dark glasses.

Dominating the town, the fort sat astride a high hill of sand, a succession of scattered buildings protected by a wandering outer rampart. It was a separate town, alien to the surrounding landscape and candidly military in aspect. The native guards at the gate looked at her with interest as she went through. The town, sand-color, was spread out below with its single-storied, flat-roofed houses. She turned in the other direction and skirted the wall, climbing for a brief distance until she was at the top of the hill. The heat and the light made her slightly dizzy, and the sand kept filling her shoes. From this point she could hear the clear, high-pitched sounds of the town below; children's voices and dogs barking. In all directions, where the earth and sky met, there was a faint, rapidly pulsating haze.

"Sbâ," she said aloud. The word meant nothing to her; it did not even represent the haphazard collection of formless huts below. When she returned to the room someone had left a mammoth white china chamber-pot in the middle of the floor. Port was lying on his back, looking up at the ceiling, and he had pushed the covers off.

She hurried to the cot and pulled them up over him. There was no way of tucking him in. She took his temperature: it had fallen somewhat.

"This bed hurts my back," he said unexpectedly, gasping a little. She stepped back and surveyed the cot: it sagged heavily between the head and the foot.

"We'll fix that in a little while," she said. "Now, be good and keep covered up."

He looked at her reproachfully. "You don't have to talk to me as if I were a child," he said. "I'm still the same person."

"It's just automatic, I suppose, when people are sick," she said, laughing uncomfortably. "I'm sorry."

He still looked at her. "I don't have to be humored in any way," he said slowly. Then he shut his eyes and sighed deeply.

When the mattress arrived, she had the Arab who had brought it go and get another man. Together they lifted Port off the cot and laid him onto the mattress which was spread on the floor. Then she had them pile some of the valises on the cot. The Arabs went out.

"Where are you going to sleep?" asked Port.

"On the floor here beside you," she said.

He did not ask her any more. She gave him his pills and said: "Now sleep." Then she went out to the gate and tried to speak with the guards; they did not understand any French, and kept saying: *"Non, m'si."* As she was gesticulating with them, Captain Broussard appeared in a nearby doorway and looked at her with a certain suspicion in his eyes. "Do you want something, madame?" he said.

"I want someone to go with me to the market and help me buy some blankets," said Kit.

"Ah, je regrette, madame," he said. "There is no one in the post here who could render you that service, and I do not advise you to go alone. But if you like I can send you blankets from my quarters."

Kit was effusive in her thanks. She went back into the inner courtyard and stood a moment looking at the door of the room, loath to enter. "It's a prison," she thought. "I'm a prisoner here, and for how long? God knows." She went in, sat down on a valise just inside the door, and stared at the floor. Then she rose, opened a bag, pulled out a fat French novel she had bought before leaving for Boussif, and tried to read. When she had got to the fifth page, she heard someone coming through the courtyard. It was a young French soldier carrying three camel blankets. She got up and stepped aside for him to enter, saying: *"Ah, merci. Comme vous êtes amiable!"* But he stood still just outside the door, holding his arm out toward her for her to take the blankets. She lifted them off and laid them on the floor at her feet. When she looked up he already had started away. She stared after him an instant, vaguely perplexed, and then set about collecting various odd pieces of clothing from among her effects, which could serve as a foundation to place underneath the blankets. She finally arranged her bed, lay down on it, and was pleasantly surprised to find it comfortable. All at once she felt an overwhelming desire to sleep. It would be another hour and a half before she must give Port his medicine. She closed her eyes and for a moment was in the back of the truck on her way from El Ga'a to Sbâ. The sensation of motion lulled her, and she immediately fell asleep.

She was awakened by feeling something brush past her face. She started up, saw that it was dark and that someone was moving about in the room. "Port!" she cried. A woman's voice said: *"Voici mangi, madame."* She was standing directly above her. Someone came through the courtyard silently bearing a carbide lamp. It was a small boy, who walked to the door, reached in, and set the light down on the floor. She looked up and saw a large-boned old woman with eyes that were still beautiful. "This is Zina," she thought, and she called her by name. The woman smiled, and stooped down, putting the tray on the floor by Kit's bed. Then she went out.

It was difficult to feed Port; much of the soup ran over his face and down his neck. "Maybe tomorrow you'll feel like sitting up to eat," she said as she wiped his mouth with a handkerchief. "Maybe," he said feebly.

"Oh, my God!" she cried. She had overslept; the pills were long overdue. She gave them to him and had him wash them down with a swallow of tepid water. He made a face. "The water," he said. She sniffed the carafe. It reeked of chlorine. She had put the Halazone tablets in twice by mistake. "It won't hurt you," she said.

She ate her food with relish: Zina was quite a good cook. While she was still eating, she looked over at Port and saw that he was already asleep. The pills seemed each time to have that effect. She thought of taking a short walk after the meal, but she was afraid that Captain Broussard might have given orders to the guards not to let her pass. She went out into the courtyard and walked around it several times, looking up at the stars. An accordion was being played somewhere at the other end of the fort; its sound was very faint. She went into the room, shut the door, locked it, undressed, and lay on her blankets beside Port's mattress, pulling the lamp over near her head so she could read. But the light was not strong enough, and it moved too much, so that her eyes began to hurt, and the smell of it disgusted her. Reluctantly she blew out the flame, and the room fell back into the profoundest darkness. She had scarcely lain down before she sprang up again, and began to scrabble about the floor with her hand, searching for matches. She lit the lamp, which seemed to be smelling stronger than ever since she had blown it out, and said to herself, but moving her lips: "Every two hours. Every two hours."

In the night she awoke sneezing. At first she thought it was the odor of the lamp, but then she put her hand to her face, and felt the grit on her skin. She moved her fingers along the pillow: it was covered with a coating of dust. Then she became conscious of the noise of the wind outside. It was like the roar of the sea. Fearful of waking Port, she tried to stifle the sneeze that was on its way; her effort was unsuccessful. She got up. It seemed cold in the room. She spread Port's bathrobe over him. Then she got two large handkerchiefs out of a suitcase and tied one over the lower part of her face, bandit-fashion. The other one she intended to arrange for Port when she woke him up to give him his pills. It would be only another twenty minutes. She lay down, sneezing again as a result of the dust raised by moving the blankets. She lay perfectly still listening to the fury of the wind as it swept by outside the door.

"Here I am, in the middle of horror," she thought, attempting to exaggerate the situation, in the hope of convincing herself that the worst had happened, was actually there with her. But it would not work. The sudden arrival of the wind was a new omen, connected only with the time to come. It began to make a singular, animal-like sound beneath the door. If she could only give up, relax, and live in the perfect knowledge that there was no hope. But there was never any knowing or any certitude; the time to come always had more than one possible direction. One could not even give up hope. The wind would blow, the sand would settle, and in some as yet unforeseen manner time would bring about a change which could only be terrifying, since it would not be a continuation of the present.

She remained awake the rest of the night, giving Port his pills regularly, and trying to relax in the periods between. Each time she woke him he moved obediently and swallowed the water and the tablet proffered him without speaking or even opening his eyes. In the pale, infected light of daybreak she heard him begin to sob. Electrified, she sat up and stared at the corner where his head lay. Her heart was beating very fast, activated by a strange emotion she could not identify. She listened a while, decided it was compassion she felt, and leaned nearer to him. The sobs came up mechanically, like hiccups or belches. Little by little the sensation of excitement died away, but she remained sitting up, listening intently to the two sounds together: the sobs inside the room and the wind without. Two impersonal, natural sounds. After a sudden, short silence she heard him say, quite distinctly: "Kit. Kit." As her eyes grew wide she said: "Yes?" But he did not answer. After a long time, clandestinely, she slid back down under the blanket and fell asleep for a while. When she awoke the morning had really begun. The inflamed shafts of distant sunlight sifted down from the sky along with the air's fine grit; the insistent wind seemed about to blow away what feeble strands of light there were.

She arose and moved about the room stiffly in the cold, trying to raise as little dust as possible while she made her toilet. But the dust lay thick on everything. She was conscious of a defect in her functioning—it was as if an entire section of her mind were numb. She felt the lack there: an enormous blind spot inside her—but she could not locate it. And as if from a distance she watched the fumbling gestures her hands made as they came in contact with the objects and the garments. "This has got to stop," she said to herself. "This has got to stop." But she did not know quite what she meant. Nothing could stop; everything always went on.

Zina arrived, completely shrouded in a great white blanket, and slamming the door behind her against the blast, drew forth from beneath the folds of her clothing a small tray which bore a teapot and a glass. *"Bonjour, madame. R'mleh bzef,"* she said, with a gesture toward the sky, and set the tray on the floor beside the mattress.

The hot tea gave her a little strength; she drank it all and sat a while listening to the wind. Suddenly she realized that there was nothing for Port. Tea would not be enough for him. She decided to go in search of Zina to see if there was any way of getting him some milk. She went out and stood in the courtyard, calling: "Zina! Zina!" in a voice rendered feeble by the wind's fury, grinding the sand between her teeth as she caught her breath.

No one appeared. After stumbling into and out of several empty niche-like rooms, she discovered a passageway that led to the kitchen. Zina was there squatting on the floor, but Kit could not make her understand what she wanted. With motions the old woman indicated that she would presently fetch Captain Broussard and send him to the room. Back in the semi-darkness she lay down on her pallet, coughing and rubbing away from her eyes the sand that had gathered on her face. Port was still sleeping.

She herself was almost asleep when the captain came in. He removed the hood of his camel's-hair burnous from around his face, and shook it, then he shut the door behind him and squinted about in the obscurity. Kit stood up. The expected queries and responses regarding the state of the patient were made. But when she asked him about the milk he merely looked at her pityingly. All canned milk was rationed, and that only to women with infants. "And the sheep's milk is always sour and undrinkable in any case," he added. It seemed to Kit that each time he looked at her it was as if he suspected her of harboring secret and reprehensible motives. The resentment she felt at his accusatory gaze helped her to regain a little of her lost sense of reality. "I'm sure he doesn't look at everybody that way," she thought. "Then why me? Damn his soul!" But she felt too utterly dependent upon the man to allow herself the satisfaction of letting him perceive anything of her reactions. She stood, trying to look forlorn, with her right hand outstretched above Port's head in a compassionate gesture, hoping the captain's heart might be moved; she was convinced that he could get her all the canned milk she wanted, if he chose.

"Milk is completely unnecessary for your husband in any case, madame," he said dryly. "The soup I have ordered is quite sufficient, and more digestible. I shall have Zina bring a bowl immediately." He went out; the sand-laden wind still roared.

Kit spent the day reading and seeing to it that Port was dosed and fed regularly. He was utterly disinclined to speak; perhaps he did not have the strength. While she was reading, sometimes she forgot the room, the situation, for minutes at a time, and on each occasion when she raised her head and remembered again, it was like being struck in the face. Once she almost laughed, it seemed so ridiculously unlikely. "Sbâ," she said, prolonging the vowel so that it sounded like the bleat of a sheep.

Toward late afternoon she tired of her book and stretched out on her bed, carefully, so as not to disturb Port. As she turned toward him, she realized with a disagreeable shock that his eyes were open, looking at her across the few inches of bedding. The sensation was so violently unpleasant that she sprang up, and staring back at him, said in a tone of forced solicitude: "How do you feel?" He frowned a little, but did not reply. Falteringly she pursued. "Do you think the pills help? At least they seem to bring the fever down a bit." And now, surprisingly enough, he answered, in a soft but clear voice. "I'm very sick," he said slowly. "I don't know whether I'll come back."

"Back?" she said stupidly. Then she patted his hot forehead, feeling disgusted with herself even as she uttered the words: "You'll be all right."

All at once she decided she must get out of the room for a while before dark—even if just for a few minutes. A change of air. She waited until he had closed his eyes. Then without looking at him again for fear she would see them open once more, she got up quickly and stepped out into the wind. It seemed to have shifted a little, and there was less sand in the air. Even so, she felt the sting of the grains on her cheeks. Briskly she walked out beneath the high mud portal, not looking at the guards, not stopping when she reached the road, but continuing downward until she came to the street that led to the market place. Down there the wind was less noticeable. Apart from an inert figure lying here and there entirely swathed in its burnous, the way was empty. As she moved along through the soft sand of the street, the remote sun fell rapidly behind the flat hammada ahead, and the walls and arches took on their twilight rose hue. She was a little ashamed of herself for having given in to her nervous impatience to be out of the room, but she banished the sentiment by arguing with herself that nurses, like everyone else, must rest occasionally.

She came to the market, a vast, square, open space enclosed on all four sides by whitewashed arcades whose innumerable arches made a monotonous pattern whichever way she turned her head. A few camels lay grumbling in the center, a few palm-branch fires flared, but the merchants and their wares were gone. Then she heard the muezzins calling in three distinct parts of the town, and saw those men who were left begin their evening prayer. Crossing the market, she wandered into a side street with its earthen buildings all orange in the momentary glow. The little shop doors were closed—all but one, in front of which she paused an instant, peering in vaguely. A man wearing a beret crouched inside over a small fire built in the middle of the floor, holding his hands fanwise almost in the flames. He glanced up and saw her, then rising, he came to the door. *"Entrez, madame,"* he said, making a wide gesture. For lack of anything else to do, she obeyed. It was a tiny shop; in the dimness she could see a few bolts of white cloth lying on the shelves. He fitted a carbide lamp together, touched a match to the spout, and watched the sharp flame spring up. "Daoud Zozeph," he said, holding forth his hand. She was faintly surprised: for some reason she had thought he was French. Certainly he was not a native of Sbâ. She sat on the stool he offered her, and they talked a few minutes. His French was quite good, and he spoke it gently in a tone of obscure reproof. Suddenly she realized he was a Jew. She asked him; he seemed astonished and amused at her question. "Of course," he said. "I stay open during the

hour of prayer. Afterward there are always a few customers." They spoke of the difficulties of being a Jew here in
Sbâ, and then she found herself telling him of her predica-
ment, of Port who lay alone up in the Poste Militaire. He
leaned against the counter above her, and it seemed to her
that his dark eyes glowed with sympathy. Even this faint
impression, unconfirmed as it was, made her aware for the
first time of how cruelly lacking in that sentiment was the
human landscape here, and of how acutely she had been
missing it without realizing she was missing it. And so she
talked on and on, even going into her feeling about omens.
She stopped abruptly, looked at him a little fearfully, and
laughed. But he was very serious; he seemed to understand
her very well. "Yes, yes," he said, stroking his beardless
chin meditatively. "You are right about all that."

Logically she should not have found such a statement
reassuring, but the fact that he agreed with her she found
deliciously comforting. However, he continued: "The mistake you make is in being afraid. That is the great mistake.
The signs are given us for our good, not for our harm. But
when you are afraid you read them wrong and make bad
things where good ones were meant to be."

"But I *am* afraid," protested Kit. "How can I change
that? It's impossible."

He looked at her and shook his head. "That is not the
way to live," he said.

"I know," she said sadly.

An Arab entered the shop, bade her good evening, and
purchased a pack of cigarettes. As he went out the door,
he turned and spat just inside it on the floor. Then he gave
a disdainful toss of his burnous over his shoulder and strode
away. Kit looked at Daoud Zozeph.

"Did he spit on purpose?" she asked him.

He laughed. "Yes. No. Who knows? I have been spat

upon so many thousand times that I do not see it when it happens. You see! You should be a Jew in Sbâ, and you would learn not to be afraid! At least you would learn not to be afraid of God. You would see that even when God is most terrible, he is never cruel, the way men are."

Suddenly what he was saying sounded ridiculous. She rose, smoothed her skirt, and said she must be going.

"One moment," he said, going behind a curtain into a room beyond. He returned presently with a small parcel. Behind the counter he resumed the anonymous air of a shopkeeper. He handed the parcel across to her, saying quietly: "You said you wanted to give your husband milk. Here are two cans. They were the ration for our baby." He raised his hand as she tried to interrupt. "But it was born dead, last week, too soon. Next year if we have another we can get more."

Seeing Kit's look of anguish, he laughed: "I promise you," he said, "as soon as my wife knows, I will apply for the coupons. There will be no trouble. *Allons!* What are you afraid of now?" And as she still stood looking at him, he raised the parcel in the air and presented it again with such an air of finality that automatically she took hold of it. "This is one of those occasions where one doesn't try to put into words what one feels," she said to herself. She thanked him saying that her husband would be very happy, and that she hoped they would meet again in a few days. Then she went out. With the coming of night, the wind had risen somewhat. She shivered climbing the hill on the way to the fort.

The first thing she did on arriving back in the room was to light the lamp. Then she took Port's temperature: she was horrified to find it higher. The pills were no longer working. He looked at her with an unaccustomed expression in his shining eyes.

"Today's my birthday," he murmured.

"No, it isn't," she said sharply; then she reflected an instant, and asked with feigned interest: "Is it, really?"

"Yes. This was the one I've been waiting for."

She did not ask him what he meant. He went on: "Is it beautiful out?"

"No."

"I wish you could have said yes."

"Why?"

"I'd have liked it to be beautiful out."

"I suppose you could call it beautiful, but it's just a little unpleasant to walk in."

"Ah, well, we're not out in it," he said.

The quietness of his dialogue made more monstrous the groans of pain which an instant later issued from within him. "What is it?" she cried in a frenzy. But he could not hear her. She knelt on her mattress and looked at him, unable to decide what to do. Little by little he grew silent, but he did not open his eyes. For a while she studied the inert body as it lay there beneath the covers, which rose and fell slightly with the rapid respiration. "He's stopped being human," she said to herself. Illness reduces man to his basic state: a cloaca in which the chemical processes continue. The meaningless hegemony of the involuntary. It was the ultimate taboo stretched out there beside her, helpless and terrifying beyond all reason. She choked back a wave of nausea that threatened her for an instant.

There was a knocking at the door: it was Zina with Port's soup, and a plate of couscous for her. Kit indicated that she wanted her to feed the invalid; the old woman seemed delighted, and began to try to coax him into sitting up. There was no response save a slight acceleration in his breathing. She was patient and persevering, but to no avail.

Kit had her take the soup away, deciding that if he wanted nourishment later she would open one of the tins of milk and mix it with hot water for him.

The wind was blowing again, but without fury, and from the other direction. It moaned spasmodically through the cracks around the window, and the folded sheet moved a bit now and then. Kit stared at the spurting white flame of the lamp, trying to conquer her powerful desire to run out of the room. It was no longer the familiar fear that she felt—it was a steadily mounting sentiment of revulsion.

But she lay perfectly still, blaming herself and thinking: "If I feel no sense of duty toward him, at least I can act as if I did." At the same time there was an element of self-chastisement in her immobility. "You're not even to move your foot if it falls asleep. And I hope it hurts." Time passed, expressed in the low cry of the wind as it sought to enter the room, the cry rising and falling in pitch but never quite ceasing. Unexpectedly Port breathed a profound sigh and shifted his position on the mattress. And incredibly, he began to speak.

"Kit." His voice was faint but in no way distorted. She held her breath, as if her least movement might snap the thread that held him to rationality.

"Kit."

"Yes."

"I've been trying to get back. Here." He kept his eyes closed.

"Yes—"

"And now I am."

"Yes!"

"I wanted to talk to you. There's nobody here?"

"No, no!"

"Is the door locked?"

"I don't know," she said. She bounded up and locked it, returning to her pallet, all in the same movement. "Yes, it's locked."

"I wanted to talk to you."

She did not know what to say. She said: "I'm glad."

"There are so many things I want to say. I don't know what they are. I've forgotten them all."

She patted his hand lightly. "It's always that way."

He lay silent a moment.

"Wouldn't you like some warm milk?" she said cheerfully.

He seemed distraught. "I don't think there's time. I don't know."

"I'll fix it for you," she announced, and she sat up, glad to be free.

"Please stay here."

She lay down again, murmuring: "I'm so glad you feel better. You don't know how different it makes *me* feel to hear you talk. I've been going crazy here. There's not a soul around—" She stopped, feeling the momentum of hysteria begin to gather in the background. But Port seemed not to have heard her.

"Please stay here," he repeated, moving his hand uncertainly along the sheet. She knew it was searching for hers, but she could not make herself reach out and let it take hold. At the same moment she became aware of her refusal, and the tears came into her eyes—tears of pity for Port. Still she did not move.

Again he sighed. "I feel very sick. I feel awful. There's no reason to be afraid, but I am. Sometimes I'm not here, and I don't like that. Because then I'm far away and all alone. No one could ever get there. It's too far. And there I'm alone."

She wanted to stop him, but behind the stream of quiet words she heard the entreaty of a moment back: "Please stay here." And she did not have the strength to stop him unless she got up and moved about. But his words made her miserable; it was like hearing him recount one of his dreams—worse, even.

"So alone I can't even remember the idea of not being alone," he was saying. His fever would go up. "I can't even think what it would be like for there to be someone else in the world. When I'm there I can't remember being here; I'm just afraid. But here I can remember being there. I wish I could stop remembering it. It's awful to be two things at once. You know that, don't you?" His hand sought hers desperately. "You do know that? You understand how awful it is? You've got to." She let him take her hand, pull it towards his mouth. He rubbed his rough lips along it with a terrible avidity that shocked her; at the same time she felt the hair at the back of her head rise and stiffen. She watched his lips opening and shutting against her knuckles, and felt the hot breath on her fingers.

"Kit, Kit. I'm afraid, but it's not only that. Kit! All these years I've been living for you. I didn't know it, and now I do. I do know it! But now you're going away." He tried to roll over and lie on top of her arm; he clutched her hand always tighter.

"I'm not!" she cried.

His legs moved spasmodically.

"I'm right here!" she shouted, even louder, trying to imagine how her voice sounded to him, whirling down his own dark halls toward chaos. And as he lay still for a while, breathing violently, she began to think: "He says it's more than just being afraid. But it isn't. He's never lived for me.

Never. Never." She held to the thought with an intensity that drove it from her mind, so that presently she found herself lying taut in every muscle without an idea in her head, listening to the wind's senseless monologue. For a time this went on; she did not relax. Then little by little she tried to draw her hand away from Port's desperate grasp. There was a sudden violent activity beside her, and she turned to see him partially sitting up.

"Port!" she cried, pushing herself up and putting her hands on his shoulders. "You've got to lie down!" She used all her strength; he did not budge. His eyes were open and he was looking at her. "Port!" she cried again in a different voice. He raised one hand and took hold of her arm.

"But Kit," he said softly. They looked at each other. She made a slight motion with her head, letting it fall onto his chest. Even as he glanced down at her, her first sob came up, and the first cleared the passage for the others. He closed his eyes again, and for a moment had the illusion of holding the world in his arms—a warm world all tropics, lashed by storm. "No, no, no, no, no, no, no," he said. It was all he had the strength to say. But even if he had been able to say more, still he would have said only: "No, no, no, no."

It was not a whole life whose loss she was mourning there in his arms, but it was a great part of one; above all it was a part whose limits she knew precisely, and her knowledge augmented the bitterness. And presently within her, deeper than the weeping for the wasted years, she found a ghastly dread all formed and growing. She raised her head and looked up at him with tenderness and terror. His head had dropped to one side; his eyes were closed. She put her arms around his neck and kissed his forehead many times.

Then, half-pulling and half-coaxing, she got him back down into bed and covered him. She gave him his pill, undressed silently and lay down facing him, leaving the lamp burning so she could see him as she fell asleep. The wind at the window celebrated her dark sensation of having attained a new depth of solitude.

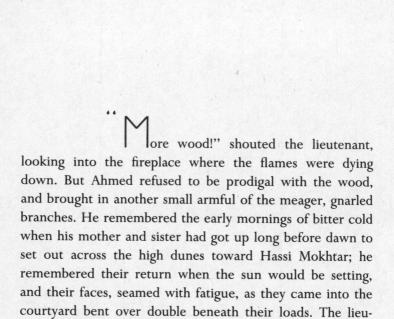

23

"More wood!" shouted the lieutenant, looking into the fireplace where the flames were dying down. But Ahmed refused to be prodigal with the wood, and brought in another small armful of the meager, gnarled branches. He remembered the early mornings of bitter cold when his mother and sister had got up long before dawn to set out across the high dunes toward Hassi Mokhtar; he remembered their return when the sun would be setting, and their faces, seamed with fatigue, as they came into the courtyard bent over double beneath their loads. The lieutenant would often throw on the fire as much wood as his sister had used to gather in the entire day, but *he* would not do it; he always brought in a scant amount. The lieutenant was quite aware that this was sheer recalcitrance on Ahmed's part. He considered it a senseless but unalterable eccentricity.

"He's a crazy boy," said Lieutenant d'Armagnac, sipping his vermouth-cassis, "but honest and faithful. Those are the prime qualities to look for in a servant. Even stupidity and stubbornness are acceptable, if he has the others. Not that Ahmed is stupid, by any means. Sometimes he has a better intuition than I. In the case of your friend, for instance. The last time he came to see me here at my house. I invited him and his wife for dinner. I told him I would send Ahmed to let him know exactly which day it would be. I was ill at the time. I think my cook had been trying to poison me. You understand everything I am saying, monsieur?"

"*Oui, oui,*" said Tunner, whose ear was superior to his tongue. He was following the lieutenant's conversation with only a slight amount of difficulty.

"After your friend had left, Ahmed said to me: 'He will never come.' I said: 'Nonsense. Of course he will, and with his wife.' 'No,' said Ahmed. 'I can tell by his face. He has no intention of coming.' And you see he was right. That very evening they both left for El Ga'a. I heard only the next day. It's astonishing, isn't it?"

"*Oui,*" said Tunner again; he was sitting forward in his chair, his hands on his knees, looking very serious.

"Ah, yes," yawned his host, rising to throw more wood on the fire. "A surprising people, the Arabs. Of course here there's a very heavy admixture of Soudanese, from the time of slavery—"

Tunner interrupted him. "But you say they're not in El Ga'a now?"

"Your friends? No. They've gone to Sbâ, as I told you. The Chef de Poste there is Captain Broussard; he is the one who telegraphed me about the typhoid. You'll find him a bit curt, but he's a fine man. Only the Sahara does not agree with him. Some it does, some not. Me, for example, I'm in my element here."

Again Tunner interrupted. "How soon do you think I can be in Sbâ?"

The lieutenant laughed indulgently. *"Vous êtes bien pressé!* But there's no hurry with typhoid. It will be several weeks before your friend will care whether he sees you or not. And he will not be needing that passport in the meantime! So you can take your time." He felt warmly toward this American, whom he found much more to his liking than the first. The first had been furtive, had made him vaguely uneasy (but perhaps that impression had been due to his own state of mind at the time). In any case, in spite of Tunner's obvious haste to leave Bou Noura, he found him a sympathetic companion, and he hoped to persuade him to stay a while.

"You will remain for dinner?" said the lieutenant.

"Oh," said Tunner distraughtly. "Thank you very much."

First of all there was the room. Nothing could change the hard little shell of its existence, its white plaster walls and its faintly arched ceiling, its concrete floor and its windows across which a sheet had been tacked, folded over many times to keep out the light. Nothing could change it because that was all there was of it, that and the mattress on which he lay. When from time to time a gust of clarity swept down upon him, and he opened his eyes and saw what was really there, and knew where he really was, he fixed the walls, the ceiling and the floor in his memory, so that he could find his way back next time. For there were so many other parts of the world, so many other moments in time to be visited; he never was certain that the way back would really be there. Counting was impossible. How many hours he had been like this, lying on the burning mattress, how many times he had seen Kit stretched out on the floor nearby, had made a sound and seen her turn over, get up and then come toward him to give him water—things like that he could not have told, even if he had thought to ask them of himself. His mind was occupied with very different problems. Sometimes he spoke aloud, but it was not satisfying; it seemed rather to hold back the natural development of the ideas. They flowed out through his mouth, and he was never sure whether they had been resolved in the right words. Words were much more alive and more difficult to handle, now; so much so that Kit did not seem to understand them when he used them. They slipped into his head like the wind blowing into a room, and extinguished the frail flame of an idea forming there in the dark. Less and less he used them in his thinking. The process became more mobile; he followed the course of thoughts because he was tied on behind. Often the way was vertiginous, but he could not let go. There was no repetition in the landscape; it was always new territory and the peril increased constantly. Slowly, pitilessly, the number of dimensions was lessening. There were fewer directions in which to move. It was not a clear process, there was nothing definite about it so that he could say: "Now up is gone." Yet he had witnessed occasions when two different dimensions had deliberately, spitefully, merged their identities, as if to say to him: "Try and tell which is which." His reaction was always the same: a sensation in which the outer parts of his being rushed inward for protection, the same movement one sometimes sees in a kaleidoscope on turning it very slowly, when the parts of the design fall headlong into the center. But the center! Sometimes it was gigantic, painful, raw and false, it extended from one side of creation to the other, there was no telling where it was; it was everywhere. And sometimes it would disappear, and the other center, the true one, the tiny burning black point, would be there in its place, unmoving and impossibly sharp, hard and distant. And each center he called "That." He knew one from the other, and which was the true, because when for a few minutes sometimes he actually came back to the room and saw it, and saw Kit, and said to himself: "I am in Sbâ," he could remember the two centers and distinguish between them, even though he hated them both, and he knew that the one which was only *there* was the true one, while the other was wrong, wrong, wrong.

It was an existence of exile from the world. He never saw a human face or figure, nor even an animal; there were no familiar objects along the way, there was no ground below, nor sky above, yet the space was full of things. Sometimes he saw them, knowing at the same time that really they could only be heard. Sometimes they were absolutely still, like the printed page, and he was conscious of their terrible invisible motion underneath, and of its portent to him because he was alone. Sometimes he could touch them with his fingers, and at the same time they poured in through his mouth. It was all utterly familiar and wholly horrible—existence unmodifiable, not to be questioned, that must be borne. It would never occur to him to cry out.

The next morning the lamp had still been burning and the wind had gone. She had been unable to rouse him to give him his medicine, but she had taken his temperature through his half-open mouth: it had gone much higher. Then she had rushed out to find Captain Broussard, had brought him to the bedside where he had been noncommittal, trying to reassure her without giving her any reason for hope. She had passed the day sitting on the edge of her pallet in an attitude of despair, looking at Port from time to time, hearing his labored breathing and seeing him twist in the throes of an inner torment. Nor could Zina tempt her with food.

When night came and Zina reported that the American lady still would not eat, Captain Broussard decided upon a simple course of action. He went to the room and knocked on the door. After a short interval he heard Kit say: *"Qui est là?"* Then she opened the door. She had not lighted the lamp; the room was black behind her.

"Is it you, madame?" He tried to make his voice pleasant.

"Yes."

"Could you come with me a moment? I should like to speak with you."

She followed him through several courtyards into a brightly lighted room with a blazing fireplace at one end. There was a profusion of native rugs which covered the walls, the divans and the floor. At the far end was a small bar attended by a tall black Soudanese in a very white turban and jacket. The captain gestured nonchalantly toward her.

"Will you take something?"

"Oh, no. Thank you."

"A little apéritif."

Kit was still blinking at the light. "I couldn't," she said.

"You'll have a Cinzano with me." He signaled to his barman. *"Deux Cinzanos.* Come, come, sit down, I beg you. I shall not detain you long."

Kit obeyed, took the glass from the proffered tray. The taste of the wine pleased her, but she did not want to be pleased, she did not want to be ripped from her apathy. Besides, she was still conscious of the peculiar light of suspicion in the captain's eyes when he looked at her. He sat studying her face as he sipped his drink: he had about come to the decision that she was not exactly what he had taken her for at first, that perhaps she really was the sick man's wife after all.

"As Chef de Poste," he said, "I am more or less obliged to verify the identity of the persons who pass through Sbâ. Of course the arrivals are very infrequent. I regret having to trouble you at such a time, naturally. It is merely a question of seeing your identity papers. Ali!" The barman stepped silently to their chairs and refilled the glasses. Kit did not reply for a moment. The apéritif had made her violently hungry.

"I have my passport."

"Excellent. Tomorrow I shall send for both passports and return them to you within the hour."

"My husband has lost his passport. I can only give you mine."

"*Ah, ça!*" cried the captain. It was as he had expected, then. He was furious; at the same time he felt a certain satisfaction in the reflection that his first impression had been correct. And how right he had been to forbid his inferior officers to have anything to do with her. He had expected just something of this sort, save that in such cases it was usually the woman's papers which were difficult to get hold of, rather than the man's.

"Madame," he said, leaning forward in his seat, "please understand that I am in no way interested in probing matters which I consider strictly personal. It is merely a formality, but one which must be carried out. I must see both passports. The names are a matter of complete indifference to me. But two people, two passports, no? Unless you have one together."

Kit thought he had not heard her correctly. "My husband's passport was stolen in Aïn Krorfa."

The captain hesitated. "I shall have to report this, of

course. To the commander of the territory." He rose to his feet. "You yourselves should have reported it as soon as it happened." He had had the servant lay a place at the table for Kit, but now he did not want to eat with her.

"Oh, but we did. Lieutenant d'Armagnac at Bou Noura knows all about it," said Kit, finishing her glass. "May I have a cigarette, please?" He gave her a Chesterfield, lighted it for her, and watched her inhale. "My cigarettes are all gone." She smiled, her eyes on the pack he held in his hand. She felt better, but the hunger inside her was planting its claws deeper each minute. The captain said nothing. She went on. "Lieutenant d'Armagnac did everything he could for my husband to try and get it back from Messad."

The captain did not believe a word she was saying; he considered it all an admirable piece of lying. He was convinced now that she was not only an adventuress, but a truly suspicious character. "I see," he said, studying the rug at his feet. "Very well, madame. I shall not detain you now."

She rose.

"Tomorrow you will give me your passport, I shall prepare my report and we shall see what the outcome will be." He escorted her back to the room and returned to eat alone, highly annoyed with her for having insisted upon trying to deceive him. Kit stood in the dark room a second, reopened the door slightly and watched the glow cast on the sand by his flashlight disappear. Then she went in search of Zina, who fed her in the kitchen.

When she had finished eating she went to the room and lighted the lamp. Port's body squirmed and his face protested against the sudden light. She put the lamp in a corner behind some valises and stood a while in the middle of the room thinking of nothing. A few minutes later she took up her coat and went out into the courtyard.

The roof of the fort was a great, flat, irregularly shaped

mud terrace whose varying heights were a projection, as it were, of the uneven ground below. The ramps and staircases between the different wings were hard to see in the dark. And although there was a low wall around the outer edge, the innumerable courtyards were merely open wells to be skirted with caution. The stars gave enough light to protect her against mishaps. She breathed deeply, feeling rather as if she were on shipboard. The town below was invisible—not a light showed—but to the north glimmered the white ereg, the vast ocean of sand with its frozen swirling crests, its unmoving silence. She turned slowly about, scanning the horizon. The air, doubly still now after the departure of the wind, was like something paralyzed. Whichever way she looked, the night's landscape suggested only one thing to her: negation of movement, suspension of continuity. But as she stood there, momentarily a part of the void she had created, little by little a doubt slipped into her mind, the sensation came to her, first faint, then sure, that some part of this landscape was moving even as she looked at it. She glanced up and grimaced. The whole, monstrous star-filled sky was turning sideways before her eyes. It looked still as death, yet it moved. Every second an invisible star edged above the earth's line on that side, and another fell below on the opposite side. She coughed self-consciously, and started to walk again, trying to remember how much she disliked Captain Broussard. He had not even offered her a pack of cigarettes, in spite of her overt remark. "Oh, God," she said aloud, wishing she had not finished her last Players in Bou Noura.

He opened his eyes. The room was malignant. It was empty. "Now, at last, I must fight against this room." But later he had a moment of vertiginous clarity. He was at the edge of a realm where each thought, each image, had an arbitrary existence, where the connection between each thing and the next had been cut. As he labored to seize the essence of that kind of consciousness, he began to slip back into its precinct without suspecting that he was no longer wholly outside in the open, no longer able to consider the idea at a distance. It seemed to him that here was an untried variety of thinking, in which there was no necessity for a relationship with life. "The thought in itself," he said—a gratuitous fact, like a painting of pure design. They were coming again, they began to flash by. He tried to hold one, believed he had it. "But a thought of what? What is it?" Even then it was pushed out of the way by the others crowding behind it. While he succumbed, struggling, he opened his eyes for help. "The room! The room! Still here!" It was in the silence of the room that he now located all those hostile forces; the very fact that the room's inert watchfulness was on all sides made him distrust it. Outside himself, it was all there was. He looked at the line made by the joining of the wall and the floor, endeavored to fix it in his mind, that he might have something to hang on to when his eyes should shut. There was a terrible disparity between the speed at which he was moving and the quiet immobility of that line, but he insisted. So as not to go. To stay behind. To overflow, take root in what would stay here. A centipede can, cut into pieces. Each part can walk by itself. Still more, each leg flexes, lying alone on the floor.

There was a screaming sound in each ear, and the difference between the two pitches was so narrow that the vibration was like running his fingernail along the edge of a new dime. In front of his eyes clusters of round spots were being born; they were the little spots that result when a photographic cut in a newspaper is enlarged many times.

Lighter agglomerations, darker masses, small regions of un-inhabited space here and there. Each spot slowly took on a third dimension. He tried to recoil from the expanding glob-ules of matter. Did he cry out? Could he move?

The thin distance between the two high screams be-came narrower, they were almost one; now the difference was the edge of a razor blade, poised against the tips of each finger. The fingers were to be sliced longitudinally.

A servant traced the cries to the room where the American lay. Captain Broussard was summoned. He walked quickly to the door, pounded on it, and hearing nothing but the continued yelling within, stepped into the room. With the aid of the servant, he succeeded in holding Port still enough to give him an injection of morphine. When he had finished, he glared about the room in an access of rage. "And that woman!" he shouted. "Where in the name of God is she?"

"I don't know, my Captain," said the servant, who thought the question had been addressed to him.

"Stay here. Stand by the door," growled the captain. He was determined to find Kit, and when he found her he was going to tell her what he thought of her. If necessary, he would place a guard outside the door, and force her to stay inside to watch the patient. He went first to the main gate, which was locked at night so that no guard was nec-essary. It stood open. *"Ah, ça, par exemple!"* he cried, beside himself. He stepped outside, and saw nothing but the night. Going within, he slammed the high portal shut and bolted it savagely. Then he went back to the room and waited while the servant fetched a blanket, and instructed him to stay there until morning. He returned to his quarters and had a glass of cognac to calm his fury before trying to sleep.

As she paced back and forth on the roof, two things

happened at once. On one side the large moon swiftly rose above the edge of the plateau, and on the other, in the distant air, an almost imperceptible humming sound became audible, was lost, became audible again. She listened: now it was gone, now it was a little stronger. And so it continued for a long time, disappearing, and coming back always a bit nearer. Now, even though it was still far away, the sound was quite recognizable as that of a motor. She could hear the shifts of speed as it climbed a slope and reached level ground again. Twenty kilometers down the trail, they had told her, you can hear a truck coming. She waited. Finally, when it seemed that the vehicle must already be in the town, she saw a tiny portion of rock far out on the hammada being swept by the headlights as the truck made a curve in its descent toward the oasis. A moment later she saw the two points of light. Then they were lost for a while behind the rocks, but the motor grew ever louder. With the moon casting more light each minute, and the truck bringing people to town, even if the people were anonymous figures in white robes, the world moved back into the realm of the possible. Suddenly she wanted to be present at the arrival down in the market. She hurried below, tiptoed through the courtyards, managed to open the heavy gate, and began to run down the side of the hill toward the town. The truck was making a great racket as it went along between the high walls in the oasis; as she came opposite the mosque it nosed above the last rise on its way up into the town. There were a few ragged men standing at the entrance of the market place. When the big vehicle roared in and stopped, the silence that followed lasted only a second before the excited voices began, all at once.

She stood back and watched the laborious getting-down of the natives and the leisurely unloading of their possessions: camel saddles that shone in the moonlight, great formless bundles done up in striped blankets, coffers and sacks, and two gigantic women so fat they could barely walk, their bosoms, arms and legs weighted down with pounds of massive silver ornaments. And all these possessions, with their owners, presently disappeared behind the dark arcades and went out of hearing. She moved around so she could see the front end of the truck, where the chauffeur and mechanic and a few other men stood in the glare of the headlights talking. She heard French being spoken—bad French—as well as Arabic. The chauffeur reached in and switched off the lights; the men began to walk slowly up into the market place. No one seemed to have noticed her. She stood still a moment, listening.

She cried: "Tunner!"

One of the figures in a burnous stopped, came running back. On its way, it called: "Kit!" She ran a few steps, saw the other man turning to look, and was being smothered in Tunner's burnous as he hugged her. She thought he would never let go, but he did, and said: "So you're really here!" Two of the men had come over. "Is this the lady you were looking for?" said one. *"Oui, oui!"* Tunner cried, and they said good night.

They stood alone in the market place. "But this is wonderful, Kit!" he said. She wanted to speak, but she felt that if she tried, her words would turn to sobs, so she nodded her head and automatically began to pull him along toward the little public garden by the mosque. She felt weak; she wanted to sit down.

"My stuff is locked in the truck for the night. I didn't know where I'd be sleeping. God, what a trip from Bou Noura! Three blowouts on the way, and these monkeys think changing a tire should always take a couple of hours at least." He went into details. They had reached the entrance to the garden. The moon shone like a cold white sun; the spearlike shadows of the palm branches were black on the sand, a sharp unvaried pattern along the garden walk.

"But let's see you!" he cried, spinning her around so the moon's light struck her face. "Ah, poor Kit! It must have been hell!" he murmured, as she squinted up into the brightness, her features distorted by the imminent outbreaking of tears.

They sat on a concrete bench and she wept for a long time, her face buried in his lap, rubbing the rough wool of the burnous. From time to time he uttered consoling words, and as he found her shivering, he enveloped her in one great wing of the robe. She hated the salt sting of the tears, and even more she hated the ignominy of her being there, demanding comfort of Tunner. But she could not, could not stop; the longer she continued to sob, the more clearly she sensed that this was a situation beyond her control. She was unable to sit up, dry her tears, and make an attempt to extricate herself from the net of involvement she felt being drawn around her. She did not want to be involved again: the taste of guilt was still strong in her memory. Yet she saw nothing ahead of her but Tunner's will awaiting her signal to take command. And she would give the signal. Even as she knew this she was aware of a pervading sense of relief, to struggle against which would have been unthinkable. What a delight, not to be responsible—not to have to decide anything of what was to happen! To know, even if there was no hope, that no action one might take or fail to take could change the outcome in the slightest degree—that it was impossible to be at fault in any way, and thus impossible to feel regret, or, above all, guilt. She realized the absurdity of still hoping to attain such a state permanently, but the hope would not leave her.

The street led up a steep hill where the hot sun was shining, the sidewalks were crowded with pedestrians looking in the shop windows. He had the feeling there was traffic in the side streets, but the shadows there were dark. An attitude of expectancy was growing in the crowd; they were waiting for something. For what, he did not know. The entire afternoon was tense, poised, ready to fall. At the top of the street a huge automobile suddenly appeared, glistening in the sunlight. It came careening over the crest and down the hill, swerving savagely from one curb to the other. A great yell rose up from the crowd. He turned and frantically sought a doorway. At the corner there was a pastry shop, its windows full of cakes and meringues. He fumbled along the wall. If he could reach the door. . . . He wheeled, stood transfixed. In the tremendous flash of sunlight reflected from the glass as it splintered he saw the metal pinning him to the stone. He heard his own ridiculous cry, and felt his bowels pierced through. As he tried to topple over, to lose consciousness, he found his face a few inches from a row of pastries, still intact on their paper-covered shelf.

They were a row of mud wells in the desert. But how near were they? He could not tell: the debris had pinned him to the earth. The pain was all of existence at that moment. All the energy he could exert would not budge him from the spot where he lay impaled, his bleeding entrails open to the sky. He imagined an enemy arriving to step into his open belly. He imagined himself rising, running through the twisting alleys between the walls. For hours in all directions in the alleys, with never a door, never the final opening. It would get dark, they would be coming nearer, his breath would be failing. And when he willed it hard enough, the gate would appear, but even as he rushed panting through it, he would realize his terrible mistake.

Too late! There was only the endless black wall rising ahead of him, the rickety iron staircase he was obliged to take, knowing that above, at the top, they were waiting with the boulder poised, ready to hurl it when he came near enough. And as he got close to the top it would come hurtling down at him, striking him with the weight of the entire world. He cried out again as it hit, holding his hands over his abdomen to protect the gaping hole there. He ceased imagining and lay still beneath the rubble. The pain could not go on. He opened his eyes, shut his eyes, saw only the thin sky stretched across to protect him. Slowly the split would occur, the sky draw back, and he would see what he never had doubted lay behind advance upon him with the speed of a million winds. His cry was a separate thing beside him in the desert. It went on and on.

The moon had reached the center of the sky when they arrived at the fort and found the gate locked. Holding Tunner's hand, Kit looked up at him. "What'll we do?"

He hesitated, and pointed to the mountain of sand above the fort. They climbed slowly upward along the dunes. The cold sand filled their shoes: they took them off and continued. Up here the brightness was intense; each grain of sand sent out a fragment of the polar light shed from above. They could not walk side by side—the ridge of the highest dune was too steep. Tunner draped his burnous around Kit's shoulders and went ahead. The crest was infinitely higher and further away than they had imagined. When finally they climbed atop it, the ereg sat with its sea of motionless waves lay all about them. They did not stop to look: absolute silence is too powerful once one has trusted oneself to it for an instant, its spell too difficult to break.

"Down here!" said Tunner.

They let themselves slide forward into a great moonlit cup. Kit rolled over and the burnous slipped off; he had to dig into the sand and climb back after it. He tried to fold it and throw it down at her playfully, but it fell halfway. She let herself roll to the bottom and lay there waiting. When he came down he spread the wide white garment out on the sand. They stretched out on it side by side and pulled the edges up around them. What conversation had eventually taken place down in the garden had centered about Port. Now Tunner looked at the moon. He took her hand.

"Do you remember our night on the train?" he said. As she did not reply, he feared he had made a tactical error, and went on quickly: "I don't think a drop of rain has fallen since that night, anywhere on the whole damned continent."

Still Kit made no answer. His mention of the night ride to Boussif had evoked the wrong memories. She saw the dim lamps swinging, smelled the coal gas, and heard the rain on the windows. She remembered the confused horror of the freight car full of natives; her mind refused to continue further.

"Kit. What's the matter?"

"Nothing. You know how I am. Really, nothing's wrong." She pressed his hand.

His voice became faintly paternal. "He's going to be all right, Kit. Only some of it's up to you, you know. You've got to keep in good shape to take care of him. Can't you see that? And how can you take care of him if you get sick?"

"I know, I know," she said.

"Then I'd have two patients on my hands—"

She sat up. "What hypocrites we are, both of us!" she cried. "You know damned well I haven't been near him for hours. How do we know he's not already dead? He could die there all alone! We'd never know. Who could stop him?"

He caught her arm, held it firmly. "Now, wait a minute, will you? Just for the record, I want to ask you: who could stop him even if we were both there beside him? Who?" He paused. "If you're going to take the worst possible view of everything, you might as well follow it through with a little logic at least, girl. But he's not going to die. You shouldn't even think of it. It's crazy." He shook her arm slowly, as one does to awaken a person from a deep sleep. "Just be sensible. You can't get in to him until morning. So relax. Try and get a little rest. Come on."

As he coaxed, she suddenly burst into tears once again, throwing both arms around him desperately. "Oh, Tunner! I love him so much!" she sobbed, clinging ever more tightly. "I love him! I love him!"

In the moonlight he smiled.

His cry went on through the final image: the spots of raw bright blood on the earth. Blood on excrement. The supreme moment, high above the desert, when the two elements, blood and excrement, long kept apart, merge. A black star appears, a point of darkness in the night sky's clarity. Point of darkness and gateway to repose. Reach out, pierce the fine fabric of the sheltering sky, take repose.

24

She opened the door. Port lay in a strange position, his legs wound tightly in the bedcovers. That corner of the room was like a still photograph suddenly flashed on the screen in the middle of the stream of moving images. She shut the door softly, locked it, turned again toward the corner, and walked slowly over to the mattress. She held her breath, bent over, and looked into the meaningless eyes. But already she knew, even to the convulsive lowering of her hand to the bare chest, even without the violent push she gave the inert torso immediately afterward. As her hands went to her own face, she cried: "No!" once—no more. She stood perfectly still for a long, long time, her head raised, facing the wall. Nothing moved inside her; she was conscious of nothing outside or in. If Zina had come to the door it is doubtful whether she would have heard the knock. But no one came. Below in the town a caravan setting out for Atar left the market place, swayed through the oasis, the camels grumbling, the bearded black men silent as they walked along thinking of the twenty days and nights that lay ahead, before the walls of Atar would rise above the rocks. A few hundred feet away in his bedroom Captain Broussard read an entire short story in a magazine that had arrived that morning in his mail, brought by last night's truck. In the room, however, nothing happened.

Much later in the morning, probably out of sheer fatigue, she began to walk in a small orbit in the middle of the room, a few steps one way and a few the other. A loud knock on the door interrupted this. She stood still, staring toward the door. The knock was repeated. Tunner's voice, carefully lowered, said: "Kit?" Again her hands rose to cover her face, and she remained standing that way during the rest of the time he stayed outside the door, now rapping softly, now faster and nervously, now pounding violently. When there was no more sound, she sat down on her pallet for a while, presently lying out flat with her head on the pillow as if to sleep. But her eyes remained open, staring upward almost as fixedly as those beside her. These were the first moments of a new existence, a strange one in which she already glimpsed the element of timelessness that would surround her. The person who frantically has been counting the seconds on his way to catch a train, and arrives panting just as it disappears, knowing the next one is not due for many hours, feels something of the same sudden surfeit of time, the momentary sensation of drowning in an element become too rich and too plentiful to be consumed, and thereby made meaningless, nonexistent. As the minutes went by, she felt no impulse to move; no thought wandered near her. Now she did not remember their many conversations built around the idea of death, perhaps because no idea about death has anything in common with the presence of death. She did not recall how they had agreed that one can *be* anything but *dead,* that the two words together created an antinomy. Nor did it occur to her how she once had thought that if Port should die before she did, she would not really believe he was dead, but rather that he had in some way gone back inside himself to stay there, and that he never would be conscious of her again; so that in reality it would be she who would have ceased to exist, at least to a great degree. She would be the one who had entered partially into the realm of death, while he would go on, an anguish inside her, a door left unopened, a chance irretrievably lost. She had quite forgotten the August afternoon only a little more than a year ago, when they had sat alone out on the grass beneath the maples, watching the thunderstorm sweep up the river valley toward them, and death had become the topic. And Port had said: "Death is always on the way, but the fact that you don't know when it will arrive seems to take away from the finiteness of life. It's that terrible precision that we hate so much. But because we don't know, we get to think of life as an inexhaustible well. Yet everything happens only a certain number of times, and a very small number, really. How many more times will you remember a certain afternoon of your childhood, some afternoon that's so deeply a part of your being that you can't even conceive of your life without it? Perhaps four or five times more. Perhaps not even that. How many more times will you watch the full moon rise? Perhaps twenty. And yet it all seems limitless." She had not listened at the time because the idea had depressed her; now if she had called it to mind it would have seemed beside the point. She was incapable now of thinking about death, and since death was there beside her, she thought of nothing at all.

And yet, deeper than the empty region which was her

consciousness, in an obscure and innermost part of her mind, an idea must already have been in gestation, since when in the late afternoon Tunner came again and hammered on the door, she got up, and standing with her hand on the knob, spoke: "Is that you, Tunner?"

"For God's sake, where were you this morning?" he cried.

"I'll see you tonight about eight in the garden," she said, speaking as low as possible.

"Is he all right?"

"Yes. He's the same."

"Good. See you at eight." He went away.

She glanced at her watch: it was quarter of five. Going to her overnight bag, she set to work removing all the fittings; one by one, brushes, bottles and manicuring implements were laid on the floor. With an air of extreme preoccupation she emptied her other valises, choosing here and there a garment or object which she carefully packed into the small bag. Occasionally she stopped moving and listened: the only sound she could hear was her own measured breathing. Each time she listened she seemed reassured, straightway resuming her deliberate movements. In the flaps at the sides of the bag she put her passport, her express checks and what money she had. Soon she went to Port's luggage and searched awhile among the clothing there, returning to her little case with a good many more thousand-franc notes which she stuffed in wherever she could.

The packing of the bag took nearly an hour. When she had finished, she closed it, spun the combination lock, and went to the door. She hesitated a second before turning the key. The door open, the key in her hand, she stepped out into the courtyard with the bag and locked the door after her. She went to the kitchen, where she found the boy who tended the lamps sitting in a corner smoking.

"Can you do an errand for me?" she said.

He jumped to his feet smiling. She handed him the bag and told him to take it to Daoud Zozeph's shop and leave it, saying it was from the American lady.

Back in the room she again locked the door behind her and went over to the little window. With a single motion she ripped away the sheet that covered it. The wall outside was turning pink as the sun dropped lower in the sky; the pinkness filled the room. During all the time she had been moving about packing she had not once glanced downward at the corner. Now she knelt and looked closely at Port's face as if she had never seen it before. Scarcely touching the skin, she moved her hand along the forehead with infinite delicacy. She bent over further and placed her lips on the smooth brow. For a while she remained thus. The room grew red. Softly she laid her cheek on the pillow and stroked his hair. No tears flowed; it was a silent leave-taking. A strangely intense buzzing in front of her made her open her eyes. She watched fascinated while two flies made their brief, frantic love on his lower lip.

Then she rose, put on her coat, took the burnous which Tunner had left with her, and without looking back went out the door. She locked it behind her and put the key into her handbag. At the big gate the guard made as if to stop her. She said good evening to him and pushed by. Immediately afterward she heard him call to another in an inner room nearby. She breathed deeply and walked ahead, down toward the town. The sun had set; the earth was like a single ember alone on the hearth, rapidly cooling and growing black. A drum beat in the oasis. There would probably be dancing in the gardens later. The season of feasts had begun. Quickly she descended the hill and went straight to Daoud Zozeph's shop without once looking around.

She went in. Daoud Zozeph stood behind the counter in the fading light. He reached across and shook her hand.

"Good evening, madame."

"Good evening."

"Your valise is here. Shall I call a boy to carry it for you?"

"No, no," she said. "At least, not now. I came to talk to you." She glanced around at the doorway behind her; he did not notice.

"I am delighted," he said. "One moment. I shall get you a chair, madame." He brought a small folding chair around from behind the counter and placed it beside her.

"Thank you," she said, but she remained standing. "I wanted to ask you about trucks leaving Sbâ."

"Ah, for El Ga'a. We have no regular service. One came last night and left again this afternoon. We never know when the next will come. But Captain Broussard is always notified at least a day in advance. He could tell you better than anyone else."

"Captain Broussard. Ah, I see."

"And your husband. Is he better? Did he enjoy the milk?"

"The milk. Yes, he enjoyed it," she said slowly, wondering a little that the words could sound so natural.

"I hope he will soon be well."

"He is already well."

"Ah, *hamdoul'lah!*"

"Yes." And starting afresh, she said: "Monsieur Daoud Zozeph, I have a favor to ask of you."

"Your favor is granted, madame," he said gallantly. She felt that he had bowed in the darkness.

"A great favor," she warned.

Daoud Zozeph, thinking that perhaps she wanted to borrow money, began to rattle objects on the counter, saying: "But we are talking in the dark. Wait. I shall light a lamp."

"No! Please!" exclaimed Kit.

"But we don't see each other!" he protested.

She put her hand on his arm. "I know, but don't light the lamp, please. I want to ask you this favor immediately. May I spend the night with you and your wife?"

Daoud Zozeph was completely taken aback—both astonished and relieved. "Tonight?" he said.

"Yes."

There was a short silence.

"You understand, madame, we should be honored to have you in our house. But you would not be comfortable. You know, a house of poor people is not like a hotel or a poste militaire. . . ."

"But since I ask you," she said reproachfully, "that means I don't care. You think that matters to me? I have been sleeping on the floor here in Sbâ."

"Ah, that you would not have to do in my house," said Daoud Zozeph energetically.

"But I should be delighted to sleep on the floor. Anywhere. It doesn't matter."

"Ah, no! No, madame! Not on the floor! *Quand-même!*" he objected. And as he struck a match to light the lamp, she touched his arm again.

"*Ecoutez, monsieur,*" she said, her voice sinking to a conspiratorial whisper, "my husband is looking for me, and I don't want him to find me. We have had a misunderstanding. I don't want to see him tonight. It's very simple. I think your wife would understand."

Daoud Zozeph laughed. "Of course! Of course!" Still laughing, he closed the door into the street, bolted it, and struck a match, holding it high in the air. Lighting matches all the way, he led her through a dark inner room and across a small court. The stars were above. He paused in front of a door. "You can sleep here." He opened the door and stepped inside. Again a match flared: she saw a tiny room in disorder, its sagging iron bed covered with a mattress that vomited excelsior.

"This is not your room, I hope?" she ventured, as the match went out.

"Ah, no! We have another bed in our room, my wife and I," he answered, a note of pride in his voice. "This is where my brother sleeps when he comes from Colomb-Béchar. Once a year he visits me for a month, sometimes longer. Wait. I shall bring a lamp." He went off, and she heard him talking in another room. Presently he returned with an oil lamp and a small tin pail of water.

With the arrival of the light, the room took on an even more piteous aspect. She had the feeling that the floor had never yet been swept since the day the mason had finished piling the mud on the walls, the ubiquitous mud that dried, crumbled, and fell in a fine powder day and night. . . . She glanced up at him and smiled.

"My wife wants to know if you like noodles," said Daoud Zozeph.

"Yes, of course," she answered, trying to look into the peeling mirror over the washstand. She could see nothing at all.

"*Bien*. You know, my wife speaks no French."

"Really. You will have to be my interpreter."

There was a dull knocking, out in the shop. Daoud Zozeph excused himself and crossed the court. She shut the door, found there was no key, stood there waiting. It would have been so easy for one of the guards at the fort to follow her. But she doubted that they had thought of it in time. She sat down on the outrageous bed and stared at the wall opposite. The lamp sent up a column of acrid smoke.

The evening meal at Daoud Zozeph's was unbelievably bad. She forced down the amorphous lumps of dough fried in deep fat and served cold, the pieces of cartilaginous meat, and the soggy bread, murmuring vague compliments which were warmly received, but which led her hosts to press more of the food upon her. Several times during the meal she glanced at her watch. Tunner would be waiting in the public garden now, and when he left there he would go up to the fort. At that moment the trouble would begin; Daoud Zozeph could not help hearing of it tomorrow from his customers.

Madame Daoud Zozeph gestured vigorously for Kit to continue eating; her bright eyes were fixed on her guest's plate. Kit looked across at her and smiled.

"Tell madame that because I am a little upset now I am not very hungry," she said to Daoud Zozeph, "but that I should like to have something in my room to eat later. Some bread would be perfect."

"But of course. Of course," he said.

When she had gone to her room, Madame Daoud Zozeph brought her a plate piled high with pieces of bread. She thanked her and said good night, but her hostess was not inclined to leave, making it clear that she was interested in seeing the interior of the traveling case. Kit was determined not to open it in front of her; the thousand-franc notes would quickly become a legend in Sbâ. She pretended not to understand, patted the case, nodded and laughed. Then she turned again toward the plate of bread and repeated her thanks. But Madame Daoud Zozeph's eyes did not leave the valise. There was a screeching and fluttering of wings outside in the court. Daoud Zozeph appeared carrying a fat hen, which he set down in the middle of the floor.

"Against the vermin," he explained, pointing at the hen.

"Vermin?" echoed Kit.

"If a scorpion shows its head anywhere along the floor—tac! She eats it!"

"Ah!" She fabricated a yawn.

"I know madame is nervous. With our friend here she will feel better."

"This evening," she said, "I am so sleepy that nothing could make me nervous."

They shook hands solemnly. Daoud Zozeph pushed his wife out of the room and shut the door. The hen scratched a minute in the dust, then scrambled up onto the rung of the washstand and remained motionless. Kit sat on the bed looking into the uneven flame of the lamp; the room was full of its smoke. She felt no anxiety—only an overwhelming impatience to put all this ludicrous décor behind her, out of her consciousness. Rising, she stood with her ear against the door. She heard the sound of voices, now and then a distant thud. She put on her coat, filled the pockets with pieces of bread, and sat down again to wait.

From time to time she sighed deeply. Once she got up to turn down the wick of the lamp. When her watch said ten o'clock, she went again to the door and listened. She opened it: the court glowed with reflected moonlight. Stepping back inside, she picked up Tunner's burnous and flung it under the bed. The resultant swirl of dust almost made her sneeze. She took her handbag and the valise and went out, taking care to shut the door after her. On her way through the inner room of the shop she stumbled over something and nearly lost her balance. Going more slowly, she moved ahead into the shop, around the end of the counter, feeling lightly along its top with the fingers of her left hand as she went. The door had a simple bolt which she drew back with difficulty; eventually it made a heavy metallic noise. Quickly she swung the door open and went out.

The light of the moon was violent—walking along the white street in it was like being in the sunlight. "Anyone could see me." But there was no one. She walked straight to the edge of town, where the oasis straggled over into the courtyards of the houses. Below, in the wide black mass formed by the tops of the palms, the drums were still going. The sound came from the direction of the ksar, the Negro village in the middle of the oasis.

She turned into a long, straight alley bordered by high walls. On the other side of them the palms rustled and the running water gurgled. Occasionally there was a white pile of dried palm branches stacked against the wall; each time she thought it was a man sitting in the moonlight. The alley swerved toward the sound of the drums, and she came out upon a square, full of little channels and aqueducts running paradoxically in all directions; it looked like a very complex toy railway. Several walks led off into the oasis from here. She chose the narrowest, which she thought might skirt the ksar rather than lead to it, and went on ahead between the walls. The path turned this way and that.

The sound of the drums was louder: now she could hear voices repeating a rhythmical refrain, always the same.

They were men's voices, and there seemed to be a great many of them. Sometimes, when she reached the heavy shadows, she stopped and listened, an inscrutable smile on her lips.

The little bag was growing heavy. More and more frequently she shifted it from one hand to the other. But she did not want to stop and rest. At each instant she was ready to turn around and go back to look for another alley, in case she should come out all at once from between the walls into the middle of the ksar. The music seemed quite nearby at times, but it was hard to tell with all the twisting walls and trees in between. Occasionally it sounded almost at hand, as if only a wall and a few hundred feet of garden separated her from it, and then it retreated into the distance and was nearly covered by the dry sound of the wind blowing through the palm leaves.

And the liquid sound of the rivulets on all sides had their effect without her knowing it: she suddenly felt dry. The cool moonlight and the softly moving shadows through which she passed did much to dispel the sensation, but it seemed to her that she would be completely content only if she could have water all around her. All at once she was looking through a wide break in the wall into a garden; the graceful palm trunks rose high into the air from the sides of a wide pool. She stood staring at the calm dark surface of water; straightway she found it impossible to know whether she had thought of bathing just before or just after seeing the pool. Whichever it was, there was the pool. She reached through the aperture in the crumbling wall and set down her bag before climbing across the pile of dirt that lay in her way. Once in the garden she found herself pulling off her clothes. She felt a vague surprise that her actions should go on so far ahead of her consciousness of them.

Every movement she made seemed the perfect expression of lightness and grace. "Look out," said a part of her. "Go carefully." But it was the same part of her that sent out the warning when she was drinking too much. At this point it was meaningless. "Habit," she thought. "Whenever I'm about to be happy I hang on instead of letting go." She kicked off her sandals and stood naked in the shadows. She felt a strange intensity being born within her. As she looked about the quiet garden she had the impression that for the first time since her childhood she was seeing objects clearly. Life was suddenly there, she was in it, not looking through the window at it. The dignity that came from feeling a part of its power and grandeur, that was a familiar sensation, but it was years ago that she had last known it. She stepped out into the moonlight and waded slowly toward the center of the pool. Its floor was slippery with clay; in the middle the water came to her waist. As she immersed herself completely, the thought came to her: "I shall never be hysterical again." That kind of tension, that degree of caring about herself, she felt she would never attain them any more in her life.

She bathed lengthily; the cool water on her skin awakened an impulse to sing. Each time she bent to get water between her cupped palms she uttered a burst of wordless song. Suddenly she stopped and listened. She no longer heard the drums—only the drops of water falling from her body into the pool. She finished her bath in silence, her excess of high spirits gone; but life did not recede from her. "It's here to stay," she murmured aloud, as she walked toward the bank. She used her coat as a towel, hopping up and down with cold as she dried herself. While she dressed she whistled under her breath. Every so often she stopped and listened for a second, to see if she could hear the sound of voices, or the drums starting up again. The wind came by, up there above her head, in the tops of the trees, and there was the faint trickle of water somewhere nearby. Nothing more. All at once she was seized with the suspicion that something had happened behind her back, that time had played a trick on her: she had spent hours in the pool instead of minutes, and never realized it. The festivities in the ksar had come to an end, the people had dispersed, and she had not even been conscious of the cessation of the drums. Absurd things like that did happen, sometimes. She bent to take her wrist watch from the stone where she had laid it. It was not there; she could not verify the hour. She searched a bit, already convinced that she would never find it: its disappearance was a part of the trick. She walked lightly over to the wall and picked up her valise, flung her coat over her arm, and said aloud to the garden: "You think it matters to me?" And she laughed before climbing back across the broken wall.

Swiftly she walked along, focusing her mind on that feeling of solid delight she had recaptured. She had always known it was there, just behind things, but long ago she had accepted not having it as a natural condition of life. Because she had found it again, the joy of being, she said to herself that she would hang on to it no matter what the effort entailed. She pulled a piece of bread from the pocket of her coat and ate it voraciously.

The alley grew wide, its wall receding to follow the line of vegetation. She had reached the oued, at this point a flat open valley dotted with small dunes. Here and there a weeping tamarisk tree lay like a mass of gray smoke along the sand. Without hesitating she made for the nearest tree and set her bag down. The feathery branches swept the sand on all sides of the trunk—it was like a tent. She put on her coat, crawled in, and pulled the valise in after her. In no time at all she was asleep.

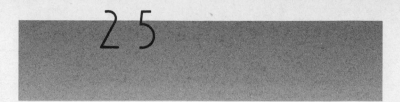

25

Lieutenant d'Armagnac stood in his garden supervising Ahmed and several native masons in the work of topping the high enclosing wall with a crown of broken glass. A hundred times his wife had suggested this added protection for their dwelling, and he like a good colonial had promised but not performed; now that she was returning from France he would have it ready for her as one more pleasant surprise. Everything was going well: the baby was healthy, Mme. d'Armagnac was happy, and he would go up to Algiers at the end of the month to meet them. At the same time they would spend a happy few days in some good little hotel there—a sort of second honeymoon—before returning to Bou Noura.

It was true that things were going well only in his own little cosmos; he pitied Captain Broussard down in Sbâ and thought with an inward shudder that but for the grace of God all that trouble would have fallen upon him. He had even urged the travelers to stay on in Bou Noura; at least he was able to feel blameless on that score. He had not known the American was ill, so that it was not his fault the man had gone on and died in Broussard's territory. But of course death from typhoid was one thing and the disappearance of a white woman into the desert was another; it was the latter which was making all the trouble. The terrain around Sbâ was not favorable to the success of searching parties conducted in jeeps; besides, there were only two such vehicles in the region, and the expeditions had not been inaugurated immediately because of the more pressing business of the dead American at the fort. And everyone had imagined that she would be found somewhere in the town. He regretted not having met the wife. She sounded amusing—a typical, high-spirited American girl. Only an American could do anything so unheard-of as to lock her sick husband into a room and run off into the desert, leaving him behind to die alone. It was inexcusable, of course, but he could not be really horrified at the idea, as it seemed Broussard was. But Broussard was a puritan. He was easily scandalized, and unpleasantly irreproachable in his own behavior. He had probably hated the girl because she was attractive and had disturbed his poise; that would be difficult for Broussard to forgive.

He wished again that he could have seen the girl before she had so successfully vanished from the face of the earth. At the same time he felt mixed emotions regarding the recent return of the third American to Bou Noura: he liked the man personally, but he hoped to avoid involvement in the affair, he wanted no part of it. Above all he prayed that the wife would not turn up in his territory, now that she was practically a cause célèbre. There was the likelihood that she, too, would be ill, and the curiosity he felt to see her was outweighed by the dreaded prospect of complications in his work and reports to be made out. *"Pourvu qu'ils la trouvent là-bas!"* he thought ardently.

There was a knock at the gate. Ahmed swung it open. The American stood there; he came each day in the hope of getting news, and each day he looked more despondent at hearing that none had been received. "I knew the other one was having trouble with his wife, and *this* was the trouble," said the lieutenant to himself when he glanced up and saw Tunner's unhappy face.

"Bonjour, monsieur," he said jovially, advancing upon his guest. "Same news as always. But that can't continue forever."

Tunner greeted him, nodding his head understandingly on hearing what he had expected to hear. The lieutenant allowed the intervention of a silence proper to the occasion, then he suggested that they repair to the salon for their usual cognac. In the short while he had been waiting here at Bou Noura, Tunner had come to rely on these morning visits to the lieutenant's house as a necessary stimulus for his morale. The lieutenant was sanguine by nature, his conversation was light and his choice of words such that he was easily understandable. It was agreeable to sit in the bright salon, and the cognac fused these elements into a pleasant experience whose regular recurrence prevented his spirits from sinking all the way into the well of despair.

His host called to Ahmed, and led the way into the house. They sat facing each other.

"Two weeks more and I shall be a married man again," said the lieutenant, beaming at him, and thinking that perhaps he might yet show the Ouled Naïl girls to an American.

"Very good, very good." Tunner was distraught. God help poor Madame d'Armagnac, he thought gloomily, if she had to spend the rest of her life here. Since Port's death and Kit's disappearance he hated the desert: in an obscure fashion he felt that it had deprived him of his friends. It was too powerful an entity not to lend itself to personification. The desert—its very silence was like a tacit admission of the half-conscious presence it harbored. (Captain Broussard had told him, one night when he was in a talkative mood, that even the Frenchmen who accompanied the peloton into the wilderness there managed to see djnoun, even though out of pride they refused to believe in them.) And what did this mean, save that such things were the imagination's simple way of interpreting that presence?

Ahmed brought in the bottle and the glasses. They drank for a moment in silence; then the lieutenant remarked, as much to break the silence as for any other reason: "Ah, yes. Life is amazing. Nothing ever happens the way one imagines it is going to. One realizes that most clearly here; all your philosophic systems crumble. At every turn one finds the unexpected. When your friend came here without his passport and accused poor Abdelkader, who ever would have thought that this short time later such a thing would have happened to him?" Then, thinking that his sequence of logic might be misinterpreted, he added: "Abdelkader was very sorry to hear of his death. He bore him no grudge, you know."

Tunner seemed not to be listening. The lieutenant's mind ambled off in another direction. "Tell me," he said, curiosity coloring his voice, "did you ever manage to convince Captain Broussard that his suspicions about the lady were unfounded? Or does he still think they were not married? In his letter to me he said some very unkind things about her. You showed him Monsieur Moresby's passport?"

"What?" said Tunner, knowing he was going to have trouble with his French. "Oh, yes. I gave it to him to send to the Consul in Algiers with his report. But he never believed they were married, because Mrs. Moresby promised to give him her passport, and in place of that, ran away. So he had no idea who she really was."

"But they were husband and wife," pursued the lieutenant softly.

"Of course. Of course," said Tunner with impatience, feeling that for him even to engage in such a conversation was disloyal.

"And even if they had not been, what difference?" He poured them each another drink, and seeing that his guest was disinclined to continue that conversation, he went on to another which might be less painful in its associations. Tunner, however, followed the new one with almost as little enthusiasm. At the back of his mind he kept reliving the day of the burial in Sbâ. Port's death had been the only truly unacceptable fact in his life. Even now he knew that he had lost a great deal, that Port really had been his closest friend (how had he failed to recognize that before?), but he felt that it would be only later, when he had come to the full acceptance of the fact of his death, that he would be able to begin reckoning his loss in detail.

Tunner was sentimental, and in accordance with this trait, his conscience troubled him for not having offered more vigorous opposition to Captain Broussard's insistence upon a certain amount of religious ceremony during the burial. He had the feeling that he had been cowardly about it; he was certain that Port would have despised the inclusion of such nonsense on that occasion and would have relied upon his friend to see that it was not carried through. To be sure, he had protested beforehand that Port was not a Catholic—was not even, strictly speaking, a Christian, and consequently had the right to be spared such goings-on at his own funeral. But Captain Broussard had replied with heat: "I have only your word for all this, monsieur. And you were not with him when he died. You have no idea what his last thoughts were, what his final wishes may have been. Even if you were willing to take upon yourself such an enormous responsibility as to pretend to know such a thing, I could not let you do it. I am a Catholic, monsieur, and I am also in command here." And Tunner had given in. So that instead of being buried anonymously and in silence out on the hammada or in the ereg, where surely he would have wished to be put, Port had been laid to rest officially in the tiny Christian cemetery behind the fort, while phrases in Latin were spoken. To Tunner's sentimental mind it had seemed grossly unfair, but he had seen no way of preventing it. Now he felt that he had been weak and somehow unfaithful. At night when he lay awake thinking about it, it had even occurred to him that he might go all the way back to Sbâ and, waiting for the right moment, break into the cemetery and destroy the absurd little cross they had put over the grave. It was the sort of gesture which would have made him happier, but he knew he never would make it.

Instead, he told himself, he would be practical, and the important thing now was to find Kit and get her back to New York. In the beginning he had felt that in some way the whole business of her vanishing was a nightmarish practical joke, that at the end of a week or so she would surely have reappeared, just as she had on the train ride to Boussif. And so he had determined to wait until she did. Now that time had elapsed and there was still no sign of her, he understood that he would wait much longer—indefinitely if necessary.

He put his glass on the coffee table beside him. Giving

voice to his thoughts, he said: "I'm going to stay here until Mrs. Moresby is found." And he asked himself why he was being so stubborn about it, why Kit's return obsessed him so utterly. Assuredly he was not in love with the poor girl. His overtures to her had been made out of pity (because she was a woman) and out of vanity (because he was a man), and the two feelings together had awakened the acquisitive desire of the trophy collector, nothing more. In fact, at this point, he realized that unless he thought carefully he was inclined to pass over the entire episode of intimacy between them, and to consider Kit purely in terms of their first meeting, when she and Port had impressed him so deeply as being the two people in the world he had wanted to know. It was less of a strain on his conscience that way; for more than once he had asked himself what had happened that crazy day at Sbâ when she had refused to open the door of the sick chamber, and whether or not she had told Port of her infidelity. Fervently he hoped not; he did not want to think of it.

"Yes," said Lieutenant d'Armagnac. "You can't very well go back to New York and have all your friends ask: 'What have you done with Mrs. Moresby?' That would be very embarrassing."

Inwardly Tunner winced. He definitely could not. Those who knew the two families might already be asking it of each other (since he had sent Port's mother both items of unfortunate news in two cables separated in time by three days, in the hope that Kit would turn up), but they were there and he was here, and he did not have to face them when they said: "So both Port and Kit are gone!" It was the sort of thing that never did, couldn't, happen, and if he remained here in Bou Noura long enough he knew she would be unearthed.

"Very embarrassing," he agreed, laughing uncomfortably. Even Port's death by itself would be difficult enough to account for. There would be those who would say: "For God's sake, couldn't you have gotten him into a plane and up to a hospital somewhere, at least as far as Algiers? Typhoid's not that quick, you know." And he would have to admit that he had left them and gone off by himself, that he hadn't been able to "take" the desert. Still, he could envisage all that without too much misery; Port had neglected to be immunized against any sort of disease before leaving. But to go back leaving Kit lost was unthinkable from every point of view.

"Of course," ventured the lieutenant, again remembering the possible complications should the lost American lady turn up in anything but perfect condition, and then be moved to Bou Noura because of Tunner's presence there, "your staying or not staying will have nothing to do with her being found." He felt ashamed as soon as he heard the words come out of his mouth, but it was too late; they had been spoken.

"I know, I know," said Tunner vehemently. "But I'm going to stay." There was no more to be said about it; Lieutenant d'Armagnac would not raise the question again.

They talked on a little while. The lieutenant brought up the possibility of a visit some evening to the quartier réservé. "One of these days," said Tunner dispassionately.

"You need a little relaxation. Too much brooding is bad. I know just the girl—" He stopped, remembering from experience that explicit suggestions of that nature generally destroy the very interest they are meant to arouse. No hunter wants his prey chosen and run to earth for him, even if it means the only assurance of a kill.

"Good. Good," said Tunner absently.

Soon he rose and took his leave. He would return tomorrow morning and the next, and every morning after that, until one day Lieutenant D'Armagnac would meet him at the door with a new light in his eyes, and say to him: "*Enfin, mon ami!* Good news at last!"

In the garden he looked down at the bare, baked earth. The huge red ants were rushing along the ground waving their front legs and mandibles belligerently in the air. Ahmed shut the gate behind him, and he walked moodily back to the pension.

He would have his lunch in the hot little dining room next to the kitchen, making the meal more digestible by drinking a whole bottle of vin rosé. Then stupefied by the wine and the heat he would go upstairs to his room, undress, and throw himself on his bed, to sleep until the sun's rays were more oblique and the countryside had lost some of the poisonous light that came out of its stones that midday. Walks to towns round about were pleasant: there were bright Igherm on the hill, the larger community of Beni Isguen down the valley, Tadjmout with its terraced pink and blue houses, and there was always the vast palmeraie where the town dwellers had built their toylike country palaces of red mud and pale palm thatch, where the creak of the wells was constant, and the sound of the water gurgling in the narrow aqueducts belied the awful dryness of the earth and air. Sometimes he would merely walk to the great market place in Bou Noura itself, and sit along the side under the arcades, following the progress of some interminable purchase; both buyer and seller employed every histrionic device short of actual tears, in their struggle to lower and raise the price. There were days when he felt contempt for these absurd people; they were unreal, not to be counted seriously among the earth's inhabitants. These were the same days he was so infuriated by the soft hands of the little children when they unconsciously clutched at his clothing and pushed against him in a street full of people. At first he had thought they were pickpockets, and then he had realized they were merely using him for leverage to propel themselves along more quickly in the crowd, as if he had been a tree or a wall. He was even more annoyed then, and pushed them away violently; there was not one among them who was free of scrofula, and most were completely bald, their dark skulls covered with a crust of sores and an outer layer of flies.

But there were other days when he felt less nervous, sat watching the calm old men walk slowly through the market, and said to himself that if he could muster that much dignity when he got to be their age he would consider that his life had been well spent. For their mien was merely a natural concomitant of inner well-being and satisfaction. Without thinking too much about it, eventually he came to the conclusion that their lives must have been worth living.

In the evenings he sat in the salon playing chess with Abdelkader, a slow-moving but by no means negligible adversary. The two had become firm friends as a result of these nightly sessions. When the boys had put out all the lamps and lanterns of the establishment except the one in the corner where they sat at the chessboard, and they were the only two left awake, they would sometimes have a Pernod together, Abdelkader smiling like a conspirator afterward as he got up to wash the glasses himself and put them away; it would never do for anyone to know he had taken a drink of something alcoholic. Tunner would go off up to bed and sleep heavily. He would awaken at sunrise thinking: "Perhaps today—" and by eight he would be on the roof in shorts taking a sunbath; he had his breakfast brought up there each day and drank his coffee while studying French verbs. Then the itch for news would grow too strong; he would have to go and make his morning inquiry.

The inevitable happened: after having made innumerable sidetrips from Messad the Lyles came to Bou Noura. Earlier in the same day a party of Frenchmen had arrived in an old command car and taken rooms at the pension. Tunner was at lunch when he heard the familiar roar of the Mercedes. He grimaced: it would be a bore to have those two around the place. He was not in a mood to force himself to politeness. With the Lyles he had never established any more than a passing acquaintanceship, partly because they had left Messad only two days after taking him there, and partly because he had no desire to push the relationship any further than it had gone. Mrs. Lyle was a sour, fat, gabby female, and Eric her spoiled sissy brat grown up; those were his sentiments, and he did not think he would change them. He had not connected Eric with the episode of the passports; he supposed they had been stolen simultaneously in the Aïn Krorfa hotel by some native who had connections with the shady elements that pandered to the Legionnaires in Messad.

Now in the hall he heard Eric say in a hushed voice: "Oh, I say, Mother, what next? That Tunner person is still mucking about here." Evidently he was looking at the room slate over the desk. And in a stage whisper she admonished him: "Eric! You fool! Shut up!" He drank his coffee and went out the side door into the stifling sunlight, hoping to avoid them and get up to his rooms while they were having lunch. This he accomplished. In the middle of his siesta there was a knock on the door. It took him a while to get awake. When he opened, Abdelkader stood outside, an apologetic smile on his face.

"Would it disturb you very much to change your room?" he asked.

Tunner wanted to know why.

"The only rooms free now are the two on each side of you. An English lady has arrived with her son, and she wants him in the room next to her. She's afraid to be alone."

This picture of Mrs. Lyle, drawn by Abdelkader, did not coincide with his own conception of her. "All right," he grumbled. "One room's like another. Send the boys up to move me." Abdelkader patted him on the shoulder with an affectionate gesture. The boys arrived, opened the door between his room and the next, and began to effect the change. In the middle of the moving Eric stepped into the room that was being vacated. He stopped short on catching sight of Tunner.

"Aha!" he exclaimed. "Fancy bumping into you, old man! I expected you'd be down in Timbuctoo by now."

Tunner said: "Hello, Lyle." Now that he was face to face with Eric, he could hardly bring himself to look at him or touch his hand. He had not realized the boy disgusted him so deeply.

"Do forgive this silly whim of Mother's. She's just exhausted from the trip. It's a ghastly lap from Messad here, and she's in a fearful state of nerves."

"That's too bad."

"You understand our putting you out."

"Yes, yes," said Tunner, angry to hear it phrased this way. "When you leave I'll move back in."

"Oh, quite. Have you heard from the Moresbys recently?"

Eric, when he looked at all into the face of the person with whom he was speaking, had a habit of peering closely, as if he placed very little importance on the words that were said, and was trying instead to read between the lines of the conversation, to discover what the other really meant. It seemed to Tunner now that he was observing him with more than a usual degree of attention.

"Yes," said Tunner forcefully. "They're fine. Excuse me. I think I'll go and finish the nap I was taking." Stepping through the connecting door he went into the next room. When the boys had carried everything in there he locked the door and lay on the bed, but he could not sleep.

"God, what a slob!" he said aloud, and then, feeling angry with himself for having capitulated: "Who the hell do they think they are?" He hoped the Lyles would not press him for news of Kit and Port; he would be forced to tell them, and he did not want to. As far as they were concerned, he hoped to keep the tragedy private; their kind of commiseration would be unbearable.

Later in the afternoon he passed by the salon. The Lyles sat in the dim subterranean light clinking their teacups. Mrs. Lyle had spread out some of her old photographs, which were propped against the stiff leather cushions along the back of the divan; she was offering one to Abdelkader to hang beside the ancient gun that adorned the wall. She caught sight of Tunner poised hesitantly in the doorway, and rose in the gloom to greet him.

"Mr. Tunner! How delightful! And what a surprise to see you! How fortunate you were, to leave Messad when you did. Or wise—I don't know which. When we got back from all our touring about, the climate there was positively beastly! Oh, horrible! And of course I got my malaria and had to take to bed. I thought we should never get away. And Eric of course made things more difficult with his silly behavior."

"It's nice to see you again," said Tunner. He thought

he had made his final adieux back in Messad, and now discovered he had very little civility left to draw upon.

"We're motoring out to some very old Garamantic ruins tomorrow. You must come along. It'll be quite thrilling."

"That's very kind of you, Mrs. Lyle—"

"Come and have tea!" she cried, seizing his sleeve.

But he begged off, and went out to the palmeraie and walked for miles between the walls under the trees, feeling that he never would get out of Bou Noura. For no reason, the likelihood of Kit's turning up seemed further removed than ever, now that the Lyles were around. He started back at sunset, and it was dark by the time he arrived at the pension. Under his door a telegram had been pushed; the message was written in lavender ink in an almost illegible hand. It was from the American Consul at Dakar, in answer to one of his many wires: No INFORMATION REGARDING KATHERINE MORESBY WILL ADVISE IF ANY RECEIVED. He threw it into the wastebasket and sat down on a pile of Kit's luggage. Some of the bags had been Port's; now they belonged to Kit, but they were all in his room, waiting.

"How much longer can all this go on?" he asked himself. He was out of his element here; the general inaction was telling on his nerves. It was all very well to do the right thing and wait for Kit to appear somewhere out of the Sahara, but suppose she never did appear? Suppose—the possibility had to be faced—she were already dead? There would have to be a limit to his waiting, a final day after which he would no longer be there. Then he saw himself walking into Hubert David's apartment on East Fifty-fifth Street, where he had first met Port and Kit. All their friends would be there: some would be noisily sympathetic; some would be indignant; some just a little knowing and super-

cilious, saying nothing but thinking a lot; some would consider the whole thing a gloriously romantic episode, tragic
only in passing. But he did not want to see any of them.
The longer he stayed here the more remote the incident
would become, and the less precise the blame that might
attach to him—that much was certain.

That evening he enjoyed his chess game less than usual.
Abdelkader saw that he was preoccupied and suddenly suggested they stop playing. He was glad of the opportunity to
get to sleep early, and he found himself hoping that the bed
in his new room would not prove to have something wrong
with it. He told Abdelkader he would see him in the morning, and slowly mounted the stairs, feeling certain now that
he would be staying in Bou Noura all winter. Living was
cheap; his money would hold out.

The first thing he noticed on stepping into his room
was the open communicating door. The lamps were lighted
in both rooms, and there was a smaller, more intense light
moving beside his bed. Eric Lyle stood there on the far side
of the bed, a flashlight in his hand. For a second neither
one moved. Then Eric said, in a voice trying to sound sure
of itself: "Yes? Who is it?"

Tunner shut the door behind him and walked toward
the bed; Eric backed against the wall. He turned the flashlight in Tunner's face.

"Who—Don't tell me I'm in the wrong room!" Eric
laughed feebly; nevertheless the sound of it seemed to give
him courage. "By the look of your face I expect I am! How
awful! I just came in from outside. I thought everything
looked a bit odd." Tunner said nothing. "I must have come
automatically to this room because my things had been in
it this noon. Good God! I'm so fagged I'm scarcely conscious."

It was natural for Tunner to believe what people told him; his sense of suspicion was not well developed, and even though it had been aroused a moment ago he had been allowing himself to be convinced by this pitiful monologue. He was about to say: "That's all right," when he glanced down at the bed. One of Port's small overnight cases lay there open; half of its contents had been piled beside it on the blanket.

Slowly Tunner looked up. At the same time he thrust his neck forward in a way that sent a thrill of fear through Eric, who said apprehensively: "Oh!" Taking four long steps around the foot of the bed he reached the corner where Eric stood transfixed.

"*You* God-damned little son of a bitch!" He grabbed the front of Eric's shirt with his left hand and rocked him back and forth. Still holding it, he took a step sideways to a comfortable distance and swung at him, not too hard. Eric fell back against the wall and remained leaning there as if he were completely paralyzed, his bright eyes on Tunner's face. When it became apparent that the youth was not going to react in any other way, Tunner stepped toward him to pull him upright, perhaps to take another swing at him, depending on how he felt the next second. As he seized his clothing, a sob came in the middle of Eric's heavy breathing, and never shifting his piercing gaze, he said in a low voice, but distinctly: "Hit me."

The words enraged Tunner. "*With* pleasure," he replied, and did so, harder than before—a good deal harder, it seemed, since Eric slumped to the floor and did not move. He looked down at the full, white face with loathing. Then he put the things back into the valise, shut it, and stood still, trying to collect his thoughts. After a moment Eric stirred, groaned. He pulled him up and propelled him toward the door, where he gave him a vicious shove into the next room. He slammed the door, and locked it, feeling slightly sick. Anyone's violence upset him—his own most of all.

The next morning the Lyles were gone. The photograph, a study in sepia of a Peulh water carrier with the famous Red Mosque of Djenné in the background, remained tacked on the salon wall above the divan all winter.

BOOK THREE

THE
SKY

*"From a certain point onward there
is no longer any turning back. That
is the point that must be reached."*

—KAFKA

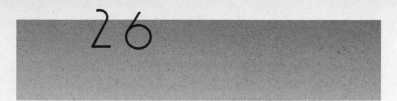

26

When she opened her eyes she knew immediately where she was. The moon was low in the sky. She pulled her coat around her legs and shivered slightly, thinking of nothing. There was a part of her mind that ached, that needed rest. It was good merely to lie there, to exist and ask no questions. She was sure that if she wanted to, she could begin remembering all that had happened. It required only a small effort. But she was comfortable there as she was, with that opaque curtain falling between. She would not be the one to lift it, to gaze down into the abyss of yesterday and suffer again its grief and remorse. At present, what had gone before was indistinct, unidentifiable. Resolutely she turned her mind away, refusing to examine it, bending all her efforts to putting a sure barrier between herself and it. Like an insect spinning its cocoon thicker and more resistant, her mind would go on strengthening the thin partition, the danger spot of her being.

She lay quietly, her feet drawn up under her. The sand

was soft, but its coldness penetrated her garments. When she felt she could no longer bear to go on shivering, she crawled out from under her protecting tree and set to striding back and forth in front of it in the hope of warming herself. The air was dead; not a breath stirred, and the cold grew by the minute. She began to walk farther afield, munching bread as she went. Each time she returned to the tamarisk tree she was tempted to slide back down under its branches and sleep. However, by the time the first light of dawn appeared, she was wide awake and warm.

The desert landscape is always at its best in the halflight of dawn or dusk. The sense of distance lacks: a ridge nearby can be a far-off mountain range, each small detail can take on the importance of a major variant on the countryside's repetitious theme. The coming of day promises a change; it is only when the day has fully arrived that the watcher suspects it is the same day returned once again— the same day he has been living for a long time, over and over, still blindingly bright and untarnished by time. Kit breathed deeply, looked around at the soft line of the little dunes, at the vast pure light rising up from behind the hammada's mineral rim, at the forest of palms behind her still immersed in night, and knew that it was not the same day. Even when it grew entirely light, even when the huge sun shot up, and the sand, trees and sky gradually resumed their familiar daytime aspect, she had no doubts whatever about its being a new and wholly separate day.

A caravan comprising two dozen or more camels laden with bulging woolen sacks appeared coming down the oued toward her. There were several men walking beside the beasts. At the rear of the procession were two riders mounted on their high mehara, whose nose rings and reins gave them an even more disdainful expression than that of the ordinary camels ahead. Even as she saw these two men she knew that she would accompany them, and the certainty gave her an unexpected sense of power: instead of feeling the omens, she now would make them, *be* them herself. But she was only faintly astonished at her discovery of this further possibility in existence. She stepped out into the path of the oncoming procession and called to it, waving her arms in the air. And before the animals had stopped walking, she rushed back to the tree and dragged out her valise. The two riders looked at her and at each other in astonishment. They drew up their respective mehara and leaned forward, staring down at her in fascinated curiosity.

Because each of her gestures was authoritative, an outward expression of utter conviction, betraying no slightest sign of hesitation, it did not occur to the masters of the caravan to interfere as she passed the valise to one of the men on foot and motioned to him to tie it atop the sacks on the nearest pack camel. The man glanced back at his masters, saw no expression on their faces indicating opposition to her command, and made the complaining animal kneel and receive the extra burden. The other camel drivers looked on in silence as she walked back to the riders and stretching her arms up toward the younger of the two, said to him in English: "Is there room for me?"

The rider smiled. Grumbling mightily, his mehari was brought to its knees; she seated herself sideways, a few inches in front of the man. When the animal rose, he was obliged to hold her on by passing one arm around her waist, or she would have fallen off. The two riders laughed a bit, and exchanged a few brief remarks as they started on their way along the oued.

After a certain length of time they left the valley and turned across a wide plantless region strewn with stones.

The yellow dunes lay ahead. There was the heat of the sun, the slow climbing to the crests and the gentle going down into the hollows, over and over—and the lively, insistent pressure of his arm about her. She raised no problem for herself; she was content to be relaxed and to see the soft unvaried landscape going by. To be sure, several times it occurred to her that they were not really moving at all, that the dune along whose sharp rim they were now traveling was the same dune they had left behind much earlier, that there was no question of going anywhere since they were nowhere. And when these sensations came to her they started an ever so slight stirring of thought. "Am I dead?" she said to herself, but without anguish, for she knew she was not. As long as she could ask herself the question: "Is there anything?" and answer: "Yes," she could not be dead. And there were the sky, the sun, the sand, the slow monotonous motion of the mehari's pace. Even if the moment came, she reflected at last, when she no longer could reply, the unanswered question would still be there before her, and she would know that she lived. The idea comforted her. Then she felt exhilarated; she leaned back against the man and became conscious of her extreme discomfort. Her legs must have been asleep for a long time. Now the rising pain made her embark on a ceaseless series of shiftings. She hitched and wriggled. The rider increased the pressure of his enfolding arm and said a few words to his companion; they both chuckled.

At the hour when the sun shone its hottest, they came within sight of an oasis. The dunes here leveled off to make the terrain nearly flat. In a landscape made gray by too much light, the few hundred palms at first were no more than a line of darker gray at the horizon—a line which varied in thickness as the eye beheld it, moving like a slow-running liquid: a wide band, a long gray cliff, nothing at all, then once more the thin penciled border between the earth and the sky. She watched the phenomenon dispassionately, extracting a piece of bread from the pocket of her coat which lay spread across the ungainly shoulders of the mehari. The bread was completely dry.

"*Stenna, stenna. Chouia, chouia,*" said the man.

Soon a solitary thing detached itself from the undecided mass on the horizon, rising suddenly like a djinn into the air. A moment later it subsided, shortened, was merely a distant palm standing quite still on the edge of the oasis. Quietly they continued another hour or so, and presently they were among the trees. The well was enclosed by a low wall. There were no people, no signs of people. The palms grew sparsely; their branches, still more gray than green, shone with a metallic glister and gave almost no shade. Glad to rest, the camels remained lying down after the packs had been removed. From the bundles the servants took huge striped rugs, a nickel tea service, paper parcels of bread, dates and meat. A black goatskin canteen with a wooden faucet was brought out, and the three drank from it; the well water was considered satisfactory for the camels and drivers. She sat on the edge of the rug, leaning against a palm trunk, and watched the leisurely preparations for the meal. When it was ready she ate heartily and found everything delicious; still she did not down enough to please her two hosts, who continued to force food upon her long after she could eat no more.

"*Smitsek? Kuli!*" they would say to her, holding small bits of food in front of her face; the younger tried to push dates between her teeth, but she laughed and shook her head, letting them fall onto the rug, whereupon the other quickly seized and ate them. Wood was brought from the packs and a fire was built so the tea could be brewed. When all this was done—the tea drunk, remade and drunk again—it was mid-afternoon. The sun still burned in the sky.

Another rug was spread beside the two supine mehara, and the men motioned to her to lie down there with them in the shade cast by the animals. She obeyed, and stretched out in the spot they indicated, which was between them. The younger one promptly seized her and held her in a fierce embrace. She cried out and attempted to sit up, but he would not let her go. The other man spoke to him sharply and pointed to the camel drivers, who were seated leaning against the wall around the well, attempting to hide their mirth.

"*Luh, Belqassim! Essbar!*" he whispered, shaking his head in disapproval, and running his hand lovingly over his black beard. Belqassim was none too pleased, but having as yet no beard of his own, he felt obliged to subscribe to the other's sage advice. Kit sat up, smoothed her dress, looked at the older man and said: "Thank you." Then she tried to climb over him so that he would lie between her and Belqassim; roughly he pushed her back down on the rug and shook his head. "*Nassi,*" he said, signaling that she sleep. She shut her eyes. The hot tea had made her drowsy, and since Belqassim gave no further sign of intending to bother her, she relaxed completely and fell into a heavy slumber.

She was cold. It was dark, and the muscles of her back and legs ached. She sat up, looked about, saw that she was alone on the rug. The moon had not yet risen. Nearby the camel drivers were building a fire, throwing whole palm branches into the already soaring flames. She lay down again and faced the sky above her, seeing the high palms flare red each time a branch was added to the blaze.

Presently the older man stood at the side of the rug,

motioning to her to get up. She obeyed, followed him across the sand a short way to a slight depression behind a clump of young palms. There Belqassim was seated, a dark form in the center of a white rug, facing the side of the sky where it was apparent that the moon would shortly rise. He reached out and took hold of her skirt, pulling her quickly down beside him. Before she could attempt to rise again she was caught in his embrace. "No, no, no!" she cried as her head was tilted backward and the stars rushed across the black space above. But he was there all around her, more powerful by far; she could make no movement not prompted by his will. At first she was stiff, gasping angrily, grimly trying to fight him, although the battle went on wholly inside her. Then she realized her helplessness and accepted it. Straightway she was conscious only of his lips and the breath coming from between them, sweet and fresh as a spring morning in childhood. There was an animal-like quality in the firmness with which he held her, affectionate, sensuous, wholly irrational—gentle but of a determination that only death could gainsay. She was alone in a vast and unrecognizable world, but alone only for a moment; then she understood that this friendly carnal presence was there with her. Little by little she found herself considering him with affection: everything he did, all his overpowering little attentions were for her. In his behavior there was a perfect balance between gentleness and violence that gave her particular delight. The moon came up, but she did not see it.

"*Yah, Belqassim!*" cried a voice impatiently. She opened her eyes: the other man was standing above them, looking down at them. The moon shone full into his eagle-like face. An unhappy intuition whispered to her what would occur. Desperately she clung to Belqassim, covering his face with kisses. But a moment later she had with her a different animal, bristling and alien, and her weeping passed unnoticed. She kept her eyes open, staring at Belqassim who leaned idly against a nearby tree, his sharp cheekbones carved brightly by the moonlight. Again and again she followed the line of his face from his forehead down to his fine neck, exploring the deep shadows in search of his eyes, hidden in the darkness. At one point she cried aloud, and then she sobbed a little because he was so near and she could not touch him.

The man's caresses were brusque, his motions uncouth, unacceptable. At last he rose. *"Yah latif! Yah latif!"* he muttered, slowly walking away. Belqassim chuckled, stepped over and threw himself down at her side. She tried to look reproachful, but she knew beforehand that it was hopeless, that even had they had a language in common, he never could understand her. She held his head between her hands. "Why did you let him?" she could not help saying.

"Habibi," he murmured, stroking her cheek tenderly.

Again she was happy for a while, floating on the surface of time, conscious of making the gestures of love only after she had discovered herself in the act of making them. Since the beginning of all things each motion had been waiting to be born, and at last was coming into existence. Later, as the round moon, mounting, grew smaller in the sky, she heard the sound of flutes by the fire. Presently the older merchant appeared again and called peevishly to Belqassim, who answered him with the same ill humor.

"Baraka!" said the other, going away again. A few moments later Belqassim sighed regretfully and sat up. She made no effort to hold him. Presently she also rose and walked toward the fire, which had died down and was being used to roast some skewers of meat. They ate quietly without conversation, and shortly afterward the packs were

closed and piled onto the camels. It was nearly the middle of the night when they set out, doubling back on their tracks to the high dunes, where they continued in the direction they had been traveling the previous day. This time she wore a burnous that Belqassim had tossed to her as they were about to start. The night was cold and miraculously clear.

They continued until mid-morning, stopping at a place in the high dunes that had not a sign of vegetation. Again they slept through the afternoon, and again the double ritual of love was observed at a distance from the camping site when dark had fallen.

And so the days went by, each one imperceptibly hotter than the one before it, as they moved southward across the desert. Mornings—the painful journey under the unbearable sun; afternoons—the soft hours beside Belqassim (the short interlude with the other no longer bothered her, since Belqassim always stood by); and nights—the setting forth under the now waning moon, toward other dunes and other plains, each more distant than the last and yet indistinguishable from it.

But if the surroundings seemed always the same, there were certain changes appearing in the situation that existed among the three of them: the ease and lack of tension in their uncomplicated relationship began to be troubled by a noticeable want of good feeling on the part of the older man. He and Belqassim had endless argumentative discussions in the hot afternoons when the camel drivers were sleeping. She also would have liked to take advantage of the hour, but they kept her awake, and although she could not understand a word they said, it seemed to her that the older man was warning Belqassim against a course of action upon which the latter was stubbornly determined. In a perfect orgy of excitement he would go through a lengthy mimicry in which a group of people successively registered astonishment, indignant disapproval and rage. Belqassim would smile indulgently and shake his head with patient disagreement; there was something both intransigent and self-assured about his attitude in the matter that infuriated the other, who, each time it seemed that further expostulation would be useless, got up and took a few steps away, only to turn a moment later and renew the attack. But it was quite clear that Belqassim had made up his mind, that no threat or prophecy of which his companion was capable would succeed in altering the decision he had made. At the same time Belqassim was adopting an increasingly proprietary attitude toward Kit. Now he made it understood that he suffered the other to take his brief nightly pleasure with her only because he was being exceptionally generous. Each evening she expected that he finally would refuse to yield her up, fail to rise and walk over to lean against a tree when the other approached. And indeed, he had taken to grumbling objections when that moment arrived, but still he let his friend have her, and she supposed that it was a gentleman's agreement, made for the duration of the voyage.

During the middle of the day it was no longer the sun alone that persecuted from above—the entire sky was like a metal dome grown white with heat. The merciless light pushed down from all directions; the sun was the whole sky. They took to traveling only at night, setting out shortly after twilight and halting at the first sign of the rising sun. The sand had been left far behind, and so had the great dead stony plains. Now there was a gray, insect-like vegetation everywhere, a tortured scrub of hard shells and stiff hairy spines that covered the earth like an excrescence of hatred. The ashen landscape as they moved through it was flat as a floor. Day by day the plants grew higher, and the thorns that sprouted from them stronger and more cruel. Now some reached the stature of trees, flat-topped and wide, and always defiant, but a puff of smoke would have afforded as much protection from the sun's attack. The nights were moonless and much warmer. Sometimes as they advanced across the dark countryside there was the startled sound of beasts fleeing from their path. She wondered what she would have seen if it had been daylight, but she did not feel any real danger. At this point, apart from a gnawing desire to be close to Belqassim all the time, it would have been hard for her to know what she did feel. It was so long since she had canalized her thoughts by speaking aloud, and she had grown accustomed to acting without the consciousness of being in the act. She did only the things she found herself already doing.

One night, having stopped the caravan to go into the bushes for a necessary moment, and seeing the outline of a large animal in the dimness near her, she cried out, and was joined instantly by Belqassim, who consoled her and then forced her savagely to the ground where he made unexpected love to her while the caravan waited. She had the impression, notwithstanding the painful thorns that remained in various parts of her flesh, that this was a usual occurrence, and she suffered calmly the rest of the night. The next day the thorns were still there and the places had festered, and when Belqassim undressed her he saw the red welts and was angry because they marred the whiteness of her body, thus diminishing greatly the intensity of his pleasure. Before he would have anything to do with her, she was forced to undergo the excruciating extraction of every thorn. Then he rubbed butter all over her back and legs.

Now that their love making was carried on in the

daytime, each morning when it was definitely over, he left the blanket where she lay and took a gourba of water with him to a spot a few yards distant, where he stood in the early sunlight and bathed assiduously. Afterwards she, too, would fetch a gourba and carry it as far away as she could, but often she found herself washing in full view of the entire camp, because there was nothing behind which she could conceal herself. But the camel drivers paid her no more attention at such moments than did the camels themselves. For all that she was a topic of intense interest and constant discussion among them, she remained a piece of property that belonged to their masters, as private and inviolable as the soft leather pouches full of silver these latter carried slung across their shoulders.

At last there came a night when the caravan turned into a well trodden road. In the distance ahead a fire blazed; when they came abreast of it they saw men and camels sleeping. Before dawn they stopped outside a village and ate. When morning came, Belqassim went on foot into the town, returning some time later with a bundle of clothing. Kit was asleep, but he woke her and spread the garments out on the blanket in the ambiguous shadow of the thorn trees, indicating that she undress and put them on. She was pleased to lay aside her own clothes, which were in an unrecognizable state of dishevelment at this point, and it was with growing delight that she pulled on the full soft trousers and got into the loose vests and the flowing robe. Belqassim watched her closely when she had finished and was walking about. He beckoned her to him, took up a long white turban and wound it around her head, hiding her hair completely. Then he sat back and watched her some more. He frowned, called her to him again and produced a woolen sash with which he bound the upper part of her body tightly, pressing it against her bare skin directly under her arms and tying it firmly in the back. She felt a certain difficulty in breathing, and wanted him to take it off, but he shook his head. Suddenly she understood that these were men's garments and that she was being made to look like a man. She began to laugh; Belqassim joined her in her merriment, and made her walk back and forth in front of him several times; each time she passed he patted her on the buttocks with satisfaction. Her own clothes they left there in the bushes, and when an hour or so later Belqassim discovered that one of the camel drivers had appropriated them, presumably with the intention of selling them as they passed through the village presently, he was very angry, and wrenched them away from the man, bidding him dig a shallow hole and bury them then and there while he watched.

She went to the camels and opened her bag for the first time, looked into the mirror on the inside of the lid, and discovered that with the heavy tan she had acquired during the past weeks she looked astonishingly like an Arab boy. The idea amused her. While she was still trying to see the ensemble effect in the small glass, Belqassim came up, and seizing her, bore her off bodily to the blanket where he showered kisses and caresses upon her for a long time, calling her "Ali" amid peals of delighted laughter.

The village was an agglomeration of round mud huts with thatched roofs; it seemed strangely deserted. The three left the camels and drivers at the entrance and went on foot to the small market, where the older man bought several packets of spices. It was unbelievably hot; the rough wool against her skin and the tightness with which the sash was bound about her chest made her feel that at any moment she would collapse into the dust. The people squatting in the market were all very black, and most of them had old, lifeless faces. When a man addressed himself to Kit, holding up a pair of used sandals (she was barefoot), Belqassim pushed forward and answered for her, indicating with accompanying gestures that the young man with him was not in his right mind and must not be bothered or spoken to. This explanation was given several times during their walk through the village; everyone accepted it without comment. At one point an aged woman whose face and hands were partially devoured by leprosy reached up and seized Kit's clothing, asking alms. She glanced down, shrieked, and clutched at Belqassim for protection. Brutally he pushed her away from him, so that she fell against the beggar; at the same time he poured forth a flood of scornful invective at her, spitting furiously on the ground when he had finished. The onlookers seemed amused; but the older man shook his head, and later when they were back at the edge of the town with the camels, he began to berate Belqassim, pointing wrathfully at each item of Kit's disguise. Still Belqassim only smiled and answered in monosyllables. But this time the other's anger was unappeasable, and she had the impression that he was delivering a final warning which he knew to be futile, that henceforth he would consider the matter outside the domain of his interest. And sure enough, neither that day or the next did he have anything to do with her.

They started at dusk. Several times during the night they met processions of men and oxen, and they passed through two smaller villages where fires burned in the streets. The following day while they rested and slept there was a constant stream of traffic moving along the road. That evening they set out even before the sun had set. By the time the moon was well up in the sky they had arrived at the top of a slight eminence from which they could see, spread out not far below, the fires and lights of a great flat city. She listened

to the men's conversation, hoping to discover its name, but
without success.

An hour or so later they passed through the gate. The
city was silent in the moonlight, and the wide streets were
deserted. She realized that the fires she had seen from the
distance had been outside the town, along the walls where
the travelers encamped. But here within, all was still, everyone slept behind the high, fortress-like façades of the big
houses. Yet when they turned into an alley and dismounted
to the sound of the mehara growling in chorus, she also
heard drums not far away.

A door was opened, Belqassim disappeared into the
dark, and soon there was life stirring within the house.
Servants arrived, each one carrying a carbide lamp which
he set down among the packs being removed from the camels. Soon the entire alley had the familiar aspect of a camp
in the desert. She leaned against the front of the house near
the door and watched the activity. Suddenly she saw her
valise among the sacks and rugs. She stepped over and took
it. One of the men eyed her distrustfully and said something
to her. She returned to her vantage point with the bag.
Belqassim did not reappear from inside for a long time.
When he came out he turned directly to her, took her arm,
and led her into the house.

Later when she was alone in the dark she remembered
a chaos of passageways, stairways and turnings, of black
spaces beside her suddenly lighted for an instant by the
lamp Belqassim carried, of wide roofs where goats wandered in the moonlight, of tiny courtyards, and of places
where she had to stoop to pass through and even then felt
the fringe of loose fibres hanging from the palmwood beams
brushing the turban on her head. They had gone up and
down, to the left and to the right, and, she thought, through

innumerable houses. Once she had seen two women in white squatting in the corner of a room by a small fire while a child stood by stark naked, fanning it with a bellows. Always there had been the hard pressure of Belqassim's hand on her arm as, in haste and with a certain apprehension it seemed to her, he guided her through the maze, deeper and deeper into the immense dwelling. She carried her bag; it bumped against her legs and against the walls. Finally they had crossed a very short stretch of open roof, climbed a few uneven dirt steps, and after he had inserted a key and pulled open a door, they had bent over and entered a small room. And here he had set the light down on the floor, turned without speaking a word, and gone out again, locking the door behind him. She had heard six retreating footsteps and the striking of a match, and that was all. For a long time she had stood hunched over (for the ceiling was too low for her to stand upright), listening to the silence that swarmed around her, profoundly troubled without knowing why, vaguely terrified, but for no reason she could identify. It was more as though she had been listening to herself, waiting for something to happen in a place she had somehow forgotten, yet dimly felt was still there with her. But nothing happened; she could not even hear her heart beat. There was only the familiar, faint hissing sound in her ears. When her neck grew tired of its uncomfortable position she sat down on the mattress at her feet and pulled small tufts of wool out of the blanket. The mud walls, smoothed by the palm of the mason's hand, had a softness that attracted her eye. She sat gazing at them until the fire of the lamp weakened, began to flutter. When the little flame had given its final gasp, she pulled up the blanket and lay down, feeling that something was wrong. Soon, in the darkness, far and near, the cocks began to crow, and the sound made her shiver.

27

The limpid, burning sky each morning when she looked out the window from where she lay, repeated identically day after day, was part of an apparatus functioning without any relationship to her, a power that had gone on, leaving her far behind. One cloudy day, she felt, would allow her to catch up with time. But there was always the immaculate, vast clarity out there when she looked, unchanging and pitiless above the city.

By her mattress was a tiny square window with iron grillwork across the opening; a nearby wall of dried brown mud cut off all but a narrow glimpse of a fairly distant section of the city. The chaos of cubical buildings with their flat roofs seemed to go on to infinity, and with the dust and heat-haze it was hard to tell just where the sky began. In spite of the glare the landscape was gray—blinding in its brilliancy, but gray in color. In the early morning for a short while the steel-yellow sun glittered distantly in the sky, fixing her like a serpent's eye as she sat propped up against the cushions staring out at the rectangle of impossible light. Then when she would look back at her hands, heavy with the massive rings and bracelets Belqassim had given her, she could hardly see them for the dark, and it would take a while for her eyes to grow used to the reduced interior light. Sometimes on a far-off roof she could distinguish minute human figures moving in silhouette against the sky, and she would lose herself in imagining what they saw as they looked out over the endless terraces of the city. Then a sound near at hand would rouse her; quickly she would pull off the silver bracelets and drop them into her valise, waiting for the footsteps to approach up the stairs, and for the key to be turned in the lock. An ancient Negro slave woman with a skin like an elephant's hide brought her food four times a day. At each meal, before she arrived bearing the huge copper tray, Kit could hear her wide feet slapping the earthen roof and the silver bangles on her ankles jangling. When she came in, she would say solemnly: *"Sbalkheir,"* or *"Msalkheir,"* close the door, hand Kit the tray, and crouch in the corner staring at the floor while she ate. Kit never spoke to her, for the old woman, along with everyone else in the house with the exception of Belqassim, was under the impression that the guest was a young man; and Belqassim had portrayed for her in vivid pantomime the reactions of the feminine members of the household should they discover otherwise.

She had not yet learned his language; indeed, she did not consider making the effort. But she had grown used to the inflection of his speech and to the sound of certain words, so that with patience he could make her understand any idea that was not too complicated. She knew, for instance, that the house belonged to Belqassim's father; that the family came from the north, from Mecheria, where they had another house; and that Belqassim and his brothers took turns conducting caravans back and forth between points in Algeria and the Soudan. She also knew that Belqassim, in spite of his youth, had a wife in Mecheria and three here in the house, and that with his own wives and those of his father and his brothers, there were twenty-two women living in the establishment, exclusive of the servants. And these must never suspect that Kit was anything but an unfortunate young traveler rescued by Belqassim as he was dying of thirst, and still not fully recovered from the effects of his ordeal.

Belqassim came to visit her at mid-afternoon each day and stayed until twilight; it would occur to her when he had left and she lay alone in the evening, remembering the intensity and insistence of his ardor, that the three wives must certainly be suffering considerable neglect, in which case they must already be both suspicious and jealous of this strange young man who for such a long time had been enjoying the hospitality of the house and the friendship of their husband. But since she lived now solely for those few fiery hours spent each day beside Belqassim, she could not bear to think of warning him to be less prodigal of his love with her in order to allay their suspicion. What she did not guess was that the three wives were not being neglected at all, and that even if such had been the case, and they had believed a boy to be the cause of it, it never would have occurred to them to be jealous of him. So that it was out of pure curiosity that they sent little Othman, a Negro urchin who often ran about the house without a stitch of clothing on him, to spy on the young stranger and report to them what he looked like.

Frog-faced Othman accordingly installed himself in the niche under the small stairway leading from the roof to the high room. The first day he saw the old slave woman carrying trays up and down, and he saw Belqassim going to visit in the afternoon and coming away again much later adjusting his robes, so that he was able to tell the wives how long their husband had spent with the stranger and what he thought was going on. But that was not what they wanted to know; they were interested in the stranger himself—was he tall and did he have light skin? The excitement they felt at having an unknown young man living in the house, particularly if their husband were sleeping with him, was more than they could endure. That he was handsome and desirable they did not doubt for an instant, otherwise Belqassim would not keep him there.

The next morning after the old slave had carried the breakfast tray down, Othman crawled out of his niche and rapped gently on the door. Then he turned the key and stood there in the open doorway with a carefully studied expression of forlorn pertness on his small black face. Kit laughed. The small naked being with the protruding stomach and the ill-matched head struck her as ridiculous. The sound of her voice was not lost on little Othman, who nevertheless grinned and pretended suddenly to be overcome by a paroxysm of shyness. She wondered if Belqassim would mind if a child like this were to come into the room; at the same time she found herself beckoning to him. Slowly he advanced, head down, finger in mouth, his huge pop-eyes rolled far upward, fixed on hers. She stepped across the room and closed the door behind him. In no time at all he was giggling, turning somersaults, singing silly, pantomimic songs, and in general acting the fool to beguile her. She was careful not to speak, but she could not help laughing from time to time, and this disturbed her a little, because her intuition had begun to whisper to her that there was something factitious about his gaiety, something faintly circumspect in the growing intimacy of his regard; his antics amused her but his eyes alarmed her. Now he was walking on his hands. When he stood upright again he flexed his arms like a gymnast. Without warning he sprang to her side where she sat on the mattress, pinched her biceps under their robes, and said innocently: *"Deba, enta,"* indicating that the young guest was to exhibit his prowess as well. She was suddenly wholly suspicious; she pushed his lingering hand away, at the same time feeling his little arm brush deliberately across her breast. Furious and frightened, she tried to hold his gaze and read his thoughts; he was still laughing and urging her to stand up and perform. But the fear in her was like a mad motor that had started up. She looked at the grimacing reptilian face with increasing terror. The emotion was a familiar feeling to have there inside her; the overwhelming memory of her intimacy with it cut her off from all sense of reality. She sat there, frozen inside her skin, knowing all at once that she did not know anything— neither where nor what she was; there was a slight, impossible step that must be taken toward one side or the other before she could be back in focus.

Perhaps she sat staring at the wall too long to please Othman, or perhaps he, having made his great discovery, felt no need of providing her with further entertainment: after a few desultory dance steps he began backing toward the door, still keeping his eyes unflinchingly fixed on hers, as if his distrust of her were so great that he believed her capable of any treachery. When he reached the doorway, he felt softly behind his back for the latch, swiftly stepped out, slammed the door shut and locked it.

The slave brought her the noonday meal, but she still sat unmoving, eyes unseeing. The old woman held up morsels of food before her face, tried to push them into her mouth. Then she went out to look for Belqassim, to tell him that the young gentleman was ill or bewitched, and would not eat. But Belqassim was lunching that day at the home of a leather merchant at the far end of the city, so she could not reach him. Deciding to take matters into her own hands, she went to her quarters off a courtyard near the stables, and prepared a small bowl of goat's butter and powdered camel dung which she mixed carefully with a pestle. This done, she made a ball of half of it and swallowed it without chewing it. With the rest she anointed the two thongs of a long leather whip she kept by her pallet. Carrying the whip she returned to the room where Kit still sat motionless on her mattress. When she had shut the door behind her she stood a while gathering her forces, and presently she broke into a monotonous, whining song, flourishing the serpentine lash slowly in the air as she chanted, watching Kit's paralyzed countenance for a sign of awareness. After a few minutes, seeing that none was forthcoming, she moved closer to the mattress and brandished the whip above her head; at the same time she began to move her feet in a slow, shuffling step that made the heavy bands of silver on her ankles ring in a rhythmical accompaniment to her song. Soon the sweat ran down the furrows of her black face, dripped onto her garments and onto the dry earthen floor where each drop slowly spread to make a large round spot. Kit sat, conscious of her presence and her musty odor, conscious of the heat and the song in the room, but none of it was anything that had to do with her—it was all like a distant, fleeting memory, far on the outside. Suddenly the old woman brought the whip down across her face with a quick, light gesture. The lithe greased leather wrapped itself around her head for the fraction of a second, stinging the skin of her cheek. She sat still. A few seconds later she slowly raised her hand to her face, and at the same time she gave a slight scream, not loud, but unmistakably a sound made by a woman. The old slave watched fearfully, perplexed; clearly the young man was under a very serious spell. She stood looking as Kit fell back on the mattress and surrendered herself to a long fit of crying.

At this point the old woman heard steps on the stairs. Terrified that Belqassim was returning and would punish her for meddling, she dropped the whip and turned toward the door. It opened, and one after the other the three wives of Belqassim strode into the room, bending their heads slightly forward to avoid scraping them on the ceiling. Paying no attention to the old woman, they rushed as one person to the mattress and threw themselves upon Kit's prostrate form, wrenching the turban from her head and ripping her garments open by sheer force, so that all at once the upper part of her body was entirely unclothed. The onslaught was so unexpected and so violent that the thing was accomplished in a very few seconds; Kit did not know what was happening. Then she felt the whip strike across her breasts. As she screamed she reached out and grasped a head that bobbed in front of her. She felt the hair, the soft features of the face beneath her clenched fingers. With all her might she pulled it downward and tried to rip the thing to shreds, but it would not tear; it merely became wet. The whip was making streaks of fire across her shoulders and back. Someone else was screaming now, and shrill voices were crying out. There was the weight of a body against her face. She bit into soft flesh. "Thank God I have good teeth," she thought, and she saw the words of the sentence printed in front of her as she clamped her jaws together, felt her teeth sinking into the mass of flesh. The sensation was delicious. She tasted the warm salt blood on her tongue, and the pain of the blows receded. There were many people in the room; the air was a jumble of sobs and screeches. Above the noise she heard Belqassim's voice shout furiously. Knowing now that he was there, she relaxed the grip of her jaws, and received a violent blow in the face. The sounds sped away and she was alone in the dark for a while, thinking she was humming a little song that Belqassim often had sung to her.

Or was it his voice, was she lying with her head in his lap, with her arms stretching upward to draw his face down to hers? Had there been a quiet night in between, or several nights, before she was sitting cross-legged in the large room lighted by many candles, in a gold dress, surrounded by all these sullen-faced women? How long would they keep filling her glass with tea as she sat there alone with them? But Belqassim was there; his eyes were grave. She watched him: in the static posture of a character in a dream he removed the jewelry from around the necks of the three wives, turning repeatedly to place the pieces gently in her lap. The gold brocade was weighted down with the heavy metal. She stared at the bright objects and then at the wives, but they kept their eyes on the floor, refusing to look up at all. Beyond the balcony in the court below, the sound of men's voices constantly augmented, the music began, and the women around her all screamed together in her honor. Even as Belqassim sat before her fastening the jewelry about her neck and bosom she knew that all the women hated her, and that he never could protect her from their hatred. Today he punished his wives by taking another woman and humiliating them before her, but the other somber woman-faces around her, even the slaves looking in from the balcony, would be waiting from this moment on, to savor her downfall.

As Belqassim fed her a cake, she sobbed and choked, showering crumbs into his face. *"G igherdh ish'ed our illi,"* sang the musicians below, over and over, while the rhythm of the hand drum changed, slowly closing in upon itself to form a circle from which she would not escape. Belqassim was looking at her with mingled concern and disgust. She coughed lengthily in the midst of her sobbing. The kohl from her eyes was streaking her face, her tears were wetting the marriage robe. The men laughing in the court below would not save her, Belqassim would not save her. Even now he was angry with her. She hid her face in her hands and she felt him seize her wrists. He was talking to her in a whisper, and the incomprehensible words made hissing sounds. Violently he pulled her hands away and her head fell forward. He would leave her alone for an hour, and the three would be waiting. Already they were thinking in unison; she could follow the vengeful direction of their thoughts as they sat there opposite her, refusing to look up. She cried out and struggled to rise to her feet, but Belqassim shoved her back fiercely. A huge black woman tottered across the room and seated herself against her, putting her massive arm around her and pinning her against the pile of cushions on the other side. She saw Belqassim leave the room; straightway she unhooked what necklaces and brooches she could; the black woman did not notice the movements of her hands. When she had several pieces in her lap she tossed them to the three sitting across from her. There was an outcry from the other women in the room; a slave went running in search of Belqassim. In no time he was back, his face dark with rage. No one had moved to touch the pieces of jewelry, which still lay in front of the three wives on the rug. *("G igherdh ish'ed our illi,"* insisted the song sadly.) She saw him stoop to pick them up, and she felt them strike her face and roll down upon the front of her dress.

Her lip was cut; the sight of the blood on her finger fascinated her and she sat quietly for a long time, conscious only of the music. Sitting quietly seemed to be the best way to avoid more pain. If there was to be pain in any case, the only way of living was to find the means of keeping it away as long as possible. No one hurt her now that she was sitting still. The woman's fat black hands bedecked her with the necklaces and charms once more. Someone passed her a glass of very hot tea, and someone else held a plate of cakes before her. The music went on, the women regularly punctuated its cadences with their yodeling screams. The candles burned down, many of them went out, and the room grew gradually darker. She dozed, leaning against the black woman.

Much later in the darkness she climbed up the four steps into an enormous enclosed bed, smelling the cloves with which its curtains had been scented, and hearing Belqassim's heavy breathing behind her as he held her arm to guide her there. Now that he owned her completely, there was a new savageness, a kind of angry abandon in his manner. The bed was a wild sea, she lay at the mercy of its violence and chaos as the heavy waves toppled upon her from above. Why, at the height of the storm, did two drowning hands press themselves tighter and tighter about her throat? Tighter, until even the huge gray music of the sea was covered by a greater, darker noise—the roar of nothingness the spirit hears as it approaches the abyss and leans over.

Afterwards, she lay wakeful in the sweet silence of the night, breathing softly while he slept. The following day she spent in the intimacy of the bed, with the curtains drawn. It was like being inside of a great box. During the morning Belqassim dressed and went out; the fat woman of the night before bolted the door after him and sat on the floor leaning against it. Each time the servants brought food, drink or washing water the woman rose with incredible slowness, panting and grunting, to pull open the big door.

The food disgusted her: it was tallowy, cloying and soft—not at all like what she had been eating in her room on the roof. Some of the dishes seemed to consist principally of lumps of half-cooked lamb fat. She ate very little, and saw the servants look at her disapprovingly when they came to collect the trays. Knowing that for the moment she was safe, she felt almost calm. She had her little valise brought her, and in the privacy of the bed she set it on her knees and opened it to examine the objects inside. Automatically she used her compact, lipstick and perfume; the folded thousand-franc notes fell out onto the bed. For a long time she stared at the other articles: small white handkerchiefs, shiny nail scissors, a pair of tan silk pajamas, little jars of facial cream. Then she handled them absently; they were like the fascinating and mysterious objects left by a vanished civilization. She felt that each one was a symbol of something forgotten. It did not even sadden her when she knew she could not remember what the things meant. She made a bundle of the thousand-franc notes and put it at the bottom of the bag, packed everything else on top and snapped the valise shut.

That evening Belqassim dined with her, forcing her to swallow the fatty food after showing her with eloquent gestures that she was undesirably thin. She rebelled; the stuff made her feel ill. But as always it was impossible not to do his bidding. She ate it then, and she ate it the following day and the days that came after that. She grew used to it and no longer questioned it. The nights and days became confused in her mind, because sometimes Belqassim came to

bed at the beginning of the afternoon and left her at night-
fall, returning in the middle of the night followed by a
servant bearing trays of food. Always she remained inside
the windowless room, and usually in the bed itself, lying
among the disordered piles of white pillows, her mind empty
of everything save the memory or anticipation of Belqassim's presence. When he climbed the steps of the bed,
parted the curtains, entered and reclined beside her to begin the slow ritual of removing her garments, the hours she
had spent doing nothing took on their full meaning. And
when he went away the delicious state of exhaustion and
fulfilment persisted for a long time afterward; she lay half
awake, bathing in an aura of mindless contentment, a state
which she quickly grew to take for granted, and then, like
a drug, to find indispensable.

One night he did not come at all. She tossed and
sighed so long and so violently that the Negro woman went
out and got her a hot glass of something strange and sour.
She fell asleep, but in the morning her head was heavy and
full of buzzing pain. During the day she ate very little. This
time the servants looked at her with sympathy.

In the evening he appeared. As he came in the door
and motioned the black woman out, Kit sprang up, bounded
across the room and threw herself upon him hysterically.
Smiling, he carried her back to the bed, methodically set
about taking off her clothing and jewelry. When she lay
before him, white-skinned and filmy-eyed, he bent over and
began to feed her candy from between his teeth. Occasionally she would try to catch his lips at the same time that
she took the sweets, but he was always too quick for her,
and drew his head away. For a long time he teased her this
way, until finally she uttered a long, low cry and lay quite
still. His eyes shining, he threw the candy aside and covered

her inert body with kisses. When she came to, the room was in darkness and he was beside her, sleeping profoundly. After this he sometimes stayed away two days at a time. Then he would tease her endlessly until she screamed and beat him with her fists. But between times she waited for these unbearable interludes with a gnawing excitement that drove every other sensation from her consciousness.

Finally there came a night when for no apparent reason the woman brought her the sour beverage and stood above her looking at her sternly while she drank it. She handed back the glass with a sinking heart. Belqassim would not be there. Nor did he come the next day. Five successive nights she was given the potion, and each time the sour taste seemed stronger. She spent her days in a feverish torpor, sitting up only to eat the food that was given her.

It seemed to her that sometimes she heard the sharp voices of women outside her door; the sound reminded her of the existence of fear, and she was haunted and unhappy for a few minutes, but when the stimulus was removed and she no longer thought she heard the voices, she forgot about it. The sixth night she suddenly decided that Belqassim never would come back. She lay dry-eyed, staring at the canopy over her head, the lines of its draperies dim in the light of the one carbide lamp by the door where the woman sat. Spinning a fantasy as she lay there, she made him come in the door, approach the bed, pull back the curtains—and was astonished to find that it was not Belqassim at all who climbed the four steps to join her, but a young man with a composite, anonymous face. Only then she realized that any creature even remotely resembling Belqassim would please her quite as much as Belqassim himself. For the first time it occurred to her that beyond the walls of the room, some-where nearby, in the streets if not in the very house, there were plenty of such creatures. And among these men surely there were some as wonderful as Belqassim, who would be quite as capable and as desirous of giving her delight. The thought that one of his brothers might be lying only a few feet from her behind the wall at the head of her bed, filled her with a tremulous anguish. But her intuition whispered to her to lie absolutely still, and she turned over quietly and pretended to be asleep.

Soon a servant knocked at the door, and she knew that her nightly glass of soporific had been handed in; a moment later the Negro woman opened the bed curtains, and seeing that her mistress was asleep, set the glass on the top step and went back to her pallet by the door. Kit did not move, but her heart was beating in an unaccustomed fashion. "It's poison," she told herself. They had been poisoning her slowly, which was the reason why they had not come to punish her. Much later, when she raised herself softly on one elbow and peered between the curtains, she saw the glass and shuddered at the nearness of it. The woman was snoring.

"I must get out," she thought. She was feeling strangely wide awake. But when she climbed down from the bed she knew she was weak. And for the first time she noticed the dry, earthen smell of the room. From the cowhide chest nearby she took the jewelry Belqassim had given her, as well as all he had taken from the other three, and spread it out on the bed. Then she lifted her little valise out of the chest and quietly stepped over to the door. The woman still slept. "Poison!" whispered Kit furiously as she turned the key. With great care she managed to close the door silently behind her. But now she was in the absolute dark, trembling with weakness, holding the bag in one hand, and lightly running the fingers of the other along the wall beside her.

"I must send a telegram," she thought. "It's the quickest way of reaching them. There must be a telegraph office here." But first it was necessary to get into the street, and the street was perhaps a long way off. Between her and the street, in the darkness ahead of her, she might meet Belqassim; now she never wanted to see him again. "He's your husband," she whispered to herself, and stood still a second in horror. Then she almost giggled: it was only a part of this ridiculous game she had been playing. But until she sent the telegram she would still be playing it. Her teeth began to chatter. "Can you possibly control yourself just until we get into the street?"

The wall at her left suddenly came to an end. She took two cautious steps forward and felt the soft edge of the floor beneath the tip of her slipper. "One of those damned stairwells without a railing!" she said. Deliberately she set down the valise, turned around, and stepped back to the wall, following it the way she had come until she felt the door beneath her hand. She opened it soundlessly and took up the little tin lamp. The woman had not moved. She managed to shut the door without a mishap. With the light she was surprised to see how near the valise was. It was at the edge of the drop, but close to the top of the stairs; she would not have fallen very far. She went down slowly, taking care not to twist her ankle on the soft, crooked steps. Below, she was in a narrow corridor with closed doors on either side. At the end it turned to the right and led into an open court whose floor was strewn with straw. A narrow moon above gave white light; she saw the large door ahead and the sleeping forms along the wall beside it, and put her lamp out, setting it on the ground. When she advanced to the door she found that she could not budge the giant bolt that fastened it.

"You've *got* to move it," she thought, but she felt weak and ill as her fingers pushed against the cold metal of the lock. She lifted the valise and hammered once with the end of it, thinking she felt it give a little. At the same time one of the nearby figures stirred.

"*Echkoun?*" said a man's voice.

Immediately she crouched down and crawled behind a pile of loaded sacks.

"*Echkoun?*" said the voice again with annoyance. The man waited a bit for a reply, and then he went back to sleep. She thought of trying again, but she was trembling too violently, her heart was beating too hard. She leaned against the sacks and closed her eyes. And all at once someone began to beat a drum back in the house.

She jumped. "The signal," she decided. "Of course. It was beating when I came." There was no doubt now that she would get out. She rested a moment, then rose and crossed the courtyard in the direction of the sound. Now there were two drums together. She stepped through a door into darkness. At the end of a long hallway there was another moonlit court, and as she approached she saw yellow light shining from under a door. In the court she stood a while listening to the nervous rhythms coming from inside the room. The drums had awakened the cocks in the vicinity, and they were beginning to crow. Faintly she tapped on the door; the drums continued, and the thin high voice of a woman started to sing a repeated querulous refrain. She waited a long time before finding the courage to knock again, but this time she rapped loudly, with determination. The drumming ceased, the door was flung open, and she stepped blinking inside the room. On the floor among the cushions sat Belqassim's three wives, staring up at her in wide-eyed surprise. She stood perfectly rigid, as though she had come face to face with a deadly snake. The girl servant pushed the door shut and remained leaning against it. Then the three threw down their drums and began talking all at once, gesticulating, pointing upward. One of them jumped up and approached her to feel among the folds of her flowing white robe, apparently in search of the jewelry. She pulled up the long sleeves, feeling for bracelets. Excitedly the other two pointed at the valise. Kit still stood unmoving, waiting for the nightmare to end. By dint of prodding and pushing her, they got her to bend down and open the combination lock, whose manipulation in itself, under any other circumstances, would have fascinated them. But now they were suspicious and impatient. When the bag was open they precipitated themselves upon it and pulled everything out on to the floor. Kit stared at them. She could scarcely believe her good luck: they were far more interested in the valise than in her. As they carefully inspected the objects, she regained some of her composure, presently taking heart sufficiently to tap one of them on the shoulder and indicate that the jewelry was upstairs. They all looked up incredulously and one of them dispatched the servant girl to verify. But as the girl turned to go out of the room Kit was seized with fear and tried to stop her. She would wake the black woman. The others jumped up angrily; there was a brief mêlée. When that had died down and all five of them stood there panting, Kit, making a grimace of desperation, put her fingers to her lips, took a few exaggeratedly cautious steps on tiptoe, and pointed repeatedly at the servant. Then she puffed out her cheeks and tried to imitate a fat woman. They all understood immediately and solemnly nodded their heads; the sense of conspiracy had been imparted to them. When the servant had left the room they tried to question Kit: *"Wen timshi?"* they said, their voices betraying more curiosity than anger. She could not answer; she shook her head hopelessly. It was not long before the girl returned, ostensibly announced that all the jewelry was on the bed—not only theirs but a lot more besides. Their expressions were mystified but joyous. As Kit knelt to pack her things into the bag, one of them crouched beside her and spoke with her in a voice that certainly was no longer inimical. She had no idea what the girl was saying; her mind was fixed on the image of the bolted door. "I've got to get out. I've got to get out," she told herself over and over. The pile of banknotes lay with her pajamas. No one paid them any attention.

When everything had been put back, she took up a lipstick and a small hand mirror, and turning toward a light, ostentatiously made up. There were cries of admiration. She passed the objects to one of them and invited her to do the same. When all three had brilliant red lips and were looking enraptured at themselves and at each other, she showed them that she would leave the lipstick as a gift for them, but that in return they must let her out into the street. Their faces reflected eagerness and consternation: they were eager to have her out of the house but fearful of Belqassim. During the consultation that followed, Kit sat beside her valise on the floor. She watched them, not feeling that their discussion had anything to do with her. The decision was being made far beyond them, far beyond this unlikely little room where they stood chattering. She ceased looking at them and stared impassively in front of her, convinced that because of the drums she would get out. Now she was merely waiting for the moment. After a long time they sent the servant girl away; she returned accompanied by a little black man so old that his back bent far forward as he shuffled along. In his shaking hand he held a huge key. He was muttering protestations, but it was clear that he had already been persuaded. Kit sprang up and took her bag. Each of the wives came to her as she stood there, and implanted a solemn kiss in the middle of her forehead. She stepped to the door where the old man stood, and together they crossed the courtyard. As they went along he said a few words to her, but she could not answer. He took her to another part of the house and opened a small door. She stood alone in the silence of the street.

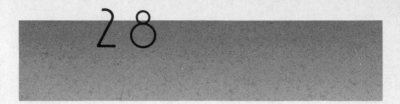

28

The blinding sea was there below, and it glistened in the silver morning light. She lay on the narrow shelf of rock, face down, head hanging over, watching the slow waves moving inward from far out there where the curving horizon rose toward the sky. Her fingernails grated on the rock; she was certain she would fall unless she hung on with every muscle. But how long could she stay there like that, suspended between sky and sea? The ledge had been growing constantly narrower; now it cut across her chest and hindered her breathing. Or was she slowly edging forward, raising herself ever so slightly on her elbows now and then to push her body a fraction of an inch nearer the edge? She was leaning out far enough now to see the sheer cliffs beneath at the sides, split into towering prisms that sprouted fat gray cacti. Directly below her, the waves broke soundlessly against the wall of rock. Night had been here in the wet air, but now it had retreated beneath the surface of the water. At the moment her balance was perfect; stiff as a plank she lay poised on the brink. She fixed her eye on one distant advancing wave. By the time it arrived at the rock her head would have begun to descend, the balance would be broken. But the wave did not move.

"Wake up! Wake up!" she screamed.

She let go.

Her eyes were already open. Dawn was breaking. The rock she leaned against hurt her back. She sighed, and shifted her position a bit. Among the rocks out there beyond the town it was very quiet at this time of the day. She looked into the sky, saw space growing ever clearer. The first slight sounds moving through that space seemed no more than variations on the basic silence of which they were made. The nearby rock forms and the more distant city walls came up slowly from the realm of the invisible, but still only as emanations of the shadowy depths beneath. The pure sky, the bushes beside her, the pebbles at her feet, all had been drawn up from the well of absolute night. And in the same fashion the strange languor in the center of her consciousness, those vaporous ideas which kept appearing as though independently of her will, were mere tentative fragments of her own presence, looming against the nothingness of a sleep not yet cold—a sleep still powerful enough to return and take her in its arms. But she remained awake, the nascent light invading her eyes, and still no corresponding aliveness awoke within her; she had no feeling of being anywhere, of being anyone.

When she was hungry, she rose, picked up her bag, and walked among the rocks along a path of sorts, probably made by goats, which ran parallel to the walls of the town. The sun had risen; already she felt its heat on the back of her neck. She raised the hood of her haïk. In the distance were the sounds of the town: voices crying out and dogs barking. Presently she passed beneath one of the flat-arched gates and was again in the city. No one noticed her. The market was full of black women in white robes. She went up to one of the women and took a jar of buttermilk out of her hand. When she had drunk it, the woman stood waiting to be paid. Kit frowned and stooped to open her bag. A few other women, some carrying babies at their backs, stopped to watch. She pulled a thousand-franc note out of the pile and offered it. But the woman stared at the paper and made a gesture of refusal. Kit still held it forth. Once the other had understood that no different money was to be given her, she set up a great cry and began to call for the police. The laughing women crowded in eagerly, and some of them took the proffered note, examining it with curiosity, and finally handing it back to Kit. Their language was soft and unfamiliar. A white horse trotted past; astride it sat a tall Negro in a khaki uniform, his face decorated with deep cicatrizations like a carved wooden mask. Kit broke away from the women and raised her arms toward him, expecting him to lift her up, but he looked at her askance and rode off. Several men joined the group of onlookers, and stood somewhat apart from the women, grinning. One of them, spotting the bill in her hand, stepped nearer and began to examine her and the valise with increasing interest. Like the others, he was tall, thin and very black, and he wore a ragged burnous slung across his shoulders, but his costume included a pair of dirty white European trousers instead of the long native undergarment. Approaching her, he tapped her on the arm and said something to her in Arabic; she did not understand. Then he said: *"Toi parles français?"* She did not move; she did not know what to do. *"Oui,"* she replied at length.

"Toi pas Arabe," he pronounced, scrutinizing her. He turned triumphantly to the crowd and announced that the lady was French. They all backed away a few steps, leaving him and Kit in the center. Then the woman renewed her demands for money. Still Kit remained motionless, the thousand-franc note in her hand.

The man drew some coins from his pocket and tossed them to the expostulating woman, who counted them and walked off slowly. The other people seemed disinclined to move; the sight of a French lady dressed in Arab clothes delighted them. But he was displeased, and indignantly tried to get them to go on about their business. He took Kit's arm and gently tugged at it.

"It's not good here," he said. "Come." He picked up the valise. She let him pull her along through the market, past the piles of vegetables and salt, past the noisy buyers and vendors.

As they came to a well where the women were filling their water jars, she tried to break away from him. In another minute life would be painful. The words were coming back, and inside the wrappings of the words there would be thoughts lying there. The hot sun would shrivel them; they must be kept inside in the dark.

"Non!" she cried, jerking her arm away.

"Madame," said the man reprovingly. "Come and sit down."

Again she allowed him to lead her through the throng. At the end of the market they went under an arcade, and in the shadows there was a door. It was cool inside in the corridor. A fat woman wearing a checked dress stood at the end, her arms akimbo. Before they reached her, she cried shrilly: "Amar! What's that *saloperie* you're bringing in here? You know very well I don't allow native women

317

in my hotel. Are you drunk? *Allez! Fous-moi le camp!*" She
advanced upon them frowning.

Momentarily taken aback, the man let go of his charge.
Kit wheeled about automatically and started to walk toward
the door, but he turned and seized her arm again. She tried
to shake him off.

"She understands French!" exclaimed the woman, surprised. "So much the better." Then she saw the valise.
"What's that?" she said.

"But it's hers. She's a French lady," Amar explained,
a note of indignation in his voice.

"*Pas possible,*" murmured the woman. She came nearer
and looked at her. Finally she said: "*Ah, pardon, madame.*
But with those clothes—" She broke off, and suspicion entered her voice again. "You know, this is a decent hotel."
She was undecided, but she shrugged her shoulders, adding
with bad grace: "*Enfin, entrez si vous voulez.*" And she
stepped aside for Kit to pass.

Kit, however, was making frantic efforts to disengage
herself from the man's grasp.

"*Non, non, non! Je ne veux pas!*" she cried hysterically,
clawing at his hand. Then she put her free arm around his
neck and laid her head on his shoulder, sobbing.

The woman stared at her, then at Amar. Her face
grew hard. "Take that creature out of here!" she said furiously. "Take her back to the bordel where you found
her! *Et ne viens plus m'emmerder avec tes sales putains! Va!*
Salaud!"

Outside the sun seemed more dazzling than before.
The mud walls and the shining black faces went past. There
was no end to the world's intense monotony.

"I'm tired," she said to Amar.

They were in a gloomy room sitting side by side on a

long cushion. A Negro wearing a fez stood before them handing them each a glass of coffee.

"I want it all to stop," she said to them both, very seriously.

"Oui, madame," said Amar, patting her shoulder.

She drank her coffee and lay back against the wall, looking at them through half-closed eyes. They were talking together, they talked interminably. She did not wonder what it was about. When Amar got up and went outside with the other, she waited a moment, until their voices were no longer audible, and then she too jumped up and walked through a door on the other side of the room. There was a tiny stairway. On the roof it was so hot she gasped. The confused babble from the market was almost covered by the buzzing of the flies around her. She sat down. In another moment she would begin to melt. She shut her eyes and the flies crawled quickly over her face, alighting, leaving, realighting with frantic intensity. She opened her eyes and saw the city out there on all sides of her. Cascades of crackling light poured over the terraced roofs.

Slowly her eyes grew accustomed to the terrible brightness. She fixed the objects beside her on the dirt floor: the bits of rags; the dried carcass of a strange gray lizard; the faded, broken matchboxes; and the piles of white chicken feathers stuck together with dark blood. There was somewhere she had to go; someone was expecting her. How could she let the people know she would be late? Because there was no question about it—she was going to arrive far behind schedule. Then she remembered that she had not sent her telegram. At that moment Amar came through the little doorway and walked toward her. She struggled to her feet. "Wait here," she said, pushing past him, and she went in because the sun made her feel ill. The man looked at the paper and then at her. "Where do you want to send it?" he repeated. She shook her head dumbly. He handed her the paper and she saw, written on it in her own hand, the words: "CANNOT GET BACK." The man was staring at her. "That's not right!" she cried, in French. "I want to add something." But the man went on staring at her—not angrily, but expectantly. He had a small moustache and blue eyes. *"Le destinataire, s'il vous plaît,"* he said again. She thrust the paper at him because she could not think of the words she needed to add, and she wanted the message to leave immediately. But already she saw that he was not going to send it. She reached out and touched his face, stroked his cheek briefly. *"Je vous en prie, monsieur,"* she said imploringly. There was a counter between them; he stepped back and she could not reach him. Then she ran out into the street and Amar, the black man, was standing there. "Quick!" she cried, not stopping. He ran after her, calling to her. Wherever she ran, he was beside her, trying to make her stop. *"Madame!"* he kept saying. But he did not understand the danger, and she could not stop to explain anything. There was no time for that. Now that she had betrayed herself, established contact with the other side, every minute counted. They would spare no effort in seeking her out, they would pry open the wall she had built and force her to look at what she had buried there. She knew by the blue-eyed man's expression that she had set in motion the mechanism which would destroy her. And now it was too late to stop it. *"Vite! Vite!"* she panted to Amar, perspiring and protesting beside her. They were in an open space by the road that led down to the river. A few nearly naked beggars squatted here and there, each one murmuring his own short sacred formula for them as they rushed by. No one else was in sight.

He finally caught up with her and took hold of her

shoulder, but she redoubled her efforts. Soon, however, she slowed down, and then he seized her firmly and brought her to a stop. She sank to her knees and wiped her wet face with the back of her hand. The expression of terror was still strong in her eyes. He crouched down beside her in the dust and tried to comfort her with clumsy pats on the arm.

"Where are you going like this?" he demanded presently. "What's the matter?"

She did not answer. The hot wind blew past. In the distance on the flat road to the river, a man and two oxen passed along slowly. Amar was saying: "That was Monsieur Geoffroy. He's a good man. You should not be afraid of him. For five years he has worked at the Postes et Télégraphes."

The sound of the last word was like a needle piercing her flesh. She jumped. "No, I won't! No, no, no!" she wailed.

"And you know," Amar went on, "that money you wanted to give him is not good here. It's Algerian money. Even in Tessalit you have to have A.O.F. francs. Algerian money is contraband."

"Contraband," she repeated; the word meant absolutely nothing.

"*Défendu!*" he said laughing, and he attempted to get her up onto her feet. The sun was painful; he, too, was sweating. She would not move at present—she was exhausted. He waited a while, made her cover her head with her haïk, and lay back wrapped in his burnous. The wind increased. The sand raced along the flat black earth like white water streaming sideways.

Suddenly she said: "Take me to your house. They won't find me there."

But he refused, saying that there was no room, that

his family was large. Instead he would take her to the place where they had had coffee earlier in the day.

"It's a café," she protested.

"But Atallah has many rooms. You can pay him. Even your Algerian money. He can change it. You have more?"

"Yes, yes. In my bag." She looked around. "Where is it?" she said vacantly.

"You left it at Atallah's. He'll give it to you." He grinned and spat. "Now, shall we walk a little?"

Atallah was in his café. A few turbaned merchants from the north sat in a corner talking. Amar and Atallah stood a moment conversing in the doorway. Then they led her into the living quarters behind the café. It was very dark and cool in the rooms, and particularly in the last one, where Atallah set her valise down and indicated a blanket in the corner on the floor for her to lie on. Even as he went out, letting the curtain fall across the doorway, she turned to Amar and pulled his face down to hers.

"You must save me," she said between kisses.

"Yes," he answered solemnly.

He was as comforting as Belqassim had been disturbing.

Atallah did not lift the curtain until evening, when by the light of his lamp he saw them both asleep on the blanket. He set the lamp down in the doorway and went out.

Some time later she awoke. It was silent and hot in the room. She sat up and looked at the long black body beside her, inert and shining as a statue. She laid her hands on the chest: the heart beat heavily, slowly. The limbs stirred. The eyes opened, the mouth broke into a smile.

"I have a big heart," he said to her, putting his hand over hers and holding it there on his chest.

"Yes," she said absently.

"When I feel well, I think I'm the best man in the world. When I'm sick, I hate myself. I say: you're no good at all, Amar. You're made of mud." He laughed.

There was a sudden sound in another part of the house. He felt her cringe. "Why are you afraid?" he said. "I know. Because you are rich. Because you have a bag full of money. Rich people are always afraid."

"I'm not rich," she said. She paused. "It's my head. It aches." She pulled her hand free and moved it from his chest to her forehead.

He looked at her and laughed again. "You should not think. *Ça c'est mauvais.* The head is like the sky. Always turning around and around inside. But very slowly. When you think, you make it go too fast. Then it aches."

"I love you," she said, running her finger along his lips. But she knew she could not really get to him.

"Moi aussi," he replied, biting her finger lightly.

She wept, and let a few tears fall on him; he watched her with curiosity, shaking his head from time to time.

"No, no," he said. "Cry a little while, but not too long. A little while is good. Too long is bad. You should never think of what is finished." The words comforted her, although she could not remember what was finished. "Women always think of what is finished instead of what is beginning. Here we say that life is a cliff, and you must never turn around and look back when you're climbing. It makes you sick." The gentle voice went on; finally she lay down again. Still she was convinced that this was the end, that it would not be long before they found her. They would stand her up before a great mirror, saying to her: "Look!" And she would be obliged to look, and then it would be all over. The dark dream would be shattered; the light of terror would be constant; a merciless beam would be turned upon her; the pain would be unendurable and endless. She lay close against him, shuddering. Shifting his body toward her, he took her tightly in his arms. When next she opened her eyes the room was in darkness.

"You can never refuse a person money to buy light," said Amar. He struck a match and held it up.

"And you are rich," said Atallah, counting her thousand-franc notes one by one.

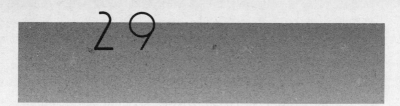

29

"*V*otre nom, madame.* Surely you remember your name."

She paid no attention; it was the only way of getting rid of them.

"*C'est inutile.* You won't get anything out of her."

"Are you certain there's no kind of identification among her clothing?"

"None, *mon capitaine.*"

"Go back to Atallah's and look some more. We know she had money and a valise."

A cracked little church bell pealed from time to time. The nun's garments made a rippling sound as she moved about the room.

"Katherine Moresby," said the sister, pronouncing the name slowly and all wrong. "*C'est bien vous, n'est-ce pas?*"

"They took everything but the passport, and we were lucky to find that."

"Open your eyes, madame."

"Drink it. It's cool. It's lemonade. It won't hurt you."
A hand smoothed her forehead.

"No!" she cried. "No!"

"Try to lie still."

"The Consul at Dakar advises sending her back to Oran. I'm waiting for a reply from Algiers."

"It's morning."

"No, no, no!" she moaned, biting the pillowcase. She would never let any of it happen.

"It's taking this long to feed her only because she refuses to open her eyes."

She knew that the constant references to her closed eyes were being made only in order to trap her into protesting: "But my eyes are open." Then they would say: "Ah, your eyes are open, are they? Then—look!" and there she would be, defenseless before the awful image of herself, and the pain would begin. This way, sometimes for a brief moment she saw Amar's luminous black body near her in the light of the lamp by the door, and sometimes she saw only the soft darkness of the room, but it was an unmoving Amar and a static room; time could not arrive there from the outside to change his posture or split the enveloping silence into fragments.

"It's arranged. The Consul has agreed to pay the Transafricaine for her passage. Demouveau goes out tomorrow morning with Estienne and Fouchet."

"But she needs a guard."

There was a significant silence.

"She'll sit still, I assure you."

"Fortunately I understand French," she heard herself saying, in that language. "Thank you for being so explicit." The sound of such a sentence coming from her own lips struck her as unbelievably ridiculous, and she began to laugh. She saw no reason to stop laughing: it felt good. There was an irresistible twitching and tickling in the center of her that made her body double up, and the laughs rolled out. It took them a long time to quiet her, because the idea of their trying to stop her from doing something so natural and delightful seemed even funnier than what she had said.

When it was all over, and she was feeling comfortable and sleepy, the sister said: "Tomorrow you are going on a trip. I hope you will not make things more difficult for me by obliging me to dress you. I know you are capable of dressing yourself."

She did not reply because she did not believe in the trip. She intended to stay in the room lying next to Amar.

The sister made her sit up, and slipped a stiff dress over her head; it smelled of laundry soap. Every so often she would say: "Look at these shoes. Do you think they will fit you?" Or: "Do you like the color of your new dress?" Kit made no answer. A man had hold of her shoulder and was shaking her.

"Will you do me the favor of opening your eyes, madame?" he said sternly.

"Vous lui faites mal," said the sister.

She was moving with others in a slow procession down an echoing corridor. The feeble church bell clanged and a cock crowed nearby. She felt the cool breeze on her cheek. Then she smelled gasoline. The men's voices sounded small in the immense morning air. Her heart began to race when she got into the car. Someone held her arm tightly, never letting go for an instant. The wind blew through the open windows, filling the car with the pungent odor of woodsmoke. As they jolted along, the men kept up a constant conversation, but she did not listen to it. When the car stopped there was a very brief silence in which she heard a dog barking. Then she was taken out, car doors were slammed, and she was led along stony ground. Her feet hurt: the shoes were too small. Occasionally she said in a low voice, as if to herself: "No." But the strong hand never let go of her arm. The smell of gasoline was very heavy here. "Sit down." She sat, and the hand continued to hold her.

Each minute she was coming nearer to the pain; there would be many minutes before she would actually have reached it, but that was no consolation. The approach could be long or short—the end would be the same. For an instant she struggled to break free.

"*Raoul! Ici!*" cried the man with her. Someone seized her other arm. Still she fought, sliding almost down to the ground between them. She scraped her spine on the tin molding of the packing case where they sat.

"*Elle est costaude, cette garce!*"

She gave up, and was lifted again to a sitting position, where she remained, her head thrown far backward. The sudden roar of the plane's motor behind her smashed the walls of the chamber where she lay. Before her eyes was the violent blue sky—nothing else. For an endless moment she looked into it. Like a great overpowering sound it destroyed everything in her mind, paralyzed her. Someone once had said to her that the sky hides the night behind it, shelters the person beneath from the horror that lies above. Unblinking, she fixed the solid emptiness, and the anguish began to move in her. At any moment the rip can occur, the edges fly back, and the giant maw will be revealed.

"*Allez! En marche!*"

She was in a standing position, she was turned about and led toward the quivering old Junkers. When she was in the co-pilot's seat in the cockpit, tight bands were fastened across her chest and arms. It took a long time; she watched dispassionately.

The plane was slow. That evening they landed at Tessalit, spending the night in quarters at the aerodrome. She would not eat.

The following day they made Adrar by mid-afternoon; the wind was against them. They landed. She had become quite docile, and ate whatever was fed her, but the men took no chances. They kept her arms bound. The hotel proprietor's wife was annoyed at having to look after her. She had soiled her clothes.

The third day they left at dawn and made the Mediterranean before sunset.

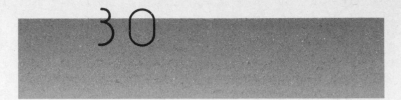

30

Miss Ferry was not pleased with the errand on which she had been sent. The airport was a good way out of town and the taxi ride there was hot and bumpy. Mr. Clarke had said: "Got a little job for you tomorrow afternoon. That crackpot who was stuck down in the Soudan. Transafricaine's bringing her up. I'm trying to get her on the *American Trader* Monday. She's sick or had a collapse or something. Better take her to the Majestic." Mr. Evans at Algiers had finally reached the family in Baltimore that very morning; everything was all right. The sun was dropping behind the bastions of Santa Cruz on the mountain when the cab left town, but it would be another hour before it set.

"Damned old idiot!" she said to herself. This was not the first time she had been sent to be officially kind to a sick or stranded female compatriot. About once a year the task fell to her, and she disliked it intensely. "There's something repulsive about an American without money in his pocket," she had said to Mr. Clarke. She asked herself what possible attraction the parched interior of Africa could have for any civilized person. She herself had once passed a week-end at Bou Saâda, and had nearly fainted from the heat.

As she approached the airport the mountains were turning red in the sunset. She fumbled in her handbag for the slip of paper Mr. Clarke had given her, found it. *Mrs. Katherine Moresby.* She dropped it back into the bag. The plane had already come in; it lay alone out there in the field. She got out of the cab, told the driver to wait, and hurried through a door marked: *Salle d'Attente.* Immediately she caught sight of the woman, sitting dejectedly on a bench, with one of the Transafricaine mechanics holding her arm. She wore a formless blue and white checked dress, the sort of thing a partially Europeanized servant would wear; Aziza, her own cleaning woman, bought better looking ones in the Jewish quarter.

"She's really hit bottom," thought Miss Ferry. At the same time she noted that the woman was a great deal younger than she had expected.

Miss Ferry walked across the small room, conscious of her own clothes; she had bought them in Paris on her last vacation. She stood before the two, and smiled at the woman.

"Mrs. Moresby?" she said. The mechanic and the woman stood up together; he still held her arm. "I'm from the American Consulate here." She extended her hand. The woman smiled wanly and took it. "You must be absolutely exhausted. How many days was it? Three?"

"Yes." The woman looked at her unhappily.

"Perfectly awful," said Miss Ferry. She turned to the mechanic, offered him her hand, and thanked him in her almost unintelligible French. He let go of his charge's arm to acknowledge her greeting, seizing it again immediately afterward. Miss Ferry frowned impatiently: sometimes the French were incredibly gauche. Jauntily she took the other arm, and the three began to walk toward the door.

"Merci," she said again to the man, pointedly, she hoped, and then to the woman: "What about your luggage? Are you all clear with the customs?"

"I have no luggage," said Mrs. Moresby, looking at her.

"You *haven't*?" She did not know what else to say.

"Everything's lost," said Mrs. Moresby in a low voice. They had reached the door. The mechanic opened it, let go of her arm, and stepped aside for them to go through.

"At last," thought Miss Ferry with satisfaction, and she began to hurry Mrs. Moresby toward the cab. "Oh, what a shame!" she said aloud. "It's really terrible. But you'll certainly get it back." The driver opened the door and they got in. From the curb the mechanic looked anxiously after them. "It's funny," went on Miss Ferry. "The desert's a big place, but nothing really ever gets lost there." The door slammed. "Things turn up sometimes months later. Not that that's of much help *now,* I'll admit." She looked at the black cotton stockings and the worn brown shoes that bulged. *"Au revoir et merci,"* she called to the mechanic, and the car started up.

When they were on the highway, the driver began to speed. Mrs. Moresby shook her head slowly back and forth and looked at her beseechingly. *"Pas si vite!"* shouted Miss Ferry to the driver. "You poor thing," she was about to say, but she felt this would not be right. "I certainly don't envy you what you've just been through," she said. "It's a perfectly awful trip."

"Yes." Her voice was hardly audible.

"Of course, some people don't seem to mind all this dirt and heat. By the time they go back home they're raving about the place. I've been trying to get sent to Copenhagen now for almost a year."

Miss Ferry stopped talking and looked out at a lumbering native bus as they overtook it. She suspected a faint, unpleasant odor about the woman beside her. "She's probably got every known disease," she said to herself. Observing her out of the corner of her eye for a moment, she finally said: "How long have you been down there?"

"A long time."

"Have you been under the weather for long?" The other looked at her. "They wired you were sick."

Neglecting to answer, Mrs. Moresby looked out at the darkening countryside. There were the many lights of the city ahead in the distance. That must be it, she thought. That was what had been the matter: she had been sick, probably for years. "But how can I be sitting here and not know it?" she thought.

When they were in the streets of the city, and the buildings and people and traffic moved past the windows, it all looked quite natural—she even had the feeling she knew the town. But something must still be quite wrong, or she would know definitely whether or not she had been here before.

"We're putting you in the Majestic. You'll be more comfortable there. It's none too good, of course, but it'll certainly be a lot more comfortable than anything down in *your* neck of the woods." Miss Ferry laughed at the force of her own understatement. "She's damned lucky to have all this fuss made about her," she was thinking to herself. "They don't all get put up at the Majestic."

As the cab drew up in front of the hotel, and a porter

stepped out to open the door, Miss Ferry said: "Oh, by the way, a friend of yours, a Mr. Tunner, has been bombarding us with wires and letters for months. A perfect barrage from down in the desert. He's been very upset about you." She looked at the face beside her as the car door opened; at the moment it was so strange and white, so clearly a battlefield for desperate warring emotions, that she felt she must have said something wrong. "I hope you don't mind my presumption," she continued, a little less sure of herself, "but we promised this gentleman we'd notify him as soon as we contacted you, *if* we did. And I never had much doubt we would. The Sahara's a small place, really, when you come right down to it. People just don't disappear there. It's not like it is here in the city, in the Casbah. . . ." She felt increasingly uncomfortable. Mrs. Moresby seemed quite oblivious of the porter standing there, of everything. "Anyway," Miss Ferry continued impatiently, "when we knew for sure you were coming I wired this Mr. Tunner, so I shouldn't be surprised if he were right here in town by now, probably at this hotel. You might ask." She held out her hand. "I'm going to keep this cab to go home in, if you don't mind," she said. "Our office has been in touch with the hotel, so everything's all right. If you'll just come around to the Consulate in the morning—" Her hand was still out; nothing happened. Mrs. Moresby sat like a stone figure. Her face, now in the shadows cast by the passersby, now full in the light of the electric sign at the hotel entrance, had changed so utterly that Miss Ferry was appalled. She peered for a second into the wide eyes. "My God, the woman's nuts!" she said to herself. She opened the door, jumped down and ran into the hotel to the desk. It took a little while for her to make herself understood.

A few minutes later two men walked out to the waiting cab. They looked inside, glanced up and down the sidewalk; then they spoke questioningly to the driver, who shrugged his shoulders. At that moment a crowded streetcar was passing by, filled largely with native dock workers in blue overalls. Inside it the dim lights flickered, the standees swayed. Rounding the corner and clanging its bell, it started up the hill past the Café d'Eckmühl-Noiseux where the awnings flapped in the evening breeze, past the Bar Métropole with its radio that roared, past the Café de France, shining with mirrors and brass. Noisily it pushed along, cleaving a passage through the crowd that filled the street, it scraped around another corner, and began the slow ascent of the Avenue Galliéni. Below, the harbor lights came into view and were distorted in the gently moving water. Then the shabbier buildings loomed, the streets were dimmer. At the edge of the Arab quarter the car, still loaded with people, made a wide U-turn and stopped; it was the end of the line.

Bab el Hadid, Fez.

VINTAGE CONTEMPORARIES

VINTAGE
CONTEMPORARIES

VINTAGE
CONTEMPORARIES

Available at your bookstore or call toll-free to order: 1-800-733-3000.
Credit cards only. Prices subject to change.